APRIL

may

FALL

APRIL may FALL

USA TODAY BESTSELLING AUTHOR

CHRISTINA HOVLAND

Entangled Publishing, LLC
10940 S Parker Road
Suite 327
Parker, CO 80134
rights@entangledpublishing.com

Amara is an imprint of Entangled Publishing, LLC.

Visit our website at www.entangledpublishing.com.

Edited by Stacy Abrams
Cover design and images by Elizabeth Turner Stokes
Interior design by Toni Kerr

ISBN 978-1-64937-092-1
Ebook ISBN 978-1-64937-110-2

Manufactured in the United States of America

First Edition October 2021

10 9 8 7 6 5 4 3 2 1

AMARA
an imprint of Entangled Publishing LLC

MORE ROMANCES BY CHRISTINA HOVLAND

MOMMY WARS SERIES

Rachel, Out of Office
April May Fall
There's Something About Molly

MILE HIGH MATCHED SERIES

Going Down on One Knee
Blow Me Away
Take It Off the Menu
Do Me a Favor

OTHER SINGLE TITLES

The Honeymoon Trap

For my kids: Britton, Ella, Sofia, and Niklas

Sofia, you also deserve a special thank you for allowing Harmony to use your song in this book.

"'Everybody has a voice,
But you just have to find it,
It won't be in the forest,
You have to find it deep down inside you,
You just have to let it free to be,
'Cause if you don't let it out,
You'll never have a voice,
And you need a voice to sing out,
Voices are the best things you'll ever find,
Yeah, 'cause everybody has a voice to find!'"

At Entangled, we want our readers to be well-informed. If you would like to know if this book contains any elements that might be of concern for you, please check the back of the book for details.

CHAPTER ONE

"Motherhood is not the same experience for every person. It's not even the same experience for yourself when you have more than one kid. Just do the best you can."
—Jennifer, Maryland, United States

April Davis used to be a catch.

Or at least that's what her husband used to say. But once upon a time was a long, long time and one *very* final divorce ago.

A year ago. Her divorce had been finalized exactly one year to the day.

She gulped down all the emotion from the past year like it was a soda at the 7-Eleven near the yoga studio where she taught classes on Tuesdays and Thursdays. Then, for the briefest of seconds, she honored the memory of what should have been... before refocusing on the future.

She had to honor that now instead.

Cell pressed to her ear in her suburban Denver kitchen, April listened as her social influencer team manager gave her last-minute updates before April left for her livestream that afternoon.

Meanwhile, she eyed her eight-year-old daughter, Harmony, as she forced her feet into one-size-too-small bright green dressy shoes that didn't match her orange outfit. They didn't match at all.

April shook her head frantically toward her daughter, gesturing at the shoes.

Harmony was patently ignoring her mother's attempts to get her attention. Her daughter might as well be coated with an entire pound of butter, because the worries of the world always slid right off her.

These days, between teaching yoga, starting her new business, and wrangling her kids, April barely had time to grab a shower and comb her hair. Or clean her house. Or mow her yard. Her nonstick coating had deserted her right along with her original life plans.

April tried to follow along with the call, but her primary concern at the moment was getting Harmony's cooperation to wear the black patent shoes April had laid out earlier. She had already caved and approved the orange outfit, even though it didn't match the blue the rest of the family wore.

She pulled the phone away from her ear and put it on speaker so she could use both hands to help Harmony.

"These squish your toes," she whispered, keeping one ear on the phone and both eyes on her daughter.

"They make me feel special." Harmony raised her gaze to meet April's with a silent resolve that April felt clearly in the depths of her bones.

Fine, if green pinchy shoes made Harmony feel special, then what did it really matter?

April's teeth seemed to find her bottom lip all on their own, chewing the lipstick clean off. Which meant she'd need to reapply before she left. The mental list of things to remember as she got out the door and stepped into her future as a social media influencer was growing by the second.

"April, you are doing fantastic." Jack Gibson joined the call, his voice throaty and deep. All business. Just before her divorce finalized, Jack was the man who had brokered the deal that would, in theory, make her a household name. He'd arranged a guest spot on the ever-popular, live morning web show *Practical Parenting*. Two weeks to the appearance that would propel her to household status.

Network morning talk shows had nothing on the audience of *Practical Parenting*. Or so Jack said. April had seen the statistics of their audience numbers and they were big. Massive. So she believed him.

"Hi," Harmony said as she skipped to the phone April had placed on the counter. "Who are you?"

Damn. Damn. Dammit.

Was it inappropriate to put her hand over her kid's mouth? Yeah, April gritted her teeth. Inappropriate.

"Mommy's on a call," she said instead, holding her finger to her lips. "Shhh."

"This is Jack," Jack said, like this was an actual introduction. "Who is this?"

"That's Harmony," April said, pressing her fingertip harder to her lips. "She's getting ready for the big shopping trip."

"Wanna see my loose tooth?" Harmony asked, reaching into the depths of her mouth to wiggle at the molar.

"It's not a video call," April said, shaking her head frantically. "He can't see your tooth."

April hated live videos. Too many variables. Oh, sure, she did them. Of course she did—she had to. But she did them in the relatively controlled environment of her home after rehearsing multiple times. And, also, most of her videos were prerecorded. Life was easier that way.

Even when it was freaking hard.

"I'm wearing my green shoes." Harmony climbed up on the stool to get closer to the cell.

There was a bit of a pause.

"Green shoes are...great," Jack finally said, sounding

excessively out of his depth.

If he saw the dress they went with, April had a feeling he'd change that tune real quick. Jack was all about appearances.

He went on about final touches, while April shooed Harmony toward the door.

A success in the world of turning social influencers into celebrities, Jack's blond-haired, blue-eyed, sun-kissed California handsome was wrapped up tight in a suit that probably cost more than her monthly mortgage. At least, that's how his photo appeared on the company website. Still, he had a way about him that soothed frayed edges.

She used to be that way, too, back in the before times. Before the divorce times. She used to soothe, too. Now, though, her edges stayed consistently frayed. Not even Jack could smooth them.

So she did what her mama and her mama before her did: she faked it. Until she made it. Dear God, please let her make it.

The Calm Mom: Mindful Motherhood, Simplified. Her brainchild and the vision that made *her* feel special. She had become a brand. A brand she'd spun out of nothing but sheer determination and the hope that someday her life would, in fact, be peaceful again. Soon.

Soon-ish.

Someday.

Maybe starting today, with this hopefully-leads-to-more-endorsements video of her shopping excursion at Earth Foods, Denver's premier organic grocery store chain.

April's company had launched only two months ago. Over twenty-thousand MyTube subscribers practiced yoga with her prerecorded videos every week. Also, she posted a biweekly meditation series that had surpassed the number of yoga followers within the first month.

Self-sufficiency as an influencer was on the horizon.

Take that, Kent. That'd be her ex. She'd make this work because she didn't need him or any future spousal support.

Back in the day, she'd made the wrong choice to put her career on hold so *he* could play alpha male and climb that corporate ladder. This would be her comeback. She would be her own alpha this time. Alpha, beta, omega…she could be everything.

Harmony bounced out of the kitchen as Jack said, "Your brand is solid. Your content is spot-on. Now *we* shine."

We. As though they were a team. Which, they sort of were, given that he was the Vice President of Influencer Strategy and she was officially now an influencer. With followers and everything.

She took him off speaker and held her phone against her ear as she lifted toddler Lola from the toy-mess she'd made on the floor and began shooing Harmony toward the garage so they could load up.

"Rachel will meet you at the store. She'll ensure everyone is briefed and ready to roll," Jack's words were smooth as honey, calming as a well-timed Savasana. "You have any problems, I'll be right here to help."

"Perfect." April gulped, stepping around a pile of Legos in the laundry room so she could slip into her own shoes, the black flats that would've matched Harmony's.

She switched the phone to her other ear as Jack-the-multitasker shuffled papers in the background and said something to someone else in his Los Angeles office she knew he rarely left.

"I can't ask her that," Jack said, but clearly not to April.

There was some mumbling in the background before he said, "Are they willing to pay for it?" More mumbling. Then to her: "They're asking that you bring the dog, April. The store's got a whole canine-food-delivery thing going to the picnic tables out front. They want to highlight it. I'm just finding out."

April's pulse paused a beat. *It's okay, girl. Pick your battles.*

But. Uh. No. No. No. April's geriatric basset hound, Mayonnaise—yes, that was her official name—had an unholy fear of riding in the car and a seriously unreliable bladder. Any outings with Mayonnaise required a solid strategy, not to mention two adults to lift her into and out of the car.

"I...I'm sorry, Jack, but that's not going to happen," April said, glancing at the hefty dog. Mayonnaise chilled near the bay window overlooking the crinkled leaves dropping from the trees onto the trampoline in the backyard.

There was a long pause on the other end of the line. Like he was waiting for her to change her mind.

Jack rarely heard the word "no" from anyone; she was certain of that. Yet, in this case, the no remained a total necessity. Mayonnaise was not invited to the grocery store.

"She just doesn't do well in public," April went on. "Maybe Rachel will let me borrow one of her dogs?"

Rachel was April's assistant and Jack's sister—that's how they'd connected. Rachel had started doing executive assistant work for April, and then she'd introduced her to Jack. Then Jack mentioned her to the CEO of his social influencer management company and things took off from there.

Rachel also had two golden retrievers that were rambunctious, but at least they had solid bladder control.

"Good call," Jack said, offhandedly. "I'll figure something out." There was more shuffling on his end, followed by a muffled, "We need a dog for the shoot. Get Rachel on the line."

"I'll have to add the new dog to the blog, podcasts, social media." Tension infused April's words as she spoke. No way was this going to work.

"April." Jack was back. Jack and his no-nonsense, make-things-happen energy. The energy that had gotten April to sign with his firm. "I solve problems; it's what I do. I've got this. We'll get through the video, then we'll deal with the rest. One thing at a time."

Great. Okay, this was good. *Everything's fine.*

"I'll be watching. Monitoring the comments," he said, his words so smooth, they could melt the glaze clean off a doughnut— the glazed kind with chocolate frosting and little pink sprinkles. Not that April was picky about her doughnut choice.

Except, fine, she was totally picky about her doughnut choice.

Mostly, she had to be, because she rarely ate doughnuts. Until recently. "Recently" being a year ago when her husband— ex-husband—abandoned their family in favor of his midlife crisis skydiving instructor.

She had learned two lessons from her divorce. One, go with your gut before you saunter down the aisle with the wrong man. Even if you're positive you love him and he loves you. That little niggle of doubt? Trust it.

And two, if you don't and do it anyway, then ensure your name is on *everything*. Or he'll be able to take it all with him when he walks away.

"I've got this." She kept the smile in her voice, even as her peripheral vision caught her five-year-old son, Rohan, lapping up Goldfish crackers with his tongue from the garage floor near her van.

He did a leapfrog hop as he flicked his tongue to the nearest cracker.

"This is going to make your career," Jack assured. "Trust me."

"I'm leaving." She averted her gaze from her frog-loving son so she could focus on Jack. "Getting the kids loaded."

As soon as she got the floor-cracker out of her son's mouth.

The kids shopping with her was part of the deal with the

promotion she'd agreed on. A simple ditty following a peace-filled single mom as she joyfully shops for organic carrots with her well-adjusted children and pretend dog. Today's little side gig Jack had booked for her would be enough to pay her mortgage that month and, hopefully, lead to more.

More being the self-sufficiency she craved.

"I'll call you after," Jack said like the hotshot mogul he totally was. Then he rehashed the specifics and reminders about what she needed to say, not say, do, and not do.

Her muscles tensed at the number of his instructions. She exhaled and focused on progressively relaxing the muscles in her back. This was only a video. One video. Nothing more. She'd done videos before. Everything would be hunky-dory.

"Ribbit," Rohan said, his enormous eyes looking up at her.

April turned back to him, catching him mid-tongue-flick with another cracker from the floor.

Dammit.

Rohan was processing his dad's betrayal by pretending he was a frog. This had concerned her at first, but the professionals assured her he wouldn't be an imaginary amphibian forever. He'd come around; he just needed to know he was loved and life would continue even without his jackass of a dad.

Not that she thought about her ex often anymore. She didn't see him in the faces of their three kids like she used to. The sparse amount of time he spent with them made this task easier.

"April?" Jack asked. "Are you with me?"

Crud, what had he been saying? "Yes, of course. All good."

Hopefully, he couldn't tell she was only yea far from a total freak-out.

"Questions?" he asked.

"Nope," she said, but didn't move. Instead, she took the deepest, most cleansing breath possible and paused, letting her mind briefly sweep clean of all thought. "I'm ready," she said, her voice radiating calm while inside she tried to remember if her older daughter had softball practice the next evening.

It was Jack's turn to pause. There was the sound of paper shuffling followed by, "I'll stick close to my phone while they're filming. Questions, just have Rachel call."

"Of course," April replied, steeping her voice in what, she hoped like hell-o, sounded like "peace-be-with-you" and not "son of a bitch I've gotta figure out how to get my five-year-old to stop licking cracker crumbs off the ground."

"Great," he said. But it came across more like "fantastic." Brilliant. Wonderful.

Breathe in Jack's promises. Breathe out hesitation.

"Great," April echoed, her voice as pure and gentle as a woman who was faking it for all she was worth.

They ended the call, and she gripped her cell in her hand. She held on to more than the phone. She latched on to the idea that there could be more to life than falling, and that made her heart-space soften and her breaths come more evenly.

April brushed a chunk of hair from her forehead where it flopped. This was her life, and she totally had this.

CHAPTER TWO

"Our house rules:
1. Don't say bad words.
2. Always wear clothes.
3. Don't lick your friends."
—Addie Yoder

April posted a quick update about the shopping excursion on Instagram, buckled her kids, reapplied her lipstick, grabbed Harmony's black shoes—just in case she could persuade her to put them on later—gave everyone a solid once-over, and backed her Honda Odyssey minivan onto the street like the calm badass she was not.

Instead of the relaxing mantra music she preferred, Lola insisted on "Baby Shark" for the bajillionth time. *Do-do-do-do* played through the van as she willed any residual stress to slide away on the drive. "Baby Shark" was ineffective for relaxation, and when she parked at Earth Foods, her chakras were still out of whack.

"Hey." Rachel met her at the grocery store entrance. "We. Are. Ready. For. You!" She punctuated each word like it was its own sentence.

"Great." With Lola on her hip and Harmony's shoes dangling from her fingertips, April gripped Rohan's hand while Harmony skipped along beside them in her bare feet.

Harmony had ditched the shoes halfway to the store and stubbornly refused to put them back on. They hurt her feet now. She also refused the black shoes April had brought, too.

"Do you need to go potty?" April asked, adjusting Lola on her hip. "Once we get started, we can't stop for the bathroom."

"No potty." Lola popped her thumb in her mouth.

April did the quick math in her head—the metrics of when Lola had last gone to the bathroom, how much she'd had to drink since, and the time the shopping trip would take.

All of it aligned with Lola's assertion that she didn't need to go. And yes, they were good.

"The dog will be here in a bit," Rachel said, directing April to the coffee aisle where they'd begin filming. "We're going to do that part first."

April grunted, adjusting the toddler, as a trickle of sweat traced the line of her bra along her spine. The blue dress with little yellow flowers did nothing to absorb the moisture.

That, right there, was why she usually wore yoga pants and a stretchy moisture-wicking top. It helped that she *was* a yoga instructor, so the yoga pants weren't quite so cliché. Though, let's be honest, even if she were a cliché, she'd still go for yoga pants. Motherhood required breathable fabric. Fact of life. Fact of motherhood.

"Let's maybe not have the kids there for that?" April suggested.

"But I like dogs." Harmony frowned, pressed her little knuckles into her hips like a mini-diva in the making.

"Puppy!" Lola shrieked way too loudly for April's eardrum health.

Rohan glanced up to his mom, tilted his head to the side, and said, "Ribbit."

She was 99 percent certain that one meant that he wanted to be with the dog, too.

Ugh.

Rachel turned, frowned, and gestured toward April's chest. "There seems to be a…" Rachel raised her eyebrows.

April glanced down.

"There's a goldfish on your boob," Rachel said matter-of-factly, like it was the time of day.

Crap. April handed off Rohan to her friend and pawed at her chest.

Rachel brushed at April's temple. "How the hell did you get a cracker in your hair, too?"

Kids. That's how.

April brushed at that spot, as well. "Good now?"

Rachel shook her head but smiled. "You're good."

I'm good. We're good. It's all good.

She squared her shoulders, hoping no additional crackers adhered to any part of her body, and introduced herself to the camera guy while Rachel convinced Harmony to put the damn black shoes on her feet.

Then they went live on social media.

Starting with the dog.

Nothing went sideways. Everyone behaved. Even Pete, one of Rachel's golden retrievers.

Though April was careful not to actually say he was her dog. She just implied. Which only put her on the fringes of a lie, right?

She'd take it because she… Well, she had to. The trip going so well was, frankly, an Earth Foods miracle. The miracle she needed. Rohan was happy to sit next to his toddler sister in the red and yellow little-kid plastic car attached in front of the normal cart. These things were fun for the kids, but a total bitch to maneuver.

The dog safely outside, April was breathing much easier, answering the camera dude's questions, relishing the ease of the filming. This wasn't so bad. Not bad at all. Maybe she should plan more outside-the-home videos.

She selected a bag of coffee beans—pre-ground—and set it in the cart. Next stop, frozen foods.

That's when she made her first mistake. Things were going well, and she got cocky. Sure, she'd almost made it out of the aisle, but the cart got too close to the shelves, and Rohan ran his hand outside the plastic vehicle, pulling a whole slew of coffee cans onto the floor. The Illy whole-bean kind that came fresh roasted from Italy. Not that the coffee brand had anything to do with anything in the moment, but it was what she noticed as the excessive crash ricocheted through her brain…and the store.

April stared at the mess scattered all over the aisle. She swallowed. Hard. "I'm just going to clean this up." She glanced at her daughter. "Harmony, why don't you tell the people on the internet a story? Like you do at school?" She looked at the camera. "Harmony tells the best stories."

She'd even won a contest once with her butterfly story: an inspirational short about a butterfly with a broken wing.

Harmony took a deep breath. Looked into the camera and said, "Mom buys the blue kind because the yellow bag is what my goddamned dad used to buy."

Harmony delivered this gem with a full-on cheerleader smile for the camera.

This was not the butterfly story.

April's entire body stilled. Straight-up, she stopped functioning as a human being in that moment. She was pretty sure her blood wasn't even pumping right then.

"Harmony, why would you say that?" April asked, pausing her cleanup to kneel at her daughter's level, while trying to keep her cheeks from flushing as red as the car cart. She was pretty sure she failed. "We don't say things like that. That's a grown-up word."

April gave a look to the guy filming her like *whatcha gonna do?* And pulled a *yeesh* face into the camera.

"That's what Grammy calls him." Harmony lifted a shoulder. She looked straight into the lens again. "Mommy calls him '*that cheating asshole.*'"

April's lips parted and her cheeks went numb.

Oh no. No, no, no.

Given that April thought her children didn't hear her when she talked to her friends on the phone about her ex, she should be absolved for the things she said in private. Her mouth went dry. This was how it ended. She would die of embarrassment on the floor of Earth Foods on Hampden Avenue.

She opened her mouth to explain—and maybe steal the camera and run far, far away, when Rohan wriggled out of the cart, belt still semi-attached. Somehow he hippity-hopped right out of it and lunged at a fly that had landed on one silver can of coffee.

He flicked his tongue at the can, tilted his head to the side, and said, "Ribbit."

There was something seriously wrong with that fly's reflexes, because Rohan got it.

"Oh my God," April screeched, crawling closer to her son.

Okay, this wasn't happening. She forbade it. And, since she was April, she hardly forbade anything. Going with the flow of life was literally her thing.

Harmony spoke again. "Mom also says—"

"Harmony!" April shouted as she dug the bug from her son's mouth with her index finger. "Play the stop-talking game."

Please, please, please make it stop.

For the first time since they'd arrived, Harmony took her cue and pressed her lips together.

Pete took that moment to sprint down the aisle toward them.

"Grab him!" Rachel yelled, missing the leash trailing behind.

Pete was on the move. Where to? April didn't know. Didn't really care, either.

Rachel's husband, Travis, slid around the corner into their aisle, stopping abruptly at the scene smeared out before him.

"Whose dog is this?" One of the supermarket attendants shouted from an aisle over.

"I'm coming," April yelled. "I'll be right there." She heaved a breath, blowing it out through her lips. "To get...our dog."

Could the floor open up now and just swallow her?

"He's not *our* dog," Harmony not-so-helpfully corrected.

No, he wasn't, but April used the word "our" in the communal sense. That was a thing, wasn't it?

"Unless we're going to bring him home?" Harmony's eyes lit right the hell-o up. "I want another dog. Can we take him home?"

"Oh my God." April's whole face, throat, chest, everything went numb. She couldn't look into the camera. Surely they'd turned off the camera by now?

"Mom?" Harmony asked, cautious as a child recognizing her mother was about to lose her shit.

April did the in-for-five-seconds, out-for-four breathing thing that usually worked when she was about to lose her mind. It didn't work this time.

"Yeah, baby?" she asked, the words breathier than normal with a subtle sprinkle of hysteria.

She really shouldn't have asked.

"I think Lola peed," Harmony said.

April glanced to the little-kid car thing with the two steering wheels, and two squeaker horns, and... the puddle of urine her daughter was soaked in.

Oh dear God.

"Please tell me you stopped filming," April said, low with a dose of wobble.

"You're still live," the camera guy said, monotone, like this was just another day at the office for him.

Oh. Oh. Hell-o.

It's okay. It's okay. This was fine. She could recover. She'd come back from worse. Hadn't she?

"It's really okay," April said, looking straight into the camera. "I mean, I've been through so much worse than this. I'm getting through it." She needed to remove that pitchy quality from her voice.

Rohan ribbited in apparent solidarity.

Rachel managed to single-handedly whisk the kids away. Thank goodness. April wasn't sure precisely where they went, but Rachel would make sure they were safe. Probably somewhere with Pete the dog.

"I'm getting through it," she said again. Maybe to herself? Maybe to the camera guy? Maybe to anyone watching the live feed. "My *son* presently thinks he's a *frog*. But I'm right there with him, helping him through it." She paused. Only briefly. "But you know what? He's got the right idea. I want to be a frog." She looked around and shouted, "Where's my fairy godmother so I can be a fuc—reaking frog!"

Rachel had apparently dumped the kids somewhere, because she was now kneeling next to April.

"Okay." She wrapped her arm around April. "We're going to turn off the video now." She gave a look to the camera guy. "Now." Nothing happened. "I said, now," she used her mom voice. The one April knew so well because she used it, too.

"No, you know what?" April said, waving her hands in front of the camera. "Let 'em film. I mean, what's the worst that could happen? My husband leaves our family for someone else? A younger, even more cliché someone else? Oh wait, that happened. I didn't matter to him. My feelings didn't matter." Her chest heaved with each passing second. "Or maybe I'll have to borrow a dog because mine is so old she can't get stressed out? Yup. Did that. Because things have to march on, right?" Her blood pressure totally spiked. "Oh. Or we could potty train for four months and literally go backward with our progress? That already happened, too."

April now knew what it was like to have her blood pressure get so high, she saw spots. That wasn't a good thing. Spots in vision were a very bad thing.

"Do you know what I learned when I googled the crap out of how to get your kid to use the potty?" She waited. For what? She didn't know. Probably the sarcasm to finish dripping from her words. "I learned that urine is sterile. All this urine." She waved to the puddle. "Totally sterile. Did you know that urine is sterile?"

"Sweetie, stop." Rachel turned April's face so they were eye to eye. She shook her head. "Stop."

Like a rubber band snapping back, April was done with this out-of-body-whatever that had happened. And, oh dear, she really did wish she could be a frog.

In that moment, the grocery store floor still did not open up and swallow her whole.

No, she just kept falling.

CHAPTER THREE

*"I just overheard a mom say this to her kids and I about died
laughing!! The kids were acting up and one was sticking
her head through the back of a chair. The mom quickly said,
'Stop that, that's how people end up on the internet!!'"*
— Stacey, Kansas, United States

Jack

Urine is sterile?

Jack froze in place at his desk in his corner office of a Los
Angeles high-rise, his eyes soldered to the monitor where April's
fledgling career was mid-implosion. His mouth hung open and
his pen dangled between his index finger and thumb. He noted
all of this with utter clarity, even as the numb that started at
the center of his face spread throughout.

Automatically, he turned his gaze to the comment feed he'd
been monitoring. The comments were now coming so quickly,
he couldn't keep up.

This is calm?

Well, she's doing her best.

This is her best?

*For someone who says to stop and take a breath, she's
not exactly doing it.*

The dog isn't even hers? What the hell? Don't lie about pets.

Are the kids her kids? I bet she lied about them too.

One-click unfollow.

He'd bet his left nut this was the calm before the storm. These comments would move straight into vitriol territory.

There was no way that April could recover from this without some serious crisis management.

Fuuuck, she was sopping up *sterile urine* with napkins on the sponsored live feed. He ran a palm over his face, a headache definitely gaining traction behind his eye sockets.

Points in her favor, though, April was very thorough with her cleanup on Aisle Two. Somehow, and he wasn't sure how she did this, she made sopping up pee sort of charming.

Unless he was the sponsor. The sponsor wouldn't be finding any of this charming.

And that company paid the bills.

He shook his head. Their opinion was the one that mattered.

This shopping trip needed to be very much *over*. How was it not already over?

His muscles finally willing to move, Jack pushed the button on his phone—the one that called the marketing manager. "Why is this shopping trip still happening?" he asked, his blood pressure kicking against the walls of his arteries. "Kill the feed."

The situation had definitely become a *situation*.

"Manually, if we have to," he shouted.

The manager said something in reply, but he didn't hear a word. What with all the blood rushing in his skull.

When he'd signed April right before her divorce, she'd been the epitome of tranquility. Perfection for what they'd planned together.

That was not now.

Her calm veneer had completely cracked. Confidence in herself gone. Because *this*, this right here? *This* was not part of his plan for her. Their plan for her.

The stressed pink hue of her skin surged to red as she held

the wet napkins, totally unsure of what to do with them. Yeah, he had no clue, either. The muscles in his lower back spasmed.

"Cut the camera!" he said to no one because he was alone in his office when he should've been in Denver. Jack should've flown to Colorado. He'd had a hunch after their last call that she was on the precipice of crumbling. It was in the little ways she seemed distracted. The uncertainty of her latest string of mom meditations.

He should've dropped everything and flown his ass to Colorado when he first noticed the drop in her self-assurance.

The feed finally—thank hell *finally*—stopped streaming.

But he'd done this gig long enough to know the damage had only begun. His mind started running scenarios. Options for fixing. A mash-up of solutions duking it out in his psyche. Because here was the thing: Jack's life revolved around the angle. The spin. Making things look the way he wanted—or needed—them to appear.

He was a modern-day magician for the digital age and was the best at what he did. And he fucking loved it.

He, however, was coming up blank on how to spin "urine is sterile."

A full headache brewed like a pot of break-room coffee. *Drip. Drip. Drip.*

"You. My house. Dinner. Tomorrow," Jack's best friend and boss, Ben, gave a delayed two-knuckled knock at the side of Jack's office door.

Jack's office was on the twentieth floor, overlooking the city, with two walls of glass. One wall separated him from the office of the executive next to him. And the other, with the door, faced a bullpen of cubicles for the rest of the support staff.

Jack peeled his focus from the now-blank computer monitor. From the remnants of the excursion that had gone totally and utterly sideways.

He ignored Ben for the two seconds it took to punch the button on his phone again. "I need to be in Denver yesterday," he said to his assistant. "Get me as close to April's place as you can find—I'm talking within walking distance. I need to be *close*."

Close enough to fix this.

His assistant gave an acknowledgment and quickly clicked off the call.

"You're running to Denver because you don't want to have dinner with us?" Ben asked, feigning hurt and with clearly no concept of what had just happened. "Little extreme, my friend."

Jack was already standing and grabbing his suit jacket. "We both know this dinner invitation isn't about me."

Ben's wife had been trying to set Jack up with her friends for forever, while Jack did his very best to dodge her fix-up attempts. Though he'd never hopped states before. But the timing of this trip just worked out.

With dating, he was definitely more of a casual guy, reserving his serious streak for work. Even if it drove his best friend's wife to throw lots of dinner parties he didn't ask for. Jack and Ben met during what Ben's wife Sarah called their oat-sowing days.

That descriptor might take it a tad too far, given that Ben had no oats to sow. He had Sarah. Even early on, she was his everything. Still, he'd rooted Jack on while Jack sowed his. They'd had a fuckuva lot of fun during those days.

Well, mostly Jack had the fun.

But he was good with that.

Jack's feelings about Sarah's friends had never shifted. They were decidedly...bland. The feelings, not the women. The women were fine. To be honest, the previous dinners and coffees and lunches and beach dates and gerbil-house-sitting-accidental-double-bookings that Sarah set up for him were all with very nice women. But they were all women looking for a future he was not interested in providing.

"Sarah has a friend coming...maybe," Ben said, all noncommittal. Jack called bullshit. Ben's eyes roamed to the left the barest of inches when he said, *maybe*.

Which meant he was lying.

"Will this *friend* be bringing her husband?" Jack shoved everything he'd need for a virtual office into his travel satchel. Why he was continuing to bait Ben, he didn't really know. He wouldn't be in town anyway.

"Husband?" Ben scoffed. "Come on, man, you know Sarah better than that. Would she invite you over if the woman who may or may not attend was hitched?"

Ben was six feet six, built, and bald, with dark brown skin. He was the smartest man Jack had ever met. The brains behind the company. He'd seen the need for influencer management long before anyone else. And also, he had the brilliant idea to put Jack in charge of selecting talent and making them shine.

"I'm good finding my own hookups." Jack pursed his lips. He just would be too busy to even consider it. He paused, mentally calculating how many days he'd need to fix this situation with April.

Ben sauntered farther into the office. "Ah, but my wife wants you to have more than a tryst. She wants you to have what I have."

"Your wife should focus on telling *you* what to do, not me." Jack said it, but they both knew he didn't mean it. Jack adored Sarah and, like Ben, would do anything to make her happy.

Except take up with one of her friends.

Ben married his high school sweetheart, and they currently lived their happily ever after in a house near Pasadena with two kids and a gerbil. He left every day by five and didn't work weekends. That's why he had Jack. Because Jack did not mind working weekends.

Jack was good with what he had in his life. His track record was spotless. He'd never failed in business—and that was enough. He didn't need a love story like Ben's.

If he were to want to meet a woman for anything remotely longer than a weekend—and he didn't think he'd ever be in that mindset—he'd like a woman like April. The way her voice always sounded like she cared. The way she didn't get too worked up about anything. Usually radiated calm confidence.

"Your wife is a troublemaker," Jack muttered, grabbing the files of a nearly washed-up celebrity chef account he'd brought in recently. The chef would not be washed up when Jack was through with him.

A tickle of an idea about the chef and April and using them both to benefit each other formed. A kid cookbook. Chef Ethan had a kid, didn't he? Yeah, he was pretty sure Ethan had a kid.

He'd focus on that later. Later, when he was in-flight with time to spare.

Not when he was on a mad dash out of the office with Ben's wife trying to set him up the whole way.

He sighed. Eventually, Sarah would get the message that he wasn't interested in any of her long-term entanglements. Wasn't interested in anything that shifted his focus away from what mattered: this gig of his.

His first love.

His only love.

"Nosy is her way. Seeing you married with four kids is her dream." Ben dropped to a chair across from Jack's desk.

"*You* don't even have four kids," Jack muttered with a shiver. Four kids was a lot of kids.

"Yet." Ben grinned a cat's-got-his-cream grin that made Jack want to gag.

"No kids for me." And fucking four of them? Not ever.

"You know what my favorite thing about your kids is?"

"I bet you're going to tell me."

"That they're not mine." Bah dum bum. Jack shook his head and grabbed his travel bag.

"Wait, so are you seriously taking off?" Ben asked, standing and coming to the side of the desk to take a peek at Jack's computer monitor.

"Yeah. Problem. Fixing it." Jack shoved his cell into the outside pocket of his bag.

"The calm lady?" Ben asked.

"Yeah."

"Huh." Ben was tracking Jack as he buzzed around the office like a semi-frantic bee around a puddle of—you know what. He didn't need to finish that thought. With any other boss, it would've stressed Jack out, but Ben wasn't a normal employer. Mostly because he trusted his staff. Well, he trusted Jack. "How are you gonna fix it?"

That was the question of the hour, wasn't it? "Someone hit the delete button on her self-confidence. I'm going to help her find her way back there with some aggressive calm."

Jack paced to the window, took a long look at Los Angeles. Hoping it'd do that grounding thing April always went on about on her feeds. All he could see was napkins drenched in urine.

No taking this back. It was out there. They either had to work with it or bury the hell out of it.

Burying it was the best option. Because...control. This was going to be about control.

Show April the path back to tranquility and control—that's what he'd do.

"How big is the mess?" Ben asked, his voice pitching to the realm of boss instead of friend.

Jack would say about a Costco-size package of napkins

worth of disaster. He turned to his boss, because that's who Ben was in this situation. Ben got it with that look. Clearly, he knew a plan was percolating.

And that Jack needed to be in Denver two hours ago.

"It's a big mess." Jack nodded. "But lucky for you, messes are my specialty."

CHAPTER FOUR

"Forget happy and healthy, sometimes I consider it a win if everyone is alive at the end of the day!"
—*Tara, Colorado, United States*

April

Funny thing about viral videos. The whole viral spreading thing happens *super* fast.

Which made sense if April were to stop and think about it. Unfortunately, during the spread, there was no time for mindful thinking. No time for any thinking at all.

Especially once Betsy Kelly—the self-appointed Queen of Mommy Land—got her hands on it. She'd already dissected the video and April's parenting on her blog. Her extremely popular mommy blog.

Yup. One second, April was sopping up a pee puddle with organic napkins while formulating a plan to discuss appropriate word choices with Harmony.

The next? Boom. Internet sensation. Thank you, Betsy.

It turned out, a second grader cussing while her frazzled, *supposed-to-be-calm* mom cleans up coffee cans, body waste, and loses her shit is pure parent-fail fodder for the internet masses following Betsy's blog.

April groaned internally.

Becoming an internet sensation for all the wrong reasons was not a good thing when she'd been carefully curating her online persona with Jack's team in preparation for the great big *Practical Parenting* episode.

Jack.

She'd have to check in with Jack. She didn't want to check in with Jack.

So, like a toddler, she'd avoided her phone, metaphorically putting her fingers in her ears and singing *la-la-la*.

Way to be a grown-up, April. But the idea of Jack made her teeth hurt.

She'd call him later. After she got home, gave her kids cold cereal for a snack, sent them out to play in the autumn leaves, and collapsed onto her laundry-strewn sofa in a mess of what-happens-next?

She'd been asking herself that a lot over the past year. Her marriage with Kent had been so...solid. Until it wasn't. And when it wasn't, oh boy, it wasn't.

Thankfully, she had good friends. Lots of excellent friends. So she got home, got the kids settled. Then Rachel came by with her boys for an April check-in. Not as an assistant, but just as Rachel.

Now the kids were all playing in the backyard leaf piles. April didn't really mind that, since the kids kept raking them back together after each decimation.

April eyed her phone for a quick social media check-in. This wasn't just time to face the music, it was time to face the entire symphony. Sift through the rubble of this mess now. See what toll this would take on her influencer score card. Finally, call Jack.

She reached for the phone, flicked it on.

The dinging started immediately. Texts, direct messages, e-mails...everything.

"Nope." Rachel grabbed the phone, sliding it from April's grip and tucking it into her bra.

In her bra. Still dinging. Still chiming. But now in Rachel's bra.

April began an internal debate about how badly she wanted the phone.

Rachel gave her a look like she knew exactly what April was thinking. Then she crossed her arms over her chest to prevent April from going for the iPhone.

"I can't believe you just did that." April fell back against the pile of clean laundry she'd dumped on the sofa cushions with every intention of folding. Last week. Okay yes, this was last week's laundry, but she'd started it when Lola had needed a snack. Harmony had needed a snuggle. Mayonnaise had needed letting out.

So the laundry remained.

She closed her eyes. *Breathe in peace. Breathe out pressure.*

"Don't look. That's why you have me. I'm watching, so you don't have to." Rachel held up her own cell. Sure enough, she was monitoring the video comments. And hoo boy, were they scrolling quickly.

April's phone still went banana pants in Rachel's bra until Rachel reached in and flicked it to silent.

"You said it wasn't that bad," April pointed out. She curled up in the fetal position with a pair of her favorite yoga pants.

"I lied." Rachel made a yeesh expression that April felt in her soul.

"Then the truth." April scrubbed the palms of her hands over her eyes, sitting up. "How bad is this?"

"Okay." Rachel spread her arms wide. "You know how we all pooled our money to send penis confetti cannons to Kent's condo?"

He'd found out it was them and was wicked pissed. He even sicced his attorneys on April. Lucky for her, his parents found that situation hilarious, and they'd paid her attorney to, and she was quoting, "make it go away."

Also, even luckier for her, there wasn't anything illegal about penis-shaped confetti.

"I recall that," April said cautiously.

"You remember how angry he was?" Rachel asked. "The way we all panicked?"

Oh yeah, April remembered. She definitely recalled the way she hadn't been able to sleep for days. She nodded.

Rachel's face fell. "This is worse than that."

April's fragile hold on control started to fail.

"Are we past twenty thousand views?" April asked, cringing inside. Usually, she had to work her ass off to get to that kind of number with her soothing meditation video series.

Rachel didn't even have to look at her phone. "You passed that a while ago."

April shivered. The whole viral experience made her skin crawl. Which was pretty standard for any kind of virus, really.

Still, April's heart fell to her knees, and she immediately *stopped* asking for updates because there was no way she'd be able to keep any sort of tranquility with those kinds of stats.

Each view was another nail in the coffin of her career. Another reason for Kent to have to continue helping her out. More proof that she'd failed, again.

"How do I even keep going with this?" she whispered. The whisper wasn't at her normal volume because she was just now realizing that she couldn't put herself through another round of live video. Definitely not on the biggest parenting web show out there. No more live anything for her.

Definitely not this kind of live...the kind that messed everything up for those involved.

"We all have times when we're embarrassed," Rachel assured, rubbing April's arm. "It's part of the human experience."

Easy for her to say. She wasn't the wild-eyed, not-so-calm

influencer trending on MyTube.

"My kid's pee is all over the internet," April moaned. Did anyone understand how hard it was to meditate when her life was self-destructing?

"Yes, I know. And *you* know you didn't have to clean it all by yourself," Rachel murmured, her lips against the edge of her wineglass. She still seemed a touch perturbed that April had insisted on cleaning it up alone. But while Rachel may have technically been hired as April's executive assistant, her job description said nothing about bodily fluids. Whereas April's job, as the child's mother, did.

"You weren't there as my friend, you were there as a professional." That was April's stance, and she stood by it.

"Couldn't I be there as both?" Rachel asked, tilting her head to the side.

April slid her gaze out the picture window to the backyard. The kids had combined all the piles into one giant leaf mountain and were diving right in.

Except…Rohan. Rohan sat to the side, flicking his tongue against a leaf.

April's throat clogged. She needed to deal with that, too.

There was always so much to deal with. None of it simple.

"Trust me when I say that accepting help when it's offered is a good thing," Rachel said.

Yes, theoretically, she understood this. But that moment at the store hadn't been theoretical, and she didn't want someone else to clean up her mess.

"My mess. My job." April closed her eyes. Kent used to be such a great partner with the kids. Until that something in him cracked, and he decided he didn't want to do it anymore.

At all.

Not even every other weekend. Taking them out for dinner twice a week hardly counted as partnership. Kent didn't do things halfway, so he didn't *only* have a midlife crisis. No, he pulled them all through his midlife catastrophe with him. Moved out. Got a damn condo and a girlfriend. Shattered little hearts. Well and truly broke the family they'd built side by side, leaving April alone to dig through the rubble and rebuild all by herself.

While he came out on the other side, the rest of them were still in the middle of the wreckage.

Still finding their way out.

This chance at being an influencer had been her golden ticket. A golden ticket she'd worked so hard to earn. Spent hours building. Hours she hadn't spent with her kids. Hours she hadn't visited with her friends. Hours and hours of time... wasted.

Like her marriage.

"You should know, the pee isn't the part trending. It's the '*goddamned dad*' part." Rachel scrolled through her cell. "And your expression when she said it. And...after she said it."

"How bad do you think this will be for me?" April asked no one in particular, but everyone all the same. "On a scale of Justin Timberlake to Justin Theroux?"

"I'd say we're a solid Bieber," Rachel said with a hefty dose of remorse. "Still volatile, but it'll probably be okay."

Probably be okay. This was what April's professional life had come to. To be honest, her personal life wasn't much better.

She closed her eyes and wished she could teleport back to when she'd originally signed the deal with Jack's company, before Kent left. When she'd still had hope. Still felt a sense of calm in her life.

Rachel poured another stream of wine into April's glass. "Everything will blow over. This really could happen to anybody. A lot of the comments say so."

That was very much not true. April's crumbs of hope were

disappearing. She shook her head.

"This wouldn't happen to you," she said, sipping the liquid balm in her wineglass.

Nuh-uh. This would never have happened to *Rachel*, because Rachel wouldn't have allowed it. Rachel had systems. She did her job with precision. Even now, when her blond hair fell over her shoulders in messy waves, it might have officially been messy, but it looked like it was supposed to be exactly as it fell. Messy chic. Even her creamy skin had just enough makeup to look like she tried without screaming *I tried!*

Yes, April wanted to believe her. Really, she did. But the bottom just kept dropping out of her world. Look, April wasn't one to wallow, but enough was e-freaking-nough.

She needed to take her own advice and think of something good that had happened in her life. Just one thing. One little thing.

The kitchen door opened and she glanced up.

Her best friend and neighbor, Simone, peeked inside. "Is it safe to come in?"

"Did you bring doughnuts?" April asked.

"It's like you don't even know me." Simone sauntered through the door, her hips swishing, dropping a box of doughnuts on the table. "Of course I brought doughnuts. Pink sprinkles and all. Has Kitty shown up with the rum yet?"

Kitty, her other neighbor, was surprisingly absent. April sort of figured she'd be on the front porch waiting for her after the implosion. Because even with a serious aversion to boundaries, Kitty was always very neighborly when life rained lemons. In truth, she was always neighborly. Sometimes she took her responsibilities as the neighborhood busybody a bit too seriously.

April eyed Simone. Simone and her wife, Yelena, moving in next door was definitely a good thing. They'd scooted right into her life and became family. Their friendship was a very good thing.

Some might even call it a calming thing.

Case in point? Simone had doughnuts and a soft smile that made April believe, for a moment, that it'd all be okay.

Simone was an artist—she weaved baskets and sold them for obnoxious amounts of cash. Yelena was a pediatrician. They had two kids who spent as much time at April's as they did at home, which was fine because April's kids were becoming free-rangers, too, spending an abundance of time next door.

"Did you see it?" April asked, already knowing the answer.

Of course Simone had watched. She gave a subtle head nod. "But you looked beautiful, and not *all* the comments were bad..."

Damn. Even Simone thought it was a lost cause.

"Simone," April said, pinning her friend with her name. She didn't want to ask, but she had to. "Am I going to come back from this?"

Simone wouldn't sugarcoat things. She was a pull-the-bandage-off kind of friend. She was that kind of mom, too.

She didn't meet April's eyes, though, just looked everywhere but at April. She *always* met April's eyes. That was her thing. Perhaps she was a nonconformist with her free-range parenting choices, but she was a straight shooter with everything else.

"You can move past anything," Simone dodged. "Hard things happen, but they don't have to break us." Okay, so apparently she was ready to go into the greeting-card-writing business. "Though sometimes things aren't salvageable."

Right. So, uh, yeah. *That* was not going on a greeting card.

"It doesn't mean that you're not The Calm Mom," Simone continued. "It just means that, perhaps, you need to rethink what your brand means."

Um. No.

April and Jack's team had spent an obscene amount of time

working out her angle. Who she was. Her mission.

She couldn't just rethink what that meant because of one stumbling block.

No, she had to figure out a way to get back on track. Preferably before she talked to Jack. See? Not reaching out to him was a good thing. It gave her time to regroup.

She let her eyelids fall closed, pulled a bucketful of oxygen into her lungs. Held it. Then released.

Her blood pressure was still way too high.

Dammit. This wasn't working. Inner peace was as far away as California at the moment.

She peeled open her eyes.

Simone and Rachel both stared at her like this time it might actually be her who imploded and not her marriage, her finances, or her grip on tranquility.

"You said Jack fixes things, right?" Simone asked.

"Yes," Rachel replied, but she didn't say the word with confidence.

"Call Jack. Let him fix it," Simone said this like it was already a done deal.

Uh… "Shouldn't I at least try to fix it myself?"

"You're past that, sweetie," Simone said, her eyes kind as could be, even if her declarations were a teensy bit harsh.

"I tried to call Jack," Rachel said. "He isn't exactly responding."

April's pulse seemed to stop beating. Say what?

"Jack always responds." April sat a little taller.

Rachel's gaze was filled with pity. "Not this time."

April didn't care for the pity or the answer. "But he's your brother."

"And?"

April rolled her shoulders back, but it did nothing for the knots tying themselves there. "That means he should respond."

"Jack gets busy." Rachel thought on that. "He's a great brother who gets overly caught up in his work. *But* he's got good intentions. *And* he's always sending me and the boys awesome treats from L.A."

"If you give me my phone, I'll call him," April said.

Simone shook her head. "Call from Rachel's phone. Your cell probably isn't the best idea for you, right now."

April firmed her posture further. "I have to handle whatever is coming at me. I've just got to dive on in."

Rachel studied April, giving her a long look before finally extracting the cell from her bra. She handed it over—reluctantly.

April turned on her phone and immediately went to her contacts list, even as the thing beeped and buzzed and practically smoked with incoming messages.

Then she paused.

Oh. Oh goodness. No.

Jack had sent her a message. Several messages, in fact.

Her mouth went dry and her heartbeat seemed to get slow and fast at the same time.

Perhaps she *couldn't* handle what was coming at her.

"April." Simone stood and moved to her. "What's going on?"

April held up the screen, Jack's message burned there. "He's coming."

"Who?" Rachel asked, pulling the cell from April's hand.

April hated this part of any catastrophe. The part after things settled when she actually had to feel the things without the benefit of an in-the-chaos adrenaline hit.

"Jack." April let the phone go. "He's coming here."

CHAPTER FIVE

*"This too shall pass. It may hurt like a kidney stone,
but you will live and be stronger tomorrow."*
— *Cindy, New York, United States*

April

April's heart was still pounding at the thought of Jack on her doorstep when the door flew open and the force of Kitty blew through.

Kitty was tiny, blond, and when she wasn't gossiping with whoever would listen, she was hitting the StairMaster she kept on her front porch or welcoming new guests to the room in her home she provided as a vacation rental.

Right then? Kitty looked ticked.

"I had to hit up the store for rum," she ranted as she tore through the entry. "Here *you* are in the middle of a *crisis* and I can't even bring you liquor. Me?" She gestured to her chest. A chest that was, even April had to concede, impressive. "*I never run out.*" She shook her head, platinum blond hair flying.

April happened to know from loads of experience that Kitty often ran out of rum.

"It was that last guest who stayed with me." Kitty waggled her finger. "I swear he took the entire bottle when he left. *And* the bottle of body wash in the shower. The special kind I buy online made of mud from the Amazon. Who does that?" She jerked her gaze between Simone and April, eyes wide, like she expected them to answer. But she obviously wasn't expecting them to answer because she just kept going. "My next guest is going to sign a soap agreement. I swear, I never thought I'd see the day when I'd have to present a contract so my guests don't five-finger discount my mud soap!" She paused. Settled. "Hey, look. You showered today. That's fabulous. Do you have any of those tropical-punch juice boxes?" She held up the fresh bottle of rum.

The fact that her grabbing a shower was news for the neighborhood was something April needed to seriously consider. She cocked her head toward the kitchen. "I have the berry fruit punch kind."

"I can work with that." Kitty nodded as she sauntered toward the pantry in the kitchen. "What'd I miss? Somebody fill me in."

Oh, where to begin?

Simone smiled that reassuring smile of hers, but it didn't quite work like it usually did. Because even Kitty's rum didn't change the fact that Jack was on his way.

To clean up April's mess.

"When will Jack be here?" Harmony asked, bouncing on her tush on the now laundry-free sofa.

Oh, it hadn't been folded; it had just been tossed onto the bed in the spare bedroom.

"Soon." April lifted her gaze to her eldest from the current post she drafted. Then she froze. Then she yelped.

"What's on your face?" she asked, already knowing the answer.

Harmony had helped herself to April's makeup. That was Coral Crush along her kiddo's cheekbones and an abundance of Paramount Pink all over her lips. "Lips" being a loose term, given that it appeared Harmony had slipped a little and then tried to recover. Poorly.

April let out an audible gasp.

Harmony's eyebrows bunched together. "It's not right?"

Not. At. All.

But April reined in her shock. In the scheme of all that was happening, this was not a big deal. It was a small deal. Minor, really.

Making an internal note to show Harmony the skill of minimalism, she rolled her lips between her teeth. "You're perfect."

Harmony smiled a lipstick-smeared grin.

April crossed and uncrossed her arms, and finally let them fall to her sides. It was what it was.

She pulled back the living room curtains, looked up and down the empty street, then closed them. She'd been doing this for ten full minutes. Ever since she got the text from Jack that he was on his way over.

Though he had officially arrived the night before. His flight from Los Angeles had been massively delayed. By the time he made it through Denver International, his flight had essentially become a red-eye. She didn't mind having a moment—a whole night, in fact—to let her armor settle back into place before she faced him.

That armor was still pretty thin, but at least it was something.

Oh God. She was going to be sick.

The dissolving of a Cinderella contract did that to a girl. She wasn't a total doomstagrammer—just a realist. Her influencer contract held a clause—something about ethics and appearances and not screwing any of that up. Her attorney friend, Sadie, had explained it all in detail, and much more eloquently after a couple of rounds of Kitty's juice box cocktails as they all immersed themselves in what was being said about her online.

The firestorm Betsy started wasn't kind, and it was definitely not tranquil. The words "fraud" and "liar" had been tossed around not-too-lightly. And that hurt the worst.

Because she didn't want to believe it, but she definitely felt like one. When Jack dismissed her from her contract, she'd go back to teaching yoga full-time. She could become a micro influencer—it wasn't the size of the audience, it was how she used it.

Oh dear God. That was the kind of thing her ex would've said. She did not need his type of thoughts rattling around in her brain. Not today, when she was doing the hard things.

Harmony stood on the sofa to get a better look out the window.

"Shoes off the sofa." April gave a pointed glance at Harmony's shoes pressing into the couch cushions. The green shoes April was prepared to burn the next time Harmony was out of the house.

"Relax," April said, smoothing Rohan's hair. "He'll be here any minute."

She stopped herself, dropping her hand mid-smooth. *Doesn't matter.*

Rohan had also gone with a green shirt, but for different— amphibious—reasons than Harmony.

Lola was wearing purple stretchy pants, for what it was worth. Her purple matched April's yoga pants from a start-up company that had been hoping April might become one of their brand ambassadors.

This was, of course, before yesterday.

Harmony scooted from the sofa and opened the door to peer onto the street, then she looked back at her mom. And April was pretty sure there was a teensy bit of accusation in little Harmony's eyes. "He's not here. Are you sure this guy's coming?"

April scratched at her neck. No, he was not there yet, but—

"He is." April picked a dog hair from the supposed-to-be-breathable poly-blend fabric suffocating her thighs.

These were definitely not her favorite. Not even the top ten, to be honest.

Harmony closed the door and slunk back to the couch.

A car door closed outside.

The bottom seemed to drop out of her stomach.

"He's here." Harmony bounced in her green-freaking-shoes.

He's here. And April was about to handle the hell-o out of some hard life stuff. Starting with Jack, followed by issuing a response to the video.

She needed to face Jack, accept his termination of their contract, and start on step two. Whatever that was going to be.

April gulped. Took a deep, not-so-calming breath and moved back to the curtains, pulled them aside, and watched as Jack adjusted his suit jacket. He did that jacket-arm shake thing guys do to wrangle their sleeves into submission. Kent used to do that. She thought it was super hot. Now, she saw it for what it was…a guy probably trying to get his shirt cuffs aligned for his own comfort.

Still, her blood all seemed to rush to her head like she was upside down.

Harmony squirmed in beside her on one side; Rohan did the same on the other. Though he wasn't so much bouncing as hopping from foot to foot.

April's entire focus shifted to Jack.

Damn. His loose-limbed gait across the asphalt of her cul-de-sac drew her attention right to his thighs. They were nice thighs. The fabric of his slacks stretched really nicely there.

The only reason she noticed the thigh thing was because she was topsy-turvy, punch-drunk after yesterday. No other reason. She forbade any other reasons. The last thing she needed was to develop a crush on Jack's thighs.

She caught the moment Jack saw her. His blue (oh so blue)

eyes pierced her right in the solar plexus like a sword to any hope she had left for being an influencer.

He waved. Did a chin lift thing that made the pressure in her chest kick so high that even an hour of the Savasana pose wouldn't remedy the damage.

April took a deep, mindful breath. It didn't help.

As a general rule, before everything in her life turned upside down, she was a bloodhound for mindful calm. A woman who refused to acknowledge the stress of life.

Today, none of that mattered.

She gave Jack a little two-finger wave.

The edges of his lips twitched.

A guy who came to give her walking papers didn't have lip twitches, did he? She was pretty sure that was a no. Then again, she clearly had no ability to understand anything at this phase of her life.

Harmony ran for the door.

April dropped the curtain, smoothed the hem of her top—a tan off-the-shoulder sweater that reminded her of that movie *Flashdance*—and headed for the door.

Harmony beat her there. She pulled open the door and stood smack-dab in the middle of the doorway.

Two things. First, Jack didn't seem to know what to do about an eight-year-old in garish makeup guarding the doorway.

And second, Rohan ribbited his greeting, holding out his fist for a bump.

Oh dear heavens.

Jack had probably never fist-bumped a kid pretending to be a frog before, either.

After only a brief moment of reconciling the situation, he gave Rohan a very energetic first bump.

And that? Dammit all to hell-o, that melted April's heart. The man was nice to her kid, and she was a sucker for anyone who was kind to Rohan and didn't question his amphibious behavior.

Rohan ribbited in gratitude.

Lola hung onto April's leg, clearly unsure of what this man was doing there. Or, perhaps she was simply hanging on to her mother in solidarity. Either way, Jack smiled at the little girl in a way that looked...frightened. Like she might tackle him and lick his eyebrows.

"Harmony, move out of the way," April said, gently scooting her daughter to the side so Jack could come in. "Jack." April held out her hand to him. "We finally meet in person."

He took her hand in his. "Thanks for making the time. We need to do some immediate triage. Let's get started, shall we?"

"Triage." Right. Right. Right. "Let's triage," she said. *Stop the bleeding. Cut her loose.*

"Triage," he repeated with a little bit of an amused grin. Probably because she'd repeated the word twice.

She blew out a breath.

So.

That voice. Jack's voice.

Her breath caught right at her chest bone, and she had to work to release it.

His voice over a video call was a wondrous thing to behold.

In person? That voice was like pouring butter over a hot pan. It soothed and sizzled at the same time. So much so that she squirmed, unable to stop the involuntary movement of her body.

She really needed to get out more. This was what nerves did to her. Made rational thinking not the priority.

Also, and this wasn't one of those good things about meeting Jack—he observed everything, therefore he caught it. Her squirm. Clocked it. And clearly filed away her body's response to him, because his crystal-blue-tidal-pool eyes sparkled.

His ability to make her body act like she'd never seen an

attractive man before was ridiculously unreasonable. Her cheeks flushing wasn't the only thing he heated inside her with the eye glitter he was tossing around with his testosterone-fueled gaze. There was not one doubt that he freaking knew the effect he was having on her hormone fluctuations.

"I like your shoes." Harmony gave a pointed glance to his loafers. "Do you still like my green shoes?"

"Uh…" Jack looked to April for help but seemed to recover quickly. "I do still like your green shoes. And…uh…thanks for liking mine."

"Are you going to fire my mom now?" Harmony asked. She looked up at him with the innocence of a meddling second grader.

April choked on saliva.

Jack's eyebrows raised. He studied Harmony. Then April.

"No," he said, the word measured. "Because your mom doesn't work for me."

Semantics. Right. Got it. He was pacifying the child. But April wasn't born yesterday; she understood who held the power in this dynamic, and it wasn't her.

It might, however, be Harmony. That much was still up for debate.

Simone took that pregnant moment to stroll through the back door. This sort of pop-in-unannounced visit was not abnormal, given that they'd added a gate between their backyards.

The kids could go back and forth at leisure and April, Simone, and Yelena could visit without using the front doors. Though Yelena worked long hours frequently, so she wasn't as likely to be the one to pop in to April's kitchen unannounced.

"Simone. Hi." April turned to Jack. "This is my friend Simone. She lives next door." April made her eyes go wide in the direction of her best friend in what she hoped was a what-the-heck-are-you-doing-here-when-you-knew-he-was-coming stare.

Simone made her eyes go wide right back at April. Not subtle at all. "I'm *here* to invite your children over to have apple cider with us."

Oh, okay. That was nice.

She twisted the thin ring Harmony had given her for her birthday. It smooshed against her skin. She bent it back into place.

April wasn't a superstitious person, but Harmony had promised the ring was lucky. Right now? April could use all the luck in the world. And look, here was Simone offering a dose of luck.

"So you two can talk without munchkin interventions," Simone continued.

Jack held his hand to Simone, tossing a good dose of eye glitter at her, too. "I'm Jack."

"I know." She gave his hand a solid shake before giving him a once-over and letting it go.

"Your timing is exceptionally suspicious," April said to her friend, tilting her head slightly to Jack.

Simone could've come over ten minutes ago to invite the kids for cider. That actually would've been even more helpful.

"I know," Simone said again, her sly smile unmistakable. She turned her attention to Lola. "What do you say, sweet cheeks? Want to come hang out with me?"

Lola released her grip on April's leg. Rohan took her other hand. They headed toward the door.

"Harmony?" Simone asked. "You coming?"

Harmony hadn't budged. She didn't look like she was going to, either. She pinched her overly painted lips together.

"This is going to require negotiation, isn't it?" Simone asked, zeroing her focus on Harmony.

Jack tucked his aviator sunglasses into the pocket of his jacket. "I'm good with negotiations."

"Yes, you are," April whispered. *Well, it's a given, right?* That was pretty much his job.

He cut his gaze to her, quirking an eyebrow in question. Then he glanced back to Simone and then to the side. His eyes widened.

"April, did you know your kid is licking the wall?" he asked.

April turned to said wall. Rohan was, in fact, lapping his tongue at the wall like the handprint Lola had left there last week was a delicious variety of insect.

"It's fine," she said, waving it off. "He does that."

It wasn't fine, though. Not really. It just...was.

"Harmony," Simone said. "Jack says he's good at negotiations. Shall we see just how good he is?"

Jack returned his focus to her oldest. "What's it going to take?"

Harmony seemed to consider his request. If April had to guess, she was wondering if Jack would finally buy her that real-life, needs-a-pasture llama that she'd been chattering about for months.

Simone, clearly grasping that Harmony was heading for a shakedown, not a negotiation, gave her that soft smile she should go ahead and patent, package, and market. She said but two words. "Chocolate chip."

Cookies. She was using cookies as a bribe.

And Jack thought *he* was good at negotiations.

CHAPTER SIX

"You are enough just as you are."
—Maria, Oregon, United States

April

"That was easier than expected," Jack said as Harmony did a two-step skip toward Simone.

April glanced at him. He was taking it all in, his expression impassive, but he followed the group to the door with a look. His mental note-making apparently engaged as he monitored Harmony and Simone. Don't ask her how she knew, she could just feel his mind calculating scenarios and following their movement. He probably had a finger on the pulse of Lola and Rohan, too. Which meant he was probably also taking the pulse of—

He moved his gaze to April.

She cleared her throat. Simone and the kids bustled across the yard to the fence, letting themselves through the gate to Simone and Yelena's three-story Victorian. The homes on the street had been original to Denver and dated back to the days when the city was founded. They'd all been updated and remodeled countless times. Modernized with an attentive eye to including the history of each home.

The moment April drove onto the street, she knew she'd call it home.

Kent had preferred the new-build community four streets

over. Then again, he had a thing for new builds, apparently. In his case, the grass wasn't just greener on the other side, it was straight-up artificial.

"Sorry about that." April brushed her low ponytail back over her shoulder. "I'm sure Harmony really likes you, too."

Jack's grin stretched wide. "But she likes chocolate chips more?"

"Cookies." April fidgeted with her hands, then dropped them to her sides. "She's a total fiend for all things cookies. Last year at her birthday she even asked for a cookie cake. The kind with extra fudge frosting and buttercream accents. And llamas. Also otters. Don't ask me why."

"Can't say I blame her. Cookies, llamas, and otters, all good things." Jack put his hands in the pockets of his slacks, lifting the edges of his suit jacket at the movement. The hands-in-pockets thing was totally innocuous, but it had the unfortunate—or fortunate—result of pulling the fabric taut over his…

April ripped her gaze away. Because the bulge there was on display. Not like it was totally inappropriate or anything. She just caught a glimpse. Then she'd been super impressed. Then she'd averted her eyes like the totally rational woman she was.

Keeping eye contact was important because being the utmost professional while watching her career implode built character. That's what she would've told her kids, anyway. "Do you want to sit? Can I get you something to drink?"

"I'm good." He moved to an armchair alongside the sofa, sitting there. "Let's have a chat, yeah?"

His eyes had a kindness to them, a dose of reality, that made her want to crawl inside them and stay for a while. Ugh. Just like that, she wanted to get comfortable in all that was… Jack.

"That's why you're here, amiright?" She sat on the sofa catty corner to his chair, propped at the edge, ensuring her posture was on pointe. "That, uh, grocery store event didn't go well."

Understatement of the century. Her palms itched at just the thought of the day before. Of Betsy and the things she'd written.

"It won't happen again. That's why I'm here." He sat forward, obviously calculating something about her, moving to just outside her personal-space bubble. Not invasive or anything. Actually, the proximity was nice. Professional, yet she could still catch the scent of his cologne—tea leaves, cedar, and vanilla.

Why couldn't he smell like bologna sandwiches or something? He had everything else going for him. Did he have to smell amazing, too?

She toyed with her fingers before pressing them against her knees. *Do it, April. Rip off the bandage. Follow the footwear slogan and "Just do it."*

"How do you want to do this?" she asked, squaring her shoulders. "Void my contract. What are the steps?"

The question seemed to surprise him. For the barest of moments, he broke his facade. The one she'd bought into of him being totally in control.

"Why would I void your contract?" he asked, slowly.

"Because I screwed up everything with the video and then it went…" She let out a long stream of air. "Well, we both know what happened then."

He paused. Shifted. Paused again.

She couldn't seem to pull her eyes away from the way his lips parted and closed.

"Do you understand just how much money our firm has put into your launch?" he asked.

She didn't. Not really. She had a hunch, of course, because she paid attention. It wasn't a little amount of money.

"I convinced Ben and the board to go all in on you." He shifted, holding her hostage with his eyes again. "And do you know why I did that?"

She shook her head because, to be honest, she really didn't.

"Because I believe in you." He enunciated the words.

Then he was a liar. She wasn't sure why he would lie about this, but she didn't believe him. He had no reason to believe in her.

"You barely know me," she said, picking at another dog hair. This fabric was like a freaking magnet.

"I believe in what you can be." He seemed serious. How could he be serious about this?

Because even she didn't have any idea what she could be. Not really. Not anymore. She brushed off his words as a line he was using to pacify her to get whatever it was he wanted. He had to have an angle here.

"You don't believe me," he said with as much confidence as before. "We'll have to work on that."

"Work on me believing you?" Because she didn't. Other than her closest friends, she didn't believe most people these days. Her post-divorce trust issues were definitely still raging.

He nodded. "You'll get there." He sat up straight, his button-down white dress shirt stretching over his pectorals. "First, we're going to get you to believe in yourself."

April would not acknowledge what that declaration did to her insides. Spoiler: it felt nice.

"In the meantime," Jack said, "I've got some thoughts on things we can do to help bring back that calm confidence I know you still have."

"My confidence is shot." So very shot.

"I've got a statement I worked up with the team. You'll read it on your blog and on an Instagram video. Then they'll handle the replies."

Er… "What kind of a statement?"

"Accept responsibility that things went wrong and deflect right into neutral territory. Then get going on that confidence boost. It's still there, and we're going to find it. But we're going to need to work closely together while we do."

Uh…

"We have been working together." They had. She'd talked to his staff daily. She'd communicated with him weekly—sometimes by phone, sometimes by email.

Jack removed a folded paper from his coat pocket and handed it over. She scanned the document. Just a few lines expressing her apology for what happened. How excited she was for the future. That there was amazing stuff coming soon she couldn't wait to talk about.

"What's the amazing stuff?" she asked.

"I've drafted a multipoint plan to get you back on track before the big *Practical Parenting* episode. Step one is for you to get comfortable in front of a live audience again."

Er… "I'm sorry. What kind of plan is this?" Because that seemed more like step twenty, not step one.

If he wasn't firing her? Great. Supremely great. She still had a gig.

However, and it was a massive *however*, there was no way she would put herself through another live example of what a failure she could be. Prerecorded video? Absolutely. She was all in. A carefully crafted live from her home that she could control? Sure thing.

Another opportunity for losing her shit? Never. Not ever. Again.

When Jack had landed this interview, she'd been so excited. That level of exposure was a dream come true.

Before.

Now she had to cancel that particular dream. Which was pretty apt for her recent life decisions. They needed a new strategy. One that didn't involve *Practical Parenting* or anything else not filmed in advance with an abundance of opportunity for editing.

"The plan is for us to move forward through this challenge," he said. "You are coming out on the other side of this with no permanent brand damage. That's not only what I'm saying—it's what I'm promising."

Brilliant idea. But—

"Is that even possible at this point?" She didn't think so. Rachel didn't think so. Simone definitely didn't think so. Kitty perched on the fence.

His blue eyes bore into hers.

"Yes. The Plan is going to work." He nodded as he spoke. His certainty nearly had her nodding along with him.

It took four tries to perfect the video of her apology and her excitement for the future. Jack filmed from his cell and forwarded to the team to edit and post.

April remained more than a little shell-shocked.

"This really isn't the part where you tell me I'm done?" She pinched at Harmony's ring again.

"April." He gave her that look of his that heated her skin in a good way, right before he went in for the kill that he delivered in most definitely not *a good way*. The haughty chin lift. The squint. The way he scrunched half of his face, causing his left dimple to pop. "This is the part where we make you shine."

CHAPTER SEVEN

"Trust your instincts and don't be afraid to ask for help."
—Elizabeth, Hornsby, Australia

Jack

Jack glanced around April's living room. Purple must be April's favorite color because she filled the entire house with it. He liked it. Appreciated the soothing feel of the house. The way a guy felt like he could take off his suit jacket and relax.

The place felt like a home—like people who loved one another lived there. The whole vibe reminded him of Sarah and Ben's house. Or Rachel's, even. Which meant there would probably be a kid screeching through at any moment to wreck the serenity. That's how it usually played out.

Though April had that calming scented stuff everywhere. Maybe that worked with kids? The house smelled like the candle shop across from Neiman-Marcus that Sarah had dragged him to when he moved into his apartment.

She'd insisted he needed candles. Though he never ended up using the ones she'd given him as a housewarming gift. She mentioned something about essential oil blends and stress levels and how his future girlfriend would appreciate his efforts in domestication.

"There's something we need to figure out." April heaved a huge lungful of air and her face paled. "With your plan."

Jack waited to see where she was going with this, but he had a strong hunch he wouldn't like it. Especially given the chatter about contract cancelling.

"The live *Practical Parenting* appearance has to go." She nodded as she said this, though her complexion paled further.

He shook his head. No. He didn't like that. "That's not a good idea."

Actually, it was a horrible idea.

"What if it's what's good for me?" she asked, resigned, like she only reluctantly believed it.

And she reluctantly believed it because she was wrong. Giving up the thing that would make her a household name, the thing they'd spent all this time working toward, was not the way to go. The exposure from this appearance would give her everything she'd told him she wanted when they first started working together.

"Is it, though?" he asked, the calming candle stuff not nearly potent enough for him in that moment.

She pursed her lips. "I can't do that again. No more viral anything for me."

Whew. All right. He shook his shoulders. They had a bigger problem than he'd originally thought. April needed to get back in the game, not throw the fourth quarter.

So, yeah. A new multipoint plan started percolating. He was a touch iffy on the details, but with a little effort it would be solid, of that he was certain. His plans were always solid. They always worked. Always made money.

Which meant he had to manipulate the hell out of this situation so it'd fall like dominoes in his favor. In April's favor.

Which, luckily for all involved, was his specialty.

"Don't cancel the best thing that will ever happen to your career." He steeped his words in the calm he needed her to embody. Because this was her big break. This was what her career needed. He knew it like he knew how to breathe. "You've got the best team behind you. *Me* behind you. We won't let you fail. Viral can be good. We're going to make that happen."

What happened before would not happen again.

"I appreciate your belief in me." April threaded her hands in her lap. "I really do. But no more risks. I'm not quitting. I'm still The Calm Mom. But…a prerecorded version."

Prerecorded didn't get the sponsorships. Didn't get the views.

"Okay." He splayed his hands. Leaned forward. "Here's what's going to happen. I'm going to stay here until I convince you that you've got this." He reached for her hands and held them in his. "Because you've got this."

He gave her hands a quick squeeze and released.

The firm headshake she gave set his back teeth on edge. "You're going to sit here in my living room until I change my mind?"

No, he had a feeling this would take more time than that. Also, eventually the kids would return, and he should probably check out before that.

"Denver," he said, with a roving glance and a tilt of his head toward the street. "I booked the vacation rental across the street for a couple of nights." When things went to shit, he immersed himself in the situation. It was what he did.

There had been the life coach he'd helped brand who needed the reminder he was the best at his job. Jack flew to New York, hired him, and let the guy coach him into remembering his own awesomeness. He was currently reveling in TikTok fame. Then there was the former television remodel carpenter who needed to finish flipping a house in time for the big Instagram reveal. Jack hung the damn drywall himself. Reveal was on time, sponsors came on board, everyone was happy.

His immersion method worked.

She pointed to where his eyes had trailed to the window. "*There?*"

He nodded.

Though he didn't think it possible, April's eye widening intensified, and the little wrinkles above her nose crinkled.

April pointed to the house across the street that his assistant had rented for him. "Over *there*."

He nodded again. "Yes."

She eyed him, clearly leery.

"I'm going to stay close so we can hash out the plan. I'm going to stay close because you matter, April."

She shifted, but she did the thinking thing where she pulled at her bottom lip with her top teeth. Which meant he was well on his way to adjusting her trajectory back in the correct direction. He'd seen her do this on their video calls. Noted it. Tracked it. One of her consistent tells that he picked up during their first meeting.

"I fix problems. It's what I do," he continued.

"Fix problems?" she asked.

He nodded. "Exactly." Voice lowered to the tone he knew would help her relax—because it worked on 99 percent of the population he'd come across—he said, "You've had a lot of change happen over the past months."

Not being an asshole, he wouldn't actually point out that most of the change had come about because her ex was a bastard.

April didn't seem to buy in to his relaxation technique. Either that or she had a helluva poker face.

"My job is to ensure your brand thrives," he said. "That *you* thrive."

There it was again. The lip nibble.

She fidgeted with her hands. Then smoothed them against her knees.

"There's a problem." She uncrossed her arms and smoothed

her palms against her knees again.

"I'm good with solving problems." He leaned in to the problem at hand.

She glanced away. Then pointed across the street. "You might consider a hotel?"

No. Close was where he needed to be. They were about to spend a whole lot of time together.

"I don't think you know what you're getting into over there," she said. "You'll definitely be more comfortable somewhere else."

"It's a rental." He eyed the perfectly normal rancher through April's front window. He didn't need the Four Seasons.

"It's *not* just a rental," she said, her gaze not meeting his. Cleared her throat then said, "The lady who owns it—Kitty—is my friend. But she's eccentric. Very eccentric."

"I can handle eccentric." He'd have his own space, and he'd be spending most of his time with April, anyway. "Is there anything else you'd like to warn me about?"

She sat tall. "There are a *lot* of kids in this neighborhood. Many of them are mine. I'm not sure you're going to be super comfortable with all the kids, all the time."

He probably wouldn't be. But he'd manage.

"It'll be fine," he assured. "Kids love me."

She frowned at him, apparently calling bullshit on his bullshit.

Ben said his kids loved Jack. And Ben lied only when he tried to get Jack to date Sarah's friends. Therefore, it must be true.

"Have you ever even been around kids before?" There she was sounding all...unconvinced.

Uh, yeah, he was around Ben's kids sometimes. Ben was there, too, or Sarah, or both. But they were normal human beings. Just of the pint-sized variety.

"I'm good with *people*," he assured.

Again, she frowned. Clearly skeptical.

"All people," he clarified.

She continued with the frownage. "They're not *people*, they're *children*."

People. Children. Children were people, last he'd heard.

"I can handle it." He was totally sure of this point. Mostly sure. Okay, mildly certain. "You won't scare me away with your children."

He'd totally handled worse.

Hell, he'd hung drywall and bungee jumped off a bridge.

CHAPTER EIGHT

*"Know that there are days when you won't be your best self.
No one is their best self, one-hundred percent of the time."*
— *Lee Ann, New Jersey, United States*

April

"**A**re you for real?" April asked, wetting her lips a little. Because he hadn't met Kitty yet. Or read the Amazonian mud soap contract for her bed-and-breakfast guests she'd had tipsy attorney Sadie draft over rum and berry-punch juice boxes.

He also hadn't really spent time with April's children yet. Or discovered all the ways they could ruin a good suit. That had been one of the final nails in the coffin of her marriage— when Kent's favorite suit got grape Kool-Aid spilled all over the sleeve. He'd just looked up at her and said he was done.

Of course, then, she'd also found out about the other woman. So it was probably more than the sugary drink mix spill. The thought made her stomach ache, so she stopped thinking about it.

"I most definitely am *for real*," Jack said, all for-real seriousness.

She squinted at him. He was clearly the king of evaluating her, but she was a queen in her own right and she had his number, too.

And because she had his number...

She didn't believe it. He was, most definitely, *not* for real.

Because if he was for real, he would already be out the door to hop on the next plane to LAX with a voided contract in hand. Ready to run a search for a woman who was the *true* calm mom.

But he was here. And he was trying to help her fix her screw-up. Even if she had no intention of following through with *Practical Parenting* in two weeks, the little tickle in her gut soured. She'd been so damn excited when she'd landed the interview.

She briefly shut her eyes.

Now she was so damn tired.

"Are you with me on this?" he asked, adding a dash of pressure.

"Fine. *Fine.* If you want to stick around, I won't stop you." She opened her eyes and shrugged, like she was laissez-faire about it. "But prerecorded is where I'm at."

"We'll get moving on the April *Live* plan." He smiled, and she had a hunch he was about to be spending a lot of time with her. "First thing."

"I think you mean the April *Prerecorded* plan." She countered.

"I meant what I said."

"We'll see." She briefly calculated how long it would take her to speed scrub her entire life, finally settling on, "Tomorrow. Let's start tomorrow."

"Don't put off until tomorrow what you can do today," he said, apparently also ready to jump into the greeting card business with Simone.

"Unless you have a whole lot to do in between," April said.

"How about, I get settled across the street. Then I'll check in with you. We'll come up with a mutually agreeable compromise." Jack's lips spread into a grin as he held his hand to her.

"Your compromise fairy dust doesn't work on me, Jack

Gibson." April did her best impression of Harmony diva. "I'm immune."

"We'll see," he said, tossing that damn imaginary fairy dust all over her.

She had a feeling they'd be starting today. And not tonight, either—*today* today. Which was why she panicked for a split second, realizing that all of this was too much too soon.

Mayonnaise took that moment to lumber into the living room, tail held high while the tips of her basset hound ears trailed along the edge of the floor. She seemed more than a little put out about the trek into the living room. But, apparently, she was ready to meet Jack.

Mayonnaise gave him a good look. And then, if a basset hound could grin, Mayonnaise did just that.

She waddled to Jack, a little more skip to her step than April had seen in the past year. Perhaps all it took was a guy in a suit ready to play Mr. Fix-It to get Mayonnaise all skippy again.

April could relate. Her not-so-canine hormones got all skippy at the prospect of the Godiva store.

"Who is this we have here?" Jack knelt, holding his closed hand for Mayonnaise to sniff.

And sniff she did, licking the whole side of his hand. Yeah, yeah, April liked how he smelled, too. But she'd never lick him.

"This is Mayonnaise," April said, eyeing the dog to ensure she was going to behave.

She did, usually. But she had a propensity for stealing April's bras from the laundry bin because they made the best chew toys, in her elderly opinion. And she had the bladder control of an elderly basset hound...or Lola.

"Isn't that an interesting name?" Jack gave her a good massage under her floppy left ear. Mayonnaise ate it up, then let out a *harrumph* and dropped to the floor.

"She came to us with the name. It just sort of stuck." Of course, Mayonnaise hated her name. At least, April was pretty certain of this once she'd learned to understand how the dog operated. But, by that time, April hadn't wanted to confuse her by changing it. Instead, she bought her a rhinestone collar in apology.

If Harmony was the queen diva of eight-year-olds, then Mayonnaise was the queen diva of basset hounds.

Temperamental to the core with a cold shoulder that could ice the entire Denver metro area. She did not accept her age, did not accept the frequent veterinarian visits that came with it, and wanted nothing to do with the car.

For goodness sakes, April even had to slip her a special pill from the vet just before loading her up for any outings. And that was a feat because Mayonnaise didn't care for the way they tasted and could sniff them out of even the most delicious Italian meatball from Barolo Grill.

"So you like dogs?" April asked, toying with the fine hairs at the base of her ponytail.

They were going to be working together, building a plan in person. So she should probably get to know him. Understand what he liked and didn't like.

He looked up at her from where he crouched, a mega smile spread across his face. "Who doesn't?"

Mayonnaise let out a sigh, totally lapping up Jack's magic.

His hand at Mayonnaise's ear scratched harder and her tail thumped faster. Given her advanced age, he needed to be careful, getting her worked up like that.

Even the littlest bit of excitement and she'd—

The dog made the sound she made right before she—

April gasped. *Oh no.* "You're going to want to step back." April doused her voice in the urgency taking over as her pulse beat faster.

"Why?" He refocused on the dog.

Mayonnaise whined and, son of a biscuit, she relieved herself all over his fancy-looking loafers.

He bolted to his feet, taking a giant leap backward.

Welcome to my life, Jack Gibson. Welcome to my life.

CHAPTER NINE

"As long as they are breathing and can move under
their own power, everything will be all right."
—Elizabeth, Texas, United States

For the second time in as many days, April handled bodily fluids like a professional.

"You should go get settled," she suggested, her cheeks still flushed from the utter humiliation of—all that would never be mentioned again.

Because everything that had happened in the past forty-eight hours was going in the vault of things she didn't talk about or think about. Like her marriage. And that time Kitty had convinced her to buy sports bras from her sister's online lingerie company.

Yes, Jack should go get settled so she could erase her memory. She needed a minute alone to handle that task. Or many minutes.

"I'm sorry I got her so excited." Jack gave April a sympathetic smile. "Point me to the paper towels?"

Since when did a man actually offer to help her clean up? Never. That's when.

April shook her head. "I'll get the mess. It's…better for me to do it. You're in a suit."

Jack didn't look convinced. "I don't—"

"I've really got it." Of all the piddle puddles she'd cleaned in the past forty-eight hours, this one was the smallest...because it got mostly on his shoes.

His mouth parted like he was about to argue the point, but then closed, like he'd thought better of it. "I'm sorry again about this. Guess I'll go get checked in across the street."

And probably change his shoes...

Well, that was nice. Offer to help, apologize when he had done nothing wrong, gloss over his ruined fancy loafers, *and* recognize when she needed a breather. Who was this guy and what was the catch? There was definitely a catch.

"Before you head over there. What...uh..." April cleared her throat and went for her best attempt at casual. "Have you been told about your vacation rental room?" Somehow she couldn't quite bring her eyes to meet his. Not when she knew all about his room at Kitty's. If one could call it a room.

"My assistant booked it." Jack strode to the door, holding it to let April pass. "And it's close. That was my only requirement."

Well, that was good. Because that's pretty much all it had going for it.

A small battle waged inside April's mind as to whether she should fully warn him before he walked into Kitty's lair, or if she should just let it be what it would be...since given the intent of his stride, he was obviously not going to be deterred on his quest to stay with her friendly neighborhood gossip goddess.

She decided to just let it be what it would be, and followed behind him as he moved with authority across their small neighborhood street.

Jack was all business. Which, if April had to guess, was how he'd ended up at Kitty's. She billed it as the premier vacation rental for business travelers. Kitty always ended up with great reviews, soap theft notwithstanding. To be honest, April didn't know how she managed it. Because the space was...interesting.

Yes. That was a good word for it. Interesting, like Kitty.

"You know the owner?" he asked, scrolling through his cell for what appeared to be instructions for checking in.

April nodded. Because she was afraid if she spoke, she'd accidentally expose something that maybe Jack should experience firsthand.

He gave a quick knock at the door and slipped off his soaked shoes—apparently, to leave them on the mat.

The whirlwind that was Kitty yanked open the door.

On a normal day, Kitty wore tight leggings and an equally tight shirt with a deep V-neckline and a chunky belt cinched tight around her waist. On a normal day, she had a thick coat of makeup airbrushed on like a professional. A professional with a commitment to Taylor Swift's red lips.

Oh, she had all of that going on today. But today she *also* had her hair in full Farrah Fawcett 1989 glory with feathers clipped under the curtain of blond. And today she was somehow painting her fingernails while opening the door. The paint in one hand and the brush in the other held between two fingers like it was a cigarette.

Jack's eyes widened for only the barest of moments before he smacked down a boardroom cover on his emotions that would've been the best mask April had ever seen—except Kitty took that second to connect the brush to the bottle and shove it between her cleavage so the top paint handle emerged from her ta-tas.

Jack's ability to hang out in neutral was wrecked. Oh, he didn't stare at her boobs. His mouth just dropped a few centimeters.

He did, however, get bonus points for not staring at the cleavage paint.

"This is Jack," April said, because Jack had apparently been rendered silent. "He has a reservation."

"Your Jack is my Jack?" Kitty purred. "Well, hot damn. What a nice surprise."

April knew Kitty well enough to call baloney. This wasn't a surprise. She just had, for possibly the first time in her life, been tight-lipped when the information would've been nice to have.

"You don't have to take off your shoes here." Kitty nodded to the loafers. "I'm not one of those people."

"Mayonnaise peed on them." April raised her eyebrows.

"Then let's go ahead and leave them outside. Shall we, handsome?" She backed into the room, gesturing to the space. "Welcome to your home away from home."

Kitty had an affinity for animal prints and minimalism. Which meant that while the outside of the house looked like the rest of the historic neighborhood, the inside was cheetah, zebra, and snakeskin...minimalism.

After her son went off to college, Kitty had had nearly all the walls of her home torn out to create one great room with slightly rusted, reclaimed aluminum roofing lining the exterior walls. She'd had to leave those walls because if she hadn't there wouldn't have been a house anymore. This was actually a conversation that Kitty had had with April during the demolition of all the other walls in the house.

April didn't let her kids play here very much because she worried that they'd come home with tetanus from the rusted aluminum walls.

"Your room is just this way." Kitty maneuvered around her leopard print sofa to what would be Jack's room.

April used the term in the stretchiest interpretation.

She and Jack followed Kitty, and the hairs on the back of April's neck prickled. She was certain Jack would run back to Los Angeles before the tour was even over.

"Your home is very..." Jack seemed to search through all the corners of his psyche for something to compliment. "Unique."

That was, in fact, the perfect word to describe the space.

"Aren't you just the sweetest?" Kitty turned her attention from painting her nails with cleavage polish to Jack. "I still charge extra for soap. One person just has to ruin it for everyone else."

Kitty gestured to Jack's space and April watched as he gulped. Hard.

Given the concern of potential blood-borne bacteria from the walls, April didn't come over frequently. Also, Kitty usually had guests for the vacation rental. More to the point, well, to be honest, April didn't have much time for visiting. There was always something she needed to get done.

The great room held normal living room furniture with a television and a La-Z-Boy and a kitchen to the left with Kitty's bedroom and bathroom to the right. Kitty's rooms were of the normal variety.

But just near the back of the enormous space, she'd set up glass panes of office cubicle walls and—boom—her vacation rental was born.

Kitty gestured to the opening that led into the cubicle.

"There aren't any walls," Jack said. For the first time since April had known him, his warm, butterscotch voice had a touch of ominous.

"There are walls." Kitty smacked the glass. It wobbled.

April stepped back a foot, just in case it all came down.

"They don't reach the ceiling." Jack strode into the clear fish-tank of a room. "And they're transparent."

"Only if you want them to be." Kitty pushed a button, and blinds tucked between the panes of glass motored down to the ground. Well, dang, April didn't know they did that.

"I can't see over the top, don't you worry about that. Your privacy is very important to me," Kitty chirped.

April totally called pickle-flavored-bubble-gum on that assertion.

No one's privacy was important to Kitty. Jack had effectively checked his at the door.

"How's that hotel looking now?" April whispered out of the side of her mouth.

Unfortunately, Jack got a flash in his eyes like her kids did when one of them dared the other to do something ridiculous and they planned on seeing it through.

"This is great. Thank you so much." Jack raised his eyebrows toward April.

Suddenly, she didn't really want that time alone. She wanted to stay right here and watch Kitty's fish bowl with her.

Unfortunately, she had kids, and she had a crap load of life scrubbing to do.

"Do you have dinner plans?" she asked, because if she could put off the start of their collaboration and all his multipronged plans, then she'd have more time to scrub her life. At this point, every minute mattered. Bonus, no negotiation, she just took the control right into her own hands.

"Dinner plans?" Kitty asked.

"You know, when you eat later in the afternoon or early evening." Or late evening, whatever worked. "I'm sure Jack knows what I mean."

She didn't dare look at him to confirm, because he'd probably counter with a late lunch instead.

"Oh, like a date." Kitty made wide eyes, her long eyelashes blinking rapidly. April was pretty sure they were the magnetic kind. "I think that's a fabulous idea."

April paused for an uncomfortably long moment. Um…

"You and Jack should go out." She pointed between them. "Just the two of you. I'll watch your kids."

"Do you even know my kids' names?" April asked, because

honestly, she never watched the kids and she'd never called them anything other than "you there" and "hey kiddo."

"Of course I do." Kitty held her hand to her chest, then adjusted it because of the paint bottle there. "You're one of my best friends."

"Then what are their names?" April asked. She gestured to Jack. "No helping her."

"Well, there's Peace," Kitty counted off on her index finger.

"Harmony," April corrected.

"That's what I said," Kitty replied. "And there's Road."

"Rohan."

"Why do you keep repeating me?" Kitty asked. "And then the little one."

"Lola," April said, giving Jack what she hoped was a see-I-told-you glance.

"That's short for The Little One." Kitty tossed her hands up. "See, I know their names."

April laughed. "*You* are not watching my kids."

"Oh, please. How else are you going to land yourself a date with this guy here?" Kitty jerked her thumb toward Jack.

"Jack," he supplied helpfully. "And I'd be happy to have dinner, April. With or without kids. It'll be a nice break after an afternoon of plotting our next moves." He turned his attention to Kitty, stuffing his hands in his pockets.

"That's wonderful." Kitty clapped gently. "We could rope Simone into helping if April is declining my offer. Now, how do you feel about being a stepdad?"

April gave a gentle smack to Kitty's shoulder. "Boundaries."

"Do I look like a fence?" Kitty asked, gesturing to herself.

I'm sorry, April mouthed to Jack.

He didn't really seem to mind the question, but he also had that boardroom mask pulled tight.

"Boundaries," Kitty muttered under her breath. "I didn't

ask him anything personal like how much money he makes or why he's still single!"

"I appreciate that." Jack said with a curt nod.

"And I didn't ask him what he weighs, because I. Am. Not. His. Doctor," Kitty continued. "So it is none of my business."

"Again, I appreciate your holding back from asking these things," Jack said, his lips twitching.

"You," Kitty said like an accusation. She pointed her glistening-with-fresh-pink-paint fingernail at April. "Are always saying you want to get back out there in the dating world."

"I have literally never said that." Out loud.

"You want your turn to play the field?" Kitty did a little Vanna White pose to show off Jack. "Here's a man who flew all the way here to see you."

"I'm not dating *Jack*," April said, and yes, it came out sounding like the reason was because he was Jack. In a bad way. What with the emphasis on the whole *Jack* thing sounding as though he was the one beneath *her* league, which was not the case. Everyone knew that's not how leagues worked.

A person could date up, but never down. And he was clearly up. A guy like him got to go to hot-guy nights where they did hot-guy things. And she got to go eat sushi and people watch.

"What's wrong with Jack?" he asked April, scowling. Boy, he didn't like her announcement at all.

"What *is* wrong with Jack?" Kitty scowled right along with Jack. "He fills out that suit very well, if you ask me. You can't do better than that. And he's here temporarily. You definitely can't do better than *that*." She refocused on him. "You're temporary, right?"

He nodded. "Yeah."

"No one is asking you to set me up." April did her best to telepathically broadcast that Kitty needed to stop.

"Perhaps we're misunderstanding each other." His hands

found his pockets. "Dinner tonight would be great. But I'm not saying April and I should *date*, because I don't date." His elbows pressed the sides of his jacket back, exposing the black silk lining.

Gah, even the inside of his jacket was the kind of fabric that would feel like…well, silk…against her hands if he were someone else and they went on a date and then did adult things afterward.

"I think we are misunderstanding." April laughed. Because she had clearly lost her grip on appropriate emotions. Kitty's house apparently had that effect.

Maybe—and this was not something she would think too hard about—she'd reach out to Molly ASAP. Molly was her dating guru friend and she would know some reasonably attractive, but still in her league, men. Molly was like Kitty light. She meddled, but she still had boundaries.

Also, if April went on a Molly-arranged date, she could have an actual conversation with a guy who didn't ask her for anything beyond eating dinner together and…well…maybe something else. Was she ready for the something else?

Perhaps.

Man, it'd been a lot of time since she had something else.

Something else that involved a scooch of spontaneity and maybe inventive use of a silk tie like the blue geometric patterned one Jack currently wore.

That silk around her wrists, holding her in place while his lips trailed down along her collarbone to her shoulder, down to her—

"Where on earth did your mind just go?" Kitty asked wryly. "Because it seems like it dropped straight into the gutter."

Blaming her body's reaction on her present lack of romantic prospects and the drought she'd been through with men was easier than acknowledging the truth, which was that Jack was just...*so* Jack.

"You can stop now," April said, seizing the fantasy and shoving it deep in that place she held for all the things she wanted but couldn't have.

Yes, she shoved the intrusive thoughts deep, deep down, because Jack was there. He wasn't just a face on a screen. And in person, she couldn't fantasize about how he might look at her with those soulful eyes and whisk her off her feet. Especially because he was not looking like he wanted to whisk her anywhere. No, he scrutinized with scrunchy eyebrows and a gaze that seemed to x-ray vision straight to her soul.

And most certainly because they were in different leagues and his league didn't date.

Best to remember that.

"We're just colleagues," Jack said, reassuring. "Who can go to dinner and talk about business."

She gave Jack a grin and stepped to the door. "Okay. I will send you a message letting you know what I come up with for supper."

What the flaming frogs was she going to serve the guy?

"You know, April, we can plan that when I'm over there *earlier*—"

"Mom," Harmony threw open Kitty's partially open door, running clean through and straight into Jack.

She knocked him back a step, but he managed to stop her forward momentum. Unfortunately, she'd left a smear of something red on his formerly pristine white shirt.

This was how it always ended.

Jack set Harmony on her feet, more than a little awkward— like he didn't quite know what to do with a child barreling face first into him while smearing God knew what across his button-down.

"What on earth?" April asked.

"Rohan ate a bee," Harmony said, out of breath.

He did— *"What?"*

"He thought it was a fly." Harmony grabbed April's hand. "Simone sent me to get you."

"Did he get stung?" Single-focused now, April started heading out without a backward glance.

Of course, he got stung. One didn't eat a bug with a stinger without getting stung.

Crap. Jack. April turned back to him. "I've got a problem to deal with—"

"It sounds like you've got a lot on your plate," Jack said, all sweet and gentlemanly. "Why don't we just plan on catching up during dinner."

"Or, you know, breakfast?" April said, rushing behind Harmony and not giving him a chance to respond.

If marriage had taught her anything, it was that sometimes this was the only way to win a compromise discussion.

April made it halfway across the street before Kitty was chasing after her. "April!"

She turned. "Kitty, I've got to get to Rohan."

"I'll walk with you." Kitty did a little jog to catch up with April, her nail polish nearly bouncing right out of her cleavage. "Because Jack needs to borrow your shower tomorrow morning."

April paused. There in the middle of the street. She paused. *"What?"*

"Why does she keep saying that?" Kitty asked Harmony.

Harmony lifted a shoulder. "I don't know."

"Walk and talk, people," April said, still hurrying to Simone's house and her bee-eating kid.

Kitty waved her hands like she was drying her nails while conversing. "I'm going to make sure there's no hot water at my place. Jack will need a shower." She leaned in like they were conspiring—which, it should be noted, they were not. "At your place."

April brushed a stray hair from her forehead. Kitty could not read a room to save a life. "You have got to stop whatever this is you're trying to do."

"I am trying to get you over whatever this is that's making you all tragic."

April huffed a breath. Stalling her momentum only a second. "I am not tragic."

"You won't be when I'm done." She flashed two perfect rows of white teeth in an expression of pure maniacal Kitty.

"Kitty," April stretched her name.

Kitty slammed her hands on her waist, somehow having the presence of mind to spread her fingertips up so the polish didn't get wrecked. "If my water heater breaks tomorrow around five a.m., do you mind if Jack borrows a shower at your house? Since you are my favorite neighbor and it would be neighborly?"

April sighed. "You know I would never refuse such a request. But Kitty. Don't do it."

Kitty said nothing. She just turned and strutted back to her house.

Back to Jack.

CHAPTER TEN

"It's okay. It's microfiber."
—*Overheard at Moms' Night Out*

April

Rohan hadn't eaten a bee. He'd eaten a flying insect that looked a whole lot like a bee but wasn't. She knew this thanks to the regurgitation of the insect. Raise the roof for fake bees. A fake bee that April thanked tremendously for buying her time to get her house together last night.

She hadn't mentioned to Jack that it was a fake-out bee. HIPAA probably covered this information somehow—at least that's what she told herself.

Now, at least symbolically, April's ducks were marching on the same side of the street. Not in a row yet, but they were at least in a huddle.

Last night she did what she could to scrub her life. Mostly, her house. Also, for reasons that had nothing to do with Jack, she shaved her legs.

Hey, it was a start.

Also, April made her bed pre-breakfast that morning—for the first time in months.

No, it was not because Jack was in her shower, thanks to the magic of Kitty.

Making her bed just used to be the first thing she did back when things were better, and the routine used to bring peace.

But when the peace had gone, so had the habits she'd formed. The alignment she'd worked so hard for turned upside down and sideways.

But that morning she'd even smoothed the corners of the sheet covering the king-size extra-soft mattress she'd bought as soon as the divorce was final. The new bed took up a good deal of the bedroom, but she didn't care. It wasn't like she needed space for anything but sleep. And she loved the feel of stretching out in her own area at night.

Her phone dinged on the countertop.

Simone: *Good morning, chickadee. Morning check-in!*

A warm feeling that always came when Simone did this wound through April. Nearly every morning—except on the days that April beat her to it—Simone would check in with her. Just to be sure she was, and she was quoting here, "Still breathing."

April appreciated having a hey-are-you-still-breathing friend. She lifted her phone and swiped her thumb over the screen to reply.

April: *Morning.*

Simone: *I saw your Jack out for a run wicked early.*

Jack was a runner? *Huh.* But it wasn't like April knew much about him or his fitness habits or any of his habits. Still, she tucked that tidbit away. Even though she wasn't really sure why.

April: *Fitness is important.*

Simone: *Indeed it is.*

April: *He's currently in my shower.*

Simone: *WHAT?*

April: *Kitty. Don't ask.*

Simone:...

April: *Tell Yelena I'm using the mascara she bought me for my birthday.*

Simone: *!!! What, may I tell my wife, is the reason you're* *wearing mascara?*

April: *No reason.*

And all the reasons.

Simone: *This is Y. I want to see.*

April moved back to her bedroom and pulled open the curtains and the blinds. Sure enough, just as she knew they'd be, Simone and Yelena stood at the window opposite April's room. Yelena was dressed in her scrubs, so it must've been hospital rotation day for her. Simone was still in her purple bathrobe—the one April and Harmony had picked out for Christmas last year.

April held her palm over the unfinished eye and did a Queen of England wave.

Yelena grinned, then gave her a thumbs-up before leaving Simone alone at the window.

Simone's eyebrows were raised. High. She glanced to her screen, tapping out another message.

This time, though, it ended up not being a message. April's phone rang.

"Girl." Simone only had to say the one word.

April ran her hand through the fine curls in her hair. She hadn't added enough hairspray, so she wasn't even certain they'd last until breakfast. "It's not a big deal."

Simone tsked. "Your hair?"

So what if she'd ditched her usual low ponytail? So what if she fixed her hair *with curls and everything*?

"I needed to be sure my curling iron still works." What if it stopped working, and she hadn't realized it?

"And the skirt?" Simone gestured to the outfit.

So what that she'd also decided to wear a skirt? A cute, short number with binding around her midsection to make it seem a size smaller.

The season was still early enough in the fall that it wasn't too cold for a skirt.

April ran a hand over the article of clothing in question. "Technically, it's not even a skirt."

Simone squinted, looking harder, even though April was sure she could probably see just fine. "Then what am I looking at that's covering your ass?"

"It's a *skort*." It *was* a skort because there were shorts underneath.

"What is a skort?" Simone looked as though April was speaking to her in Sanskrit.

April struck a pose.

"It's cute. Shows your legs. You never show your legs." Simone grinned. "I bet Jack will eat you up."

The skort set was cute. Pale blue in the shade that matched her logo.

April's heart sank a little. "I didn't do this for Jack."

She did it for herself, so she'd feel more confident around Jack.

"If you're dressing up for you, I like that all the better." Simone's tone turned comforting.

"I needed to figure out how to wear the skorts in case we have to do photoshoots. I've never worn a skort before." Because an athletic skirt—while comfortable—didn't really fit into her usual routine. Sure, it was perfectly appropriate for a woman who taught yoga, she just hadn't been sure where to wear it.

"Girl, stop saying that. It's not a word." Simone chuckled.

"It is a word!" And Simone was making this a much bigger deal than necessary. So what that she hadn't quite known where to wear the skorts when they arrived because she was, through and through, a yoga-pants woman?

"Baby," Simone held the phone away from her mouth and hollered over her shoulder. "Is the word skorts a word?"

April sighed, but she didn't really mean it. Simone just

needed to get through her drama. "It's a word. Google it."

"I don't need to. I have Yelena." Simone grinned. Then she held the phone away as she leaned toward Yelena's muffled voice. When she held it back to her ear, she said, "You'll be happy to know that Yelena said that if you want skorts to be a word, then I need to leave you alone about it."

"I've got to go finish my right eye," she said, ready to track down her kids and get them breakfast.

"Go, girl." Simone waved and hung up.

April pulled her curtains closed. Leaning back against the fabric, she let her feet root into the floor, let her eyelids drift closed, and allowed her focus to become a pinprick at the end of her nose. Then she breathed.

"Make room for me," Harmony's hissing voice carried across the hall from April's bedroom.

April opened her eyes, glancing around the room.

There seemed to be some kind of scuffle going on in the hallway on the landing. She uprooted her feet and headed in that direction.

The house had four rooms at the top of the stairs. Two on one side—that's where the kids slept. Lola and Harmony in one room, Rohan in the other. They had their own shared bathroom between their rooms.

On the other side of the landing was April's bedroom, with its own en suite bath. And the guest bedroom across the hall that used to be Kent's office. That bedroom did not have an attached bath.

She stepped onto the landing and—

Oh, for goodness' sake. Three children were lined up crisscross-applesauce, a campfire-style semicircle, ass to carpet, in the hallway outside the bathroom where Jack was showering. At least, that's what April assumed he was doing, given she could hear the shower running.

April's pulse sped up, even as she commanded it to remain steady.

Her kids were all in on their Jack curiosity. Once he'd showed up for his shower, he unwittingly adopted three little people shadows and one canine shadow. Because, yes, Mayonnaise had even made the trek up the stairs to sit with the kids outside the bathroom door. And Mayonnaise never came up the stairs. Stairs were beneath her.

April eyed where Jack had hung his suit right outside the bathroom door. Apparently, he didn't want it to get steamed by the shower.

If she had a suit that expensive, she'd probably not want it to get steamed by her shower water, either. But if she had a suit that expensive, she sure as heck wouldn't wear it around her kids. Or her. Or her house. She just wouldn't wear it, *ever*.

"Don't wait outside the door like this," April whispered, trying to shoo her kids along. But they were, all three of them, clearly not interested in moving, because no one budged at her request.

The man enthralled her kids.

To be honest, it was sort of hard not to be. What with him being new and shiny and… No, she refused to think of the odds of him being naked behind that door.

She'd just bet that Jack's body was as good as his voice—and that was saying bunches.

"C'mon," she continued, shooing only air with her hands. "You cannot wait for him *here*."

Lola shoved her thumb in her mouth. Rohan licked at a spot on the wall. Harmony squeezed one side of her mouth into her I-do-what-I-want smirk.

"I like Jack." Harmony's words were dreamy. Like Jack was a celebrity, and he deserved all sorts of adoration.

Fine, so the kids weren't about to move. She would've sworn

all four of them—dog included—seemed to settle their bottoms firmer into the carpet. Even little Lola, who usually went with whatever flow April needed her to, happily munched her thumb instead of moseying along down to the kitchen.

"Kids…" April shoved her hands into the curls she'd worked so hard on.

None of them met her gaze.

"What if I said this hallway is now the home of time-out?" Because usually she couldn't get them to sit in time-out for any length of time. Usually, in the mornings, they were all energetic balls of childhood bouncing off the walls.

"If this is time-out, are we prepaying?" Harmony asked.

What on earth was Harmony talking about? And why on earth wasn't she *moving*?

"Prepaying?" April asked.

"Like at school if we give extra money to the lunch lady so we can use it the next day?"

Oh, well then—

"No, you are not prepaying." April lifted a reluctant Lola into her arms. "And you can say good morning to Jack at breakfast."

"Jack." Lola pointed at the door, squirming to get April to release her grip. When that didn't work, Lola went totally limp, which had the odd result of making her three times heavier. Thus she slid down the length of April until her bare feet were back on the floor. April released her because…man, what else was she supposed to do? Lola cemented her bottom to the carpet once more.

"Ribbit," Rohan said, with a pointed look at the door.

The shower turned off. Gah. Jack would come out here and there was this whole audience thing going on.

April kneeled next to her son. "I get it. Jack's interesting. But you can't wait for him like this. It's rude to stand outside the bathroom door."

Also, a touch creepy.

"That's why we're not standing," Harmony stage-whispered back. "We're sitting."

April pointed to the staircase. "Downstairs. Breakfast."

She used her best-she-could-do firm tone. But even three kids into this mom thing, she hadn't quite mastered it.

April sat beside Harmony, matching her cross-legged seat, to better explain all the reasons they needed to skedaddle right out of there and get downstairs. Lola plopped down in April's lap.

"Harmony, I'll let you pick whatever you want for breakfast. Even a toaster tart, if that's what you really want." April rarely gave in to Harmony's toaster tart addiction. "Rohan, I think I saw a new frog in the backyard. You should go check."

If both of the older two left, Lola would follow. The dog, however, was probably not moving.

"There aren't any new frogs in the backyard." Harmony straight-up rolled her eyes. "Don't fall for it, Ro."

Rohan had a thing with trying to collect frogs. He'd been on a bit of a bender lately with the backyard frog hunts. He loved animals, though, so he was fine with the whole catch and release rule April had insisted on. Given that he hunted frogs only in her backyard and Simone's, she was fairly certain he *might* be catching the same frog over and over again. They all looked the same to her, anyway.

"Ribbit," he said, pointing to the door.

Right. Okay. So Jack-intrigue trumped frogs. Good to know. She might even use this knowledge to her advantage.

Once she got them all to move.

The doorknob clicked with the release of the lock, and April's head drained of all feeling.

She started to stand, but with Lola unmoving on her lap, it

was more of a baby deer style attempt at standing.

The door to the bathroom opened and there was Jack in all his glory reaching for his suit...wrapped in a white cotton towel.

Here's the thing. When April had chosen white doors for the remodel, she'd chosen them because she thought they'd be bright and cheery. When she elected to paint the bathroom yellow, she'd done it because she thought it would make the small space feel bigger. Adding the skylight? That had been to ensure enough lighting.

She had done none of those things knowing that when Jack Gibson stepped onto that threshold between the bathroom and the landing, he'd look like an angel. An angel *with* a halo and everything.

Harmony gasped.

Mayonnaise let out a low growl.

Yeah, that.

Halo or not, crap on a crumpet, shirtless Jack was breathtaking.

The ambiance of the makeshift halo was simply the cherry on top of the ice cream sundae of Jack.

"Uh." His gaze moved around the semicircle of Davises sitting right outside the door—April included. "Good morning, everyone." He drew that last word out.

Mayonnaise hefted herself up on her paws to meander over toward Jack.

"Do you want to have a tea party?" Harmony asked as she stood. "With me." She pointed to her little eight-year-old chest.

"Um..." Jack frowned, then caught himself and grinned a half smile, his gaze slipping to April. He frowned again before recovering.

Right. Her eye.

Shit. She covered her non-made-up eyelid with her palm. Of course, here was Jack in his towel of glory while she sat outside with her kids like they'd been ready to have a campfire on the landing and sing camp songs, all with eye makeup on only one eyelid.

Nice. Excellent. Very smooth, April.

This is precisely what happened when a woman tried too hard. She ended up with one eye made up and one eye not, and a whole passel of kids who listened only when it suited them.

She filled her lungs with a large gulp of air, grounding herself in her home. Allowing the feeling of each toe sinking into the carpet to become her foundation, starting with her pinky toe and ending with her big toe mound.

"Kids. Downstairs. Now." Well, damn. April finally nailed the tone because Harmony, Rohan, *and* Lola all hopped to and scampered down the stairs. Harmony grumbled something about her tea party invitation during her evacuation. April would figure out what to do about that later.

After Jack got dressed and the kids went to school.

She couldn't put off the inevitable fixing Jack was so insistent he could accomplish.

Mayonnaise did not follow the children. She did, however, appear to give April a doggie version of stink eye.

The traitor.

"Was that the welcome committee?" Jack asked, his naked torso right on display. The heat steaming from him finished her off and melted her like a creamsicle ice cream cone, rendering her momentarily speechless.

"Because if we're doing this officially with invitations to tea parties," he said, "let me know next time. I should probably put pants on."

Thank God he did not gesture to his pant-less legs because then she'd have had to look.

April swallowed hard and dropped the palm covering her eye. "I was just finishing my makeup when I heard the kids out here." She sighed. "I was trying to get them to leave before you…you know…"

Jack's eyes searched hers and held them to his. "Let's get started on the agenda for the day. Talk about goals, how we're going to get there, all that."

"After you get dressed?" April asked.

He nodded. "Obviously."

"Then I need to feed my children. Get them to school. Return home. Check my socials. Do the dishes. Check my socials again. Then we'll talk about agendas and goals?" Hey, she was nothing if not the queen of deflecting.

"Can I hire a car to take the kids to school so we can focus?" Jack asked, clearly not liking that she had to continue with her life even though he was right there.

Right there in a towel.

Here's the thing, Jack was perfectly decent. A white terry cloth towel covered his entire lower torso.

"You want to hire a driver to take my kids to school?" Not that she'd object, it just seemed like painting the fence while her house was on fire.

"And pick them up. So we can focus," Jack added.

She shook her head. "Then I'd have to fill out a bunch of paperwork at each school for this *driver*." That would take another half hour, at the very least. Probably more because they'd have to hire the driver, and then they'd have to get their information for the schools, and then the paperwork.

Jack let out a long breath. "Fine. Okay. Once you get back, we'll get going."

"Perfect." April gave a curt nod.

"No more putting this off," he said, softly. "Are we in this together?" The gentle way he said the words had her rethinking why she had become the queen of deflecting discomfort. She'd need to work on that.

"Yes." She held out her pinky. "Pinky swear."

He linked his pinky with hers like he did this all the time. She was certain he didn't do that all too often.

Mayonnaise eyed Jack's towel like it was one of April's bras left in the laundry.

"Mayonnaise," April said, releasing her pinky with a clipped, "Come."

Mayonnaise did not come.

No, she seemed to study a droplet of water as it trailed between the hairs along Jack's shins. For the record, Jack had excellent shins.

Clearly, Mayonnaise thought so too, because she reached her tongue out...and. She. Licked. It.

CHAPTER ELEVEN

"How many times do I need to say the same thing?"
—*Shelley, Kent, United Kingdom*

Jack

Jack could deal with slow going, but this was ridiculous. He couldn't actually fix things if he couldn't get an audience with the woman herself.

The Band-Aid apology had done the job of staunching the immediate viral bleeding, but they needed to get moving or it wouldn't hold.

He clicked send on his most recent pitch for April's brand, to the network news this time.

Then the cursor on his laptop blinked at him from the farmhouse table in April's kitchen. The family obviously used the table, given the number of scuffs in the wood, but it wasn't worn. Scuffs added character he hadn't realized was possible when it came to furniture. All of his furniture looked like it had the day the interior decorator helped him choose it from the showroom floor. Fine. She picked it. He didn't really care, so he went along with whatever she suggested.

Where his walls were the gray the designer had picked out, April's white kitchen walls contrasted with a multitude of purple. April sure loved her purple. Purple plates, mugs, even flatware.

He finished returning emails and texting Ben, all while sipping on his not-so-hot coffee out of a mug covered in a dozen yoga-posed stick figures.

April had offered her kitchen table for his workspace until she returned, and he was all on board with that. Not that he was avoiding Kitty's, but it wasn't so—*Kitty*—here at April's. Which meant he'd get more done without being peppered with questions about…everything.

Like she was waiting for him to think of her, Kitty breezed right on through the back door.

"There you are," she sang, hips swaying.

"Here I am," he replied before refocusing on the task at hand.

He had his not-so-celebrity-anymore chef up in Vail, and he had April here in Denver. He was pretty sure there was a way to loop this situation to benefit them both. Kid cookbook. Relaxing foods—was that a thing? It should be a thing. Relaxing. Kid. Foods.

Bam.

Brilliant.

As soon as April actually met with him, he'd pitch it.

Kitty poured herself a cup of coffee from April's coffeemaker and sat across from him. "I've been thinking."

He glanced away from his screen. "Do I want to know what you've been thinking?"

Because last night when she got to thinking, she'd tried to set him and April up on a date and it'd made everything very uncomfortable. He hadn't been sure exactly why it had rubbed him so wrong when April announced she didn't want to date *him*, but it had. Perhaps it was the emphasis on the *Jack* part of her declaration. Not that he was interested in dating. Clearly, he was not. Still, a little pin pricked his chest at her declaration that made him start to wonder what was wrong with *him*?

He would ask Ben, but then he'd tell his wife and wouldn't that just be a whole thing?

"What I've been thinking is excellent." Kitty scooted her

chair in, sitting taller. "Because it has to do with April, and you're Mr. Fix It."

Curious, he closed his laptop and gave her his full attention. Funny thing about people like Kitty—the unique lot who didn't march to their own drum, but decided they'd rather march to a tambourine—those were the ones who sometimes had the best ideas.

They were also the ones who sometimes had the worst ideas.

"What about April?" He took Kitty's bait.

"She's overworked." Kitty took a sip of her coffee, pulled a face, and set it aside. "That's not good."

"It's coffee." He took a sip of his own. Tasted fine. A little cold, but not the worst he'd had.

"I don't care for coffee." Kitty waved her hand to the mug. "Here's the thing. April is in a rut of laundry. You should see this place when you're not here. I mean, it's like a laundromat bomb went off." She made an impressive *ka-pow* sound. "And the kids make messes everywhere." She leaned in to him. "I mean everywhere."

He leaned in to her. "What's your idea?"

"You. Fix. It." She punctuated each word with a smack on the table.

Wait. What? "I hire April a housekeeper?"

Kitty pursed her lips. "Here I thought you were a smart one." She gave him a once-over that made him shiver. "No, gumdrop, *you're* going to have to do it. Because lord knows she won't let me do it. Or Simone. Or any of the others who have offered to help. You might be just the man to get away with it. You've got to be sly. Can you be sly?"

He grinned. "I can be sly."

Especially when it made things work in his favor.

"Build her confidence slowly," Kitty stretched out the word. "So she doesn't even know it's happening."

He grinned. "I like the way you think."

"Have you ever cooked a lobster?" she asked, totally serious, tilting her head to the side.

Nope. And he was not sure what that had to do with laundry and messes, but this was Kitty, so he let that slide. "No."

"You turn up the heat just a little every so often until it's ready for supper." She nodded firmly, her hair bouncing with the motion. "The thing never even knows it got cooked." She, again, tapped out each word with her fingernail on the table. "Can you believe that? He's just in there one minute having a spa day and the next he's ready for the main course."

"Kitty." He speared her with a glance. "I have no idea what that means for April."

"*You* just turn up the heat a puny trace at a time so she gets her confidence back and then, boom." She smacked her hands together with a good deal of force.

He jumped.

"She's that calm mom thingy again. The one she's always going on about." She barely took a breath, but she made a come-here motion with her index finger. "Tell you a secret."

He nodded but did not lean forward.

"She's not very calm anymore." She looked around the totally wrecked kitchen. Yeah, the kids were like a hurricane at breakfast. There were only three of them, but they made enough noise for an entire elementary school cafeteria. And the mess. Dear God, the mess. He shuddered.

"I think you have some work to do." Kitty raised her eyebrows.

"Can I at least send out the laundry to be done?" he asked. That's what he did in L.A. The service was great—dirty clothes left, clean clothes came back, folded and pressed and ready to go.

Kitty scowled. "Not smart at all. This guy."

"Fine." He could fold the hell out of some laundry. How hard could it be? He used to do it all the time back when he'd been in business school. He'd worked a second job at Mervyn's in the menswear section, and he used to be decent at folding those collared shirts for the displays. He was sure he still had it.

Probably still had it.

She held out her pinky. "No sending the laundry away and no housekeepers, pinky swear?"

What were they, ten years old? Apparently, this was a Denver thing. He didn't leave her hanging, though, he linked his pinky with hers. That got him a massive Kitty purr. Saying nothing else, she sauntered to the front door and let herself right out, leaving him to stare at her barely touched coffee cup.

Kitty was truly out there, but she wasn't wrong. And her plan wasn't bad. If he added it to his current multipoint plan, it might actually make things easier.

He'd been chewing on the fact that he'd probably have to stick around longer than a few days—more like at least through her *Practical Parenting* appearance. He couldn't really spare two weeks away, but he'd make it work.

Mayonnaise lifted an eyelid when he glanced at her.

"This is not a bad idea," he said to the dog.

The dog did not respond.

"It's actually a good idea," he continued.

Again the dog did not respond.

The back door opened and April bustled through. "Hey, sorry that took so long. Lola had a meltdown at drop-off." The edges of her lips turned down at that statement before she apparently recovered and blasted through the frown with a gentle smile. "Thanks for waiting."

He shifted in his seat, since his body had reacted in an entirely surprising way when he'd seen her in the skirt in the hall that morning. Yeah, it was inappropriate, but his body didn't seem to care about inappropriate with the way the skirt rode up the slightest bit along her thigh.

She had a freckle there on the left leg, just above the knee. He knew because he had forced himself to stop his upward gaze at that point and skip to her face.

Unfortunately, seeing her in the short skirt again was doing the same damn thing to him now.

"Is she okay?" he asked, willing his body to behave like a fucking professional.

April nodded. Swallowed hard. Then toyed with the tea bag in her own yoga stick-figure mug. "This is our normal."

"Are you okay?" he asked.

The way she leaned to the left, stared at the string on her tea bag, and never actually took a sip—this wasn't the April he'd signed.

She nodded. "I'm fine."

Just like every person on the planet knew—or should know—when the woman in front of them said she was fine in that tone? She wasn't okay.

"Do you want to talk about it?" he asked, standing, grabbing his mug and joining her at the counter.

She wrapped her hands around her cup but didn't take a drink.

"No." The look she gave him with the watery eyes and the soft shake of her head made him want to give her a hug. And, to be clear about one thing, Jack did not give hugs.

She seemed to shake off whatever was making it not okay. Sipping what had to be tepid tea.

He should've warmed it up for her.

That's probably what Kitty would've told him to do. And, if he was learning anything, he should probably start helping April by thinking a little more about what Kitty would do.

"What's on the agenda for today?" April asked, sticking the

mug in the microwave and pressing the button labeled beverage.

"Well, to start, I want to talk to you about a cookbook opportunity." He leaned against the counter, crossing his socked feet. He'd learned his lesson about wearing shoes around Mayonnaise.

Since he wasn't wearing shoes, his suit jacket felt more than a little out of place.

But he was at work—even if he was at April's place—so he'd put it on.

"What kind of opportunity?" She scrunched her forehead. Apparently, she didn't know what to do with that.

If he were Kitty, he probably wouldn't jump right in to cookbooks—he'd get to know a little more of April's day.

"We'll get to that. Tell me more about what you would normally do once the kids are at school," he said.

Her bottom lip must've been chocolate flavored, what with the way she gnawed at it.

"First, I need to check my social media accounts. I haven't *really* looked at them since the...you know. I've looked. But not *looked*. Then I need to ensure the new posts went up as scheduled. Then I'll do thirty minutes of yoga class planning and write up a five-minute meditation for next Monday. Then I'll answer email, fold as much laundry as I can in the thirty minutes that are left before I pick up Lola. Oh, and I try to remember to throw a load in the washer between emails and folding, so at least someone in the house will have clean clothes tomorrow." She took a deep breath. "Then it's lunch for Lola and me. I work while she naps—reply to comments, check attendance at my Tuesday and Thursday in-person class, and send a personal note to everyone who signed up in advance. Then it's time to start the evening shift." She said all of this in what seemed to be a well-practiced recitation.

He got it. He did. He worked more than a person really

should. But he thrived on his job. She…didn't. At least, not the way he did. Because if she did, she wouldn't have been frowning the entire time she laid out her day.

Some people—like Jack—found immense joy in what they created at work. His gut said April didn't have time to appreciate the joy in what she did.

The microwave dinged, and she pulled out her now steaming mug of what smelled like some kind of herbal concoction. She blew at the rising steam, her pink lips attracting the tiniest bit of condensation.

He couldn't quite pull his gaze away from her mouth as she parted it, lifted the rim of the blue mug to her mouth, and let her lips close over the edge like two soft pillows of goodness.

His mouth went dry, and he suddenly had a hankering for tea.

Which was not normal. Coffee was his beverage of choice.

But he wanted to lean in to April and brush his mouth against hers, to experience firsthand the herbal flavor on her lips.

He shook his head.

What was this about? The first order of business on this gig was for him to get a fucking grip.

"What's on the evening shift?" He cleared his throat, yanked his gaze away from her mouth.

She laughed, a low rumbly sound that made his skin tingle.

The tingle was unreasonable, so he did what he did with unreasonable things. He ignored it.

"You don't want to know." She blew again at the steam rising from the surface.

Elbows braced against the counter, he leaned forward. Closer to her. "Have to know to do my job."

She set the mug down and turned toward the refrigerator, pulling out two Ziploc-type bags. She held them up. "Somehow I make this into an edible dinner for the family using my trusty slow cooker. Then I take Harmony to ballet, Rohan has Little League, and—hopefully—Lola won't get too crabby before I can get her bathed and in bed."

"And then?"

"And then I go to bed."

For a woman who did not thrive on chaos, this was an interesting way for her to live.

"And then you do it all again tomorrow?" He grabbed his notepad from the kitchen table.

April nodded. "And the day after that. And the day after that. Except on Tuesdays and Thursdays—those nights I teach evening classes, so my parents help with getting the kids where they need to be. Sometimes Kent helps, too, depending on his schedule. Or his parents. They adore the kids and always want to see them more often, so I make sure they're involved pretty regularly."

He tapped his pen against the notepad. "And what about you?"

She frowned. His stomach hurt a little with that movement of her mouth.

"What do *you* want, April?" he asked, tone even, his full attention on her.

The tea bag dunked up and down in her hand, once, then twice, before she let it sink to the bottom. Her brown eyes tried to look everywhere but at him. "What do you mean?"

Finally, her gaze met his, and with that movement he pinned her with his stare. How it worked? He did not know. But it seemed to help her escape the anxious energy she'd created in the space.

"I mean, what do *you* want?" he asked again.

Fingertips drumming on the counter, her eyes moved to the left. "Like right now?"

"Sure. Let's start there."

"To drink my tea on the porch and watch the trees turn color." She laughed softly. "But that's a little self-indulgent."

Not really. They could probably talk about cookbooks while they were out there.

"And after that?" He pushed just a touch harder.

"I don't know."

She stared into space, but the look on her face implied that she clearly had an idea.

"What about long-term? What is that thing you want? The *thing* you feel deep inside you that you want more than anything?"

"My kids to be happy." She recited the words but her heart wasn't in them. She may as well have announced she needed another tea bag.

He stood, stepped to the edge of the counter, and moved closer. "For you, April. What do you want *for you*?"

"I don't know." The flash of panic implied she actually did know but didn't want to say. "What do you want, Jack?" she asked, totally deflecting his question.

Points to her for the maneuver, but he had her number. He also knew the answer to this question, because what he wanted was simple—more of what he already had. More of the success. More of what that meant for him—the bone-deep feeling of accomplishment. Picking the winner from a sea of options and elevating them to become a force, a force that was firmly on Team Jack. *That's* what he wanted. He didn't say that, though. Because this was not about him.

"This is about you," he said.

She toyed with the string on her tea bag, running it between her fingers. "*I* want to be happy."

Not able to help it or keep his poker face engaged, he smiled.

There she was. Now they were getting somewhere. "What's going to make you happy?"

"I want to matter."

He leaned forward, into her space, because what he was about to say was important. "April."

The column of her throat moved as she swallowed a thick gulp of nothing, but he had her attention.

"You matter," he said, offering the words and hoping she would believe them.

She nodded, but the wet was back in her eyes.

First rule of working with Jack: don't expect him to hug or hold your hand, because that's just not the guy he was. Yet he found his hand settling over April's. The warm tingling along his skin intensified with the touch. He ignored everything going on inside him—he'd deal with that later—and kept this about her. "Who do you want to matter to?"

Another flash of heat hit her eyes.

He'd just bet that April had a fire that would blaze when she got ticked. Something about that thought had him wishing he could see that blaze up close and personal. Not this minor flash, but the whole blaze of April.

She pulled her hand away and pushed it through the curls he'd never seen her wear before that day. Not on any of their video calls. She was about as low maintenance as a woman came. In the good way—the way that the beauty of her glowed clear through without effort. That was why she made the perfect influencer. Because she didn't need the extra—the goop on her eyes and the new hairstyle.

She crossed her arms. "I don't like this."

"Tell me and we'll drop it."

"You'll drop it now." She stood up, ripped open the Ziploc bag, then dumped the frozen contents into the slow cooker and flicked the dial to low.

Her chest heaved as she rinsed the used plastic in the sink before crumpling it in a ball and tossing it into a trash under the sink.

He backed up and backed off. She wasn't ready. But he'd be sure she would be. And soon.

For now, there came a time when a man recognized when pushing would allow him to win and when pushing would force him to lose. This was not a winning moment.

So he dropped it.

For now.

"What do you say we go sit on the porch and make a *new* plan for your day."

CHAPTER TWELVE

"Don't pee on your breakfast!"
—*April Davis*

Jack could not be for real. First, because she had invited him to breakfast with her kids and he'd accepted. But he had arrived at breakfast in a boardroom-ready navy-blue suit, all the heat of Bruce Wayne or Christian Grey—she couldn't decide which. In that moment April figured his blue suit was her favorite.

Which was silly because she wasn't into suits anymore. Not at all. Not when there was any possibility of grape Kool-Aid spilling.

Then he'd poured himself a bowl of Toasty O's and ate it with her children like it was a completely normal thing to do. Though, he did ask a whole lot of questions when Harmony mentioned Rohan liked to use the Toasty O's for toilet targets when he peed. Hey, potty training was freaking hard, and he had no ability to aim when he was younger. That's why April used the cereal O's for target practice.

Rohan simply continued on with his game apparently.

While Jack chatted about things to pee on with her kid, April scheduled two new meditation session promo posts.

How he managed to not get even a drop of milk on his tie with her kids flinging food everywhere, she did not know.

And, second, he could not be for real because April had

just laid out all that needed to be done. She did not have time to sit on the porch and drink her tea. She had time to drink her tea and get things done.

"I just told you all that I have to get done today," she said, instead of asking what the heck was wrong with him like she wanted to.

He lifted one shoulder. "I'm here to fix things."

His phone buzzed. He checked it.

"So you keep saying," she mumbled.

A few strokes to his cell screen, a frown, then a grin, and he finally tucked the phone back in his pocket.

He leaned in, caught her eyes with his, and held them. "We should go outside."

"For a planning meeting?" At least then she could check that off her list.

Again with the Jack shoulder lift. "Yeah, we'll plan a little."

"Aren't you Mr. Get Things Done?" she asked, rolling her shoulders back to release the tension that was building. "Because I'm ready to start working, and sitting out on the back patio is not getting things done."

"I'm going to tell you a secret." He made a come-here motion with his index finger. "Sometimes the way to get things done is to do nothing."

Funny thing about that...she used to say those kinds of things. Little soundbites of wisdom. But that was no longer the reality of her life and, as she'd recently learned, the way to get things done was actually just to do them.

"I don't think that means what you think it means," she said.

His coffee cup in one hand, he snatched her tea from where it sat abandoned on the counter. Then he started toward the door to the backyard. "Let's go work on a very important lesson."

"You know I can just make another cup of tea, right?" she said with a huff. "I don't have to follow you."

He paused his forward momentum but did not turn around. Instead, he said to the air in front of him, "But you want to, don't you?"

"Can't you teach me this lesson after my career is back online, *and* I fold the laundry?" she asked, but dammit, she was already following him.

"April." He turned to her and skewered her resolve with his icy blue eyes.

She skewered him right back. "Jack."

He didn't seem to mind her skewer, not really, but the hard angles of his expression softened.

"Take a breath," he said gently, before he turned and, with her tea in hand, finished his trek to the back porch.

April stood still, totally unmoving. Really, her chest probably wasn't even going up and down. She was a statue.

Because it'd been too long since she stopped to take a breath. Really, breathe.

Because when you took that time, you felt things. Things she wasn't sure she'd ever be ready to feel.

Gah. She hated that she had forgotten this part of her life. She hated that she was going to have to stay up late to get everything done. But, mostly, she hated that Jack was right about this.

For the first time that day, she closed her eyes and inhaled deeply, letting the oxygen fill her lungs. She held the breath before releasing. Then she did it again.

Breathe in the now. Breathe out the past. Breathe in Jack. Breathe out Kent.

And then she followed Jack.

He'd pulled two of the Adirondack chairs onto the lawn, and he was removing his socks. April slipped off her sneakers and toed off her own socks, leaving them on the concrete patio before stepping onto the lawn. The trees were losing their leaves and the sprinklers had been off for weeks to prepare for winter.

Making her way to her chair, the soles of her feet sank against the cool blades of brittle grass.

She paused. Closed her eyes. Positioned herself in mountain pose before raising her arms to *Urdhva Hastasana*—upward salute.

And she just…breathed. There was no divorce. No meltdown at preschool. No eating bees that weren't really bees.

Erasing all thoughts from her mind, she moved every ounce of focus to her muscles and to her breaths. In for four counts. Hold for four counts. Release for four counts. Pause for four counts. And again.

The cool earth rooting her in place as the crown of her head pointed to the sky, her blood pressure didn't seem so intense, her entire body felt lighter, and the crisp autumn air didn't feel so cold.

The edges of her lips ticked up as she finished a sun salutation, moving through the poses to downward dog and then back to forward fold and then to mountain.

Her chest rose and fell with each inhale and exhale. Finally, she opened her eyes and released the practice. She turned to Jack.

If she wasn't mistaken, he had the look of a man who had just gotten his way.

That's when she noted that his cell phone was trained on her. He raised an eyebrow and tapped the screen. "Perfection."

"Did you just record me?" she asked, eyeing him with a touch of what-the-heck? He should totally have given her a heads-up first.

"I believe we have your next post all ready to go." He shook the cell. "Once you give your stamp of approval."

She hated that this was a good idea: the calm mom being all calm and unaware of the outside world. "And if I don't like it?"

"Then we delete it and you do the thing again."

"The sun salutation," she said, edging toward her chair. This actually did solve one of her pressing issues of the morning. That being: what to post next?

"Yeah, that. The sun salutation." Small crinkles at the corners of his eyes fanned as he smiled, but he didn't say another word.

"Can we enjoy the morning without any more surreptitious filming?" April asked.

He nodded. "Unless you do something else that reinforces your brand, your image, and I happen to be holding my cell."

She chuckled. Low. The kind of sound that she used to make all the time. "That wasn't a commitment, Jack."

"Nope." Then he closed his eyes, set his cell aside, and let his head fall back against the stained-wood chair.

She sat, settled, and let her own head rest, eyes focused on the bright blue Colorado sky.

Then she took a breath.

And another.

And, dammit, Jack was right. She needed this.

"Are you filming me?" she said softly.

"No," he replied, also whispering. "Should I be?"

"I'm feeling very calm," she whispered. More peaceful than she'd been in a long time, actually.

This was nice. She and Jack sitting in her Adirondack chairs in her little back yard, feeling the shift of early morning to midmorning settle over the space. Slipping her toes down through the grass until they reached the dirt, she settled them there.

Grounded.

This was grounded.

She inhaled deeply, the cool Denver mountain air doing its job.

The innate feeling someone was watching had her peeking out of her left eye. Jack had his cell up again.

"Just a quick photo," he said, his eyes sparkling. "You'll get to approve everything before we take it live."

She ignored how just that word—live—made her whole body tense. Focusing instead on progressively relaxing each and every muscle in her body.

"It's hard to relax when you're taking my picture," she said, closing her eyes and letting the earth do its thing.

"You seemed to be doing just fine." His voice coated the air between them and settled in the morning sun.

She needed to call Lola's school to ensure she'd relaxed into the routine. Drop-offs when the kids struggled set the tone for April's day, and theirs as well. If history was any indication, Lola would have settled just fine. But April needed to be sure.

And she would be sure…later.

April released the image of her daughter's drop-off tantrum at the school that morning. Mentally putting the image in an envelope and allowing it to float away.

"She's back," Jack murmured low.

April glanced around her yard. "Who?"

He continued staring at the sky as they spoke. "You."

"Me?" she asked because she'd been there the whole time.

"This is the first time I've seen the real April since I arrived," he said, still doing the low soothing thing.

"What do you mean, the real April?" She shifted to face him.

"Just that." Jack finally turned to her. "This is the real April. Authentic April."

CHAPTER THIRTEEN

"Your authenticity is one of your most powerful tools.
Don't be so quick to put it away."
— Gaylene, Colorado, United States

She didn't know what to say to Jack's comment, so she said nothing and tried to go back to the place of peace where she'd been moments earlier.

"Why don't you start all your mornings like this?" Jack asked, his butterscotch voice sliding straight into her peace bubble.

"With you taking my photo while I try to chill?"

"You know what I mean."

She did. And the laugh that escaped her lips sort of wrecked the grounded peace she'd been building.

She flopped her arms onto the armrests and shook her head. Of course, she'd *like* to start her mornings like this, but there were the demands of the world outside of her backyard. Demands that she had to manage. Demands only she understood. "Too much to do on a normal day."

There was a long pause. A pause she didn't feel the desire to fill.

"Why isn't this a normal day?" Jack finally asked.

"Because you're here making me relax." She turned her head toward him, opening her eyes the barest of millimeters. Jack, in her backyard, sitting in the morning light, did not suck. The angle of his clean-shaven jaw made her fingers itch to reach over and touch the skin there. Apparently, this pull to him was something that would not be going away.

Which was a bummer and a complication. But something she'd manage. She always managed.

"How do *you* usually start your mornings?" April asked.

A slip of a lopsided grin settled on his mouth. "I'm in the office before the sun. But I watch it through the windows of my office sometimes."

April closed her eyes again, letting her mind settle on the grass blades between her toes. Feeling the cool pull of gravity and wishing every moment could be like this one. "You work a lot."

"I love what I do." He paused for another long moment. "That's why I came here to Denver."

April was being handled. She knew it. Understood it. And, also, hated it more than a little. Yet, oddly, on some level she appreciated Jack's handling. Now, how could she appreciate it and also hate it? Well, that was one of those great mysteries of emotion.

But Jack's physical presence made her feel as though she were truly part of a team.

Sure, she had friends. And, to some extent, her parents. But it'd been awhile since she really felt like part of a *team*.

She sat taller, reaching for her mug that he'd held onto for her and cradling it in her palms, ready to move on to the next part of her day. She sipped the delicate herbal brew.

Jack lifted his coffee mug to his lips. "The team can monitor your comments this morning."

She stilled mid-swallow, the chamomile suddenly too hot against her tongue. She shook her head, swallowing it down. "I sort of have to. I have to respond to things."

He gave a subtle head shake. "Comments get in your head."

"I'm already in my head." And wasn't that just the truth?

"Not just now." He gestured to her backyard with his cup. "I don't know where you were just now, but you were not thinking about comments that will only drag you down."

"At least my numbers are up." They were, too. She'd taken a teensy tiny peek at her follower numbers, and they were better than they'd ever been. The apology video had worked.

Because it wasn't live, and there wasn't an opportunity to muck it up.

"Mm-hmm." He made the sound deep in his throat. "Numbers are up."

"Do you think they're just following me hoping I'll mess up again?" She scratched at the bridge of her nose.

"Maybe." He moved his head from side to side in thought. "Our initial statement helped, but we need to do more to really get you back on track. Find you a cause. Deflect. Get good media out there—directed and well placed—to draw attention away from the video."

Huh. He hadn't even brought up *Practical Parenting* yet. She'd been waiting for him to broach that subject, since that was the one he seemed to be most interested in yesterday.

"What kind of cause?" Because here's the thing, April was very much into giving back and paying it forward. She'd subscribed to karmic law long before she knew it had a name.

However.

She wasn't at all into using philanthropy as an angle for her career. The whole idea left a sour taste in her mouth and, instead of grounded, her feet just felt dirty.

"Pick something that accents with your brand. Adds value to what you're doing."

That didn't sound very altruistic.

"Ideally, it would be something you're already involved in," he said. "We need to get it rolling quickly—"

"I don't know that I feel comfortable with this." She held up a hand.

Her abrupt change apparently got his attention. He tilted his head to the side. "Why?"

"Because I give to give, not to fix what happened on an internet video." She leaned forward, elbows to her knees, sifting her fingers through her now not-so-curled curls.

"Can't we do both?" She might be mistaken, but he'd forgotten to use the caramel tone in his voice that time. Oh, he may have been handling her, but she had three kids—she knew a thing or two about recognizing manipulation techniques.

April shifted, mentally grasping for the peace she'd found earlier. "It *feels* wrong."

His expression turned distant before he resettled back in the present. "Sometimes things that feel wrong can still be right."

Well, true, but also, "Sometimes things that feel wrong are also wrong."

Jack set his now empty cup on the wide armrest of his chair, but he didn't move his hand away from it. He stroked the handle between his thumb and forefinger, and April could've sworn she felt that touch of his fingertips on porcelain against her own skin. Everywhere on her own skin. This time the breath she inhaled was not mindful.

"You have a platform, yes?" he asked.

She nodded, refusing to watch his fingertips seduce the handle of her favorite yoga mug any longer.

"It's a decently sized platform, right?" he asked.

She nodded again. Totally failing because her eyes trailed back to the seduction of her mug. He'd moved on to tracing the stick figures with the pad of his index finger.

This was inappropriate, these thoughts. This whole thing. *Nip it in the bud, April.*

Either he sensed her watching his love affair with yoga stick figures with his touch, or he was simply done. In any case, his hand rested beside the mug, not tracing anything but mesmerizing her all the same.

And that really shouldn't have been such a bummer for her.

Which meant, maybe she really needed to get out with a man who might actually trace his fingertips over her skin. Someone in her league, who wasn't also her brand manager. Someone definitely not Jack.

"All I'm suggesting is that we take your platform and we use it to bring attention to a worthy cause—something that really matters to you," he said. "I'm feeling like a family yoga night with proceeds benefitting your favorite cause will be a good start."

"And as a bonus, my good intentions help scrub my reputation?"

She continued to stare at his hand, waiting to see what it would touch next. What the lucky object would be.

"Now you're getting it." He snapped his fingers together softly and, dear goodness, she jumped.

Once her heart rate settled back to normal—not relaxed, but normal—range, she raised her eyes to the sky and said, "It still doesn't feel right. I know the real reason we'd be doing this and it would be a charade, not philanthropy." Her voice rose in tone as she spoke. "It wouldn't be from the depths of my heart, it'd be because I wanted something in return." She made a conscious effort to rein in the frustration, finishing with a quiet, "That's literally the antithesis of charity."

"You're complicating something that's really pretty simple."

"You're complicating something that doesn't need complicating."

Jack laced his fingertips and rested them behind his head. This was a good thing, because then April wasn't following them with her gaze like Mayonnaise on Jack.

"Okay. Let's pause. You're getting upset…" Jack said, which was the truth.

"I am."

"The foot thing helped you relax before," he said to the sky.

She frowned. "What foot thing?"

"The thing with the grass?" He released his right hand long enough to point to the grass before he put it right back behind his head. "The toe-foot thing you did when you first sat down."

"The grounding?"

"Sure. If that's what you call it."

Her shoulders felt a touch heavier. "You noticed that?"

"Hard not to." He still wasn't looking at her, just gazing at the sky.

She would not do the foot-toe thing simply because he asked. That was something she'd do because she wanted to do it.

Which is why she did it.

"I don't want to argue," she said, settling her toes into the earth once more.

He gave a subtle shoulder shrug. "Then don't."

"But I don't want to do the right thing for the wrong reason."

"Okay. Then let's do the right thing for the right reason and let the rest go."

Suddenly the comfort of the outdoors seemed a little chilly because—

"Is this that lesson you wanted to teach me?"

He grinned at the sky. "Maybe."

"I don't like this lesson." She crossed her arms, a move that totally closed her off to the energy of the universe.

His phone buzzed in his pocket. He did not check it.

"You're all about providing a place to find calm, yeah?" he asked, still staring up into the sky.

"I am." Well, it was the truth.

"Calm for moms who aren't feeling so calm, uh-huh?" he asked in his warm butterscotch let-me-just-go-ahead-and-get-my-way tone.

"That's accurate." She may have lost her cool, but her goal was that other moms didn't have to. To give them the tools so they could keep a level head all through motherhood.

"You've done a yoga series. A meditation series..."

"I'm not really seeing your point here." Because weren't they supposed to be talking about what she should do, not what she had done?

"What about music?" he asked. "Music's calming, right?"

"Uh...yeah. And the kids love the free concerts over at the park. They go from spring through the fall. I'll drag you there if you're here for the next one."

"The concerts are free?" he asked, sitting up, not seeming to buy it.

They were mostly free. "Well...they ask for a donation to the local food bank. You bring a bag of new groceries as the price of admission. Everybody wins."

The kids even got such a kick out of buying for other families.

He lifted his eyebrows like she'd just gotten the point. "Everybody, huh?"

"I'm not a musician, Jack." She couldn't just do her own concert. What would she... Oh. Yoga. Right.

And...aw, damn. This was a good idea.

"Are you saying that I should do a yoga class and ask people to bring groceries instead of paying to attend?" She squinted at him.

"What do you think?" he asked, looking back at the sky.

"Are you doing that thing where you let the idea be mine so I want to do it, but really it was your idea?"

"I'm just talking," he said, those blue eyes of his sparkling in the morning sun.

"This plan has nothing to do with music. I've done yoga before."

"Yup." His lips stretched into a wry smile. "That's why it's perfect for you."

"I thought I was supposed to come up with something new?"

"And you did."

She didn't hate the idea. Not in the least.

"I already teach yoga a few times a week...maybe adding another class isn't a bad idea." She settled back to her chair, still keeping her feet grounded.

"Maybe not."

She turned her body toward him. "I don't like that you just got your way."

"Is everybody going to win?" he asked. Again, not even looking at her. Just staring at the sky.

"Yes," she admitted reluctantly.

"Then I can live with that."

They sat in the silence as she processed how she could turn her Tuesday class into a food drive. Maybe she just did a bonus class earlier in the day? That would work. This week the kids were going to be with Kent anyway, and she could send an email to everyone who had signed up, letting them know about the change. The logistics were surprisingly simple.

"Sometimes the best lessons are the hardest to accept," Jack said with a small smile. "And the easiest to learn."

April groaned. And, yes, it may have been out loud. "Does your wisdom always come in one-line sound bites?"

"Not all of it." He grinned because they both knew he had already won this one. Everyone would win in this one. "*Sometimes* my wisdom comes in two-line sound bites."

CHAPTER FOURTEEN

"When my twins were little, the boy twin pissed off the girl twin. She went on a rant about going to jail and having only water and bread and ended up screaming, 'There's no jelly in jail!' So now, when I feel like I'm about to strangle somebody, I remind myself 'there's no jelly in jail' and if I say it to the twins, they know I'm talking myself off a ledge and they need to scatter and lie low for a while."
—Anonymous, Alabama, United States

Jack

The problem with April Davis was her button nose. See, a button nose like April's led a guy like Jack to believe that she was sweet and innocent. April was neither. No, April Davis had some kick to her. A dash of spice in her sweet.

And, he'd learned from spending a day with her, underneath that veneer of calm was a flame.

A super stressed-out flame. Which was why he didn't broach the subject of the cookbook with her quite yet. Or the new MyTube channel he'd cooked up in his brain. First, they needed to keep the pressure on her brand. Get it back to solid. They were well on their way there.

Now, he needed to help her relax. Apparently, according to Kitty, that meant doing the laundry.

While he didn't see how one plus one equaled two on this point, he decided to try. Because...well...he didn't have a better idea yet.

So he shot off another email, handled a client Twitter situation—and the accompanying Facebook emergency—then he went back to the...laundry.

Thank fuck, his phone rang.

"Hi," he greeted his sister, Rachel, as he picked up her call and covertly shoved a load into the washing machine while April finished her pitch to a very excited food bank about to get a large donation. He adjusted the phone against his cheek. "What's up?"

"Did you figure out the whole whites versus colors thing?" Rachel asked.

She'd been 100 percent on board with him helping April on the down low.

"Har," he said. Just because he'd needed a little hand-holding from his sister with laundry meant nothing. He owned a washing machine and dryer, he just never had time to do his own.

It wasn't that he didn't know the difference between a load of colors and a load of whites, it'd just been a while since he'd had to deal with it. Back when he had dealt with it, he'd been younger, a grad student, and didn't care if his black T-shirts got mixed with his whites. It just made gray.

"Have you given any more thought to moving to Denver?" Rachel prodded. She'd been on his case about it since *she'd* moved to Denver.

"Have you given any more thought to calling our parents?" he countered.

"No," she said slowly. "Because when I call them, I start to question my life choices. But I like my life choices, so I don't want to call them."

"Fair enough." He could relate to all of that. Their parents were...a little judgy. About all things, nothing specific. It was just their way.

"Have *you* called them?" she asked.

"Nope." He shook his head even though she couldn't see. "They also question my life choices. But I like my life choices, so I don't want to call them."

Rachel snickered.

"What's up, Rach?" he asked, instead of answering her original question. The answer was the same as it always was: he lived in L.A. "I get the feeling you're not just calling me about the laundry."

"We want to take April out tonight," Rachel said.

He grabbed a pink sock that somehow had made it in with the whites. Fuck. Lola was probably better with colors than he was.

"Okay, yes, take April out," he said. "I'll come too. Give me a chance to talk to her without..." He glanced around. This.

"Actually," Rachel said in that tone of hers that he did not like one bit. "Can you watch her kids?"

He stilled. Spying a pair of blue panties in with the whites, he pulled them out. Definitely not white. Also, not something he should probably have his hands on. He put them with the pastels pile.

"Did I break your brain with my request?" Rachel asked.

"The kids? All of them?"

"Yes?"

Uh... Well, sure, he *could*. He, however, figured that perhaps he should sort out what the hell to do with kids before being left totally alone with them.

"And, maybe, Simone and Yelena's kids, too? So they can come along," Rachel said, like it wasn't a big deal.

"How many kids do they have?" he asked cautiously.

"Just the two."

He wasn't a mathematician, but that took the total up to five. Five small humans that he would be responsible for keeping alive.

"Um…" He was *pretty* sure he could do it.

He could always ask Kitty for help. But he was actually uncertain that they'd all be in one piece if he drafted her.

The little tickle in his gut was telling him he would be in way over his head. As Jack always tried to listen to his gut—

"Travis can come help, if you're not sure," Rachel added with a whole heaping of cheerful. Travis was his brother-in-law and actually had experience with children. "C'mon, big brother," Rachel continued. "April hasn't been out to a girls' night with us in months. She needs this. We need this. And you owe me for all the ridiculous knock-knock jokes I had to listen to when we were teenagers."

He had gone through a phase. He readily admitted that. He also had moved past that phase a couple of decades ago.

"That was a long time ago—"

"Seriously. You and Travis can handle the kids. He's practically a professional. And as a bonus, it'll give you two some male bonding time."

Two of them with five kids wasn't too bad. And Travis understood how the little monsters ticked, so he could definitely provide the backup Jack would most likely need.

"Does April know about this?" he asked. Because this seemed like an ask that should come from her.

"Not yet. But she will." Rachel said with a gigantic smile in her voice. He knew that smile. His little sister's smile made him feel lighter.

"Do you want me to talk to April about it?" he asked.

"Nope." Rachel popped the *p* at the end of the word. "I will handle April. You just handle feeding the children dinner, keeping them alive, and if you want bonus points, you'll fold all of April's laundry and vacuum the house."

"Why do I feel like I'm being used?" he asked. Also, where was the vacuum and how did it operate? It couldn't be that hard.

Most of those things were push a button and go. That's what the commercials said anyway.

He was pretty sure.

"Because you've known me long enough to know that's precisely what's going on."

"Have you talked to Kitty?" he asked, because he had a hunch she had.

"Yes." She didn't even try to deny it. "And I concur with her plan."

He chuckled. Dang, he missed his sister. "Tell Travis I'm looking forward to some male bonding."

"He'll love that."

"And you'll help April relax?" he asked.

"Uh...yeah." Rachel said something to someone in the background. It sounded like Travis because she mentioned Jack and helping and then something about flight time. Travis was a pilot who loved the skies.

"April isn't coming back from girls' night stressed, I guarantee," she said when she returned. "And Travis said he's good to come help."

They said their goodbyes, and he closed the washing machine, turned it on, and headed toward the kitchen. If he were in charge of dinner, then he'd have to figure out how to make the brown stuff she'd dumped in the slow cooker palatable for everyone.

He lifted the lid and gave a sniff. Chili. It actually smelled pretty good—cumin and tomato and warm spice. Though it still looked like goop and had the consistency of slush.

He enjoyed chili, so this was a good turn of events, since he'd get to eat that chili. And, though he liked it, he couldn't recall the last time he'd actually eaten it. Usually, he either made a protein shake or ordered in, unless Sarah took pity on him and brought him dinner—which she did often enough for his meals to be decently well-rounded.

Sarah had never brought him chili, though. And he hadn't thought to order it in. So, yeah, this was excellent.

He grabbed a wooden spoon out of the carousel in the middle of the counter and nudged at the mass. There was still a decent chunk of coagulated frozen tomato and kidney beans floating in the middle. He turned the knob from low to high and gave himself an internal high five.

Laundry. Check.

Load started. Load folded…sort of. It didn't look much like the neat piles he got back from the laundry company. Actually, it didn't look at all like that. His piles were pretty lopsided. He gave himself a pass, since he didn't know what the fuck he was doing.

Good enough was good enough. On to fixing dinner so he could spend a night in with the kids.

Look at him being Mr. Domesticated. If only Sarah and Ben could see him now.

Mayonnaise ambled through the kitchen, plopping down on her bed by the window.

He smiled, did an impromptu turn and Risky Business spin—his socks making the move extra smooth on the glossy tile floor.

She stared at him with an extremely unimpressed look.

"Tough audience, huh?" He did another socked slide for her benefit.

Still nothing, so he ignored her, too. If there was one thing he knew about females—and he was pretty sure this went for the canine variety, too—it was to leave them alone if they weren't into him.

At least, that was his experience.

So, yeah, he ignored Mayonnaise and paired socks, rolling them into balls and tossing them over his shoulder into the laundry bin.

If he added a few slides in the process, well, he might as well be having a good time.

Growing up, they'd had this same type of tile. The kind that got extra slick when he and his brothers used furniture polish on it. Then they'd skate around the kitchen in their socks.

Until that moment, he'd totally forgotten about how they used to do that. His littlest brother had nearly taken out their mom's china hutch with his spin and twist maneuver.

It'd been epic.

April's floor wasn't covered in furniture oil, so he couldn't exactly manage quite the same, but he did a mini version of it that wouldn't land him on his ass or in the wreckage of April's good dishes.

April's slow clapping broke him from his sock spins.

Jack didn't do embarrassed, but his body didn't get that message and his face went hot. He stopped spinning immediately. Cleared his throat. Leaned against the wall like he had not just embarrassed the hell out of himself.

"By all means, continue." April made a go-on-ahead hand gesture, and he couldn't help but notice the glimmer in her eye.

If he wasn't mistaken, there was dare beneath those rich brown eyes.

He shook his head and jerked his chin toward the table where he'd dropped the latest laundry bin. "I've got socks to fold."

"Jack?" She scratched at her temple. "Those socks don't go together at all. The little ones? Those are Lola's. They don't go with the frog pair. Those are Rohan's."

Right. "They were matched together before I threw them in."

Once in the bin? They'd sort of disassembled the rolled balls into a mess of chaos.

April scratched at her temple again. "The dancing looks like more fun, anyway."

"I agree with that."

April mimicked his stance, crossing her arms and leaning against the doorframe. "Jack?"

"Yes?"

"Why are you doing my laundry?" she asked, eyebrows raised. "Poorly?"

He glanced at the bin. "Because it needed to be done."

"You don't have to do my laundry."

"What if I told you I like to do laundry?" It wouldn't be true, but he could still ask the question.

"Then I'd say thank you." She shook her head with a slight smile. "But no one actually likes doing laundry."

"Yeah, you're right. Tell you what." He dropped his arms, kicked off from the wall, and moved toward her. "Let's have some fun instead." He made the statement knowing she wouldn't even entertain the idea. She had, as she'd pointed out multiple times that day, too much to get done. "Let's try out your socks." He glanced pointedly to her sock-covered feet.

If she agreed, and if his entire purpose here was to help her relax, there wasn't anything better to accomplish that task than sock slides.

"I'm not doing that." She shook her head.

"Because you don't want to have fun or because you don't want me to see you having fun?" he asked.

She pursed her lips and glanced to the side. "Neither."

"Then why not?" He landed a particularly good slide and held out his hand. "You've got the socks for it."

Reluctantly, she placed her hand in his and moved forward. "How do you do it?"

"Put your weight on the sides of your feet and let the socks and the tile do the rest."

"I'm going to break my neck doing this."

"Or you might have fun."

She gave it a little running start and slid a few inches.

"See?" he said. Once she got a taste of it, there was no way she'd be a ball of stressed-out socks.

She did it again, this time with more of a running start.

"It's fun," she conceded.

While her words were not enthusiastic, the gleam in her eyes was back.

"Try a spin." He stepped back, so she had more of the floor.

"I seriously cannot break my neck. Who would fix dinner?"

"I seriously will not let that happen. And me."

"How?" she asked. "Exactly how do I...?" She made a slide motion with her hands.

"C'mere," he said, holding his hand out again.

She took it—without the reluctance this time. He moved in to her like they were going to dance. The glimmer from her eyes dimmed as he moved into her space, moving into something else. Something heated.

His entire body tingled with the zing of her contact.

The air seemed thicker when they were this close. For some reason, that didn't deter him.

Platonic, this was platonic. He repeated it over and over in his mind like one of April's mantras as he pulled her in to him like a dance partner and, when she was close enough, he spun her back out. She squealed, and he loved it. Loved her expression. The exhilaration and bliss. That's what he expected he'd looked like back in the day when he did his first sock spin.

Still gripping her hand, he pulled her back to him before spinning her again. She squealed again, high and rich before laughing like he'd never heard. The sound that made a guy proud and ready to do anything in his power to make it happen again.

That's when he got brave, because he added an extra twist on her way back to him. This time she tripped the smallest of millimeters. He moved quickly, catching her around the waist before she could biff it.

Instead, she fell right into him, her chest pressed against his in a way that had his body responding like he was truly a teenager again. A teenager with no restraint.

The scent of her—lavender and something floral—enveloped the space in a way that made him not want to let her go.

She parted her lips, and they were *right* there. Only inches from him. And the air was crackling and his body was responding and her body—if her quick breaths, flushed skin, and dilated pupils were any sign—was also in on the game.

So, yeah, she was right there smelling so good and feeling even better.

His hand trailed up her back to the base of her neck, his fingertips tracing along where her shirt met her neck.

Her chest heaved against him and he flashed back to the morning and their conversation about right and wrong. For the life of him, he couldn't figure out where this situation landed on that spectrum.

Because the way his body reacted to her was definitely wrong, but the way it felt was very, very right.

Her hands smoothing the cotton fabric of his button-down shirt, she said, "Ja—"

But she got no further because the front door opened and she froze. Utterly froze.

He did, too.

"Mom?" Harmony called from the vicinity of the front door.

All color drained from April's face.

"Grandpa says hi, and he didn't cuss around me today," Harmony added.

Well, that was good. Grandpa was still in the doghouse and April was still gripping...Jack.

"The afternoon shift," she whispered, the horror in her tone a cold-water wrecking ball through his body's previous response to her proximity.

"Mom?" Harmony called again, slamming the door behind her.

Jack moved his hands to where hers white-knuckled his shirt. He moved her hands from the fabric, squeezing them in his own before April pulled them away.

"In here, baby." April stepped entirely out of his embrace, running her hands along her abdomen to the edge of her skirt at her thighs, adjusting the fabric that neither of them had messed up.

"What are you guys doing?" Harmony asked, her voice getting closer. She breezed to the doorway. "Hi, Jack." She gave him a toothy grin.

"Harmony." He moved his hands to his hips because, frankly, he didn't know what else to do with them.

"Jack was just teaching me to spin on the tile in my socks," April said, her skin still flushed but nothing like it'd been moments earlier.

Her expression had become unreadable—even for Jack.

He didn't like that at all.

Harmony dropped her backpack on a chair. "Can I play, too?"

CHAPTER FIFTEEN

*"On the hard days, pretend you're the babysitter: ice cream for
dinner, don't do the dishes, just keep the kids alive."*
—Cathi, Louisiana, United States

"Jack?" April had changed into a pair of tighter-than-they-
were-last-month jeans with a purple flounce-sleeved peek-
a-boo shirt and bounced down the stairs.

"In here," he called back.

It'd been ages since she'd been out with her friends. *They*
went often, sure. And they always invited her. She just…

She just hadn't had time.

It'd been forever since she attended their Sunday morning
get-togethers, too. Those had also fallen from the priorities of
April's new life. Again, not from lack of invitation. They always
let her know when and where and that they wanted her to show.
She just hadn't had the time to make it happen.

That all needed remedying because…hurrying down the
staircase, she realized abruptly that she missed them. She
missed who she was when she was with them.

"April?" Jack called from the kitchen. "I'm in here." He
sounded like something was off.

One last glance in the mirror in the hallway—yes, she had
eye makeup on both eyes this time—and she headed his way.

"What's wrong?" she asked as she sauntered through the

door, the purple flats that matched her shirt dangling from her fingertips.

"I think the chili burned." The cover was off the slow cooker and he was nudging a black crust around the edges with a wooden spoon.

"How's that even possible?" She knew her slow cooker like she knew how to breathe. They had a symbiotic relationship, even when she forgot about it.

Actually, she could probably even marry the thing and have a more stable relationship than she'd had with her ex. Her Crock-Pot wasn't going to shock her by running off with anyone else. Of that she was certain.

She moved closer and, sure enough, the unmistakable scent of singed chili met her nostrils.

"Who turned the knob to high?" She hurried to the cooker, flicked off the switch, grabbed pot holders, and pulled the ceramic crock from the base. "I asked Harmony not to mess with it anymore. This is what happens."

Damn. Damn. Dammit. She had been planning to take a picture and post it with the recipe. That was her end-of-the-day, everyone-will-eat-it plan.

She couldn't exactly post *this*.

"Uh." Jack had the look of guilt plastered on his face. Maybe he'd tried to hide it, maybe he hadn't. It didn't matter because she saw it all the same. This wasn't Harmony's fault.

"It wasn't Harmony, was it?" She scraped at the burnt edge with a spatula. This was fine. Totally fine. There was always a plan B when it came to supper, and she could do something else for the post. She just needed to think of something. Not a big deal.

This is fine.

"It was frozen earlier," he said, like that was a reasonable explanation.

Yes, that's how these things worked. Frozen meal in. Cook

on low. Dinner comes out. "That's how slow cookers work. They take frozen and make it dinner."

In Los Angeles things moved quicker. They probably didn't use slow cookers there.

"I'm sorry," he said, and he truly sounded like he was.

"Hey, it happens." April nodded, let out a long breath. "It's fine. Really."

Plan B.

She tried to salvage the middle of the chili, but the thick crust around the edge was seriously black. The flavor had likely permeated the entire meal.

"My slow cooker thinks it's the terminator. You have to keep it on low if you want it to be on high."

Jack looked at her like she was speaking gibberish. No, it didn't make a ton of sense, but she had figured out how to make the whole thing work long ago.

"Well, it terminated dinner," Jack said, deadpan. His tone was light, but was she mistaken or did he look disappointed?

"Crud." April ran her hand over her face.

"I'll cook," Jack said.

"You already folded all the laundry. I think you're off the hook." She shook her head, because this was her problem to solve. The kids were picky and then there was the whole gluten and no-dairy thing.

"I'll make pizza by calling my friends at Dominos," he said like it wasn't a big deal.

"That's not cooking," she said with a chuckle. "But good effort."

"Hey, it'll work."

"Harmony doesn't do gluten," she said, resigned. It would sure be easier if it would work.

"Gluten-free crust." Jack lifted his hands like he'd solved the problem. "Doesn't everywhere have that now?"

Yes. Mostly. Except...

"Rohan is lactose intolerant. When we do pizza, it's a whole thing and I have to make it here because otherwise we'd all just have sauce."

Jack frowned.

She knew that feeling.

"Where do you order in from when you don't cook?" he asked, pulling his cell from his slacks pocket. "I'll order that."

He crossed his arms, and she had no idea how he'd kept the white button-down clean throughout the entire day, but he had. At this point, with the number of kids coming to the house, he was really just testing the fates.

"I don't order in." Some things were just too complicated. "We do cold cereal or sandwiches or sometimes I can do gluten-free spaghetti in a quick pinch."

"I bet I could make cereal," he suggested, the edges of his lips twitching. "Unless I burn it in your fast-cooking slow cooker."

Look at him being adorably domestic.

She held up the spatula. "Don't mock my slow cooker. It's the closest thing I've had to a relationship in a year."

Well, that sounded a helluva lot sadder than she'd intended.

"It'll be sandwiches for dinner." She set down the spatula and began pulling the gluten-free bread and the dairy-free cheese from the refrigerator. "Sandwiches are easy."

Jack moved alongside her, opening the cupboard where she kept the trash bags. Then to the cupboard where she kept her pens and paper.

"What are you looking for?" she asked.

"Plates," he said.

He was really helping. Huh. It'd been a long time since she'd had a man's help getting dinner together.

Toward the end there, Kent had really checked out—even

before she'd ever noticed.

She pointed to the cabinet to the left of the sink. "There."

He nodded. "On it."

While April layered cheese and turkey breast together on the bread, Rohan took that moment to hop into the room. He looked straight at April and said, "Banana."

April's pulse skipped. She dropped the cheese. Then she recovered quickly and picked the cheese back up. But that was his first non-ribbit at home since...

She couldn't really say when.

He didn't ribbit at school—he never could pass kindergarten if he spent all day ribbiting. But whenever he wasn't in the classroom, he always reverted to his amphibious protective instincts.

And, unless she was mistaken—and she wasn't mistaken—frogs didn't say banana.

"Banana," he said again, with more *oomph*, giving Jack a pointed look before licking the side of the wall.

"You know that talk we had about wall germs?" Jack asked, now done separating the plates. "Still applies when you say banana." He moved to Rohan and lifted him from his squat near the wall.

Rohan nodded, looping his arms around Jack's neck.

April would not let her heart get in the middle of this mess. Absolutely not.

Rohan looked at her and flicked his tongue over his lips.

"Do you want a banana?" April asked, because while she couldn't give him a frog—or rather, she could but had decided months ago that the only inside pet she really wanted was of the Mayonnaise variety—she could give him a banana.

Rohan shook his head. "Banana."

Okay, what?

Jack smiled. "I taught the kids banana language while you

were making your posts."

"Do I want to know?" April asked.

"Banana," Rohan said in a tone that somehow sounded like, *probably not.*

"It's the language my brothers and I made up when we were kids. To mess with Rachel. And our parents."

April frowned; that didn't sound promising. "How does the banana language work?"

"Banana means everything." Harmony plowed through Jack and Rohan to clamber onto one of the barstools.

Jack set Rohan down so he could climb on the one beside her.

Lola followed them, climbing up on the third stool. A big, huge really, three-year-old smile adhered to her lips.

"Banana," she announced as though to say, *"I'm here!"*

"Banana," Harmony said with a curt head nod.

April squinted toward Jack. "Banana?" she asked. Because, really?

"Banana." He shrugged.

"Well, it's better than the ribbiting; I'll give you that," April muttered under her breath, handing Jack the turkey cold cuts so he could work on Harmony's sandwich.

"This could be good for him," Jack whispered in the air over her ear as he moved beside her.

She nodded, since Rohan was only part amphibious at the moment. They'd absolutely call that a win. "I like it. But perhaps next time we have a brief chat about which words become languages."

Jack thought on that for the briefest of seconds before saying, "Fair enough."

She couldn't help it—

"Banana," she said, hoping it came through as close to *fine* as possible.

"See, that's why I like you." Jack squeezed her shoulders. The move was totally platonic, but it still made her skin tingle every-freaking-where. "Rachel would've been all over my ass for teaching this to her kids."

"I'm not allowed to use that word," Harmony said around a giant mouthful of sandwich. "I can't say ass."

"You're right." April skewered Jack with her glare before handing him his very own sandwich. "It is a grown-up word. That means only grown-ups can use it."

Jack stood there, his jaw a little slacker than usual. He mouthed he was *sorry*, but April had a hunch that Harmony wouldn't let this one go. Thus, she wasn't going to let it go, either.

"There are consequences to bad word choices," April continued. "We all have to remember that." She gave a pointed glance at Jack. "Or we get stuck on laundry duty again." She ended with a wink.

Harmony continued picking the turkey from the sandwich Jack had just handed her. "That's Jack's consequence for saying ass?"

"Harmony." April dropped her voice. "Unacceptable. Stop saying the word."

"I feel like this is my fault." Jack grimaced, the cords of his neck popping a little as he did.

"I was just saying what Jack said." Harmony gave a shoulder lift just like Jack had done thirty seconds earlier.

"Maybe we all forget what Jack said and remind ourselves that bad words are bad words for a reason," Jack said. "And then Jack can stop referring to himself in the third person."

He took a bite out of his sandwich.

Harmony had now picked every last bit of the turkey from between her pieces of bread, leaving only the cheese and mustard and lettuce. "I know lots of grown-up words."

"What do you say we don't run through them all," April

suggested. Firmly. With no banana.

"Yeah," Jack said, nodding.

"Yeah." Harmony used the exact same *yeah* he had. "Because then Mom would make me go to time-out."

"Tell you what, you don't repeat that word and after your mom leaves, I will teach you to color outside the lines." He flashed her a Jack-infused grin before noshing on his sandwich.

Who was this guy? And why was he being so amazing?

There had to be a catch. There was always a catch. Wasn't there?

Jack was all about business. Why was he being sweet?

But, April supposed, as long as he wasn't teaching Harmony to use the word "ass," he could teach her daughter to color in the wrong places. She'd just pick it up on the playground anyway.

"Banana." Rohan raised his include-me-please hand.

Lola did the same.

"Everyone's in." Jack gave high fives all around.

April shook her head and started clearing away the remnants of sandwich making.

"Uh, April, where is time-out?" Jack leaned back to see her. He glanced around the room. "That seems like excellent information for the sitter to have."

She pointed to the naughty spot in the corner by Mayonnaise's bed. "One minute per age of life."

"Wow." He squinted at her. "Seriously?"

She laughed. "Yeah, Jack. Seriously."

"But then I'd be in time-out all night."

She held his stare for a beat. "Then don't do anything too bad."

Oh dear, that had sounded kinda dirty. She didn't mean for it to sound dirty. Just…you know, he needed to behave.

"Can I have some?" Lola asked, eyeballing the sandwich in Jack's hand.

April opened her mouth to tell him he should probably not do that because—

Lola went right in for it without waiting for permission.

"Lola," April said with a hiss. "That's Jack's."

Lola took a bite and gave it two solid chews before she opened her jaw and let the residual mess fall back on Jack's plate. "I no like that kind."

Jack eyed his sandwich then the plate, then he raised his gaze to meet April's.

She gave him one of his own shrugs. "Banana."

"Ketchup please?" Lola asked, extremely politely given that she'd just spit Jack's sandwich back on his plate.

"Sure." April grabbed the container and squirted a dollop on Lola's plate.

"I do it!" Lola grabbed for the ketchup and, with a great deal of reluctance, April let her squirt her own dollop. A dollop that was really more of a mountain. A mountain with a ketchup ski slope that trailed all along April's counter.

April waited. Not-so-patiently, but understanding that if she chose not to wait patiently, then there would be a battle of wills. And no one wanted a battle of wills before she got her first moms' night out in ages.

"Where's my spoon?" Lola asked.

"Dip your sandwich." April made a circle motion with her fingertip between the sandwich and the pile of ketchup.

"I don't want my sandwich." Lola was all big eyes like her sister.

"What are you going to eat with your ketchup?" Jack asked, already getting the spoon and handing it over.

"My spoon."

Jack looked to April for help.

"Just maybe try to get her to eat something else later?" April scraped the half-chewed bite of sandwich from his plate while

Lola ate a spoonful of ketchup.

"We're here!" Rachel called from the front door. The clomp of her boys' feet headed in the direction of the kitchen.

"Finish eating and you guys can all go outside and play." April handed Lola a napkin for the ketchup smudge on her chin.

Brady and Kellan, Rachel's kids, barely stopped on their way through the kitchen, pausing only long enough to say hello so their mom wouldn't make them come back. They'd done this dance before and knew she really would make them do it.

"Why are my nephews here?" Jack stopped polishing off his sandwich, a frown marring the line of his lips.

"Because I'm taking their mom to girls' night and Travis is here."

Jack's eyes turned to slits. "*Plus* the neighbor kids?"

Well... "Yes?"

Hadn't Rachel talked to him about this? She'd said he'd given the go-ahead.

"That's, like, seven kids," he said to no one in particular.

"You can count. Good job." Rachel had sauntered in and now patted him on the shoulder.

"I thought we'd have five kids and two adults. That Travis came to help me, not bring more children with him." Jack's complexion had gone more than a little pale.

"Are you scared, Jack?" Harmony asked like she was in a long, empty hall in the middle of a horror movie. "You look scared."

"Yeah." He nodded. "I am."

"Travis has lots of experience with kids," April assured. "And Harmony will help you, if you ask her nicely and ply her with candy."

"We can have candy?" Harmony asked, because apparently she was listening.

April gave her a don't-interrupt look. "If Jack says yes and agrees to stick around."

"Jack's not saying yes to any of this," Jack said, still clearly freaked.

April wasn't going to make him babysit if he wasn't comfortable with it. "It's okay if we can't go out—"

"No, it's not okay. Jack and Travis will be fine," Rachel assured her.

"Jack's talking about himself in the third person again," Harmony said. "Are you sure he's fine?"

He looked like he might actually pass out. Which was sort of cute, actually. He could face down anyone in the boardroom, but the thought of being in a room full of children scared the pants off him.

But Travis was here, and Harmony wouldn't let anything really bad happen. Besides, the kids were all good kids.

"What was it you said to me when you convinced me to let you do this?" April asked, pressing her lips together.

"I can totally handle this." The words fell out of his mouth with the confidence of a half-chewed Lola sandwich.

That was to say—

"Banana!" Lola announced around a mouthful of ketchup.

Yes. That.

CHAPTER SIXTEEN

*"Why color inside the lines when coloring
outside the lines is so much fun?"*
—Not Most Moms

April

"The expression on Jack's face was totally worth the price of admission." Rachel looped her arm through April's as they trekked up the sidewalk, past the convenience store, to the entrance of Brek's Bar.

Since it was a weeknight, the band would probably not be A-list. But, since it was Brek's, one could never really be sure. Brek's Bar was the best place in Denver to hear live music—except for The Pepsi Center when Dimefront played the arena.

April had actually never been to Brek's.

It seemed like it was for the crowd about a generation behind her. But attorney-friend Sadie had an in with Brek. So she'd made the *arrangements*. She used that term specifically because when April had called them "reservations," Sadie laughed like April intentionally told an exceptionally funny joke. (She hadn't.)

Apparently, Brek's Bar was not the type of place where one made reservations. It was the type of place that had bouncers and a biker-looking guy tending bar.

The bouncers took one look at Sadie and let her walk straight on through the cordoned-off entrance, totally skirting the line that trailed around the side of the building.

Sadie had decided to get dressed up for girls' night—ditching her usual pantsuit for a cute yellow sheath dress that looked amazing with the rich depth of her brown skin.

April followed behind Sadie, Rachel and the rest of the girls at her back.

Yes, it was a weekday. They'd never know, given the packed bar.

Sadie found a booth at the back, her name on a table tent. See? That was just like a reservation. April said nothing, though, as she squeezed herself into the booth without jamming an elbow into too many other patrons.

Simone slid in next to April, Yelena joining right beside her.

Sadie and Rachel took the bench across from them.

"Where's Kaiya?" April had to yell the question to be heard over the noise of the bar.

Rachel yelled right on back. "She had a party."

Kaiya was their multilevel marketing mom friend—every group needed one. She also sold an amazing skin care line that April absolutely adored.

"Molly?" April asked.

Molly, their dating guru friend, had her own MyTube channel and was April's biggest cheerleader as she launched her brand.

"School night and a science project." Rachel pursed her lips. "I know. I'm bummed, too."

"This is still fun," Simone elbowed April in the ribs.

April grabbed her cell and checked for messages. Check on the kids. That kind of thing. "It's something."

Rachel waved the phone away. "Put that down. They'll call if they need us."

April pinched her lips to the side. "What if they're all unconscious?"

If Simone and Yelena had worn off on her about anything, it was their free-range parenting style, but this was the first time in forever that April had been out. Her job description definitely included a line of worrying for her kids while she was out having fun.

"Jack may be Jack, and as his sister I have to give him plenty of crap," Rachel said, swirling her fingertip in the air over April's silent phone. "But I trust him. He'll have all of those kids—and Trav—eating out of his hand before we get back."

"Now *that* I would like to see," Kitty said, also sliding into the booth. "Thanks for the invitation." She sucked a gulp of whatever she was drinking.

"Would it be girls' night without you, Kitty?" April asked.

"No, it would not." Kitty grinned. "I came earlier to pregame and scope out the male specimens for you."

"Kitty…" April said her name, but she also did a quick scope. What? She was single. It was now totally appropriate for her to peruse. She'd been totally faithful to Kent, even when she'd found out about his… Yeah. But while Kent was the one to walk away, when push came to shove, she and Kent let each other go. She just hadn't realized it. Would've kept fighting for it, if she'd had the chance.

Which was why she now had Jack.

Not that Jack was hers or would ever be hers.

He was just Jack.

Super helpful Jack.

"Are you thinking about a guy?" Sadie asked. "You sort of look like you're thinking about a guy."

"No." April shook her head. "I'm not thinking about a guy. I'm thinking about Jack."

"Jack's a guy." Rachel laughed. "A guy who folded your laundry all afternoon." Rachel paused. "'Folded' being a general term."

Yes, some of it was more like rolled and tucked, but he was oddly precise about Rohan's little polo dress-up shirts. Besides, it wasn't like April had found the time to fold anything herself, so she'd take anything she could get. "I don't know why he was so insistent about it. But it was sweet of him to help out."

For the record, she'd hidden all of her bras before he got to that bin for folding—there were some things a girl just needed to handle herself. That, and she didn't want to have to explain how Mayonnaise would steal her bras to use them for chew toys.

"I'm surprised he doesn't know how to fold." Rachel nodded. "He's always been so precise. Of all of us kids, he was the one who actually picked up after himself when we were little."

"Tell us other things about Jack," Simone said, tapping her fingers along her cheekbone. "I have lotsa questions."

Yelena elbowed her in the side. "Not subtle."

"What?" Simone asked. "I think I should know about the guy who is taking care of our children. Don't you?"

"I think the time to ask those questions was about four hours ago," Yelena said, grabbing the attention of a server so they could put in their drink orders.

"Can I get you anything else?" the waitress asked as she finished with Rachel's order.

"I'd give a kidney for a salad," April mumbled. She'd missed out on chili and hadn't had time to eat her sandwich before they left.

Sadie laughed. "You don't come to a bar like *this* to order a salad."

"I bet I can wrangle something. Let me see what I can do." The waitress gave a wink and finished up orders before returning through the swarm of bodies toward the bartender.

"So." Rachel pulled her phone out of her bag and set it in the middle of the table. Everyone else followed the maneuver. Everyone except April.

"We all talked about you earlier and we sort of decided on something." Rachel motioned around the table.

Funny, she said *you* while looking straight at April. April mouthed, *Me*? She pointed at her chest.

Simone nodded. "Hand over your phone."

April handed over her phone because, well, she trusted Simone implicitly. Though, with the glimmer in her eye and the way Yelena shook her head, April was starting to question that trust.

Simone held up the cell camera. "Smile."

April didn't smile, she scowled. "Why?"

"Smile," Simone said, firmer this time.

"You might as well do it." Yelena's expression was soft. "So they'll get it over with and we can move on with our night."

April smiled. A quick sort of smile that she was certain didn't reach her eyes. The blinding flash probably filled in any sort of blank on that front.

"C'mon," Rachel prodded. "Think of something that makes you happy."

Without even trying, Jack's face floated to the front of her mind. Which was to say, not a good thing. But it made her smile.

"Whatever you were just thinking about," Kitty said, as Simone tapped on April's cell screen. "Keep thinking it."

"As long as it's not my brother." Rachel gave April a raised-eyebrow once-over. "Because—"

"I know." April waved her hand, welcoming the beverages that appeared at the table. She'd gone with a vodka tonic. "He's so far out of my league, it's not funny."

Kitty scowled. "In what universe?"

"I'd also like to know the answer to that," Simone said with a growl.

"Because *I* was going to say that you are out of his league," Rachel said, also scowling. "Maybe we need to go over how the leagues work."

April pointed at her chest. "I have three kids."

"And a house and a job and a life." Rachel speared April with the look she gave.

"And those bazoongas." Kitty gave April's chest a long stare. "Don't forget to add those to the list."

"Jack doesn't have any of that," Rachel continued.

"Jack has a job," April said, for some reason feeling the need to defend him.

"So he gets one point," Rachel agreed.

This was really a ridiculous conversation but… "Jack has Jack and that puts him in his own league," April said.

"He's *just* Jack." Rachel shook away whatever she was thinking. "It doesn't matter, anyway. Because, while I love my brother, he is not good for you. Not because of any league thing. Because he is hell on relationships. Hell being that he just never has them."

Jack might be hell on relationships, but they were also in this repair project together, and any outside fraternization would muddy those waters so badly, they'd need a whole crate of Kitty's Amazon soap to clean it up.

"*We* are going to find you someone else," Rachel said. "Molly gave us some advice on how to get started."

A tingle of awareness started at the outer layer of April's skin, because she'd seen that look in matchmaking Kitty's eyes before, but never Rachel's. "I'm not out here to meet anyone."

"Of course you're not," Simone said, reaching across the table to grab April's hand and give it a quick squeeze. "Not tonight, anyway. But we are going to get you all set up with some online dating so you can get your feet wet. Talk to a few people who don't want you to whip them up a PB and J."

April's pulse seemed to stop doing the whole pulsing thing that was required for consciousness, because her head felt light.

Yes, she'd considered it, but, "I can't date."

"Give me one reason," Kitty said, using that tone of hers that usually meant she was going to get her way. Which was to say, her only tone.

It didn't matter, though, because April could give her a whole slew of reasons. "I haven't been on a first date in ten years."

"So we'll ease you in," Rachel said, picking up the baton. "Get you started talking to a few guys, and you can test the waters."

Did she want to meet someone? Talk to someone? Maybe she was ready for that.

Yes. Yes. Especially if he looked like Jack, and the kids took to him like they did to Jack.

"She looks terrified," Yelena said, apparently allying herself with April, which was good, except April didn't really know where she stood, so neither could Yelena. "Maybe we should just go back to drinking and pretending not to talk about our kids."

Kitty smacked the table. "No." She handed a scrap of paper to April. "I've started a special email address for you—all you have to do is check it sometimes. Simone is already setting you up on Loving Arrow as I speak. And we've all pitched in to buy you a three-month subscription."

Her friends each looked at her a little funny.

"That's a lie," Kitty said with a sigh. "I bought the subscription hoping you might share it with me so I don't have to renew mine."

Was sharing a dating profile with your friend even allowed?

"And if I decide I don't want to do any of this?" April asked. Because maybe she'd rather use the subscription money to go grab sushi another night.

"Don't worry," Kitty said, her confidence infectious. "What's the worst thing that could happen?"

"I fall in love with a guy, have three of his children, and then he leaves me for a skydiving instructor?" That's what came to mind first, anyway.

"The odds of that exact scenario happening again are really, really slim." Kitty fished an ice cube out of her drink and started crunching it.

"Ladies!" Simone held up the screen. "We are online."

Kitty squealed and stomped her feet.

"Oh God." April snatched her phone. "Who is this guy?"

"His name is Tim." Simone pointed to where it did, in fact, say "Tim" underneath his photo.

"Okay, hello, Tim," April said to his photo. She held her thumb over the screen. "Now what?"

"Do you want to match with Tim?" Simone asked.

Tim looked nice enough. He had a really sweet smile. "Maybe."

"Then swipe left," Simone said.

"No, you swipe right." Kitty nodded to the screen. "Left is for the nos."

"Are you sure?" Simone didn't seem so sure.

"When was the last time you participated in online dating?" Yelena asked her wife with eyebrows raised.

"Never." Simone shook her head.

"So you know how to swipe, how?" Yelena asked.

"You're correct, listen to Kitty," Simone agreed.

April must've looked a little green because Yelena stopped tilting her Coors bottle to her mouth and said, "It's just talking. And we're here, too."

Except Yelena's uncertainty was wearing off on April because, heck, she wasn't sure about any of this. What if she spent her entire online dating foray swiping the wrong direction?

"Leave 'em at the left," Kitty recited. "Receive 'em at the

right." She brushed her hands together. "Super easy to remember that way."

"Okay, so I want to receive this man." April swiped her thumb to the right. "Oh. Look, there's another one."

"That's how this game works," Kitty said, her smile wry.

April swiped to the left.

"What was wrong with him?" Kitty asked.

"Nothing, I just wanted to see what happened when I went to the left instead of the right."

A new man arrived on the screen, and April didn't like the way his smile looked like he wanted to come through the phone and eat her. She swiped to the left.

"Okay, let's do this." April held the phone up, swiping left and right at what felt like pretty random intervals.

But was anything in her life really ever random? The time to figure that out was probably not the first time she swiped on a dating app. "Onward," she said.

CHAPTER SEVENTEEN

"Cheese and crackers are a food group, right?"
— *Lauren, Johannesburg, South Africa*

April

"Hold up," Sadie said as April continued to swipe with abandon. She moved to perch on the side of the booth behind April. "Does that guy have a chainsaw?"

April turned the screen. "It says the picture's from last Halloween."

The chainsaw was concerning, but not overly so. He had a nice chin. Strong jaw.

Like Jack.

Gah. No. No Jack thoughts allowed.

"Oh, that's Dale. I know him." Kitty gave a look, and it became clear she knew him in the carnal sense. "Let's just go left on that one." Kitty leaned over and used her own thumb to swipe left.

All righty then, onward.

April's heart beat a little faster because… Actually, this was fun. Like a safe way to see if she might be interested and he might be interested without all the blah blah of life.

She swiped again, because she could.

And oh.

Yeesh.

They were all intently staring at a man who looked to be

snuggling a teddy bear, but one couldn't be entirely certain that was a bear. *What to do? What to do?*

The phone in April's hand chimed. They all shrieked. Especially her.

Her heart was racing for all the wrong reasons.

"You got a message." Simone practically splayed across the table to get a view.

"Uhh…" April scrolled to find the messages. "Oh, crap." She scowled. "It's chainsaw guy."

"Freaking Dale." Kitty did not look happy.

"Are you sure?" Simone was full-court splayed on the table, but no one seemed to particularly mind.

"But I swiped left." April frowned at the image of chainsaw guy. Her pulse stuttered. Was she swiping the wrong way this whole time? Oh goodness. Some of those nos were *really* nos.

"Are you sure we're swiping the right direction?" Simone asked. "Because it seems like we might not be doing this correctly."

April couldn't help it. She laughed. Put her palm over her mouth. "I'm not very good at this game."

Kitty slipped the phone from April's hand. "Drink your tonic while I figure out what's going on."

"Kitty, you can't just take my dating app."

"Can and will," Kitty sang as she flounced away.

April didn't argue because, well, for the first time in a while she was actually having some fun. And even if the one guy interested in her was chainsaw guy, did it really matter? He was interested. Nice chin.

When was the last time a guy was interested?

She might just have to deal with a Halloween chainsaw if it meant she could get laid.

Wait.

"Are you guys trying to get me laid?" she asked, unfortunately loud given the pause of the jukebox.

Everyone in the room seemed to look in her direction.

Her cheeks heated and she shrank in the booth. "Are you?"

"No, we didn't put you on Let's Hook Up." Rachel sucked at her straw. "That *was* a discussion, though. Guess which team Kitty was on?"

"I think you're doing pretty well handling the let's-get-you-laid part yourself." Kitty said. When had she returned? Her eyes twinkled as she glanced around the bar. "Because every eligible man here is checking out you and your ta-tas."

"I think some of them aren't eligible, too," Simone whispered. And, for the record, that did not help the nerves brewing in April's stomach. She took a heady gulp of her vodka tonic. Maybe she should skip the tonic? Really let loose.

She decided against it. Because, kids.

"Okay, this guy." Kitty held up the phone and, oh…

If Jack was out of April's league with his handsome blond good looks, then this guy may as well have been from Mars. Because, seriously, he looked just like that guy who played that guy in the car movies with one of the Chris-Hollywood guys.

"What would I do with all those muscles?" April asked, sort of entranced by the mountains and valleys of this man's sinew.

"You would lick them," Sadie said over the edge of her glass. "And you would enjoy it. And so would he."

"Says the woman whose husband is built like a tank."

"I'm just sayin'." Sadie held up her hand. "Muscles on men are a definite benefit."

"I can get on board with a good dad bod, too," Rachel said. "Sometimes."

"Travis doesn't have a dad bod." Yelena pointed out.

"But if he did, I'd be on board with it." Rachel reached for the fried pickles as they arrived at the table. April poked at the salad, which was pretty good given that they were in a dive bar.

"Don't you worry that this guy is not who he says he is?" April asked. "I mean, why would a guy who looks like that be interested in somebody like me?"

"Shit." Simone shook her head. "We're going to have to do this here."

"Do what?" April forked a bite of salad.

"Tell you all the reasons we love you and you are perfection and you deserve all the happiness in the world," Simone said in one breath.

"And if that happiness comes from a guy with muscles for his muscles, then that's just how it's going to be." Rachel held April's gaze and nodded until April nodded, too.

"And if the guy has a dad bod—and you love him and he treats you awesome—then that's how it'll be," Yelena said. "Because you can lick a dad bod, too."

"But, in the meantime, totally lick this guy's arms." Kitty held up the screen showing muscle guy. "Actually..."

The moment Kitty got an idea was written across her face plain as day. She scooted out of the booth, April's phone still in her grip. She was tapping something on the screen while she chewed on her lower lip.

"What are you doing?" Simone asked, sliding out of the booth to peer over the screen. "Oh."

"What *is* she doing?" April asked, more than a little concerned about what was happening on the cell screen.

"She's talking to Mr. Muscles," Simone whispered.

Oh no. No. No. April was feeling a little numb—and not the good kind of vodka numb.

"Does Mr. Muscles have a name?" April asked, because if she were having a fake conversation with the guy through Kitty, she should probably at least know his name.

"He said to call him Beast," Kitty said from the side of her mouth. "Hallo, Mr. Beast."

"Oh my god, I am not calling him Beast." April made a gimme motion for her phone. "And do you really think we should be talking to a guy named Beast?"

"Yes, I do." Kitty lifted her face and grinned at April in that way of hers that made April sort of think everything just might be okay after all of this.

"What's he saying now?" Simone asked, moving to get a better look. "Oh, he misses campfires."

"Why are you talking about campfires?" April asked, sliding from the booth. Look at that. Now they were all pouring from the booth to watch whatever Kitty was saying on her phone to this guy who April did not know.

"Probably because he doesn't know how to make one," Yelena said, holding her hands up. "I'm not judging. I'm just saying."

"I think"—Sadie spoke as though she were the authority on all things relationships, which, she sort of was, given that she used to specialize as a divorce attorney—"that this man likes the outdoors. And you like the outdoors. And together maybe you could like the outdoors as a *we* instead of a *you*."

"And *I* think that perhaps before I go making camping trips with a guy who can't make a campfire, we should seriously reevaluate what we do for moms' night out."

"He wants to know how your cuddle skills are," Kitty said, finger poised over the screen. "I was thinking like a 4.5 out of ten?"

No, they were way higher than that. Thank you.

"Uh…" April couldn't seem to get her tongue to move so she could answer. She cleared her throat, took a gulp of her drink, and said, "Cuddle with him or just in general?"

"I'll just tell him that's a second date question." Kitty stuck the tip of her tongue at the side of her mouth as she thought hard and typed vigorously.

"Maybe even third date." Rachel nodded her agreement.

"Are you hating this?" Simone asked, slinging her arm over April's shoulders. "I hope you're not hating this."

April let out a nose laugh. "No. I'm just not even sure what I'd do after I cuddled him and licked his arm and made him a campfire. I mean, what do you do after that?"

Other than a little canoodling of the adult variety?

"Do you really want a play-by-play?" Yelena asked. "Because I know Kent was pretty lax in a lot of the departments, but given that you have the three children and the sex pillows, I figured he had that part covered."

Hold up.

"Sex pillows?" April drew her eyebrows together and gave her friend a look like she had lost her ever-loving mind. Because if April had come near Kent with anything other than a mattress and missionary, he'd probably have had a heart attack.

"You know, you use them for yoga." Yelena was totally serious here, and April had literally no idea what the hell-o she was talking about.

"I do not use sex pillows for yoga." If she did, she'd certainly have remembered.

"I think she means the pillow things you sit on," Rachel said, pointing to her sit bones.

"How would you have sex on a pillow like that?" April asked, because, seriously, how would that work?

"Oh." Rachel tilted her head from ear to ear. "You'd be surprised. Travis gets creative about things like that."

"I'm lost, too," Simone said. Then Yelena raised her eyebrows and some kind of silent exchange went down between them. "Oh, *right*." Simone gave her wife some big owl eyes. "I hadn't thought of that."

Lost. April was so lost.

She didn't care for being lost.

"Thought of what, *exactly*?" April cried, again with the being too loud.

She closed her eyes. Rooted her feet. Took three deep breaths. And let her mind flit over what exactly one would do with the bolster that would be even remotely comfortable during sex.

Maybe the cuddling Beast would know.

But given his size, she'd need to be on top because otherwise he'd probably crush her with all those muscles.

After she got done licking them?

Which, to be honest, really didn't sound like that much fun. Not really. Though she'd lick ketchup off Jack nearly any day.

Which was a problem.

Definitely a problem.

A muddy as all hell-o problem.

"Can I talk to Beast?" She held her hand out. Her fingertips shook a little from fear of what this Beast might do to her with a yoga sex pillow, but they were just talking. He was a single man (she really hoped) and she was a single woman (much to her dismay) and they'd both swiped the correct direction (whichever that was). "I'm going to need another vodka tonic." Maybe four of them. "Without the tonic."

"On it," Rachel said, heading toward the bar.

April skimmed the conversation Kitty had started. She'd said nothing and got him to say everything. Huh. She was great at this kind of thing. April held her hand up for a Kitty high five.

"You don't have to say it," Kitty said, all singsong.

"I'm not going to say anything," April murmured, typing a question to Beast about his thoughts on yoga as fitness. To be honest, a guy who was totally committed to weight lifting was fine, but—

Her phone buzzed.

Jack's face flashed across the screen, removing all thoughts of Beast and sex pillows and campfires.

Although...Jack would probably know what to do with the sex pillow.

"Hey," she said, pushing a lock of hair behind her ear. "Everything okay?"

"Uh-huh," he said, "everything's fine." His voice held a note of panic that didn't really have her believing that everything was, in fact, fine.

"Travis asked where Yelena keeps the laceration kit at her house?" Jack asked, again with a heavy dose of fear infusing his tone.

"The *what*?" April shrieked. Then she wasn't thinking of anything, because all she could see was Lola in the emergency room getting her forehead stitched up because April talked to a guy named Beast. "Which kid? What happened?"

That announcement got all the mom attention turned her way.

"No, not a kid. Travis was supposed to go left, and he went right and hit his arm on the... You know, that part isn't really something we need to go into here. He mentioned that Yelena probably has a laceration repair kit we can use?"

"You can't sew yourself back up," April said, her voice getting pitchy.

"Did Travis ask for my laceration repair kit again?" Yelena asked with an eye roll. "Tell him downstairs bathroom under the sink, but if he needs the needle, he has to wait until I get there."

"What did he do this time?" Rachel asked, hands on her hips. "I swear I should just buy stock in sutures."

"But the kids are fine?" April asked into the phone.

"Yep, they're all fine. But be careful coming in the house because I'm still trying to get the furniture polish off the tile in the entryway. And don't worry about the cat, we caught Rohan before he put him in the dryer. Had a good long talk about how to properly dry a cat and why the dryer isn't a good choice. He swears he won't do it again. So I put the cat in your bedroom until you get back. Oh, crap—" There was an indistinct crash in the background. "Don't worry. That was just Travis again."

The hinge on April's jaw seemed to be broken because she couldn't get the thing to close.

"See you in a bit," Jack said, hanging up.

Beast's muscles filled the screen again. April stared at them. "Travis needs stitching up and"—she turned her attention to Simone—"I don't have a cat."

CHAPTER EIGHTEEN

"Always remember that you're a work in progress, just like everyone else is still a work in progress."
—Lee Ann, New Jersey, United States

Right. So, it turned out, Jack wasn't the best babysitter. And Travis wasn't the best co-babysitter. Even though Jack would point out, Travis had kids living at his house *and* had been doing this whole schtick longer than twenty-four hours.

Jack figured he deserved a little leeway as the newbie on board.

He shook his head as he gave Travis an assist with the butterfly bandage they'd found in Yelena's laceration repair kit. The gash was deep, and they didn't cover this type of thing in business school, but Jack was still pretty sure it didn't need stitches. Not *that* deep. Mostly just ugly.

"Good as new." Jack snapped the med kit closed.

"Eh." Travis opened and closed his hand, apparently testing out the butterfly bandage. "We'll just call it better than it was three minutes ago."

"Works for me." Jack stood, stepped around where Mayonnaise had flopped on the floor, and poked his head out into the backyard where the kids ran laps between the two yards. For some reason—and he couldn't say exactly why—the kids had all agreed to this game when Harmony suggested it as an alternative to fighting over who got to pick the next show on the television. This was during the time Travis had hunted for a laceration repair kit and Jack had scrubbed the tile.

"They still running?" Travis asked, moving alongside him.

Jack nodded. "Harmony's a better babysitter than we are."

"I don't think that was ever a question." Travis lifted a shoulder, still holding his hand higher than his elbow as though hoping gravity would help with the intense amount of blood flow from earlier. "Next time, let's just hire her first thing."

Ha. Because—

"That would imply I'm going to be doing this again." Yeah, no. Jack didn't think he'd ever agree to supervise seven children again. Or any children again.

Hang drywall, sure.

Bungee jump, absolutely.

Become a makeshift Jack daycare? No.

Yes, he could actually say with confidence he wasn't going to agree to that. But, thank fuck, it turned out Harmony was a better babysitter than either of the adults in the house.

"How much did you pay her?" Travis asked, as one of his stepkids finished yet another lap, giving Harmony a high five on the way past. She didn't have a stopwatch, but she was holding a pine cone up like a stopwatch and shouting made-up numbers.

That twenty-dollar bill Jack had slipped her to keep the other kids busy outside was well worth it.

Actually, he'd offered ten. She'd negotiated up to twenty.

"I don't think I want to admit how much she got out of me." That got him a half grin from Travis. "Rachel always says that her kids are going to rule the universe when they're older. But I think they're gonna have to get past Harmony and her minions first."

Jack nodded. "Maybe they'll just team up and really do it right."

"That's probable."

"How much money did she get from *you*?" Jack asked, now curious exactly how much of a shakedown Harmony had on the adults.

"I don't think I want to admit how much," he said, echoing Jack's words. Travis gave a subtle head shake. "I'm a sucker. She saw me coming from a mile away."

"You know..." Jack held up his hands. "Maybe it's better if none of us knows the full details. Plausible deniability could be our friend."

"Still worth it." Travis stretched his arm, wiggling his fingers a bit more.

Given that the kids were all occupied, and no one new was bleeding in the past fifteen minutes, whatever Harmony's fee had ballooned to was worth every penny.

The front door to the house opened, and a whole gaggle of women poured themselves through the entryway.

"Whoa," Rachel said, her voice traveling all the way to the kitchen.

"Hey ladies," Travis said. "You're back early."

"We sort of had to when we got the call from Jack looking for sutures," Yelena said, but the light lift to her voice showed she found the fact that Travis needed the kit amusing.

"They cleaned," Simone said with awe. "Like, a lot."

Yeah, they'd sort of been forced into that, what with furniture polish coating most of the tile, the glass shards everywhere, and Travis's blood all over the place.

Yes, the sock and furniture polish version of a Slip 'N Slide had been Jack's suggestion. Yes, he had regretted it. No, he didn't particularly want to dive into the specifics of who did what and when.

Though it should be noted that Harmony had been opposed to this suggestion. It should also be noted that she had gone along with it anyway in the end, because they'd all had a pretty killer time. Until the vase broke, and Travis bled all over the place. Then Harmony gave them a dressing down about roughhousing inside that was truly inspired.

He had a feeling she'd gotten the ability to put them in their place straight from her mother.

Rachel sauntered into the kitchen.

"How did it go?" Jack asked, patting her on the back as she strolled to Travis.

"I think I am out entirely too late on a school night," Rachel muttered, heading straight for her husband. "How bad is it?"

Travis grimaced a little too dramatically—if Jack had to say—before letting her inspect the bandage. "We owe April a vase."

"Which vase?" April asked, testing the tile in the kitchen before fully committing to her step. That was a good call, because thirty minutes earlier, it'd been slippery as all hell.

"Purple one," Travis replied.

Even Jack knew that description didn't help much. Everything in April's house was purple.

"The one by the stairs." Jack gestured to the now-empty, also broken, pedestal thing at the bottom of the staircase.

April stared at the vacant pedestal for a beat too long.

"Was it special?" Jack asked, suddenly feeling like a total tool for the hand he'd had in breaking it.

April lifted her shoulder a touch. "Don't worry about it."

He *was* going to worry about it. Judging by the expression on Travis's face, he was going to worry about it, too.

"More importantly: what's the story with the cat?" April asked, her words oddly cautious. Like she was sticking her toe on the tile to ensure she wouldn't fall on her ass, but in word form about the cat.

"Yeah." He shoved his hands in the pockets of his slacks, already making plans to hit up Buckle and grab a few pairs of jeans for while he was in town.

Turned out taking care of kids was hell on a good suit.

His button-down wouldn't be the same since Lola used him as a napkin for her ketchup dinner.

Less than two weeks to *Practical Parenting*. Not a ton of time, and he could handle anything for a couple of weeks. Then he'd be back in his Los Angeles apartment where his shirts were safe.

"Seriously. The cat?" April asked, scratching at her temple.

Jack jerked his chin toward the top of the stairs. "He's in your room."

And he hadn't gone very willingly.

April shook her head. "But Jack—"

"I'm sorry that you had to cut your night short." He was. His job was to make things easier and encourage her to relax so she could get back to the business of being calm.

"We'll make it up to you," Travis said, letting his southern accent hang right on out there.

Funny, that thing hadn't been so pronounced until just then. Jack had a hunch that bit of an accent was one of the things that had drawn his sister to this guy in the first place. Because it wasn't his coordination when it came to sock surfing on tile.

"I know, but—"

April was cut off as a whole passel of kids barged through the room on the way to the television.

"Harmony?" Jack asked.

She shrugged and held out her palm. "Another twenty if you want me to pick the show for them."

"Harmony." April scowled at her daughter. "Go help the kids with the show and do it out of the goodness of your heart."

Harmony rolled her eyes like only an eight-year-old denied her twenty dollars could. "Fine." She stomped toward the television.

"Okay, serious now." April clapped her hands in a one-two, one-two-three rhythm that Jack remembered from elementary school.

Muscle memory kicked in because he gave her his full attention.

That was a neat little trick he should add to his arsenal. Would it work in a boardroom with a bunch of fund managers?

"The cat," April said, expression earnest. "I don't have one."

"Then whose cat is upstairs in your bedroom?" Jack asked, looking to the top of the stairs. There was definitely a cat up there.

"That's what I'm asking you." April held his gaze with hers, eyes wide, a slight tilt to her mouth.

"Damn." Jack turned and bolted up the stairs, praying the cat hadn't scratched the hell out of April's bedroom.

He jerked open the door and there was one remarkably pissed feline staring at him. A cat with no collar. A cat who, while looking remarkably ticked off, didn't seem to have an inclination to leave.

April moved behind him, Lola in her arms.

"Cat." Lola pointed to the cat.

Jack immediately sneezed because, while he liked to think of himself as invincible, he puffed up like a balloon when he was around cats. That's most of the reason he'd put the cat in April's room to begin with.

"Yes, it is." April raised her eyebrows at Jack. "A cat who should probably go back outside so he can return to his family."

Outside was a great idea. Jack bent to pick up the cat, but the feline wasn't having it. He hissed like Jack had tried to neuter him, not break him out of April's room.

Though, to be honest, April's bedroom smelled very, very nice and Jack probably wouldn't have wanted to leave, either.

Jack sneezed again as he unfolded himself, standing. Huh.

How did someone move a cat who didn't want to budge?

"Uh..." Jack slid his gaze to April.

"What's wrong?" Simone climbed the stairs, Yelena at her side.

"Jack brought a cat inside, and now he won't let anyone in my bedroom," April said dryly.

"Jack or the cat?" Simone asked. "Because we can call Beast if we need to."

This made no sense, but that was pretty much how the night had gone. So Jack rolled with it.

"Jack's also allergic to cats." April seemed to evaluate him closely, and he sort of hoped Yelena had an allergic reaction kit in the cabinet of her downstairs bathroom, too.

"Cat." Lola pointed to the cat again.

April held out her hands. "What is the protocol when you find a strange cat in your bedroom?"

Jack sneezed, his nose tickling and his throat itching. He should probably move away from the cat. Which he would've, if there were anywhere to go. Unfortunately, there was only the big bed in front of him and a group of women behind him blocking his exit.

Simone studied the cat, then she crouched down and held her hand to the dude. "Hey," she said. "Come to Auntie Simone."

The cat hissed at her.

Jack sneezed.

Kitty—where the hell had she come from?—pushed her way through the growing crowd. "Here kitty, kitty," she sang, leaning down and putting her hand out.

Well, fuck him on a Tuesday—the cat sauntered toward her.

Right past Jack, which, again, made him *ah-choo.*

"He's all skin and bones." Kitty lifted the cat so she could speak directly in his face. "This guy needs to put some meat on him."

"Jack?" April asked. "Maybe you should go someplace else."

"You need an antihistamine," Yelena said matter-of-factly.

He agreed. No one, however, moved so he could get through.

"Should we call the police or something to report that we accidentally stole a cat?" Simone asked.

Ah hell, if there were cops involved, Jack was really dreading the answers he was going to have to give about furniture polish and blood and how he should probably never be allowed to supervise children again.

"You didn't steal him." Kitty continued scratching the cat's neck. "He looks like a stray. He's too much of a lovebug to be feral."

Jack's eyes watered further. He started to head past Simone and Yelena, but no one moved to let him past them on the stairs. And now he was just closer to the cat.

"Maybe we should report that we found him," Simone suggested. She stepped closer, hand out to give the little guy a pet.

He hissed at her and snuggled into Kitty's...uh...cleavage.

"You are all a bunch of sillies." Still snuggling the cat, Kitty started down the stairs. "He can stay with me until tomorrow, then I'll take him down to the shelter for a checkup."

Uh...Jack lived in a glass room with half walls at Kitty's. Having the cat there was a terrible idea for him. He'd never had anaphylaxis before, but it didn't seem like it would be the best way to end this evening.

"What's going to happen to him if he doesn't have a family?" April asked, her brows furrowing in concern. For the cat.

Jack scratched at the hives forming along his neck. Was the air thicker? He seemed to be having a hard time catching a breath. "I'm sure he'll find a home. He's...*achoo*...sweet."

Yes, Jack felt sad, too, because the guy deserved a home. Everybody deserved a home.

"What should we call you?" Kitty asked the cat, as though the cat was actually going to answer the question.

"Jack," Lola said, pointing at the cat.

Kitty shook her head. "That'll be too confusing, little one. We'll say, 'Jack, come here,' and no one will know who we're talking to."

"Banana," Lola said, her tone low and nearly a snarl. Then she pointed to the cat again. "Jack."

Kitty gave Lola an odd look. Apparently, no one had briefed her on the banana language.

"I think Jack's a great name," Jack said, slipping his hands in his pockets. The itching at his neck was getting worse.

"We'll see." Kitty rubbed at the feline's head and totally ignored Jack. "Which is my way of saying no." She headed back to her house. Which was, unfortunately, also Jack's house.

He rubbed at his chest. Maybe he should really insist on getting out of there. Somewhere without a cat.

"What do you think the odds are that guy has a family?" April asked, looking up at Jack, and then her eyes went comically wide. "Oh my god, Jack. Your face is all swollen."

Was it? Maybe that's why he was getting a bit dizzy?

Probably.

He should sit. Here. Right there. On the landing.

Good idea, Jack. Solving problems.

CHAPTER NINETEEN

"I may not like you or your choice right now but I will always love you no matter what."
—Anonymous, Michigan, United States

Jack

Everything else happened in a blur of what-the-hell, as some pink tablets were forced on him by Yelena. He made it a policy not to take pills from random women he'd only recently met but, since she had a medical license and a syringe of some kind in hand that she seemed ready to wield, he figured it was a safe bet to take the meds.

By the time the swelling had gone down, the kids were in bed, and everyone had gone home, he was sitting on April's couch searching for a hotel room on the phone app he used sometimes to book rooms.

"Hey." April sat next to him.

"Hey." He wanted to reach for her hand, to apologize for the girls' night interrupted, but he refrained from touching her. Because he was starting to worry that if he began touching her, he wouldn't want to stop. And he was not the guy who should touch April. "I'm sorry about the vase, really. I'd like to replace it."

April shrugged. "Don't worry about it." She gave a little laugh that made his own throat go thick.

"It was special to you." Clearly it was.

April nodded. "The first thing I bought when Kent left. Spent more money than I should've because he hates purple and it was so pretty in the window of the pottery shop. He definitely didn't approve of purchases like that, so it was a little bit of a silly rebellion against him. But it's fine. I knew better than to leave it out where the kids could reach it."

But it wasn't the kids who'd broken it. Jack gritted his teeth, mentally reprimanding himself for being a dunce about it.

"I'm so sorry, April." He was, too.

"Don't think twice about it. I knew the risks when I put it out." She laughed, but it didn't quite meet her eyes. "And I can just get another one. Stick it to Kent all over again."

He'd need to figure out how to fix this.

She lifted her phone tentatively. "I figured out a post for tonight." She'd done an all-made-up-for-girls'-night selfie with an inspirational tag and a reminder she had the food bank fundraiser coming up with her classes next week.

"Look at you. You're on a roll." He nudged her with his elbow.

The flash of pride in her eyes suited her and made his stomach feel funny. Happy-funny. Not antihistamine-funny.

They sat there for a long time in that moment, because it was one of those moments that felt important. So he just let it be what it was for the few seconds it lasted.

"Do you…" April paused, pushed her hair behind her ear. "Do you want to stay here tonight? I have a spare bedroom. And with the cat over there, I'm not sure…"

"I can get a hotel."

"But it's late."

"I don't want to intrude."

"Jack, I have the spare room. You've done my laundry and cleaned my floors, and you made a really good effort at watching my kids. Giving you a place to sleep is the least I can do to say thank you." She looked up at him then with her big brown eyes, and the world seemed to click into place in a way he'd never felt before.

He wasn't sure at all what to do with that. Wasn't sure he wanted to know what to do with it.

So he simply said, "If it's not a pain, I'd appreciate the bed."

She nodded. "Not a pain."

"Thank you." He cleared his throat because the moment seemed heavier than all the others that had come before. More important.

"No, Jack. Thank *you*." She totally broke the moment and chucked him on the shoulder in an incredibly odd gesture. But the move was so April that he couldn't help but let the feeling of her touching him sink right down into his soul.

And by the time Jack had flopped face first onto the mattress in April's guest bedroom, he didn't move for a solid thirty minutes.

Kitty dropped off his bag, so when he finally pulled his ass from the bed, he changed into his lounge pants and white cotton T-shirt that served as his pajamas. He spent some time replying to email, answering messages, and checking in with his team about the other projects. But he was…distracted. So he headed to the bathroom to brush his teeth.

The house was quiet. The type of quiet that a person could sink into. The kind of quiet that took over from the busy pace at which he usually lived his life.

Very unlike the constant movement that went on when the kids were awake.

April's door was open and she was mid–yoga practice, moving through a series of poses that totally mesmerized him. Forced him to stay in place instead of heading to his toothbrush.

An enormous bed filled most of her room. But she also had an open space along the far wall where she moved through her poses. He would've suggested she put a cozy armchair there. An armchair she could drape herself over while he stood behind and—

He gulped away that thought.

Inappropriate.

There was no armchair. There was only a black yoga mat she'd unrolled next to three salt lamps under the window. The walls in this room, like the rest of the house, were purple.

She moved through the sun salutation. From mountain pose to Chaturanga and back to plank.

That he knew all about the poses said a lot more than he was ready to admit. A lot more about everything, but mostly April.

She was…

She was a distraction from what he should be doing.

But he didn't care. Her seamless movements mesmerized him to such a degree that he stood rooted in place, unable to bring his feet to move. The beauty of the motion her body made was stark against the purple curtains. They matched the walls.

She seemed to sense his presence, because her gaze snagged against his, but she didn't stop. She moved into a push-up before hovering for a beat. Then she dropped to the mat in one swift motion, raising her chest like a goddess at the bow of a ship.

He should've looked away.

He should've gone to brush his teeth.

But he couldn't bring himself to move.

She finished the series of poses on her feet, hands like a prayer at her chest.

"Everything okay?" she asked, her voice even. Not even a hint of anxiousness.

He nodded. "I'm good. Just saw you and…"

And what? Decided to watch you because I couldn't not?

"You got so much done, I finally had a moment to myself that didn't involve laundry." Her hair tied back in a low ponytail,

Lola's letter blocks scattered around the landing, and here they were alone in the middle of the night. "I'm really thankful for it all." The feeling that this was exactly where he was supposed to be flowed through him. And *that* left him suddenly feeling very out of place.

"You look relaxed." He crossed his arms because he couldn't think of what else to do with them and leaned against the edge of her door.

She smiled a soft smile. This one touched her eyes and her lips. "Well, the laundry is folded, and the tile is cleaner than I've seen it since we had it installed. You even got the grout. That's impressive."

Jack chuckled. "I did my best." Also, the blood. He'd had to clean up Travis's blood.

"And you're here."

"That I am."

"And some guy with muscles asked me out for next week."

Jack paused. "What?"

Any feelings of contentment vanished in a snap.

"Don't worry. Simone and Kitty are vetting him before we get together." April was smooth and calm and suddenly he… wasn't.

He didn't like this. And he didn't have a reason not to like this. Yet, here he was, not liking it. Nope. Zero stars. Do not recommend.

"That's good, then," he said, even though he didn't mean it, not one iota.

"It is." She didn't sound too excited.

He needed to figure out what the hell was going on with him. Because his reactions around April were totally wrong.

"I guess I should…uh…" He tilted his head toward the bathroom, toward his toothbrush. But he didn't want to go.

"Night, Jack," April said, her voice even.

"Night, April," he replied, his voice even.

They stood there for a long second, neither of them saying anything.

But it wasn't him who moved away. He didn't seem capable of it.

It was April who smiled, shook her head the tiniest of inches, and knelt to roll her mat.

It took everything in him, but he moved his feet and walked away.

CHAPTER TWENTY

"People are going to give you their opinions on everything. Listen politely, then do what you think is best. As long as you love your baby/child, and are doing what you think is best, then you are doing the right thing."
—Elizabeth, Louisiana, United States

If she were being totally honest, the problem with Jack Gibson was that he wasn't a dick. Life would be so much easier if he were a straight-up jerk. She was good at handling jerks. Practically a professional after going through the divorce. Instead, he was just a good guy helping to fix her reputation.

A guy who spent the whole night, and the world hadn't collapsed in on itself because of the hot-guy-across-the-hall shift to her ecosystem.

She eyed the closed door of the guest room.

Her phone chimed.

Simone: *So...*

April: *So...*

Simone: *Jack. Your house. All night.*

April: *I felt bad for him.*

Simone: *Ask him to stay.*

April: *He'll be more comfortable at a hotel.*

She was pretty sure. Fewer kids to distract him and all that.

Simone: *He told you this?*

April: *He didn't have to.*

The phone in April's palm rang. Simone, of course.

She didn't answer right away. Instead, she let it ring two more times while she moved to her window and pulled back the curtain. Sure enough, Simone stood there in her robe looking extremely expectantly at her friend. She pointed to her phone.

April was not curled with eye makeup. No, she had returned to her yoga pants uniform with her hair tucked into a high bun instead of her low ponytail.

"Hey, Simone," she said into the receiver as she watched her friend through the glass.

"Jack needs a place to stay," Simone said, with no preamble or *good morning* or *did you sleep well?* "You should offer him your hospitality. It's the hospitable thing to do."

Perhaps. And it wasn't that she hadn't thought of offering her hospitality more long-term to Jack. Actually, she'd had dreams of offering her hospitality to Jack all night. Dreams that did not involve missionary and her mattress. Well...not only her mattress. Also the sex pillows—bolsters. She'd had some ideas. Excellent ideas.

She shivered.

"Even assuming that Jack is staying in town longer"—which she was pretty certain would not be happening—"he's not going to be comfortable here."

She had kids in every crevice. She had laundry in all the others.

"He was giving you the eyes last night," Simone said, all low and sultry.

April glanced at the ceiling. *Giving me the eyes?* "I have no idea what that even means."

Though, she did have a *slight* idea.

"*He* was looking at you like you were not just a work project for him." Simone pursed her lips and nodded.

"*He* was having an allergic reaction to the cat." April turned to sit on the bedspread. She'd made her bed that morning, too, and she wasn't going to make a big deal about it. Reestablishing a good habit was not something she needed to make a fuss over.

"I should also note that you were making eyes at him, as well," Simone continued.

Gah. *Had* April been making eyes at Jack? Yes, she was attracted to the guy. He was the kind of guy a girl who was into guys got attracted to. Even Mayonnaise was attracted to him. You didn't see Mayonnaise inviting him to live with her on her dog bed, though.

"I will ask Jack what his plans are," April conceded. "And if he needs a place to stay because Kitty is convalescing a cat—"

"You will offer your house. Because if you don't, then I will, and I think he'd rather stay with you than with us."

"Where would you offer him?" Because every room in Simone and Yelena's house was currently in use by them or one of their children.

"We have a sofa," Simone said, like she was explaining something that shouldn't need explanation. "But it's totally ridiculous that he stays on our sofa because Kitty is housing a cat who may or may not have a family and you are too stubborn to offer him his very own room." She paused, clearly for dramatic effect. "A room that he has already slept in."

Guilt seeped through April's pores. The kind of guilt that happened to a woman because she knew her best friend was not wrong.

"I'll talk to Jack," she said. "Not to ask him to stay," she added quickly.

"Then what are you going to talk to him about?" Simone asked.

"I guess I'll figure that out as we *talk*."

Simone smiled, and the hint of that motion through the panes of glass made it all the way to April's bedroom. "That's all I ask. One other thing…"

April waited while Simone started and stopped.

"What's up?" April asked.

"Rachel thinks you plus Jack plus anything other than your professional business relationship is a bad idea," Simone finished quickly, "because of his track record. Not because of yours."

"What do *you* think?" April asked, actually really interested in the answer.

"I think Jack could be your rebound—the no-expectations person who helps you move forward. Then you can find someone else if you want. Someone local. Or not. You don't have to be with someone to be happy. We both know that."

Did she, though? Really?

They said their goodbyes and April headed downstairs.

She paused mid-step halfway down the staircase. Her bare feet simply wouldn't move. From where she stood, she had an eagle's view of her living room. Lola serving Jack what April hoped like hell-o was water from her plastic Beauty and the Beast teapot. Straight into a yellow, plastic teacup that looked like it could decorate the top of a cake.

"Drink." Lola nudged it up toward Jack's mouth.

Jack looked like she may as well have poured sludge into the cup. "What if I just pretend?"

"Banana," Lola said on a growl, her dark brown not-quite-a-baby curls bouncing as she glared.

Rohan had his eyes glued to the cartoons on television while Harmony was splayed tummy down on the carpet, coloring.

"She's not going to leave you alone until you try a sip," Harmony said. "It won't kill you. I drank it and I'm fine."

"She put crayons in it," Jack murmured, squinting at the liquid.

"Because they add flavor," Harmony said, still focused on her coloring.

Jack stared into the little cup that seemed so out of place in his big hands.

Kent never would've done this. He would've pretended a sip, maybe, but that was it. He wouldn't actually consider doing it.

"Banana," Lola said, again.

April should probably go relieve him. He didn't need to drink crayon water from her preschooler. But she didn't even get to take a step because Jack lifted the teacup to his lips and—

Holy crap, he drank it. Downed it like a tequila shot.

He *drank* the crayon water.

The face he made afterward indicated it was not top-shelf crayon. Not at all.

"Smooth," he said, handing the cup back.

Lola smiled a toothy grin and made up another cup for her teddy bear. Unlike Jack, the teddy bear got away with pretend sips.

April's lungs got tight, and the blood whooshed in her head. The whole scene laid out before her like something from a dream she didn't remember until right then, in that moment.

No one clamored for her attention. Or needed her to take care of all the things.

This was peace.

Today was a school day and everyone needed to hop to it so they wouldn't be late, but April couldn't seem to catch her breath, the peace effectively a splash of ice water against the chaos she'd been living.

It had been like they'd stopped breathing when Kent left. Still moved forward because time pushed them on. But no matter how hard she tried, her life seemed stalled in his betrayal.

She squeezed her eyes shut. Tight.

Her heart stuck like peanut butter in her throat.

She started up the stairs, backward. Unable to pull her eyes from the view, but also not able to jump in and be part of it.

She thought, somewhere in the recesses of her mind, that Jack said her name. Certainly that was an illusion, though. He was in the middle of the peace while she stood outside in the free-for-all.

At the top of the stairs, she stepped into her room and turned her back to the wall by the door. She tried to catch a breath, but the peanut butter wouldn't let the air through.

"April?" Jack asked with his butterscotch warmth. "What just happened?"

Eyes shut tight, she was mid-hyperventilation. Thus she wasn't in the best place to deal with his honeyed voice.

"One second." She held up her one second fingertip.

"Give me a hint because I'm getting worried," he said.

She drew a huge gulp of air. "I'm in the middle of an internal crisis." She waved her hands at her chest because that seemed to be where the crisis focused.

"Um." She sensed his movement closer. There in the air around her. Comforting there.

"I'm here when you're ready to tell me what happened," he said, close but not touching.

"Give me a sec," she whispered, blinking her eyes open and staring into his.

And, goodness bless the man, he waited.

He didn't move, didn't come closer, didn't leave. Who knew how he kept the kids from crashing into the room? He just... waited for her to finish with the peanut-butter-flavored chaos.

When it finally ebbed, she said, "Jack?"

"I'm right here." He *was* right there, like a boulder of a rock just waiting for her to grab on instead of rushing by in the river.

She opened her eyes and fell headfirst into the crystal blue depths of his. The kids weren't fussing for her. No one was demanding her attention. There were only the two of them there in her bedroom.

That's when she realized.

Realized what she'd missed this whole time.

"I'm ready for you to help me," she said, the last word cracking on her vocal cords.

He captured that acknowledgment with a flicker in his eyes.

"That's why I'm here." He tilted his forehead a little so their gazes met at the same level.

"I think…"

What was it she thought?

How could she even hope that maybe she might be enough to be just April and also…everything they'd built for her as The Calm Mom? She was April. And he was Jack. And he was there to help her be who she dreamed she could be.

"If I agree to *Practical Parenting*…" She ran her teeth along her lip gloss.

"When you agree…" he countered with a grin.

"I think…" She was generally so much better with words than this.

"What do you think, April?"

"Will you help me get ready?" she asked. And goodness gracious, just asking made her stomach turn over on itself in the nerve-wracking way she'd become accustomed to.

"That's why I'm here," he repeated.

"Will you stay and coach me so I don't mess up again?" Holy hell-o, it took more than she'd ever expected to say those words.

Jack, though? Jack didn't hesitate as he answered, "I will."

He would.

"Your schedule, though." She was back to noshing on cherry-flavored gloss from her lips.

"I'll figure it out." The confidence in his words was enough to have her nodding.

"Thank you," she said, meaning every syllable. They weren't touching, but there wasn't more than a breath of space between the two of them.

The whole ask should've been uncomfortable—like touching a hot pan and just having to deal with the pain. She'd expected the discomfort. But after she said the words, all she felt was relief.

The pan wasn't that hot after all.

"You can stay here," she said, and oh, Simone would be so proud. She just went all in and tossed it out. "If you want."

The little lines between his eyes deepened, prompting her to jump in further.

"So you don't have to worry about Kitty adopting a cat"— because it was pretty clear last night that if that feline did not have a home before, he was going to have one now—"or a hotel or Simone's couch."

He studied her for a long moment. An *uncomfortably* long moment.

He could also have stayed with his sister. But Rachel didn't exactly have an extra room at her house, either. What with Travis and the boys and her two golden retrievers.

"You don't have to. But you can." She wrung her fingers.

He'd say no. He was going to say no. This was why she didn't just offer her guest room to random men—because they'd say no.

"That would be great." He took a small move forward. Deeper into her personal-space bubble.

"Really?" she asked, the word breathier than she'd intended. Because had he really just agreed? How had he just agreed?

"I think it's a good solution." For the first time—or rather, ever that she'd seen—he pulled his bottom lip between his teeth. "I'm allergic to Kitty's right now, and this is where you need me."

She wouldn't think too hard on the idea that she wasn't April to him. She was his job.

No, she would not.

"Jack?"

"Yeah?" His mouth wasn't anywhere near hers, but she still, somehow, felt the word like a breath across her skin.

"Ask me what I want," she said, the question lodging in her larynx.

That got her a lopsided Jack grin. He slipped his hands into his pockets. If he was going to be around her kids for longer than a few days, he'd probably need to get some non–Wall Street clothing.

"What do you want?" he asked.

"I want to be the fucking phoenix," she said softly.

He said nothing. Letting her announcement settle over the room. Because, *yes*. There it was. She'd tossed it out there.

"Tell me about this phoenix," he finally said.

"I want to rise from the chaos that's become my reality."

The chaos that Kent left her alone to deal with.

She started talking with her hands. Animatedly. "I want to rise from the ashes and I want to prove to him that I have this." She jerked her arm wide in what she hoped was a clear illustration. "And he gave it up. And *I'm* fine. *The kids* are fine. *We're all fine!*"

"*Who* do you want to prove that to?" he asked with an air of calm.

Her chest heaved as she steamed like a cup of tea. "Kent."

"Kent's not here," he pointed out.

Maybe he was right, because Kent wasn't there anymore. This was about April, and she needed to admit that.

"Who do you want to prove it to?" Jack asked again.

"*Me*." Thankfully, the word came out with a resolution she wasn't entirely sure she felt. "Me," she said again.

"I can work with that." He gave her a solid once-over. "Yup, I can."

She wasn't entirely sure she'd make it, but she was willing to grab on to hope. For now.

CHAPTER TWENTY-ONE

"Stupidity is painful."
— *Cindy, Colorado, United States*

Jack

Unlike April's life and his current living situation, the best brand restorations were always simple. This was one of the rules Jack lived by in his career. April's case was no different.

Spending more time getting cozy with livestreams so she would be perceived as easily accessible. Linking herself as a giving platform so she would be likable. Expanding her platform to MyTube and print media like cookbooks and magazines.

This was all within reach.

No more live-cleaning urine, cussing children, or other unscheduled catastrophes. And this was an idea Jack was pretty confident would work in everyone's favor, promoting her with an already loved figure.

He had just such a figure in mind. Bonus for everyone involved, he was also Jack's client.

Now, all he had to do was show April the beauty of this strategy.

Calmly.

With yoga.

Maybe some meditation.

Then, bah-da-bing, they'd be on their way. He'd already sent the message to Ben that he'd be in Denver until April's appearance on *Practical Parenting* and her brand launched to the stratosphere, cementing her as the calmest of all the calm mothers.

Two yoga mats, the block things she kept with them, a couple of straps, and the pillows were all set up on her backyard lawn. He'd made her tea as well. A steaming cup, ready for her relaxation.

While he'd never actually practiced yoga, he'd seen enough of her content to understand the basics. So he sat cross-legged on his yoga mat and waited for her to get back from dropping the kids at school.

The amount of time he waited was, honestly, probably only thirty seconds before he started squirming.

Jack was not the kind of guy meant for slow. He was definitely not the kind of guy meant for doing nothing. Still, he tried to immerse himself in the experience of April's backyard. Closed his eyes, did the breath thing April was so fond of…

Well, this just didn't work for him at all. He stood, grabbed his cell, and checked his emails.

That was precisely how April found him around fifteen minutes later when she hurried from the garage to the back door, stuffing her keys in her purse and mumbling something about turn signals and things that were not optional.

There was definitely an under-her-breath mention of wearing pants in public and shoes in restaurants as being not optional, either.

She continued her rant, rummaging through her purse, not looking up.

He slipped his hands to his hips and waited. The suit he'd planned for the day had been scrapped in favor of his running shorts and T-shirt. Not that he couldn't do a lot of things in a suit, but yoga was not one of them.

Almost through the back door to the kitchen, she finally

glanced up and gasped. "What are you doing?"

"Impromptu yoga lesson." He held his hands up. "If you're game."

Her hair on the top of her head in a bun, she was already the picture of a walking athleisure advertisement. *He'd* buy what she was selling, the rant about turn signals notwithstanding.

She scrunched her nose adorably. "You want me to teach you?"

"I've never had a lesson before."

"Are you going to take my picture while I teach you?"

"Probably." But not right away. He pointedly set his phone to the side.

"Okay. Sure. But I get to approve the pictures." She slid her purse from her shoulder, dropping it beside his phone.

"I wouldn't have it any other way." He settled in. "I look forward to learning from the best."

The edges of her lips twitched at that. "I'm hardly a transcended yogi."

"I've heard only good things about you."

"First thing, no shoes." She slipped her tennis shoes from her feet. "No socks, either."

He followed her instructions.

She gave him a rundown of the basic poses. He gave them a decent effort but was pretty sure he'd slaughtered them. Though he continued his effort and followed her lead.

The movement appeared to come effortlessly from her body. She was an artist, there was no doubt.

"Ground yourself. Feel the connection," she said on an upward move that he followed.

He wobbled when he reached the same pose she held effortlessly. "Connection with what?"

"With everything." Turning her focus to him, she tilted her head. "Can I adjust your stance?"

He nodded. Might as well, given that he wasn't doing a bang-up job on his own.

Stepping to him, she moved his hands, then trailed her palm along the outside muscles of his abs, to his waistband, giving a slight correction to his hips so they faced forward with more prominence.

The correction was innocent.

His body's response was not.

"Now breathe." She inhaled deeply. "Feel that connection."

He must've jacked up her correction because the length of her torso pressed lightly against his to move him back to where he apparently should have been.

The connection. Oh, hell, he felt that connection. Hell, yes, he felt the power. Felt it in the marrow of his bones.

"Release," she said, stepping back and rejoining him in the pose on her own mat. "Release the tension."

He let out a long exhale. And with that loss of breath, he released.

And he got harder.

And he was pretty sure his running shorts hid nothing.

But she wasn't paying attention to him anymore. Closed eyes, perfect posture, she still recited directions so he could follow along.

"Yoga at the park," she said, coming down to a plank and then lowering herself to the ground.

"Sorry?" he asked, following her lead.

She didn't continue to press into downward dog as he'd expected.

Instead, she moved to sit in a butterfly stretch.

"We could do yoga at the park." She started talking with her hands. Animated yet serene. "For that fundraiser thing you were talking about. I could scale up after this week to yoga in the park."

"I'm listening." He moved to sit in the same stretch, thankful as all hell that the situation below his waistband had resolved itself when she moved back to her mat.

"I used to go to the park all the time with the girls. We'd sit around on the yoga mats and gab, but we didn't really ever practice. I wish I could set up something so everyone could take a minute and just…"

"Breathe," he finished for her.

She nodded. "Exactly. Sometimes I could convince the girls to do some practice with me. But mostly we just breathed together. Showed up for one another. But maybe I could provide that opportunity for yoga practice and donate proceeds to something that matters."

"Or charge a bag of groceries."

"Exactly."

He wanted to clap his hands and cheer her on, but it would have totally wrecked the mood, so he just listened. This was what they needed. This was the soul-deep thing he needed her to tap into.

"Yoga in the park," he said. "With The Calm Mom."

Face lifted to the sky, she smiled.

"What if you could make it so moms everywhere could participate?" he asked cautiously.

She kept her face lifted, the smile not faltering as she said, "I see the fairy-dust magic you're throwing around, and I am not sure I'm ready for it."

"Hear me out." He moved so he faced her more fully. "You do the fundraiser, and we stream the practice so moms everywhere can participate. Yoga in the park. Yoga on the go."

Her expression shuttered a smidgen. Not a total shutdown, but she was clearly still leery of anything streamed. But she only needed to get some confidence back, and she'd be good as gold.

"Trust me on this, April," he said.

She gave him a small affirmative.

"You grow your base. You give back. You get some more practice with livestreaming. The confidence will come." He went with calm and careful with his explanation when he really wanted to give her a high five and tell her this was so going to work.

"I'm willing to try this your way." A slight autumn breeze teased the tendrils of hair that had escaped the knot she'd tied.

"I have another client. You may have heard of him, Ethan Greene?"

Her eyelids cracked open at that. "Chef Ethan Greene?"

"One and the same." A few years ago, Ethan had been at the top of the celebrity food pyramid. He'd had to take a break to refocus priorities, and by the time he'd returned, the pyramid had restacked itself.

Enter Jack.

Jack was helping Ethan return to the top.

"I've always wanted to go to his restaurant in Vail." April opened her eyes fully, and they were a little dreamy. Which he did not like. At all.

She waved her hand. "It's never worked out. Every time I go through Vail, I've got munchkins." She gave him a look like he should know exactly what she was talking about. And, after two breakfasts together, he absolutely knew what she was talking about. "Michelin Starred restaurants aren't the place for my kids."

He chuckled because she was right.

"I want to ask him here to work on some mindful meal prep with you." Ethan was in the midst of his own brand remix. They could be a powerhouse collaboration with the right direction. "Then we pitch a joint cookbook. Food to help your kid chill out."

The tagline needed some work, but he had a team for that.

"Ethan Greene, at my house?" April asked, apparently still fixated on the first part.

"If you're game."

"Of course I'm game. Who wouldn't be game?"

"I want to stream it live." Ethan was nearby, used to the lens, needed the exposure, and he'd do a great job helping April in front of the camera. Jack would help her behind the camera.

"Oh." April looked up to the sky and let the midmorning sun play across her face. She seemed to come to a conclusion. "All right. Let's try it."

The right conclusion.

"You're bringing Ethan Greene into my house." She smiled a smile that he could live on for days. "I could seriously hug you right now."

Jack held his arms wide. "By all means."

He couldn't quite say what had come over him. Maybe it was that he was seriously jealous with how excited April was to have a celebrity chef in her home, when he'd really prefer that excitement point his way. Maybe it was because he had no idea why he wanted that excitement pointed his way. In any case, he'd offered and was totally committed to this.

April scooted over the small space to him—clearly more well-versed in the art of hugging, because she wasn't awkward about it at all, while he had a feeling like he'd just hopped on a bicycle for the first time and was about to take a header into the bushes.

She let him embrace her, and the world righted itself. He hadn't even noticed it'd been off-kilter. The scent of lavender and candles enveloped him. With the apparent experience of giving quick hugs, she gave a squeeze and began to back up. He wasn't ready to let her go, though—not when she felt so right—but he released her.

Something must've caught her attention. Probably that he wasn't moving, because he wasn't sure at all what to do with the way he was feeling inside. The way his stomach felt like he was in one of the headstand-style poses she'd had him do earlier. The way he couldn't pull his gaze from her glossed lips.

He couldn't kiss her. That would be horribly inappropriate given all they had to accomplish together. But he wanted to.

She parted her lips the slightest of millimeters and reached for his hand, pulling it to her jaw. He ran his thumb along the apple of her cheek. The morning air totally stilled between them.

"I want to kiss you." He laid it out there, let it settle between them. Let her decide what she wanted to do with it. Whatever she decided, he'd follow her direction.

"That would complicate everything," she said, her mouth only a hairsbreadth from his.

"It's already complicated," he admitted. It became complicated that morning in her bedroom. The minute this chemistry between them became undeniable.

"Everything in my life is complicated," she added, but the way she said it implied that in this minute, she didn't particularly mind. Instead of backing away, she rose to her knees and pressed her mouth to his, taking the power of the kiss into her own hands.

So they were doing this? He should probably do some evaluating before jumping right in, but he decided to just go with it for now.

Let her explore his mouth. Let her fingertips trace the planes of his jaw down to his shoulders. Let her control the kiss.

Until he didn't.

He couldn't quite say when he took over, probably when she yielded to the pressure of his lips. Maybe when his hands moved from her jaw to the back of her head. Most likely when she crawled into his lap and melted against him.

It didn't really matter because they were both breathing heavily. While the world continued to move around them, the only thing that mattered to him was more.

More of this. More of her.

CHAPTER TWENTY-TWO

"Home is not a place, it's a feeling."
—*Nicole, Ontario, Canada*

April

The last time April had made out in her backyard, she was sixteen and she'd gotten caught by her dad and the porch light.

This time, the sun was already in the sky, so there would be no porch light. And as her mouth melded with Jack's, there was no one to lecture her about the only thing boys wanted. Because in this moment, there was only one thing *she* wanted.

Oh yes, he continued to kiss the knot of stress right out of her. So what if they were in different leagues? Nothing mattered but the press of their bodies, the feel of his mouth, and the heat of his breath.

She was a grown-ass adult and she could make out with her brand manager on a yoga mat if she damn well pleased.

With the way Jack used his tongue? *Oh yes, I damn well please.*

"I actually thought I'd have to work at this." Kitty gave a squee from somewhere near the kitchen door.

April's entire body stilled. So, unfortunately, did Jack's.

"Here you two are just scooting right along without even a Kitty nudge," Kitty said with a great deal of zeal.

"I think I'm allergic to her, too," Jack muttered against

April's mouth. "All things cat, kitty, or feline."

April peeled herself off him, begrudgingly willing to move back to her own mat, since public displays of affection were decidedly in Kitty's realm, not April's.

"Stay?" Jack asked, softly, so the question was only for April. An oddly uncertain expression flashed across his face.

So she nodded. She stayed.

Oh, she climbed off him, for sure. But Jack didn't release her hand as she moved. Instead, he tugged her beside him and tucked her there under his arm. He absolutely staked his claim on her. She felt heat rush to her cheeks, because this was all so different. She'd never felt like this with Kent. Kissing him the first time had just been the thing to do. Second date, it was time.

Then again, that was pretty much her relationship with Kent. It was time, and then it wasn't. She could see that clearly now. Where had that clarity come from? Well, she wasn't entirely certain.

But with Jack, this was...comfortable.

Comfortably temporary. She'd gone and fallen in love with the perfect man for her with Kent. To her surprise and dismay, it hadn't worked out.

She might as well dive into this thing with Jack, knowing full well it wasn't going to work out. He was committed to leaving. There was no permanence here, no risk.

This was perfect.

"I guess you'll have to cancel with Beast, then." Kitty sighed an overdramatic sigh. "I'll let him know."

"Who?" Jack asked.

"The guy with the muscles," April reminded him. "I mentioned him last night."

"His name is Beast?" Jack looked less than thrilled.

"Uh-huh," Kitty said, strutting toward them.

"And he's a real guy?" Jack didn't seem certain.

"Whether he is real is actually up for debate," April said. This part was true. She hadn't actually met the man. As far as she knew, neither had Simone or Kitty. As of now, he was only an image on a screen.

And, really, it'd been Kitty chatting with him.

Not catfishing him. She had been up-front that she was April's friend vetting prospects for her because April did not know what she was doing.

Except with Jack, apparently.

Her body knew just what to do with Jack. She shivered.

"Do you want me to let Beast know?" April asked, clearing her throat because at that exact moment, Jack trailed his fingertips along her forearm. She felt echoes of those touches throughout her body.

Kitty waved away April's question. "I'll tell him. It'll go over better coming from me."

April didn't even want to think about how Kitty would let him know, or why it would be better coming from her...

She knew she would prefer if Kitty left so she and Jack could go back to their de-stress session.

Yes. What she wanted to do was crawl back into Jack's lap and do more of what they'd been doing before Kitty showed up.

"Hey all," Simone strolled through the gate.

April let out a noise that sounded a lot like *gah* and even more like *seriously?*

"My thoughts exactly," Jack said against April's earlobe.

Her skin reacted by flaunting an entire array of goose bumps.

Given that Jack noticed everything, he pressed himself closer to her. "Cold?"

April shook her head. She was not cold. She loved her neighbors, loved that they took care of her. But she would really appreciate it if they would skedaddle.

He chuckled, low and light and pure caramel candy.

Simone had paused mid-stride through the gate at the sight of April tucked up against Jack's side. She didn't move through the entire goose-bump exchange. Finally, she turned to Kitty. "When did this happen?"

"When he pulled into the neighborhood days ago, gumdrop." Kitty did not turn to leave, as April had really hoped she would. No, Kitty sauntered right over to them and plopped her hot-pants-covered tush on April's mat.

"You coming?" She gestured to Simone and patted the space beside her.

"I was hoping they'd leave," April said over her shoulder to Jack.

She didn't even try to be quiet about it.

Simone moved to stand beside Kitty, but she did not sit.

"This will only take a sec." Kitty held out a stack of yellow photocopied pages. "Then you two can get back to your hankering for a pankering." She tapped the top page of the stack of FOUND posters featuring the cat Kitty had apparently named Captain Jack.

The picture featured on the pages was Captain Jack with Kitty while she took a selfie.

Unfortunately, Kitty was wearing one of her more low-cut shirts, so there was a lot of side boob with the photo of Captain Jack.

April gasped. Kitty could not hang these around the neighborhood.

Jack coughed. "Captain Jack?"

Kitty lifted a shoulder. "What can I say? It fit." She moved into a technically perfect lotus pose while she spoke. "Captain Jack's in the slammer while he serves his waiting time before I can adopt him. No microchip. No one's filed a missing report." Kitty frowned. "I think he was abandoned. And that doesn't make any sense to me because he's just the sweetest. Why would anyone abandon him?"

April reached for Kitty's hand because she looked genuinely distraught.

Kitty never got distraught.

Except over soap theft. But that was more pissed off than distraught.

"He had ear mites, too. I think he was so embarrassed. But I got him all cleaned up and assured him that we all get mites sometimes and it isn't his fault," Kitty continued.

April had, to her knowledge, never had mites. Although, should she maybe ask Jack if he'd had mites before they took this thing between them further? Gah, she'd been out of the dating scene way too long.

"It'll be okay. He's going to find a wonderful family if his doesn't claim him." Simone had knelt down to see the poster and was still staring at it like she wasn't sure quite what to say.

April squeezed Kitty's hand. "Simone's right."

"He doesn't need a wonderful family." Kitty shook her head. "He's got me."

"Are you going to adopt him?" Simone asked, adding her hand on top of April's like they were one for all and all for one.

"Of course not." Kitty balked. "I'll see if *he* wants to adopt *me*."

April wasn't entirely sure what the difference was, but she knew better than to ask. Because if she did, it would probably take an hour for Kitty to explain. And then they'd likely have to get Sadie tipsy so she'd draft a cat-adopts-human legal document and the whole thing would take an entire day.

"I'm sure that if Captain Jack doesn't get claimed, then he'll most definitely want to adopt you." Simone gave another squeeze. Then she pulled Kitty up to stand with her. "Kitty, why don't I help you hang these posters? We'll give him his best chance at being found."

Kitty nodded and her lower lip trembled as she gripped the yellow pages to her chest. "You are just the best friends I've ever had. And Cher used to be my Girl Scout leader, so I've known a lot of really exceptional women."

"Cher was your Girl Scout leader?" Simone asked, raising her eyebrows at April.

They knew little about Kitty's past, so it actually could be true.

"Not the real Cher." Kitty sniffled. "But she looked a lot like Cher and she sang in the choir at the Baptist church, so basically the same thing."

April closed her eyes and smiled, because even fake Cher couldn't ruin her morning.

She stood to join her friends. "I'll walk you out."

This would serve two purposes. One, she could show her support for Kitty's Captain Jack distress. And two, she could lock the deadbolt and the privacy bar on all the doors to her house on her way back through.

A quick glance at Jack and she nearly tripped backward because of the heat of the look he was giving her. Like he wanted to meditate the hell-o out of their morning. All morning. And well into the afternoon. Until she was so relaxed that she was a puddle of April-flavored ice cream with pink sprinkles.

Instead of attempting to give him a heated glance in return— which would have turned into her looking like a complete fool— she trudged after Kitty and Simone.

Once inside her house, Simone closed the door to the backyard. She stood in front of it, arms crossed, toe tapping. "One night and you're jumping him?"

"I was *not* jumping him." She wasn't. She was sitting on him, sure. But there was no jumping involved.

"Yet." Kitty's distress apparently dissolved because she had a nice new bone to nibble on and it was called April. "But if what I walked in on is any sign, I'd say you are about to go all *I Got You Babe* on him. In the yard, of all places. Which, I one-hundred-and-twenty-two percent endorse because you put down the yoga mats so you wouldn't get grass burn on your tush. That's even worse than rug burn. Believe me, I should know."

"I'm not even sure how to address any of the things you just said." April blinked hard.

"Give us the ten-second version of what happened for us to get from point A to point one-hundred-and-twenty-two in the space of one night." Simone uncrossed her arms. "I'll wait."

"It literally just happened." April tossed her hands up. "One second we were in downward dog and the next he's bringing Ethan Greene to my kitchen and then we were making out."

"I prefer bridge pose for that kind of thing," Kitty said. "It's my favorite yoga position in the bedroom. You have to have great core strength to pull it off—but let's be honest, you totally could. That's a good one to start with." Kitty nodded along with herself. "Don't go straight to downward dog. It raises his expectations entirely too high at the beginning. Keep them low long enough so he appreciates when you try. Then when you pull out the downward dog, he'll think you're a goddess."

April tried, really tried, to wrap her head around how one would do a bridge pose while in any sex act and have it be remotely comfortable. She was going to break her brain if she kept trying to figure that out.

"Ethan Greene is coming to your kitchen?" Simone asked, clearly oblivious to the conversation about yoga sex.

Now it was apparently Simone's turn to blink hard.

"Ethan Greene!" Simone yelled his name loud enough that Jack probably heard it.

April shushed her. "Don't make a thing about it."

"You made out with Jack because of it," Simone accused,

jerking her thumb behind her. "And frankly, I'm about ready to go do the same. Can Ethan Greene come to my kitchen, too? Because I stopped at his restaurant in Vail last year and his scallops were so tender, they were practically loved by Elvis."

"I love good scallops," Kitty said.

April enjoyed a good scallop, too, however—

"You may not make out with Jack." April figured she should just get that out there right up-front because she wouldn't care for that and she was nearly certain that Yelena wouldn't, either. She pointed to Kitty for good measure. "You either."

Simone nodded sagely. "You're in deeper than I thought."

"Oh girl," Kitty said. "Yes, you are."

"I'm not *in* anything. It was just a kiss. He's here temporarily and is going to leave. This whole thing is very shallow—a kiddie pool. No one is in deep." And now her voice was pitching higher, showing her for the liar she was because, while the rest of what she said was true, that was *not* just a kiss. That was *the* kiss. The toe-curling, heel-kick kind of kiss. "We'll never know if it would have been more, because we had kissus interruptus."

"I am sorry for that." Kitty held up her palm. "Next time I won't say a word until you finish."

That made it official—April would never make out in her backyard again.

"We just don't want you to get hurt, gumdrop," Kitty said, soft like a purr. "And Jack's at a level five ocean when we were trying to go level one with Beast in the shallow end. Ease you back in. But then you just went and jumped off a cliff right into the water. I'm not opposed to that. Just as long as you know where you're floating."

"Jack isn't level five," April said. "Jack's so easy to be with, he's totally a kiddie pool." This Kitty logic was, however, oddly making sense to April. Which meant she probably needed to go get an MRI or something. "I also didn't jump. It happened without me even trying."

"You weren't trying, but I have a hunch…" Kitty said low under her breath.

"Jack is practically training wheels," April assured them, going with her own metaphor. "There's no risk of my heart getting involved. He's here to help me find my calm, and I can say that before the interruption, I was extremely calm. So calm. The calmest mom I've ever been."

Simone was studying April with genuine concern.

Kitty, however, grinned. "I think what she's saying is that she's feeling pretty groovy right about now."

"Well, I *was*." The groovy feeling dissolved with all the talk of cliff diving and kiddie pools.

"Then we'll leave and let you get back to your zenification," Kitty said with a wink. "Keep relaxing."

April had studied a good deal of Sanskrit and—"Zenification is not a word."

"The act of becoming Zen? It's a word," Kitty said.

April shook her head. It really wasn't.

"It doesn't matter, though, because what I mean is that I only want you to be happy," Kitty said with a huff. "I would also love it if you stocked the fruit punch juice boxes a little more regularly for my rum punch." With that, Kitty turned on her heel and flounced out.

Simone did not.

April bit her lips. Because Simone looked like she had something to say, and April probably would not like it.

Simone continued to study her, then the tile. Like she was taking an inventory of her thoughts. Finally, she said, "If he hurts you, I will send penis confetti cannons to his office every single day for the rest of his life. Not the nice ones, either. The glitter kind that gets in *everything*."

April knew Simone would follow through with that threat.

But Jack would not hurt her. Her heart was locked up tighter than Fort Knox.

"While I appreciate the sentiment," April said carefully, "we will not be entangling ourselves like that. Training wheels, Simone. He's just training wheels."

Simone pinched her lips to the side. "Can I make a suggestion?"

"Aren't you going to anyway?"

She lifted her hands to April's shoulders. "Tell him what you need. Be specific. He seems like a guy who will appreciate that."

Since she sounded so serious about this, April nodded. She did not know how she would go about telling Jack what she needed or how to be specific about it. But she would try.

Apparently appeased with April's reaction, Simone left. She left out the *front door*, clearly not interested in going back through the gate, since that would require passing Jack. If she went past Jack, April knew her well enough to know she'd start talking about penis glitter, and they both knew that was not the kind of conversation that would end with April continuing on with her calm.

April followed behind her friends, engaging all the locks.

Then she went to find Jack.

CHAPTER TWENTY-THREE

"No one has ever lived in the past
or in the future—only the now."
—*Thich Nhat Hanh*

April

Jack was not waiting for her outside, ready to continue the cuddle session they'd started on the mat.

No, Jack was on his cell phone in her kitchen. Sitting at the table, frantically typing on his laptop while he gave direction into the phone. Giving orders and taking charge of whatever was making the vein on the left side of his temple pulse visibly.

His tone was eerily calm, given the pulsing of his temple, even as he gave instruction after instruction. The words, "Somebody get legal on the line," and "What are the odds that might not happen?" were both said multiple times.

Her heart rate hitched a little higher that this could've been about her. But she hadn't done anything recently to warrant that level of attention…she was pretty sure.

She didn't make any noise to break his concentration because, clearly, whatever the situation was, it seemed important. Still, he must have sensed her there because he glanced up to her and his expression softened. His tone did too. Even if he probably hadn't meant for it to.

I had to take this, he mouthed in her direction. *Another client.*

She nodded, pointed upstairs, and left to give him some uninterrupted space.

She reached into her file of premade graphics, selected one, posted it. Glanced quickly at the comments marked for her review. There were a lot of them, so before she got started, she tossed a new load of laundry into the washer, got towels folded and put away, and did a quick pickup of the kids' rooms. She was actually ahead of her daily chores. Apparently, she had Jack's fairy-dust kisses to thank for that.

On that wonderful blissed-out Jack thought, she'd set up her workstation on her bed. The couch would've worked, but then she could still overhear him, and it seemed to be the type of crisis that required privacy and a wardrobe change. He'd switched into his power suit.

Besides, her bed worked just fine. And if she propped her laptop up on two pillows, it was nearly ergonomic.

Which was important, since she was going to spend the next hours submersed in her social networks, not letting anything anyone said about her ruin the day.

Really, it could've been worse. In fact, it had been worse. But Jack's team had spent the last days wrangling the channels into submission and scrubbing comments. That all helped quell the wave. And just as quickly as the video had come, a woman accidentally glued her socks to her feet. Her video was quickly replacing April's.

Viral videos were clearly fickle things.

Don't even ask April how the sock gluing was possible. But it was, and #sockwoman had taken the spotlight from #urinemom. That would, of course, be what the internet had taken to calling her.

April did not mind this shift of attention one bit. Especially because where April hated that limelight, Sock Woman seemed to revel in the attention. So she could just keep it.

Though, now that the seed had been planted, April could see her kids trying to glue clothing on their bodies. Actually, after hearing about it herself, she was surprised they hadn't already given it a whirl.

That was precisely how April found herself elbow deep in researching adhesive removal on clothing and skin for her next blog post when Jack appeared at her bedroom door.

A frustrated Jack.

"Everything okay?" she asked. Which was a ridiculous question. Given his conversation downstairs, everything was *not* okay.

"No," he said briskly.

She did the thing she did with Harmony after she'd had a bad day at school. She said…nothing. Waited for Jack to sort out his thoughts and tell her himself.

He sighed. Ran his hand over the back of his hair, resting it at the base of his neck. The muscles in his triceps pulled against the perfectly fitted suit jacket.

"In my line of work, things are rarely *okay*," he said. "Another day, another fire to put out." He smiled a terse smile.

That worked more quickly on Jack than it did on Harmony. She could stomp around for a solid hour before she gave in and talked to April.

"Do you need to talk about it?" April asked, since that seemed like the right thing to say.

He shook his head. "It's handled."

"Are you going to leave?" she asked, hoping like heck he wouldn't be leaving her for the next fire. Not yet. She needed a little more time before the training wheels came off.

"I got it covered." He moved into the room, but he didn't sit. Instead, he put his hands in his pockets and studied the floor.

"Hey, I'm sorry about before with Kitty and Simone. They mean well and—"

"You're clearly an important part of their lives," Jack said, a new awkwardness settling between them.

Neither of them said anything.

They'd disagreed over brand direction. They'd had many, many conversations over all kinds of subjects. Heck, they'd even played tongue twister.

They'd never had awkward before, though, and she wasn't entirely sure what to do with it.

"Jack, I—" she said at the same time he said, "We should address—"

They both halted.

"Jack," she said, giving him a second to ensure he wouldn't speak, too.

He nodded. "You go first."

"I enjoyed what happened outside." She stumbled over the words because *enjoyed* was the least appropriate word ever. What had happened was the best thing she'd experienced since... well... It'd been awhile.

He nodded, his expression still clipped like his words were before when he was at the table. "I did as well."

Wasn't that just the glowing review a girl wanted after macking on a guy?

"Good." She closed her laptop and set it aside, redistributing the pillows she had propped it on so they weren't a theoretical mountain between the two of them.

She opened her mouth. Best to just get it out there. Lay down the parameters of what they might consider doing with each other physically. "I was thinking—"

"It probably shouldn't—" He chuckled. "You go first."

Going for breezy, she said, "I went first last time."

The bashful expression he gave her—the puppy-dog eyes and the unusual innocence stopped the argument she was about to make before it slipped to her tongue and out of her mouth.

So she went first.

"I enjoyed what happened." She kept her gaze on his. "A lot more than I thought I would." Wait, that didn't come out quite right. "I mean when I imagined kissing someone other than..." She needed to stop and maybe get her words together first.

She held up her one-second finger and heaved a deep breath. Sometimes she swore she forgot to breathe. Which was really random, given her dedication to the practice of breath.

Finally she said, "If you want to do that again, I'd be game." She couldn't quite meet his eyes, though. "We could also do more. I'd be game for that, too."

He didn't move and his face totally shuttered. The blinds firmly closed. Poker face engaged.

"Unless you don't want to. That'd be fine, too," she said.

But would it? Because if he turned her down this far into whatever it was they were doing, she'd fall right on her theoretical face and there would be some definite emotional bruising.

Quickly recapping the morning, she may have been the one to actually hug him first, and that hug had led to kissing. But he'd been the one who asked her to sit next to him afterward. And by the rules of kissing, that meant he wanted to do it again, didn't it? Gah, it'd been so long since she'd done any of this.

No, they weren't in middle school anymore, but the rules of sitting next to a guy you just kissed still applied when a girl was going on forty. Didn't they? She should probably ask Kitty. Kitty would know.

"I should be up-front. I don't do the whole relationship thing." Jack sounded sorry about that. Which was silly because she wasn't into the whole *relationship thing*, either. "I'm not step-dad material. Kids are great, as long as they're not mine."

Well, ouch. But at least they were on the same page here.

"I don't want a step-dad for my kids. And I don't want a

relationship out of this." She pointed to herself like there was someone else she could be referring to with the whole "I" thing. "I'm *never* doing the relationship thing again. I've been there, done that. Rode the ride. Wouldn't recommend it."

He frowned at that, the vein in his forehead pulsing again like it had before when he was dealing with whatever it was he was dealing with.

"I know relationships work for some people," she said, a lot more gently than her previous not-gonna-happen tirade. "But you don't have to worry about that with me. I'm never doing that again."

Never.

"What exactly do you want, then?" He gestured between them. "From this thing."

Uh...a little more of what they'd already done. Heck, a few orgasms wouldn't be an awful place to start. Maybe dinner that someone else would fix for her. Plate for her. Serve to her. Clean up after her.

"I could ask you the same," she said, instead of the other things she'd considered.

The Adam's apple at his throat bobbed. "Prior to what happened *before*, I was content for things to be as they were between us."

So was she, but it wasn't like they could take it all back. Not after she'd learned how nice his lips felt against hers.

"And now?" She patted the bed. "You can sit. I won't bite."

Unless he asked.

Holy goodness. Who was this person invading her thoughts?

He sat at the edge. Close to her, but not touching her.

"I think it's pretty clear this attraction happening between us is going to continue to tempt," he said.

"Tempt" being the understatement of the millennium.

"My job here is to help you get back to calm."

She could definitely think of one thing that would help with that, and it wasn't this conversation.

"Do you think that perhaps we're making this whole thing more complicated than it needs to be?" she asked. What was wrong with what they'd done before? He wanted to kiss her. She wanted to kiss him. In the end, they both wanted the same thing from this. They'd said as much.

"We still have to work together when all this is over," he said, reaching for her hand.

"I think we can both manage separation of bedroom and office." She winked at him.

A smile tickled the edges of his lips. "It can get more complex than that."

"I don't want forever, Jack." She sighed. She had no visions of a future with a husband who sat with her through their twilight years. That would not happen for her, and she'd come to terms with it a long time ago.

"I'm good with having today," she continued. "After *Practical Parenting*, you'll go home. I'll stay here. *And* I'll have a sparkling clean reputation with a whole slew of Jack-inspired confidence. Everybody wins and nobody has to worry about messing up our work relationship."

The heated look they shared stirred something in her that made her question that assertion. But she was being real, laying out what she wanted. Simone would be so proud.

Kitty would be disappointed she hadn't pounced on him yet.

Some kind of internal debate seemed to war inside him, and she wasn't sure which side was winning.

"Why can't it just be fun?" she asked. "Everyone's always riding me about relaxing and having fun and getting back to that. This is me trying."

"April." He squeezed her hand. "I know you. You do everything with emotion."

"Not this." She scooted closer to him. "We're both adults. We're both single. We're on *my* bed. There's practically a whole chemistry set igniting between us. What do you want to do about it, Mr. Fix It?"

What could she say? She'd tried for sultry. It came out a little wonky, but she'd made the effort.

He said nothing, but his thumb stroked the inside of her wrist, so that was probably a pretty good sign. Also, it felt amazing.

"I have two choices right now," he said, the words seeming to stroke her skin along with his thumb. He watched the movement along her inner wrist.

What he did not do was continue speaking.

She shifted. "Are you going to tell me what they are? The choices?"

He made a deep *mmm-hmm* noise in his throat. "The correct choice is that I stand up, go to the kitchen table, and get back to work." He lifted his eyes to search hers. "The second choice is that I stay here."

"I vote the second choice," she said, more than a little too quickly. She didn't hold her hand up like she was actually voting, but it took a great deal of restraint to keep it back.

He moved closer to her, his lips just a breath from hers. "I guess life isn't always about making the correct choice."

CHAPTER TWENTY-FOUR

"Being a mom is damn hard. Sometimes you'll want to sit on your closet floor with a bottle of wine and cry. When you do, choose a Chardonnay. That way you don't have to deal with red wine stains if you spill."
—Dylann Crush

April

"You're sure?" he asked, more than a little too late.

"Yes," she said as she pulled him to her, hooking her leg over his hip. The snug fabric of her pants pressed against his thick erection.

He looked to her with an expectant gaze, his eyes unsure, his expression relaxed.

"I shouldn't have started this." He ran his hands over his face. For a guy whose job it was to get things right, he kept saying the wrong thing.

She stilled under him.

"Why?" she asked, the question one of genuine curiosity.

He moved his hand from her jaw. "Because I'm about to mess everything up."

"I don't think that means what you think it means." She smiled because Simone would have been all in with *The Princess Bride* references.

His erection pressed against her center and she wasn't thinking about anything else except him. The feel of him between her thighs. They were both still fully dressed—which was a complete shame—but she was more turned on than she'd been in for*ever*.

And then there was the press of his mouth against hers, his hands in her hair, her hands yanking at his shirt to untuck it from his pants.

Something made him pause, and he stopped kissing her. His breaths came ragged against her throat.

"What's wrong?" she asked. Actually, she sort of croaked it because it came out on a moan.

He didn't respond at first, seemed to attempt to get control over some part of him.

"Give me a second," he said finally.

"Tell me what you're thinking," she said softly.

"That I want what I can't have," he admitted. "And I'm taking what I shouldn't."

The world seemed to turn topsy-turvy at this. Somehow, she forced his gaze to meet the deep depths of her brown eyes.

"Why can't you have me?" she asked.

"There are reasons." He paused, his gaze still stuck to hers. "But I just decided that none of them matter."

He didn't share the reasons because his mouth moved to hers and he picked up right where they left off.

"You should know that there *were* a lot of reasons," he said, breaking the kiss long enough to unbutton his shirt. "I just can't think of any right now." He pulled the undershirt over his head and returned to her. "Give me an hour and I'll remember."

"An hour, huh?" She toyed with the hair at his ears because… well…she could. "That's a little ambitious."

He did a very nice *Chaturanga* press-up over the top of her, holding himself there.

"An hour is only the beginning. I just decided." His mouth moved to hers and there was definite tongue happening. More than he'd used outside. Because, apparently, outside, he'd held back.

Inside, now?

He was a force.

Also, superb at getting her undressed while still kissing her. She barely had to do anything but lift her hips and let him work his Jack magic. There wasn't even an opportunity to show him her flexibility—the one unique thing she could bring to the bedroom.

He held her head right where he wanted her, kissing the bejeezus right out of her. Frantic. This was frantic. In a good way. Like they were both going to ignite if they didn't get undressed, and she would combust if he wasn't inside her in five, four, three, two—

He dealt with the condom as she parted her thighs to allow him entrance, a little disappointed they were going to end up in missionary when she hadn't even given Kitty's forward bend a shot.

She paused momentarily.

No, she absolutely did not want her first time postdivorce to be missionary.

Taking over the kiss, Jack released his grip on control, passing it to her when her mouth and hands and body demanded. She rolled him to his back.

He went willingly, seemingly with no issue handing her the reins.

The power of control was brilliant. Better than she'd ever imagined. Reveling in it, she let her inner vixen run free and straddled him, holding his erection in her hand to slide him inside inch by inch.

His eyes rolled and his hands gripped the blankets as she made it all the way to the base. Frankly, her eyes rolled, too.

His hands found her hips, and he made groaning noises

that may as well have been a gold medal in the April sexual Olympics. So she moved, spurred on by her pleasure and his encouragement.

And then.

She got brazen.

Adding in a backbend as he was still inside her, because she could. All that practice, all that flexibility had to be good for something. She held her hands at his knees. Then he moved inside her. The balance precarious, but the feeling more than anything she'd ever experienced.

Her internal muscles clenched around him as he moved.

And she breathed.

"Holy hell," he said on a groan. "April…"

Her name on his lips sent her over the edge, an orgasm rippling through her.

He followed without hesitation. Pulling her to him and kissing the living daylights out of her. There was kissing—so much kissing. Panting and…was he petting her? He was totally petting her. Running his hand along her hair, down her arm, tangling his fingers with hers.

"That was… Holy hell…" He paused his invasion of her mouth to hold her head to the groove of his neck. "I didn't even know that was possible."

Well, until two minutes ago, neither had she.

"How did you even—?"

"I get to have secrets, too," she whispered against his neck.

And then.

The full force of what she'd done grabbed her around the throat and made it impossible to catch a breath.

She'd had sex with Jack. Which, it should be noted, she did not regret. Not one bit.

But she'd done a backbend on him when she rode him cowgirl. This was definitely a questionable maneuver, and not a first-time sex position. What the hell-o had she been thinking?

And she'd had sex in the middle of the freaking day. What if her kids' school called? What if there was a delivery to sign for?

The breaths that had come so easily before suddenly clogged her throat.

"April?" he asked, apparently sensing something was off.

"I can't catch my breath," she said, sitting up but deciding that wasn't a good idea and so falling back against him.

She was heaving extremely heavy air through her lungs, her chest rising and falling against him. Her skin seemed too tight, and her pulse pounded in her ears.

"Hey." He held her jaw with his hand so her eyes met his, his voice tender. "What's going on?"

She pressed the heels of her hands against her eyelids. "Minor haven't-done-this-in-a-while panic. Give me a second to get myself together."

He pulled her closer for a cuddle. Even though they were naked and they'd just done that, the move felt comfortably platonic.

"Do you regret what just happened?" he asked, using his butterscotch tone that made her not able to form a coherent thought.

Which was good, since all her thoughts jumbled.

"I just did a backbend with you *inside me*." She gripped his shoulders. "What if I'd hurt you?"

His eyebrows drew together. "You pulled off *that* maneuver and you're worried you could've hurt *me*?"

"I could've slipped." That wasn't totally out of the realm of possibility.

His expression turned to utter seriousness. "Would you have gotten hurt?"

"Of course not." She shook her head. This wasn't about her getting hurt. She could have maimed him during sex.

"Then it would've been worth the trip to the emergency room," he said, as though this whole thing was a joke.

She frowned.

"Trust me. You ever want to do *that* again, I will take the risk."

Oh, well…that was nice, then. Maybe it was okay after all.

"It's been *so* long since I've had sex," April said. "And now I'm mucking it all up."

"There is literally no way you could muck anything up after *that*." He nuzzled her neck. "Please know that was the hottest thing I've ever experienced in my life."

Now he was just messing with her.

"April." He reached for her hands, pulled them to his chest. Right over his heart.

She let him.

Then she ruined it.

"I bet *you* get to have sex all the time," she said. "And I haven't had sex in forever. *Forever.*"

Darn, she didn't really mean for that to sound so accusatory.

His eyebrows furrowed. "You think I have sex all the time?"

She looked him over from the tips of his perfect blond hair to the muscles of his abs. "Uh." She paused. "I mean, you're you." She waved her hand up and down his torso to illustrate how *him* he was. "Women must fall all over themselves to get your attention."

"That's not true." He moved her closer, which she hadn't thought was possible.

This was nice. She was mid-panic, and he didn't run away.

"You could have all the sex you wanted, whenever you wanted," she continued, but this time it didn't sound like an accusation. More like a fact of life.

His mouth pressed into a thin line like he'd didn't believe her. But it was the truth. Take her, for instance. She'd curled her hair and put on eye makeup *and* did a backbend in bed. She didn't do *that* for anyone else.

He opened his mouth. Closed it. Opened it again. Finally settling on, "I would very much like to continue doing what we just did. But I feel like I need to clarify a few things," he said. "Are you in a headspace we can talk about this? Or do you need a minute?"

She held a breath, then released it.

"I'm good." Her blood pressure was returning to normal levels. No risk of imminent stroke.

"There aren't any other women in my bed at night." He paused, clearly tested that statement. "Or during the day."

Oh. Well, that was nice of him to say.

"I'm here with you because I want to be here with *you*," he continued. "I'm the one who should question what I'm bringing to this bed. Because I can never live up to what you just did."

"Jack…"

"That's not to say I'm unwilling to try." He waggled his eyebrows, and the move was so adorably dorky she dissolved against him.

Her words from before—from outside—echoed in her ears. *Ground yourself. Feel the connection.*

She did that. Grounded herself with him. In her room. In her house. Just the two of them.

The funny thing was, with Jack there, the grounding came easier. Especially when his arms wrapped around her and held her against him. She missed that—someone to hold on to.

"I really miss being held," she said to the air. "I'm the one who is always holding now."

"April," he said her name on a growl. "You shouldn't say things like that."

"Why?"

"Because it makes me want to fix things for you." His hand

stroked up and down her side, comforting. Grounding.

She moved her fingertips through his and brought their joined hands to her mouth to kiss his knuckles. "Does anyone ever fix things for you, Jack?"

That got her a low rumble of a laugh. "Now you sound like Rachel."

"Thank you for coming here and showing me how to breathe again." For showing her how to want again. Not to settle.

She had never been the kind of person to hold back. She used to shoot straight.

Back in the day.

Back when things were...calmer.

Back...before.

"You're welcome." He brushed the tip of his nose against hers in a silly, intimate gesture that made her warm and fuzzy all over. "Thank you for teaching me I've been having sex wrong my entire adult life."

She squirmed beside him. "You, uh, want me to show *you* how to do a backbend?"

"Will it involve another illustration?" he asked. "For scientific purposes, of course."

"I could probably do another illustration for you." She shrugged and it sort of actually came off as sultry. *Yay, me.*

That got her a full-confidence Jack grin before she gave him a lesson.

And then he gave her a lesson.

Two more of them, actually.

CHAPTER TWENTY-FIVE

"Motherhood is the exquisite inconvenience of being another person's everything."
—Unknown

April

April's day was pretty freaking outstanding. By the time the end of the evening rolled around and she headed home from teaching her classes, donating a shed-load of food to the food bank, a perma-smile seemed plastered to her mouth.

Philanthropy was amazing.

Even those who couldn't attend her class tonight had dropped off a donation. She'd snapped a picture, and Jack took a video of the massive haul.

At his gentle prodding, she'd pitched the idea of yoga in the park to her students. There was a good vibe going with that.

He'd been thrilled with how it turned out. He even stuck around for the class before heading over to spend time with Rachel and her family.

"See what I meant?" he'd asked her, once the final tally was done and before he took off.

She did see. This wasn't really about fixing her image. This was about using what she had for a good cause.

That was the spin.

She got that now.

Everyone benefited. Except Betsy. Which was fine.

Today was about being happy.

Even dropping the kids at Kent's condo hadn't stirred up a slurry of emotions like it had in the past. If anyone had asked last week, she'd have said that Kent broke her heart. Now, she was wondering if maybe he just bruised her ego and crushed her spirit? Today it was harder to remember the dreams she used to harbor in his presence.

Tonight? Tonight the drop-off was an emotional breeze. And not just because Jack was superb with bedroom activities.

Exceptional.

He even went for extra credit, which was unnecessary for him to get the highest possible grade.

Not that April had particularly questioned that. But it was good to know from firsthand knowledge that their little... whatever this was...would continue to be spectacular. Fireworks spectacular.

She deserved a dash of spectacular after the past year.

Jack was all amazing but not the reason for the light feeling of the day.

Something inside her had clicked into place again. That something that reminded her life didn't always have to be so hard.

She'd just forgotten for a bit when life's blinders knocked her down.

With what had to be a goofy smile on her face, she let herself in her house. The kids were with Kent for another hour, Jack had gone to Rachel's to hang with Travis and their boys, and April had the entire house to herself.

Bliss.

She'd planned a bubble bath the entire drive home. Update her stats. Share her enthusiasm for all things charitable—and then...warm bubbles.

The last time she'd had a bubble bath? She couldn't quite remember.

With the promise of the rest of her night floating through her thoughts, she came up short at the sound of Kitty's voice.

"Hello?" April called.

"In here, gumdrop," Kitty called from the kitchen.

April sighed, mentally shelving her bubble bath to trudge to the kitchen. She refused to let a Kitty takeover ruin her vibe. There would be time for bubbles later.

Kitty, however, wasn't alone. Simone and Yelena joined her at her kitchen table with what looked like glasses of margaritas.

"Are we having a party you forgot to invite me to?" April asked, breezing to the table.

Yelena had even made up a plate of crudités, so it was definitely a party.

"We missed you at yoga class, Kitty," April said, since it was rare for Kitty to miss a session. "Thank you for your check, though."

Kitty had given a nice fat contribution to the food bank.

"You're welcome. I love food. I'm not sorry I missed this week, though—I had a coffee date." Kitty lifted a pre-poured margarita, slipping it into April's hand. "It was divine."

"I can't wait to hear all about it," April said, dabbing her tongue to the salt rim. Yes, it was salt. Not sugar.

Really, with Kitty, you never knew.

"Tonight we are not discussing me or my phenomenally wonderful coffee talk with Mr. Perfect," Kitty said dramatically. "We are discussing *you*. And your day."

April groaned out loud. "Can't we just talk about you instead?"

Kitty shook her head in that Kitty way that brooked no questions. "Rachel would like to inform you she does not want any details of what we are about to discuss."

Simone swirled her margarita like it was a fine wine. "She said, and I'm quoting, 'Ew, that's my brother.'"

"She mentioned something about how she supports you in all you do but reminds you that Jack holds a certification in heartbreaking." Yelena nodded. "Just adding that to the conversation."

April didn't have plans to discuss with anyone all the things she'd done with Jack, but especially not with his sister. So there was no worry there. Her afternoon was officially in the vault. As for the other? The chains around her heart were locked tight.

Lifting her fingers, she mimed zipping her lips.

"You're really not going to tell us?" Simone asked, looking appalled.

"Maybe we should just respect that April gets to have her privacy?" Yelena asked, even though they all knew that no one got privacy in this group.

Kitty balked. "We don't keep secrets. What kind of neighborhood do you think this is?"

April took a sip of her drink and immediately spit it back into the glass. "What is wrong with this?"

"You didn't have the right juice boxes," Kitty said, waving a hand toward the little pantry where April kept the juice and snacks for the kids. "I had to make do."

"With apple juice," Simone said dryly, pointing to her drink. "This is apple juice with a salt rim."

"Why?" April looked at her glass, utterly confused. "Why would you make this?"

"Kitty didn't believe me when I explained they don't make lime juice boxes for children, and even if they did, you wouldn't likely stock them for yours." Yelena stood. "Also, she forgot to get tequila. I'll fix some tea."

"Tea sounds good," April said. Better than Kitty's salted apple juice.

She dropped to the chair next to Simone, flopping against the back. "I'm exhausted."

"I bet you are," Simone said, not adding anything else.

Actually, no one said anything else.

April would not break the seal because, if she did, then by the rules of their friendship, she'd have to tell them things. Was she ready to tell them things? Ack. This was hard. So she refused to open her mouth and let words flow.

They said nothing, either.

Nope. All three of her friends stared at her with wide eyes, blinking in solidarity.

Even Yelena while she waited for the water to boil.

Finally, April shook her head. "You guys are impossible. You know I can't share the intimate details—that wouldn't be fair to Jack."

"Of course not." Kitty patted April's hand. "You get to have some secrets. The respect for him is a nice touch. We don't need all the details or anything that *he* did; let's start with which yoga moves *you* went with."

April choked. She absolutely couldn't tell them about that. With Jack, she got brave. Now? Now she was pretty sure her cheeks were crimson.

"Oh, it's a good one," Simone said, her tone knowing.

Yelena nodded sagely as she pulled mugs from April's cupboards. Clean mugs that didn't even need washing before use.

"Tell me you didn't jump right into downward dog." Kitty tapped her fingertip on the table to punctuate each word. "You listened to me about that, right? I hope so. I know a thing or three about this type of activity—in fact, I'm practically a professional." She paused. "Not like that. No one pays me or anything."

"I did not go right into downward dog." April could tell them that much. That had come later in the afternoon.

"I hope you began with Savasana." Kitty licked at the salt

along the rim of her glass. "That's a good one to start with. Sets a very low standard."

"I did not start with Savasana." Give her some credit, she could do better than just lying there on her back.

"You're gonna have to spill it," Yelena said, leaning forward. "Or these two will never let you live it down."

"These two and you," April said. Yelena played good cop, but she also brought a vegetable platter to butter April up. So. Yeah.

These women were the team who had held April's hand through all the muck of the last year. She'd hung all of her dirty laundry out for them to see, and they'd never once judged her. They'd just helped her through it. And if the roles were reversed, she would've been clamoring for details, too. Except from Kitty. She wouldn't have had to clamor for details on that front.

"Backward bend," she mumbled, running her hand over her shoulder to her neck. "I also know how to use the bolster now. Thanks for the tip."

Jack hadn't managed his own backbend, but he'd known just what to do with the bolster when she mentioned she wasn't sure how it could be used during intimate activity. He'd propped it under her hips, which lifted them to just the right angle so when he entered her—oh, dear wow, she'd never be able to look at a bolster the same way again.

All three of the women in her kitchen hadn't moved after her announcement. Even Yelena stood completely motionless when the kettle whistled.

"What?" April asked, lifting her shoulders. "You wanted to know. If that's TMI, that's your fault."

"A backbend?" Kitty shrieked.

Simone began a slow clap.

Yelena finished the tea with eyes wide the entire time.

"I thought we discussed level one?" Kitty smacked the table.

"Forward bend. Savasana. Easy." Kitty stood and paced to the tea. "Now he's going to have expectations." She brought the mug to April and set it down next to her salted apple juice. "I can't even figure out how that would work. How do you even *do that*? The logistics don't track."

Oh, they tracked all right.

Inexplicably, Kitty lay down on the tile floor. "Climb on top and show me."

Simone snorted.

"I'm not doing that, Kitty," April said, staring down at her friend. "Sit up here with us and tell us all about your date." April went for the big guns, using her mom voice so even Kitty would listen to her.

"Do I want to know why Kitty is on the floor?" Jack asked as he strode into the kitchen.

April yelped, jumping three inches even though her tush was on the seat.

"I thought you were going to Rachel's," she said. Well, really, she squeaked.

"Change of plans," he said. And that look in his eye?

Oh. Yes. He was *not* thinking a bubble bath.

Though with that glint? His change of plans meant they'd probably have ended up naked all the same.

Except she was hosting an impromptu party.

"Hi, Jack." Kitty waved at him, still on the floor. Still not getting up.

"Don't ask her questions," April said, shaking her head and silently pleading for him to do as she said. "You don't want to know."

"Understood." He paused, pushed his hands onto his hips, and surveyed them all, his gaze landing gently on April. "You did great today."

"Ohhh," Kitty said. "Dish!"

"He meant with the fundraiser and the donations." April shook her head. "Welcome to the after-party, Jack."

"There's tea." Yelena pointed to the kettle.

"And salted apple juice." Simone lifted April's cup of spit-in juice.

An expression of confusion passed over his features, but he didn't ask questions. "I'll take the tea."

"Good call," April said, giving him a look that she hoped broadcast her thanks for his not questioning Kitty further or inquiring about salted apple juice.

He moved to the teakettle, fixing himself a cup.

The back door opened and April's children all streamed through, followed by her ex-husband. Unfortunately, Kent looked great. Casual in a plain gray tee and jeans. How he was tanned in Colorado in the fall made no sense, but April wasn't going to ask questions about it. He'd also let his dark brown hair grow longer than he'd kept it when they were together.

He took in the room and made the same *ick* face he had when he'd first seen how she'd made the place purple.

She loved the color. He hated it.

When he'd moved out, she made everything as purple as she could. It felt good.

"We finished dinner early," Harmony sang. She'd been on a singing kick that day. She paused, her little eyebrows furrowing. "Why is Aunt Kitty on the floor?"

"Auntie Kitty was doing an experiment," Kitty said, sitting up. "It failed." She glared at April like the failure was April's fault.

"Aunt Kitty is just being silly," April said, then mouthed *Help me* to Simone.

Simone loathed Kent, since it was her duty as best friend. Thus she had no problem taking the opportunity to leave.

"Let's get you guys ready for bed," Simone said, shooing the kids up the stairs as April rose to say the necessary goodbye.

"April, I wanted to ask you why our kids are all using the word 'banana' for everything." Kent asked.

"That's on me." Jack raised his hand. "April wasn't involved."

"I'm Kent," Kent said, holding his hand to Jack, "and you are?"

Jack waited a moment too long before shaking Kent's hand. "Jack."

"And you're here because...?" Kent asked.

"Because it's none of your business," Kitty said. "Don't you have a hole to crawl back into?" She gestured regally toward the door.

"Probably time to skedaddle"—Yelena looked pointedly at the door—"Kent."

Kent's expression soured. "I see nothing's changed but the wall color."

April didn't like that. Didn't like it at all. Lots had changed.

"Jack's here, too, now." Kitty had a look on her face like she was about to spill all the backbend beans to April's ex. "That's changed. And he taught your kids a secret language."

"I'll walk you out," April said, already heading for the door.

Of course, she briefly questioned leaving Kitty alone in a room with Jack. But Yelena would be a buffer for anything Kitty decided to say.

Kent followed April's lead for what had to be the first time ever, and he let her walk him out. Oddly, this felt nice, her making the call that he should go.

He said nothing on the walk to his new convertible. No questions about Jack or what Kitty was doing on the floor. This was good, since Jack was, as Kitty said, none of his business. And Kitty was Kitty.

"I saw your...video," he said.

Great. Fabulous. So he'd been witness to her humiliation.

She refused to let him make her feel crappier than he already had. So, yeah, she'd screwed up royally. She was fixing it.

Tonight had been a giant leap in that direction.

The power was still hers.

He pursed his lips as they approached his car. The thing was going to be a bitch to manage in the snow this winter.

"Yeah." She didn't say anything else, because what was there to say that the video hadn't already said?

"You know, I didn't want it to be like this." He shoved his hands in the pockets of his jeans.

"Like what? You leaving, the kids struggling, and me alone?"

He had the audacity to look sincere. "I don't want to be the bad guy."

"I think it's too late for that," she said, the words strong and with an edge, because he'd sucked the happy right out of her awesome day.

He climbed into his car and rolled down the window. He looked like he wanted to say something but refrained. This was good, because she didn't need him talking down to her. She had vigilante mommy bloggers for that.

She stood there, arms crossed, holding herself up.

"You know," she said, "if you wanted to call your kids sometimes, they'd probably like that."

He nodded. "Yeah."

Then he left without making a commitment. Because he'd become king of no commitments.

And, right then, she wasn't entirely sure if she was still sad about that.

Instead of stewing on it, she hurried back to the kitchen. By the time she got there, Jack was missing, leaving only Kitty and Yelena.

"Simone's tucking them in," Yelena said, lifting her mug to her lips. "Jack's phone rang," she added with a shrug. "Sounded important. Something about socks?"

It always sounded important. Even the bits about socks.

"I said nothing to him," Kitty added, holding her hand up like she was swearing in. "I figured you'd want to know."

"It's true," Yelena said. "She didn't."

"And Kitty has something she should probably tell you," Simone said. "Something important."

"No, I—"

April couldn't be certain, but it looked like Yelena kicked Kitty under the table.

"Ow," Kitty finished with.

"Kitty?" Yelena said. "Tell her. She's going to find out."

Uh... "Going to find out what?"

"I went on a date with Beast," Kitty said. "But you have backbend Jack, so I'm sure you don't mind."

April's lips tilted into a grin. "Beast? My Beast?"

"I think he's her Beast now," Yelena said with a wry smile.

Huh.

"That's kind of perfect," April said, lifting her tea to her lips to blow on it.

Kitty and Beast? Who would've thought? Then again, it made about as much sense as what April and Jack were doing. So what did she know?

The steam from her tea rose to tickle her nose. There was a lot of space between a dating app and what she'd promised Kent when they'd made vows for him to break.

Apparently, inside that space was where she found Jack.

CHAPTER TWENTY-SIX

*"This has great potential for shit, but we can't deny the
potential for awesome based on the potential for shit.
So let's do this thing."*
—Sarah, California, United States

April

he kids came down from their Disneyland Dad sugar rush
and oh boy did they crash hard. She wasn't sure precisely
what Kent had sugared them up with, but given how high they
peaked, the tantrums they threw, and how hard they all went
to sleep, she'd bet her sex pillow on jelly beans.

She did not look at her open door that pointed right to
Jack's bedroom. His door was, of course, closed. She knew this
not because she'd looked, but because she hadn't heard it open.

Gah.

April hadn't seen Jack since he'd disappeared into his room
earlier before the meltdowns of the century. He hadn't come
out for any of those, not that she blamed him. The only reason
she came out was because, as their mother, she was required to.

Now, she lay in bed, flipping through her news feed socials
and replying to comments. Patently not glancing at his closed
door. Definitely not pushing her ear against it to see if he was
still on the phone.

Her mind wouldn't settle.

Not when Jack was right across the hall. Right across the

hall with that mouth and those hands and…all the rest.

To hell with it. She yanked herself out of bed, rolled out her yoga mat, and opened her door farther.

What? Maybe Jack might come looking for her later.

Maybe.

She attempted to center herself in lotus position on the purple yoga mat, her palms pressed together near her heart's center, her sit bones anchored to the ground.

She inhaled. She exhaled.

Let the thoughts come, and encouraged them to go. Counted her breaths.

Funny, usually she couldn't sleep because her mind raced with everything that needed to be done. Tonight, her mind raced hoping that Jack might come and handle her.

She squirmed. Then she tried to refocus.

In through the nose. Out through the mouth.

Jack's door creaked. Her eyes flew open.

He looked delightfully disheveled.

"Hey," he said.

"Hi." She dropped her hands, not having a hard time at all focusing on the moment in front of her.

"I…" He grinned uncomfortably. "Sorry, I had to make some calls…"

"Also, my house was a little intense there for a minute."

He nodded. "That's one way to put it."

"They crashed, though. I'll put them through a sugar detox for the next week so that doesn't happen again…until the next time they go to their dad's house."

Jack stepped forward, to the edge of her doorframe. He leaned against it. Crossed his arms. "I don't know what is allowed between us when the kids are here. I'm going to need some help navigating this."

"Are you asking me for my help, Jack Gibson?"

He rolled his tongue along his bottom lip. "I am."

"So…" She stretched her left leg to the side. "If the kids are asleep, we can still do things together—just quietly. With ample use of the door lock mechanisms. If they're awake, we can't show any PDA."

"Got it."

"I know what it is we're doing here. They don't." April studied her fingernails. She should paint them tomorrow. Pale pink would be pretty. "I don't want them to think there's a chance you might stay longer or for them to get attached to someone else who will leave."

"I'm on board with all of that." He held the thread of their gazes together as he moved into the room, pushing the door closed and pressing the lock.

"Good," she said, breathy as her heart pounded against her ribs.

"Is now a good time?" he asked.

"The best we're going to get." April chewed at her lips.

Jack was moving slower than usual, pulling his T-shirt over his head so his abs were fully exposed. She enjoyed his abs. She should probably take Kitty's advice and lick them.

She'd do that. First, though, she followed his lead, pulling her pajama top over her own head. She wasn't wearing a bra, not to bed, so the girls were just right there. Hanging out with them.

The appreciation in Jack's expression made everything right in her world.

He shucked his pants, and apparently had no problem with nudity or multiple performances in a day because he was ready and willing.

He knelt beside her, kissed her, and laid her back on the mat. His mouth didn't leave hers—thank goodness—as his erection pressed the cloth between her legs.

Damn. She should've ditched the sleep shorts, too.

Though the way the friction against the center of her pressed her to the mat was really delicious.

She swallowed a low moan, because she had to be quiet. Jack seemed to understand what she needed, because he kissed the moans away, muffling them with his mouth.

"Do you want to move to the bed?" he asked, nipping along her jawline.

"I kinda like this," she said as the length of him nudged against the cotton between her legs. "Strike that. I really like this."

He chuckled, low and rumbly, his hand moving to stroke the side of her breast. "I really like this, too."

April had likely made a whole slew of expressions over the time she'd been sexually active with her partners. But she couldn't recall a time she spent the whole encounter with a silly grin on her face.

But that's exactly what it was like there on her bedroom floor, with Jack.

He handled the condom, while she pulled off her pajama bottoms. After that, things got frantic. Hands and tongues and, yes, she licked his abs right up to his nipple.

He didn't seem to mind the licking thing because he repaid the favor. Twice. Before he laid her back on the mat and slid between her parted thighs.

The sound he made deep down in his throat radiated through her, but he kept his lips sealed tight.

"Like that," she said, pulling him tighter against her, letting each of his thrusts unwind her spooled muscles.

Technically, this was missionary position and she was naturally averse to that position, given...everything. But with Jack, she smiled.

He looped his hands behind her back, pulling her up against his chest in one smooth motion, settling her in his lap in a reverse lotus pose she... Oh, yes...she liked this. She'd never had a man so deep inside her.

And they'd done the pillow thing earlier. So that was saying something.

"Jack." She gasped his name, then pressed her mouth against his shoulder because he'd just introduced her to her very favorite sexual position ever. They didn't even need a sex pillow in the future, not with this pose. Not to have him seated so deep inside her she couldn't quite tell where he ended and where she started. In a good way. A tantric experience kind of way.

"Shhh," he said against her earlobe as he continued thrusting. "I've got you."

"I'm there," she whispered back, the noises coming from the back of her throat sounding like a growl as her body tensed around his, milking him and shaking. She pressed her mouth against his shoulder so she wouldn't cry out as her body tensed again and again.

That's when he laid her back against the mat as she leveled her breathing. Coming down from the pinnacle of pleasure.

Instead of hurrying up so he could get his part over with and get to sleep, he seemed to savor her body. Studying her as he moved in and out, like he had all the time in the world to spend there. Building her up again in a way she wasn't sure possible before that moment.

The next time she reached that elusive spot where stars danced behind her eyelids and her body clenched and fluttered, he came, too.

CHAPTER TWENTY-SEVEN

"We're off like a herd of turtles."
—Julie Rowe

Jack

Jack had already responded to twenty emails that had come in overnight as he took the steps two at a time toward the kitchen.

He'd left April tucked in her bed and then he'd gone to his own. Just in case. She didn't want to confuse the kids, and he didn't, either.

The telltale clang of dishes and noise of a Davis family breakfast were in full swing.

He strode through the entry, and while the clangs and the noises were the usual, the atmosphere was impressively dark.

"Good morning everybody."

He got two "bananas" in response and one "morning" from April.

Harmony was eating her cereal like it personally offended her.

"What happened in here?" he asked.

"The tooth fairy didn't come," April whispered. "Kent forgot to mention that Harmony lost a tooth at his house."

"I told Dad. That's the rule—tell a parent." Harmony shoved another spoonful of cereal into her mouth.

"Then, in theory, that parent gives permission for the

tooth fairy to come into the house." April pursed her lips. "Unfortunately, that system no longer works for us."

"Ahhh," Jack said. "Did you check under all the pillows?"

"I checked under mine," Harmony said with a huff. "The tooth is still there."

"A molar. I didn't realize it'd come out," April whispered.

"When I was a kid"—Jack pulled up a chair to the table— "our tooth fairy got so confused all the time. Sometimes she forgot to take the teeth, but she'd leave the loot somewhere else. I found it under my mom's pillow once. Under Rachel's pillow. Once I even found it in my shoe."

"What's loot?" Rohan asked.

"Money," April replied.

"Why don't you go check under Rohan's pillow?" Jack suggested. "See if maybe your tooth fairy got mixed up."

"Fine." Harmony stood and stalked out of the room. "I'll look. But it won't be there."

No, it wouldn't. But Jack had a plan.

"Ribbit," Rohan said, following his sister.

"What are you doing?" April said urgently, like a late tooth fairy.

He strode to the living room like he knew exactly what he was doing. He pulled a bill from his wallet and shoved it deep in the couch cushion.

"You're serious right now?" April asked.

"My mom used to do this. It always worked for us." He shooed April back into the kitchen. "When they come down, you've got to go up there and get the tooth."

"Why don't you go get the tooth? They won't suspect you," April said.

"Because then I'd have to touch it." He shivered. Nope. Not for him.

"I'll check the couch," Harmony said, issuing orders to her

brother from the stairs. "You check the shoes."

See? Jack mouthed. This was already going better than he could've ever planned.

"Mom!" Harmony called. "She left money in the couch. She didn't forget me."

Jack lifted his eyebrows toward April. *You're welcome*, he mouthed.

Thank you, she mouthed back.

"That's fantastic!" April was a touch too cheerful sauntering to see what her daughter had uncovered. "Oh my gosh, she left you a twenty-dollar bill." April didn't sound so excited about that.

"Usually, I only get a dollar." Harmony waved the bill toward Jack. "She must've gotten *really* confused this time."

"Hey, it happens to the best tooth fairies." Jack shoved his hands in his pockets. "I'm sure she doesn't mind if you keep it all."

"How many more teeth do you think I can rip out of my mouth today?" Harmony asked, eyes glittering.

"Let's let them come out when they're ready," April said. "Now go eat your breakfast, Toothless."

Harmony and Rohan went back to the kitchen and April whacked Jack on his arm with the back of her palm. "You can't just leave a *twenty*," she whispered. "That's setting a precedent for all future teeth—times three kids. That's a lot of cash."

"Maybe next time she won't be confused. She'll leave the correct amount."

See? Problem solving and a spin at the same time. He had this crisis management thing *down*. Did his chest puff up? Yes. Yes, it did.

Though it'd never felt quite *this* good to solve an issue. This one seemed to matter a whole lot more than the others he'd worked through.

Which was odd, given that this one had nothing to do with the things that usually mattered to him most. No life coaching, no hanging drywall...

"Confused, huh?" April gave a sly smile and nodded. "Maybe." Then she turned backward as she got to the doorway. "And thank you. For saving the day."

The difficulty in reconciling who he believed himself to be with who he was becoming when he was with April was getting harder and harder as the hours turned to days. He worried that as the days turned to weeks, the man he thought he was would disappear. Well, maybe it wasn't so much a worry but an understanding. Because the thing was, he wasn't sure he would mind.

They'd made it through most of their time together. At this point? His hours in Denver were numbered. Only a handful more days until *Practical Parenting* and then he'd be back in the land of sun and ocean and...office. Boardroom meetings. Lunches that didn't really matter with sandwiches that weren't cut into fun shapes.

Denver was a great place. Rachel was here. His nephews. His brother-in-law.

April. Harmony. Rohan. Lola.

The kids had grown on him. He wasn't ready to touch their yanked-out teeth, but he'd had more crayon-flavored water than he cared to admit.

He could work remotely from anywhere. Perhaps Denver could be his permanent anywhere? Rachel would be over the moon about it.

Jack should just communicate with April about how he was feeling. That's precisely what he should do. He paced from his bedroom to the hallway to do just that. Then he paused.

He would not do that.

Over the past few days, things had changed for him. Things he'd like to explore. The feeling that he'd prefer to stay for a while longer.

Not forever. No. Nuh-uh. April had been clear about wanting nothing permanent.

He didn't necessarily want to be permanent, anyway. He just…wasn't ready to leave.

He paced back to his room and shut the door, leaning against it.

He had nearly completed the work here. Her accounts had gone through a thorough scrubbing by his team. She'd worked up a plan for an abundance of new content that was Calm Mom perfection. Ethan Greene would come by to show her some tricks for keeping it all together during live feeds. They'd talk cookbooks. The MyTube channel was in the works. And then the granddaddy of them all—*Practical Parenting*—would propel her right where she needed to thrive.

The plan was on track. Honestly, if it was any other account, he'd already be moving on to the next job.

But the thought of driving away, getting on a plane, and going back to how things were before made his cotton T-shirt itch like a cheap suit.

A quick trip to the Cherry Creek mall had provided him with casual clothing more fitting to April's home than his suits. These clothes were comfortable. So it made little sense why his fingertip seemed to search out the collar all on its own and yank it away from his skin.

Though maybe it made *some* sense. He wasn't there for her anymore. Now, he stayed for himself. To give them a shot as a *them*. A temporary them was still a them.

And *that* was uncomfortable.

CHAPTER TWENTY-EIGHT

*"Parenting is great and everyone is having fun until the
fundraising forms come home from school."*
—Anonymous, Florida, United States

Jack

Jack stepped back in the hall, unsure of what he was actually
going to do or say or become. Which was unlike him. The
cotton of his tee scratched more.

April rounded the corner with a basket of laundry under
one arm, and then the itch disappeared. He straight-up grinned,
uncertainty falling away.

She had piled her hair in a bun at the crown of her head with
a few loose tendrils kissing the length of skin exposed along
her neckline. A pair of athletic pants with a long-sleeved crew
neck weren't particularly seductive. But on her? They hugged
every inch in just the right places. Places he knew intimately.

"Morning," April greeted, as though they hadn't woken up
together around four a.m. before she booted him back to his
bed so her children didn't see him emerge from her bedroom
and start asking questions.

"Hey you." He did not lean in and kiss her like he wanted
to. Like his lips urged him to. "Can I help?" He gestured to
the laundry basket.

She shook her head. "I've got it. Thanks, though."

He followed her to the laundry room, opening and closing

his mouth to make a point that he hoped she'd agree to. In the end, he probably just looked like a trout following her upstream.

"I think I might actually be ahead after this load," April said with a mellow chuckle.

Before coming to April's house, he had thoroughly underestimated the amount of soiled clothing a family of four could create. Adding him into the mix, the laundry and the dishes never seemed finished. There was always one or thirty more. For some reason, because he had apparently lost his mind, it didn't drive him bonkers.

All that led to the realization that he thrived here. The idea of his cold apartment with no one there to keep him company, the laundry service picking up his clothing, and a once-every-three-days housekeeper handling the dishes all sat starkly against the backdrop of April's chaos. The warm, cozy comfort that embraced him during it all.

When he was a kid, the family used to take a winter ski trip up to Big Bear for a weekend every January and rent an oversized cabin with an enormous fireplace. The thing had seemed massive. While everyone was out on the slopes, Jack would often hang out with Rachel by the fireplace to keep her company. She'd hated skiing. He'd hated that they left her alone. So he stuck around with her.

The feeling of a thick blanket of snow outside the walls had contrasted with the warmth inside. And that's precisely what he experienced with April.

Yet the reality of the imminent future when he would have to leave loomed heavy.

"What do you have on tap for today?" she asked, apparently oblivious to the internal mess he trudged through.

He pulled the laundry soap from the shelf and poured it into the cup for her. "A call with Ethan later to go over a plan for your cooking segment."

Her eyes lit up at Ethan's name, like they always did. Jack should've been insecure about the obvious celebrity infatuation, but he'd told himself that he didn't get to be insecure. And, while April may have been excited about Ethan, she'd also been excited about other Jack-exclusive things. *More* excited, even.

So he nipped that jealousy in the bud.

"I wanted to talk to you about maybe sticking around for a little while longer," Jack said, shoveling a whole heap of dirt over his pride.

April's expression fell. "Jack."

"Not for long," he assured quickly.

She stared into the depths of the washing machine. "That's not a good idea."

He said nothing, because he thought it was a fantastic idea.

"We can't confuse what we are." She gestured between them. "What we're doing."

What she didn't say, but what she broadcasted loud and clear, was that she hadn't changed her stance on what her future looked like.

Okay, fine. Point made. He'd promised himself he wouldn't push her. He'd promised her he wouldn't push.

This was him, absolutely not pushing.

She was right.

"We can't get attached," she said, lifting her gaze to his. "This can't be that."

Of course not. He nodded.

Of. Course. Not.

This thing he had with April *was* easy. But even Jack wouldn't rearrange what she wanted because, he sighed, there was nothing to fix there. Anything he attempted would just be manipulation for his own sake, and that's not who he was.

The thing that was right for him wasn't right for her. It was what it was. So he'd take what she'd give and move along.

"Hey, I had an idea for Rohan," he said, setting the cup of detergent on the edge of the machine for her.

He hadn't realized her shoulders had tensed until he changed the subject and they relaxed. She dumped the contents of the basket into the machine. "What's that?"

"Do you trust me?" he asked, covertly swirling a fingertip over her elbow. Playful. They could do playful. They'd agreed to playful. Playful was safe. Temporary. Just for now.

She shivered, then smiled. Though she probably didn't do it intentionally, she let her warmth wrap around him.

He liked that. Enjoyed having that ability to cause a reaction with only the barest of touches. Their bodies were in tune in a way that should be illegal.

Lucky for them, it wasn't.

He'd enjoy it while he could.

"Of course I trust you." She paused, dumping in the cup of detergent he'd prepared. "As long as it doesn't involve using more Pledge on my tile floors."

No, he'd well and truly learned his lesson on that front.

"It'll just take a bit of the backyard." About four feet, if he had to give specific measurements.

"Like a trampoline amount or a kiddie pool amount?" she asked.

Actually, a kiddie pool was an excellent idea. He hadn't thought of that. One of the hard, plastic pools would be perfect.

"Kiddie pool." He closed the washer as she wrapped up and turned it on. "You have one Rohan and I could use?"

The edges of her lips quirked. "In the shed, all the way in the back. Behind the mower."

"You don't mind if we use it?" he confirmed.

"Lola's too big for it now, anyway. You can have it."

"Perfect." He needed to grab the kid and hit up the hardware store.

"You're really not going to tell me what you're up to?" she asked as he walked away.

He stopped. Turned. "It'll be more fun as a surprise."

Given that the other surprises he'd handed her had all been excessively abundant in the fun department, he hoped she'd leave it at that.

She didn't look convinced.

"It'll be good," he assured. He was also pretty certain it would help Rohan.

"Okay." She headed toward him, looked both ways down the hall like she was crossing the street. Then she rolled up on her toes and pressed a quick kiss to his lips. "Thank you."

"What are you thanking me for?"

"For whatever it is you're going to go do with Rohan. He needs the attention."

His chest softened at that. And, since he didn't know what to say that wouldn't add a whole helping of awkward with their arrangement, he said nothing at all.

"Can he have doughnuts?" he asked. Because it wasn't a trip to the hardware store without a pastry.

She let out a breathy laugh. "Yeah, he can. No dairy, though. There's a vegan bakery up on the corner he likes."

Jack pressed a kiss to her forehead because he still could. "We'll be back."

"Why does your breath smell like crayons?" she whispered.

Well, that would be because, "Lola had an impromptu tea party."

April apparently tried to hold in a laugh. She failed.

"Do you want to taste a crayon?" he asked, closing the door behind her and leaning in for a full mouth kiss.

"Crayon has never tasted so good," she said, running her hands along his back, cupping him in the front.

This was like he was in high school hiding out in his bedroom with his first (and really, only) girlfriend so his parents wouldn't catch him. Except this time they were hiding from April's kids and he tasted like crayons.

"I'm going to get the doughnuts," he said with a quick kiss on her lips.

"Bring some for the rest of us," she called as he walked away, adjusting himself.

He turned. "Anything in particular?"

"Gluten-free for Harmony," she said. "You might as well get extra of those, just in case." She paused, thoughtful. "Probably grab something for Kitty, too. She'll want one of the cherry fritters."

The amount of grub and juice boxes the kids, and Kitty, went through had him convinced April was going to need another batch of sponsors for the podcast she'd agreed to host, just to keep them all in snacks.

"For you?" he asked, and yes, he used the deep tone he knew turned her right the hell on.

She studied him for a beat before whispering, "Surprise me."

He could do that. Yes, he could do that.

When he'd come to Denver, he figured that he'd raise April's confidence. As she'd said, helping her emerge from the ashes as a better, stronger version of herself.

He didn't have to build her confidence, though—not when she had an abundance of it. She had just tucked it down deep and, apparently, forgotten it was there.

But as they'd spent the time on her image, her social accounts, and in the bedroom—also out of the bedroom—he hadn't seen her confidence grow from ashes.

No, it'd bloomed from within.

• • •

"I've never heard of a frog sanctuary before." Rohan helped Jack unwind the wire mesh over the top of the plastic pool.

They'd come to an agreement that Rohan would use human words with Jack, like he did at school, since Jack didn't speak frog. In return, Jack had bought Rohan a whole cup of dairy-free doughnut holes.

"I hadn't heard of a neighbor like Kitty before I came here," Jack said. "That doesn't mean she didn't exist."

Rohan grinned up at him. "Kitty doesn't usually make sense."

That was the truth. Jack stapled the wire to the plastic. That should hold, even against the Colorado snowpack coming in a few months.

"You know, when I was your age, I liked to pretend I was a dinosaur." He'd spent a whole summer wearing nothing but dinosaur-inspired clothes. "Life is easier when you're a dinosaur, you know?"

"I know." Rohan sighed. "Why aren't you a dinosaur now?"

"It made Rachel uncomfortable when I roared at her all the time."

Rohan nodded.

They'd added sand to the bottom of the small pool, a terra-cotta tray from a planter he found at Home Depot, and a bunch of rocks all around. The mesh had holes big enough for a toad to slip through, but the holes weren't so big that Captain Jack would make it in.

Jack figured his namesake would absolutely love to try, since he hadn't found his family. Kitty had put in all the paperwork to adopt him. Jack figured he'd be a permanent part of the neighborhood, so Rohan's garden frogs would need a little help to stay out of his clutches.

"Do you think they'll like these friends?" Rohan asked,

moving three of his plastic toy frogs around the edge. Repositioning them for the twentieth time since they'd begun.

Jack didn't mind. He knew what it was like to need to get something exactly right. Sometimes a guy didn't know what that was until he kept trying.

"I think so." Jack picked one up, turned it over in his palm. "Do *you* think so? You're the amphibian expert."

Rohan puffed up at that. He nodded. "If they come by themselves, they won't get lonely."

"Agreed." Jack pressed the edge of the final wire to hold it in place.

Rohan adjusted frog number three a touch to the right.

"I was thinking," Jack said, careful because where he was about to venture could be considered parental territory and not visiting-Jack territory. "Your mom gets a little worried when you speak frog."

Rohan nodded. "Sometimes I forget."

"Maybe we can talk to her—in human—and see how she'd feel if you came out here to talk frog with your frogs?" Jack asked. "This could be your frog-talking space."

Rohan said nothing; he was too busy adjusting toy frog one.

"Just an idea," Jack added.

"This is where frogs come to talk to each other," Rohan said, matter-of-fact.

"I think so." Jack gentled his voice, sounding cautious. He really didn't want to fuck this up. "People can talk to one another anywhere, but frogs can come here to accomplish frog things in a safe space."

Rohan didn't look up from frog number two that had taken all his attention.

"Ribbit," Rohan said. He flicked his tongue, looked at Jack, and said solemnly, "Banana."

There was a lot of understanding in that word. Jack had a

feeling they understood each other.

He held out his knuckles for the kid. "Banana."

Rohan bumped them. "You have to go back home soon, huh?"

The question wasn't really a question. It sounded more like a confirmation. And yes, only a few more days. April didn't want this to be anything more than what it was. He had to respect that.

"My home is in Los Angeles. Like your home is here." He nodded toward the house. Jack sat back on his ass, checking out their handiwork. "And the frog home is here." He gestured to the pool.

"I get that," Rohan said, like he was a little man instead of a five-year-old kid. He sat back on his heels mirroring Jack.

Jack couldn't quite put his finger on the feeling seeping into his skin. Talking about Los Angeles didn't feel right when they were at the frog sanctuary. He shook the cobwebbed thoughts from his brain.

"What do you think is wrong with us?" Rohan asked, pressing his chin to his knees.

Uh. Well... So many things. And also nothing.

"What do you mean, what's wrong with us?" Jack asked. This time he mirrored Rohan, putting his own chin on his knees.

"I like us." Rohan sighed. "Mom makes good sandwiches. Harmony's okay. Lola doesn't even hardly talk."

"You've definitely got a good thing going here, bud." Jack clapped him gently on the back.

Rohan frowned. "Something's wrong. People keep leaving."

Well shit. Jack's throat got tight. "Everyone hasn't left."

"Dad did." Rohan picked up frog toy number one. "You will."

"I'm just here to visit," Jack said in a weak attempt at explanation. "I don't know what happened with your dad." He paused, extra cautious with his words. "sometimes grown-ups make choices that don't make sense."

Rohan's dad was a goddamned idiot for walking away from all of this.

"That's why I wish I was a frog." Rohan picked up frog number two. "Frogs don't make mistakes. They just hop."

Jack said nothing because he did not know what to say. His chest was tight, though, like Captain Jack had sauntered by, triggering a systemic reaction in his body.

"Everybody likes frogs," Rohan said, a touch dreamy.

For that moment, Jack sort of wished he was a frog, too.

He scooted closer to the kiddo, tossing his arm around Rohan's shoulders. "Everybody likes you, too."

"And doughnuts," Rohan continued. "Everybody likes doughnuts."

"Dinosaurs, too," Jack added. "Except Rachel."

Rohan nodded. "She doesn't understand."

"You know what else is good?" Jack asked, pulling Rohan closer to his side. "You are." He said the words so there was no mistaking he meant them. "There's no frog that compares to you."

He really could do better than that with compliments, but it seemed to be the thing he thought Rohan needed to hear.

As for himself? He wasn't sure what he needed to hear.

Not with the Captain Jack pressure in his chest making him question if he ever would.

CHAPTER TWENTY-NINE

"'You'll eat a pound of dirt before you die—might as well start now.' My mom's response to my toddler picking up stray Cheerios off the floor."
—Jo, Connecticut, United States

April

"**K**eep your eyes closed, Mom," Rohan said, even though her eyes were sealed shut.

"They're shut," she assured, wishing she wasn't being so closely monitored because she would very much like to see where she was going. To do that, she'd need to be able to take a peek. Just a small one. She didn't have to go full looky-loo.

They led her through the backyard and both of them insisted she keep her peepers shut. They'd insisted before she even got close to the back door.

Rohan's hand held the one on her right, Jack held her left. She leaned a bit heavier to Jack's side, since she trusted him way more not to let her take a header into the flower beds. Rohan wouldn't mean to, but he had the attention span of an, *ahem*, five-year-old.

They must've reached wherever it was they were going, and the boys stopped the forward momentum. There was shuffling. Rohan dropped her hand. She, however, awaited instructions and did not look.

"Open your eyes," Jack said, giving her hand a gentle squeeze.

She opened them.

Rohan had a gleam of excitement in his expression she hadn't seen on his face in forever. That one hint made her feel like she wasn't totally failing as a mother.

As a mother of multiple children, it was a nice feeling to be failing only a little.

She looked from Rohan to the—

Aaaand… She had no idea what she was looking at. None at all.

Her expression must've conveyed this, because Rohan's eyebrows crumpled.

"I think it's great," she said in that way moms did that implied while they were proud, they had no clue what they were proud of.

The plastic pool Lola had played in over the summer was filled with soil, and it had wire across the top, tacked down at the edges to hold it in place. Rohan's plastic frogs sat situated around a terra-cotta plate in the middle.

Ah. She came up blank. Nothing. She had nothing. Of all the things she expected, this was not anywhere near the list. Not even on the paper.

What on earth could they do with this contraption?

"It's a frog habitat," Rohan said, thankfully relieving her of her I-have-no-idea-what-this-is stupor. "For the frogs," he added, helpfully.

Oh. That was…

"Wow." April slid her gaze to Jack.

He had a look of immense pride in his expression that echoed Rohan's. It was adorable on them both.

Still, she didn't get it. She wanted to get it. But she wasn't there yet.

"This is for frogs?" she confirmed, gesturing a circle in the air over the pool.

Jack nodded. "To keep them safe from Captain Jack."

Well, that was actually really sweet. She'd been a bit worried about what might happen if Captain Jack actually caught one of Rohan's garden toads.

"I can come here to be a frog, too." Rohan beamed up at her with a smile that turned her heart to melted butter. "Whenever I want."

Oh. Well. That was the most perfect thing Jack had done so far.

"I think the frogs will love it." She pulled Rohan to her side and hoped she gave the appropriate enthusiasm. Mostly she was trying to figure out how to thank Jack for doing this with her kid. "If you love it, we know they will."

"Jack has the best ideas." Rohan knelt by the edge to rearrange his toy frogs.

"Rohan was thinking he might just talk with human words when he's not here at the habitat," Jack added, clearing his throat. "We thought you might appreciate having him speak human words in human situations." He pursed his lips and shifted on his feet. "Keep the frog behavior to here, with the frogs."

April's mouth opened the slightest bit. "You're okay with that, honey?" She kneeled so she was closer to Rohan's eye level.

He didn't look away from his toys, but his forehead crinkled like it did when he was deep in thought.

"It makes sense." He lifted a shoulder. "I don't want to upset you when I turn frog."

A wet stinging pricked at the edges of her eyelids.

Don't cry. Don't cry.

"I love this." She wrapped Rohan in a side hug she didn't want to release.

Rohan was not a show-your-feelings-with-physical-touch kind of kid. He preferred his space. So when he turned in to her embrace and hugged her right back, it meant more than an entire frog habitat. He held onto her as much as she held onto him.

They were okay. Dear goodness, they were okay. And they were going to keep being okay. Even without a frog habitat, they were fine.

Not in the sense of the word when a person said it because everything was a mess. They really were making it. How had she not seen it?

Thank you, she mouthed to Jack.

Since Rohan was receptive to her embrace, she savored it as long as he would allow.

"I wrote you a song, Jack." Harmony skipped to their group huddled around the frog habitat. She gave a cursory glance at the new addition in the garden, but kept her enthusiasm thoroughly curbed. Clearly, she had other things on her mind.

This was Harmony, though. Therefore, this was not a surprise.

She held out her pink glittered notebook for Jack.

Rohan must've recognized they had an audience, because hugging time was over. He quickly released his mom, but she didn't feel the pinch of loss. Rohan wouldn't want to be seen as a baby around his sister. Hugging mom broached into baby Lola territory.

What she found interesting was that he was fine doing the hugging around Jack. That was interesting. She'd have thought he would've tried to impress him with outdated ideas of amphibious masculinity.

"I love songs," Jack said, turning his attention to Harmony.

Mayonnaise meandered to their group with Lola, who followed behind and plopped her tush down to play with Rohan's plastic frogs.

He allowed it, even sitting next to her to show how the habitat worked.

Yes, they were fine.

A sigh released from her chest.

With the whole crew present, the only one they missed was Kitty. Though Kitty had been more absent since she'd found Beast and adopted Captain Jack. Those three had spent a lot of time together. It seemed that Kitty had found her match. Matches, as it were.

"Let's get to this song," April said, channeling every bit of the good mood of her day.

"I can't wait to hear it," Jack added.

Harmony stood there, her big eyes boring right into Jack like he'd lost all his marbles in the frog habitat. She held her glittered notebook out to him. "*I* can't sing it."

Jack took the notebook with such reverence that those tears April had held back were coming closer and closer to the surface.

"Why can't you sing it?" Jack asked, reading over the top page.

Harmony shrugged her little shoulders. "Because there's no music."

April gave Jack a well-it-does-make-sense look.

"You have to read it out loud," Harmony said, a touch of disappointment already lacing her tone. "You're the guest. That's the rules."

Jack's eyes caught April's, and there was a whole lot of exchange in that look between them. Her kids adored him. She adored him. Mayonnaise adored him. If Kitty had a vote, she'd say that she adored him.

So what exactly was April's problem with further exploration of what they could become?

She glanced at the grass. As winter approached, it got crunchier by the day.

Which was precisely what would eventually happen to this thing between her and Jack. Right now, it was new and pretty—shiny, even. But eventually they'd argue. One of them would raise their voice. Probably both of them.

She couldn't do that again. Couldn't wonder, when Jack stomped out of the room because of a misspoken word or unkind argument, if he would be leaving for good. Leaving to go to someone else shinier and newer. Someone *not* her.

A weighted feeling of unease settled over her. That wasn't the whole truth, though. Not all of it. Maybe just a corner piece of it.

More than anything, she needed to prove to herself that she *could* do this by herself. That she didn't need someone to be her training wheels.

"Jack?" Harmony asked.

April tore her thoughts from where they'd traveled.

"Yeah." His Adam's apple bobbed.

April bit her lower lip and pressed her hands together as though warming them. Really, she was holding herself together.

Then Jack read Harmony's words out loud for them all.

"'Everybody Has a Voice' by Harmony Davis," he read, then paused, skimming over the paper before diving back in with his toffee-coated tone.

"'*Everybody has a voice,*
But you just have to find it,
It won't be in the forest,
You have to find it deep down inside you,
You just have to let it free to be,
'Cause if you don't let it out,
You'll never have a voice,
And you need a voice to sing out,
Voices are the best things you'll ever find,
Yeah, 'cause everybody has a voice to find!'"

April couldn't pull her gaze from the graphite slashes Harmony had written on the paper. Erased. Then rewritten. All precisely within the wide-ruled lines.

April was a woman who had lost her voice. That's what had

happened. Her heart ached at the realization.

Kent hadn't taken it with him. Kent hadn't taken *anything* with him. She'd just tucked it away and thought it burned with the rest of her hopes, dreams, and wishes.

Maybe it hadn't.

Her head spun. Rohan seemed to be well on his way to stopping his ribbiting and licking things. Harmony was writing songs more poignant than many professionals.

And April... April was fine.

Really and truly okay.

When had that happened? And why hadn't she fully realized it?

"Harmony." Jack scraped his hand over his face, kneeling to her level.

"Is it not good?" she asked, her face scrunching up just like April knew hers did when she got frustrated. Everyone pointed it out, from Kitty to Simone to her parents. Harmony was her mini-me if ever there was one.

"No." His voice cracked a little and April's heart seemed to grow.

April hopped right in to help him. "What Jack means is—"

"I want to hear it from Jack." Harmony crossed her arms and firmed her chin. Clearly she was ready to take the hit if it came. April understood exactly how that felt.

"What I mean is," he said, glancing back at the paper, "this is *excellent*."

Harmony's eyes flickered back from the precipice of broken into the realm of hope. "Will you help me with the music?"

"I don't know much about music, but I bet we can figure something out." He held his hand to hers.

Harmony took it. "Yay," she whispered.

April's heart seemed to shrink and grow at the same time.

"Yay," she echoed.

CHAPTER THIRTY

"Owning our story and loving ourselves through that process is the bravest thing we'll ever do."
—Brene Brown

"Jack?" April called to him as she took the steps two at a time. Then she paused, inhaled deeply, and moved slower down the stairs.

The Calm Mom did not need to take the steps two at a time. The Calm Mom would arrive in her kitchen with an abundance of serenity.

Oh, who was she kidding? She squeed and hurried.

It'd now been a full week that Jack had been staying with April and her kids. A full week of help. A full week of Jack. And today was Ethan Greene day. Ethan Greene *in her house* day.

Livestream with Ethan Greene day, to be exact.

Oh, for sure, the livestream still set her teeth on edge. But her kids were safely spending the day with their auntie Simone, so there was no risk of underage cussing or potty training mishaps. And Kitty had accepted her banishment, after a promise she could come meet Ethan once they were done.

That left only Mayonnaise as their wild card.

Mayonnaise was not a wild card. She was a sleepy, Jack-infatuated, basset hound card. One that could be easily put away in a room with a lock.

April would make it through the livestream—her first since that-which-shall-never-be-mentioned-again. Jack assured her that once she experienced a live that went well, she'd relax about *Practical Parenting.*

Honestly, though, the out-of-control shaking and buzz rolling through her wasn't anxious energy over all the things that could go wrong. And the nerves didn't come from Ethan-freaking-Greene coming to her house to make a kid-friendly, gluten-free, dairy-free mac and not-so-cheese.

The nerves were aftershocks from the, *ahem*, earlier activities with Jack once the kids had gone with their honorary aunt.

He'd made an attempt at de-stressing her.

Good news: it worked.

"You getting all of that out of your system now?" Jack asked from the bottom of the steps with a sly grin, because he'd been present earlier and knew precisely what they'd done for and to each other.

Her Ethan infatuation had become something of a running joke between them. Which was good, because it took the focus and subsequent ache away from Jack's impending departure.

He wanted to stay—she'd gotten the message. But Jack needed to leave so she could prove to herself that the change was because of her, not because of him. The training wheels had to come off for her to prove she could do this herself.

She didn't let her emotions take hold on this, because that's not what it was about. He would leave after the *Practical Parenting* appearance. They'd already discussed it. The plan was solidly in place.

She liked the plan. Appreciated the plan. Had committed herself to the plan.

"I've been practicing my it's-gross-but-I'm-going-to-pretend-it's-not face." She manipulated her expression into the one she'd practiced in the mirror.

Jack smirked. He shook his head.

She bit her lower lip. "You don't like it?"

"Don't ever do that face around anyone with a camera," he said with utter seriousness.

"What's wrong with it?" She pulled the face again.

"April?" he asked, clearly trying to hold back a laugh.

"Jack?" She said his name deeply, with an effort at his butterscotch timbre.

"You'll have to trust me on this." He gave her a subtle head-shake. "Just don't."

"Then I guess if I don't like what Ethan Greene makes, I have no face to hide it." She bounded down the rest of the stairs.

How was he going to pull off the mac and not-so-cheese and make it palatable? She did not know.

She'd mastered a lot of kitchen magic so her kids could enjoy regular-type foods, but never something as brazen as this.

After the main course, they were creating a non-peanut, no-nut, still-tastes-good butter for a non-peanut PB and J. She had more faith in that than the not-exactly-cheese cheese.

"You'll like what he makes," Jack assured her. "He could cook dirt and make it delicious."

April flung herself into Jack's arms.

Since they'd had a week of togetherness, learning from each other, understanding how they each ticked, there was no hesitation in his catching her. He seemed to know she was going to pounce, so he had his arms open for her impromptu hug-slash-mounting before she had even jumped.

He held her, and she wrapped her legs around his waist, because she could. Because no one was there. And because, for now, she still had her training wheels for a few more days. She figured she'd roll with them. Enjoy them. Appreciate them. Before she had to let them go.

"Ethan Greene is coming to my house," she said with another squee.

Jack pressed a solid kiss to her mouth, cutting her off. To be honest, this was a fabulous way for him to get her to stop talking about Ethan. When Jack kissed her? The world fell away until it was just them.

Butterflies in her stomach and heated desire between her legs had become a normal part of time with Jack. She'd never had training wheels quite like this before.

He broke the kiss and held her gaze before nuzzling her jawline.

"You give the best hugs," he whispered into her hair.

She squeezed him harder, pinching her eyes closed. "How's that?"

"Your hugs lift a person up." The words were the soft kind. The kind meant for only her.

Her heart melted into a mess of Ethan Greene's not-peanut-butter peanut butter. She pulled back enough to look straight into his eyes. "That's the nicest thing anyone's ever said to me."

Jack ran his thumb along her lower lip, their faces nearly touching. "Gotta keep my edge sharp with that chef guy showing up any minute."

"Ethan Greene"—she enunciated each syllable of his name—"is not 'that chef guy.'"

He bopped her on the nose with his index finger. "So you're one of those, huh?"

"One of what?" She moved to her kitchen, where the film crew had set up earlier. Then they'd taken off with Rachel to grab doughnuts at the bakery up the street.

"One who always uses the first and last name of a celebrity." He tagged along with her to the kitchen, even though she could hear his phone buzzing in his pocket.

"Well, he's not just any Ethan. So yes, I think it's important to clarify." She paused at the entrance to her kitchen. For the record, the kitchen did not look like her kitchen anymore.

First, the dishwasher matched the rest of the appliances. She wasn't precisely sure how in the hell-o that had happened. In the time it took her to change into the sponsor's athletic gear and add mascara to her eyelashes, someone had added a professional-grade stainless steel face to the front.

Honestly, it looked great, but her kids would have that piece of adhesive off ten minutes after they got home.

Second, the kitchen was spotless. That was thanks to her and Jack staying up late cleaning absolutely everything. Cleaning with Jack wasn't normal cleaning, because it involved a decent amount of illicit touches and more than a few kisses.

Then she'd barricaded the doorway from children and Kitty.

Kitty was grumpier about that than the kids.

Third, there were lights with the umbrella things all around the island.

They definitely made the space appear to be a professional studio. Jack wasn't taking any chances with this one. He'd said that many, many times.

The doorbell rang.

Her heart seemed to stop.

"Is it him?" She rotated toward the door quickly, Jack on her heels.

The unmistakable outline of Ethan Greene appeared through the etched glass of the side window. Her heart went from stopping to beating way too fast.

Holy crap, this was happening.

"Don't pass out." Jack pressed a kiss to her temple as he strode past her to open the door.

And then, *then* Ethan Greene meandered into her home like it wasn't a big deal. Ethan, with his messy blond hair, clothed in his signature blue jeans and white chef's jacket with the sleeves rolled up, exposing a sleeve tattoo along his forearm that she'd seen when he was on the Nosh Network. Two brown sacks of groceries in his arms. When he spoke, he sounded like a Foster's beer commercial. He. Had. An. Australian. Accent.

The accent had nothing on Jack's butterscotch, but she was still going to be swimming in double hot guy heaven for a while. Might as well enjoy it.

The polite thing to do would've been to offer to carry a bag. That's what Jack did. She, however, stood stock still with her mouth open, ready to catch some of Rohan's flies. She'd never, not ever, thought she'd see Ethan Greene up close, let alone in her own home.

"This is April," Jack said, giving her an encouraging look that probably meant she should say something. Her mouth was still hanging open and her tongue wouldn't move, so she wasn't sure how to remedy that.

Then *Ethan Greene* waved. At her. "Good to meet you."

Four breaths in. Hold for four. Four breaths out. Don't faint.

"You too," she said, totally normal, like she was a totally normal person in a totally normal situation. "Ethan Greene."

"Kitchen's over here," Jack said, leading the way.

Ethan in his chef's outfit followed behind Jack—a total contrast in his pressed suit and red silk tie with little cream polka dots. A contrast that made her mouth water. While she might've been starstruck over Ethan Greene, her body clearly preferred the refined Jack Gibson.

Jack caught her gaze and gave her a reassuring wink.

She tried to wink back but, truth be told, she was never very good at winking, so it always looked like she was just having a hard time blinking.

The chuckle from Jack echoed in her marrow, and her body seemed to liquefy, her knees going weak, like it did whenever they were in the same room together.

Truly, when she thought about it—which she didn't do often—she'd never had that reaction to any other person before.

For the first time in forever, she was consistently...relaxed. The Calm Mom was more than a name: it had become *her.*

"April mentioned she wanted to visit your restaurant," Jack said, jolting April from her wandering thoughts. Jack was staring at her with his eyebrows raised.

Ethan also had a look of great expectation etched across his features.

"It's true." She couldn't figure out what to do with her hands, so she pressed them into the counter. "It's just never worked out."

"You and Jack should come up," Ethan said, unbagging the groceries on the counter.

Jack was... Jack would not be there much longer. She swallowed. "Maybe we can fit it in before Jack has to leave."

Ethan might have believed it, but she and Jack knew it would not happen. The clock was running out of hours. She had ensured that would not change because it was the fact of the visit. What she'd signed up for. The expiration date loomed closer, minute by minute.

"Vail isn't that far," Ethan said, when neither of them responded.

"I guess that would depend on how many kids are in the minivan," she replied with what she hoped was a hey-I'm-still-fun smile.

Ethan laughed, low and rumbly and well, most women probably would've found that laugh pretty freaking yummy. "I love kids."

April glanced to Jack. He looked a little put out over something, but she wasn't sure what. Usually when he got that expression, it was because he was checking his phone and then making a follow-up phone call.

"I happen to have several," she said. "They just keep showing up."

Ethan chuckled. "You are funny, April Davis."

"Funny *and* calm," Jack said, effectively slicing through the jovial atmosphere she'd been brewing with Ethan.

He slid into the space behind her, leaning against the countertop by the sink. Not close enough for it to be perceived as anything other than him joining the conversation, but to her it felt like more. She slid her gaze to Ethan. He raised his eyebrows and went back to unpacking the bags. Clearly, it felt like more to him, too.

"You two are a thing, huh?" Ethan asked. "Never thought I'd see the day Jack focused on something other than work."

April turned to Jack, his expression inscrutable as he looked between the two of them.

His cell buzzed again, breaking his attention. He pulled it from his pocket. Frowned—he did that a lot when his cell interrupted lately—and mouthed, *One minute.*

She didn't ask him about his work because it was absolutely not her place.

He strode to the other room, cell to his ear, leaving April and Ethan alone.

"I am his work," April said when the moment dragged on a little too long.

Ethan's gaze tracked Jack's pacing in the other room. April followed where he looked. Jack was on the phone, yes, and he was frowning, of course, but he also clearly kept tabs on what was happening in the kitchen.

"You know," Ethan said, pulling out a head of cauliflower and setting it to the side. "This guy—" He jerked his thumb toward the living room where Jack paced. "He saved my bacon."

"Jack's good at what he does," April said, taking a cue from Ethan and unloading the other grocery sack.

He'd saved her bacon, too.

"That he is." Ethan made his way around the kitchen with practiced ease, as though he'd cooked there a thousand times before. "He mentioned you're not so keen on the whole live-stream-for-all-to-see thing." This was not a question. The statement stood on its own.

April nodded. "The whole viral-for-all-the-wrong-reasons thing will do that to a person."

Ethan had one of his bigger knives in his hand. The man brought his own knives!

He twirled it impressively by the handle. "That it will. Viruses are assholes."

He began chopping the cauliflower into small chunks of florets. Ethan had his own nightmare under the microscope—she knew this like everyone else who followed the Nosh Network did. Seeing as she didn't particularly want him to rehash her viral episode, she didn't push to dive into his.

"The key to being chill when the red light rolls"—he furrowed his brows—"is to pretend like you're talking to your favorite person in the world. Then whatever you say doesn't matter because everyone on the other side of the film believes you're talking to them. That you care about them. That they are the one who matters to you." He stopped the fierce chopping that, to be honest, had her worried about the future of his thumbs. "Everyone wants to matter."

Then he looked at her, and she experienced a shock of understanding. *Everyone wants to matter.*

"Everyone wants to be heard, too," she said, placing a bag of unshelled sunflower seeds to the side.

He nodded sagely. Which was a total juxtaposition to his bad-boy-chef outer image. "Everyone wants to have a voice. But it's hard to find your voice when the noise of the world is giving directions."

Boy, oh boy, could she relate to that.

They worked in silence. He gave direction where needed, and she acted as his assistant chef.

"The key to making the mac and cheese creamy without cream is grated potato with avocado oil," he finally spoke. "Took me awhile to get the ratios to work out. But my daughter loves this stuff." He paused, grating a russet potato. "Dairy gives her a stomachache, so I avoid it where I can."

"You have a kiddo?" April asked, already knowing the answer. He had a kid. A little girl. The scandal surrounding her had cost him his show on The Nosh Network.

"Uh-huh."

That's all he said, and she did not push because she understood better than most how having your life implode could make you not want to talk about certain things.

"April makes fantastic chili," Jack said, coming back to the kitchen. "You should grab the recipe before you leave."

April's entire presence bloomed under Jack's compliment. She was pretty sure her cheeks were red because they were ten degrees warmer than they had been three seconds ago.

"That's sweet." She gave him a grin, hoping he knew how much she appreciated his compliment.

"I don't think anyone has ever called Jack sweet." Ethan laughed and went about pouring a box of gluten-free pasta into a bowl.

Jack's jaw clenched at the comment, but he seemed to recover. "I can be sweet."

Yes, she knew firsthand that he could be extremely sweet. Nearly saccharine.

"It's a shame no one gets to see that side of you." April heard her words but didn't really focus on anything other than the warmth of Jack's attention when it settled on her. The way she wanted to unbutton the pressed white shirt he always seemed to wear and wreck his precise image.

To meld his world with hers.

She gave a tiny headshake to rearrange her mind, because thoughts like these were not allowed. She'd savor what they had, while they had it. Then she'd get back to living her life.

CHAPTER THIRTY-ONE

"Why do kids face all the 'world is falling apart' problems only when I step inside the bathroom? I need ten minutes for the world to not be on fire. Just ten. I'll be super mom after that, I promise."
—*Sapna Bhog*

"I think your sweet potato is not good." April eyed the musty green veins inside the potato that were most definitely not supposed to be there.

The camera was rolling. They were live. And the sweet potato was rotten.

She was not going to panic about it. Not like either of them had peed on anything or started cussing.

"I tend to agree." Ethan tossed the potato into the bowl he used for discard. "I don't suppose you have a spare we could use?"

Actually, she totally did. She headed for the pantry to dig out the two she'd purchased to make sweet potato fries later that week.

She emerged from the pantry with two potatoes she hoped to heck weren't rotted inside.

Ethan did a shimmy dance. She stared at him. Did he actually expect her to jump on in with something like that?

Fine. She did half a shimmy and tossed him a potato.

Ethan caught it like a football, eating up her impromptu pass. Which, she hoped, would mean that the viewers would, too.

April even gave a quick meditation lesson before they made the not-really-peanut butter. Also, turned out that meditating absolutely made the food taste better. At least, that's what she'd said and it just came out of her mouth and was so witty and—

"And that is a wrap." Jack did a slow clap with a huge grin that made April feel twenty feet tall. Given that her kitchen didn't have vaulted ceilings, that was a particularly noteworthy feat.

They were done. She'd survived.

Rachel clapped along with Jack. She'd come to help out before the filming began.

"That was perfection," Rachel said.

April gave a small bow. Yes, it was perfect.

Ethan joined in on the clapping. "She's a natural."

"How many viewers?" April asked, hoping it wasn't only ten.

"It's a big number," Rachel said, a huge smile pinned to her lips. She held her phone so April could see.

Holy fake mac and cheese, the number wasn't big. "Huge" and "enormous" were better words.

April's rib cage expanded, puffed up with pride. Dear goodness, she'd done it. No one peed. No one cussed. No one yelled. She'd actually done it.

With Ethan.

Ethan, who had agreed to cowrite a relaxing, Calm Kids cookbook with her.

Jack was right. Of course he was. *Practical Parenting* had nothing on her. She felt like she could do anything.

Presently, she helped clean up the mess. Before, when the camera was on and the sweet potato was no good inside, she and Ethan had rolled with it. But she'd been the one to take the lead because she had the spare in her produce basket. They'd laughed off the gaff like it wasn't a big deal. Rolled with it.

Here she was, rolling along without a need for training wheels. She hadn't even had to look at Jack for reassurance the entire time. She'd focused on Ethan. And the food. And the viewers.

She'd been...*calm*.

Good luck trying to wipe the perma-grin from her face over the next few days until the *Practical Parenting* appearance.

With his own happiness etched on his face, Ethan held his hand out to her.

She shook it.

"April, it's been a pleasure." He released her grip, then moved to clean up. Which absolutely got him bonus April points—of course, those meant nothing but were not easily earned. "We can cook together anytime."

Coming from a chef of his magnitude, that was the best compliment he could've given. Wasn't this day just the best ever?

Nothing was going to ruin her buzz.

Jack's cell vibrated. He glowered at it. "Give me a minute."

While Jack left to fix the world, April helped Ethan with cleanup, their easy rapport marching along even now that the cameras had stopped rolling.

"Jack's trying to get you to do a philanthropic project, too?" He chuckled. "Maybe we team up and give him a two-for-one?"

"That would be—" April swallowed, tamping down her excitement because Ethan Greene wanted to team up. And not just because Jack told him to. "Great."

"April," Kitty called. The front door slammed. "We need to have words."

April squeezed the slotted spoon in her hand so tightly, she thought it'd break. "I am so sorry."

Rachel was already moving toward the front door. April knew anything she tried was futile. Kitty was a force of her own.

"What are you sorry about?" Ethan asked, confusion clear in his tone and sketched right across his face.

April dropped the spoon into the sink, the metal clanking as it hit the ceramic. "My friend."

Kitty stormed into the kitchen with as much drama as only Kitty could produce. Generally, that drama was directed at the juice box choices in the pantry or soap theft. Today, not so much.

Though she seemed pissed, she'd clearly dressed to impress—the feathers were clipped in her hair, her jeans painted on, and her shirt so low-cut, April was pretty sure if she looked closely enough, she'd catch a glimpse of nipple. She did not look closer. Best not to know some things.

She couldn't speak for Ethan, though, and how closely he looked.

"Who's this guy?" Kitty asked, her eyebrows drawn together, a very accusing finger pointing at Ethan Greene.

"This is Ethan," April said. She rolled her bottom lip because Kitty was on a tear and she knew from loads of experience that anything she said could feed into it.

"Ethan Greene is the chef helping April," Rachel said as though speaking to one of the kids.

"I was told Emeril Lagasse would be here!" Kitty gestured wildly. "I watched your whole macaroni show and there was no Emeril. Unless you're keeping him in the pantry with the potatoes." She strutted to the pantry, pulled open the door, poked her head inside. "Nope. Not here."

"I never said Emeril." April suddenly felt an intense desire to defend herself. "I told you *Ethan*, the celebrity chef."

She pointed to the celebrity in question. The celebrity who watched the whole thing with wide eyes and an odd purse to his lips that was part smirk, part horror. Clearly, he hadn't decided how he felt about the Kitty invasion.

"She did." Rachel nodded. "I was there when she told you."

"No." Kitty shook her head, feathers clinking against massive hoop earrings. "I would've remembered that."

"Kitty." April channeled all the patience that motherhood afforded. "Why would I tell you Emeril would be here when it's Ethan who was coming?"

Kitty seemed to percolate on that, her stiletto-covered foot tap-tappa-tapping as she pondered.

"You're a celebrity?" she asked in Ethan's direction. Though the toaster was there, too, and this was Kitty, so...

Ethan pointed to his chef-jacket-covered chest in question.

"Of course, you." Kitty sighed.

"On behalf of all of Denver, I'd like to apologize for Kitty," Rachel said, glaring at Kitty with wide eyes.

April wasn't certain, but she wouldn't be totally shocked if Rachel figured out how to muzzle Kitty with a dish towel.

"I've been told that 'celebrity' is a term some use to describe me." Ethan settled on a smirk for his expression. April wasn't certain that was the best choice. She'd have probably gone with horror. "I don't particularly like labels, however," he finished.

Kitty gave him a once-over that would've peeled paint. "Do you have an air fryer named after you?"

For pity's sake. April opened her mouth to tell Kitty she could—

"Uh, no," Ethan said. "I prefer the oven. Like they taught us at cooking school."

"*Emeril* has an air fryer named after him." Her eyes turned to eyelinered slits. "Do you at least have a catchphrase like *bam*?" She smacked the counter as she said the word. The camera guy taking down the umbrella things dropped one.

He scrambled to pick it up.

"*Nooo.*" Ethan shook his head. "But I could work on one of those."

"The shimmy thing could be your calling card," April suggested. Although, since he was Ethan Greene, he probably didn't need a calling card. His food was enough.

Kitty gave a curt nod. "That would work."

She pointed her manicured talon at April. "Do you have any of those Capri Suns I like so much? The tropical ones?" She turned to Ethan. "Mix 'em with a little Captain Morgan and they are divine. Do you like cats?"

Oh God. April groaned.

Ethan nodded an affirmative because anyone in their right mind in that kitchen with Kitty would have done the same.

"Uh. Yes." He nabbed a fork and handed it to Kitty, pushing the tray of macaroni toward her.

April laughed on the inside. While she may have been horrified, Ethan was a smart man. He was feeding Kitty to get her to calm down. *Good job, Ethan Greene.*

"Do you want one?" Kitty asked, taking a big ol' bite of casserole. She paused. Pulled a face. Then took another bite. "A cat."

"Uh..."

"This is good," Kitty announced, pointing at the tray with her fork. "You should sell it."

Ethan grinned. "I might do that."

"After you adopt a cat," Kitty added for good measure because she was Kitty and of course she did.

"Stop trying to adopt out all the homeless cats in the greater Denver area to my guests." April pried the fork from Kitty's hand, tossing it in the sink. She pulled the tray away as well, because she didn't trust that Kitty wouldn't just dig in with her hands.

Some of this needed to make it to dinner tonight. Her kids would actually eat it, and they'd enjoy it, and she really wanted there to be some left when they got home.

"Cats need families." Kitty lifted her arms like *whatcha gonna do?* "Doesn't hurt to ask. If he's such a celebrity, then he can have his butler take care of it for him."

"Actually," Ethan said, embracing an air of seriousness, "I've been considering adopting a pet for my kid. I only started to take a gander at the adoption sites. We should continue this conversation."

"I changed my mind," Kitty announced abruptly. She turned to April.

"About what?" April muttered. "This time."

"I like him." Kitty jerked her thumb toward the "him" in question. The "him" being Ethan.

April glowered at her friendly neighborhood busybody. "That's good, because he's a very nice *celebrity* chef."

"Well, he'll do," Kitty said, turning to Ethan. "You get yourself an air fryer named after you and I guarantee things will start looking up."

"I'll keep that in mind," Ethan said with the crooked smile that used to melt the lingerie right off millions of Nosh Network viewers.

Since Kitty had Beast now, apparently she was impervious to the charms of Ethan Greene. Because she didn't even give him a Kitty purr in response to his smolder.

"And you can't have Captain Jack," Kitty added.

"I have no idea who or what that is, but I am perfectly fine not...having him." Ethan began to unbutton his chef's jacket. The move was certainly for comfort, but he exposed a T-shirt that stretched taut across his chest, and even April had to appreciate that the guy took care of himself.

Kitty stopped. Stared. "I might be willing to share Captain Jack."

"You have Beast, Kitty," Rachel reminded her, nudging Kitty's arm.

Kitty'd been going on and on and on about her new special friend.

"I didn't say I'd share *me*." Kitty huffed. "Though—"

"Mom," Harmony called. "I'm back." She trotted into the kitchen, not even pausing to take in the scene. "We watched your thing. Why didn't you make cookies?"

"Because cookies weren't on the menu today, sweets," April said, leaning in so Harmony could give her a hug.

Harmony scowled. "Cookies should always be on the menu."

April didn't disagree with that.

"Where's your aunt Simone?" April craned her neck around Harmony, but there was no Simone. No Lola or Rohan, either.

"I'm guessing Aunt Simone is missing a kid and probably hasn't realized it yet," Rachel said, reaching for Harmony's hand. "I should probably return you before she gets worried."

"Aunt Simone had to go potty and your thing was over. I don't see what's the big deal." Harmony pressed her hands on her hips. "I live here, too."

"I've got this." Rachel scooted a reluctant Harmony toward the door. "Kitty, why don't you come help me? I bet Simone has those Capri Suns."

Kitty sighed. "Fine." She pressed her hands on her hips just like Harmony and, thank all the cheesy crackers, she followed. "I hope she has the rum, too."

As quickly as April's previous online experience went viral, the crew had dismantled their equipment and skedaddled. Ethan evacuated soon afterward, too.

Which left just her and Jack.

She didn't move from where her back pressed against the front door. This was partially because she didn't want one of the children, Kitty, or any of the others who regularly breezed through to come back quite yet.

Also, Jack stalked toward her like a predator.

A really yummy predator.

He trailed a fingertip along her jawline. "You were fantastic."

"I was, wasn't I?" Without any care that he'd had his suits dry-cleaned and pressed recently, she gripped his lapels and drew his face toward hers.

He got the message. It wasn't exactly encoded in secret ink or anything, and he was a smart guy. So yes, he absolutely got her message, pressing his mouth to hers.

She drank him in. Confident and calm and they had days to just be them. The work done, *Practical Parenting* would never meet such a calm mom.

Bonus, tonight was Kent's night with the kids, so she and Jack could enjoy the victory and the promises their lips currently made to each other.

He gazed at her with such intense longing, she thought she might break in two from the pressure. That was the kind of gaze that made promises before words were spoken.

She pulled away. Held his head in her hands. "Jack. Don't."

Don't ruin the time we've got left.

He pressed his forehead to hers, eyes closed, breathing heavy. Generally speaking, they had to get a whole lot hotter and heavier before he got to that point.

"I received a call." His eyes remained closed, but the intimacy of their shared space remained.

She drew her palms along the broad width of his shoulders. "I know, I saw."

He opened his eyes, and she tipped topsy-turvy into those crystal blue pools, treading water.

His lips parted, closed, then parted again. Like he regretted what he was about to say. "It's a client in L.A.…."

A little fissure in her newly restored heart opened up to a low ache.

"You have to go," she finished for him. This was what they

knew would be coming. What she'd braced herself for.

He pinched his eyes closed again, then opened them. "Yeah."

"They need you?" she asked. Of course they needed him.

He nodded.

"Then you have to go. Go help them like you helped me."

"I…" He rubbed at the back of his head. "I was considering not going this time."

Why on earth wouldn't he? He had to go. They all knew he'd be leaving soon. Today showed that she'd be fine, and she was ready to prove that to herself and to everyone.

"I was thinking I could come back afterward." He bit into his bottom lip. "Spend a little more time here—with you. With the kids. Maybe see where that takes us."

"I…" April's fingertips went cold. Numb. Then her arms. Then her chest. Then her lips. But, inexplicably, the part of her that did not lose feeling was her heart. The one part of her that she would've preferred to stop feeling was all in on the ache. "No. That's not…"

She sighed, because of course she wanted more time with him. Who wouldn't? He was *Jack*. All business on the outside, but aware of everyone and what they needed on the inside, especially her.

But no. She wasn't doing the forever thing again. Not when it had failed so spectacularly the first time. This was better—him leaving now before they got in any deeper.

When Kent had left, she broke. Her whole life had collapsed because he wasn't shouldering his portion of the weight any longer.

That would never happen again; she wouldn't allow it.

This life thing, this job of hers, both could be done without help. She didn't need her training wheels.

"Okay. I get it." He said the words, but they weren't smooth. He stepped away, holding up his hands and taking away the warmth of his touch.

She lifted her chin. This was the absolute right thing, because training wheels had to come off someday. Otherwise, they weren't training wheels.

They were just...wheels.

CHAPTER THIRTY-TWO

"I've been crossing things off my to-do list, and I just discovered it was yesterday's to-do list."
—*Serena Bell*

Jack

Jack didn't screw up often. Apparently, however, when he did screw up, he did it in an epic way.

He could fix things for his clients. But he couldn't fix his heart. Not when he'd fallen for April.

The feeling wasn't mutual.

How could he go back to his career and his office and his work hours knowing that a few states away, a woman and her children were eating Crock-Pot chili without him?

On that thought, he opened the fridge at his sister's house and grabbed a beer for him and for Travis. A beer and a goodbye and he'd be on his way.

"Tell the boys I'm sorry I missed them." Jack had grabbed a few of their favorite candy bars before he headed over for goodbyes. If they'd been home he would've showed off his newfound skills at cutting sandwiches into shapes. Harmony had been teaching him. He had a hunch this wasn't for his benefit though—she just liked her sandwiches cut into shapes and didn't like to do it herself.

The little girl was sly, that was certain. Sly and awesome. She'd crawled right into a space in his heart he hadn't even realized he'd saved for her. Right next to spaces for Rohan and Lola and, yes, even Mayonnaise.

Rachel knew better than to ask him to stay longer. Apparently, she'd shared that information with Travis, because he took Jack's leaving with resigned understanding.

"You can come back, you know." Travis sat on the sofa, crossing his ankle over his knee. "Anytime. If you make it a habit, we'll even buy you an air mattress so you don't have to sleep on the couch."

Jack grinned, but he didn't feel it. Not really.

"How did you know my sister was the one for you?" he asked, offering Travis a brew.

Travis and Rachel had a love story that wasn't of the usual variety. They'd taken the back roads to find each other, realizing somewhere down the line that happiness overcame everything else.

"I didn't." Travis popped the top and took a pull from the bottle. "Sometimes I think it must all be some big universal mistake, because there's no way I deserve her."

"As her big brother, I can agree to that." Jack grinned at his brother-in-law, then toyed with his bottle top before cracking it open. "But she's happier than I've ever seen her, so I'm good with the arrangement."

"I'm glad we have your approval." Rachel rolled her eyes and dropped to the sofa beside her husband. He wrapped his arm around her and leaned in for a forehead kiss.

Jack had never thought he would want that kind of intimacy. He'd seen it with Ben and Sarah lots of times—the little touches, the innocent kisses—but he'd never wished it for himself.

Until now.

"I like the kids." Jack cleared his throat. Took another pull from the bottle. "April's kids."

"Is my big never-having-kids-ever brother softening to the

idea?" Rachel quirked her eyebrows.

"They've definitely grown on me."

He even liked when Lola smeared her ketchup dinner all over him. Because it meant he was there. Living. Not only working and fixing things for everyone else.

Rachel shared a look with Travis before refocusing on him. "You're always welcome here. You know that."

He'd love that. But he couldn't come back for a while. Not until whatever was going on with his heart settled down.

He shook his head, going for subtle. "April's ready for me to leave. I got the call. So I'm taking off." He mimed an airplane takeoff with his palm.

"Do you ever tell people to fix their own messes?" Travis asked. "Seems like the kind of thing you might try."

"That's my job. And I'm good at it." He understood it. Didn't question himself when he was working.

"You love her." Rachel said this without any filter and without any hesitation.

He nodded, staring into the tiny bubbles of foam along the surface of his Coors. "I love her."

Though he hadn't thought it was possible to fall in love with someone that quickly, it'd happened. He'd figured that type of thing took months or even years to cultivate. But with April? One moment he was staying in her guest room, the next he couldn't stop thinking about her. Then he realized his heart had gotten involved.

Worse than that? He loved the kids, too. Not like he loved his nephews—in that drop-off-presents-uncle kind of way. No, he loved them like he wanted to burn their chili and figure out how to make them cheese-less mac and cheese.

"You know." Rachel shifted. Leaned forward, her hands on her knees. "Sometimes it just happens—like with us." She slid her gaze to her husband. "You can't manage it. It just is."

He stood. Moved to the sink and set his not-even-remotely-empty beer bottle there. "I manage things. It's what I do."

"That's why you've never had a successful relationship," Rachel said softly. She probably didn't mean for the gentle words to sting, but they did. Oh brother, they did.

"Yeah." He shoved his hands in his pockets. "I guess so."

Maybe that's why he'd never have a relationship.

This was for the best.

If he couldn't have April? He didn't want one anyway.

CHAPTER THIRTY-THREE

*"If your children don't hate you at least once a month,
you're probably not doing your job."*
—Mona, Maryland, United States

April

April's pulse seemed to pound faster as the kids fidgeted in the living room. Moments marched by, each one impressing a tread mark on her thoughts.

Jack's leaving.

She had dinner already made. Thank you, Ethan Greene.

Jack's leaving.

The laundry was done. For the first time in ever.

Jack's leaving.

She scrubbed her hands together because they felt so, so numbingly cold whenever she really stopped to think about that. It made little sense. This is what she wanted.

Sure, Jack had fit in so seamlessly with them. And yes, his leaving would be a seam ripper for what they'd gotten used to. No matter how easy she tried to make this on her kids, it would be a transition. Like coming home from a vacation. When the reality of the real world settled in after too much Mickey Mouse.

But it'd been only a little while. Not like he'd had time to wiggle permanently into the fabric of their family.

So you tell yourself...

"I thought Jack was here until the weekend." Rohan's feet

dangled from the sofa. He still had his Paw Patrol sneakers on his feet as he clunked them against the upholstery. April hadn't said a word about it, what with the whole impromptu Jack goodbye going on.

Trying to reconcile her body's odd reaction to Jack's abrupt departure to what she knew she had to do was brewing a headache. The full-body kind of headache.

"Things change, baby." April fussed with Harmony's lucky ring, bending and twisting it on her finger. "Sometimes they change quickly."

Boy, oh boy, did she know that.

Rohan frowned, but he nodded. "I know."

Good. This was good. He understood. Yay. One kid down, one to go. That'd be Harmony who wouldn't stop stewing, since Lola would roll with anything.

Jack trotted down the stairs with his carry-on in one hand and a box in the other. A good-size corrugated cardboard box, but small enough to still fit under one arm.

He stopped at the bottom of the stairs and took in all the kids staring at him. The smile on his face had to be one of the fakest she'd ever seen.

"I have something for you." He left the bag and strode to April, holding out the box.

She took it. Not heavy, just a bit of weight to it. She shook it, but he caught her hand against the cardboard.

"Probably don't do that." His eyes seemed to trace the lines of her face, warming away the cold from before. "Fragile."

"What is it?" Rohan asked, crawling up on his knees for a better look.

April didn't get impromptu gifts often, so she wasn't entirely sure of the protocol. Kent wasn't a just-because-gift kind of guy. She set the box on the coffee table and pulled the tape sealing the side. Dipping her hand around the long tube, she pulled it free from the bubble wrap and gasped.

The vase.

She'd thought Jack had tossed it when it broke, since that's what she would've done. What good would pieces of a vase be to anyone?

But Jack had had it fixed. He'd had her fuck-you-Kent vase fixed.

No…not that. Her chest heaved with the realization… He'd had her I'm-April-Davis vase fixed.

"Kintsugi." He touched the gold filling the cracks, holding the pottery back together. "There's an artist near here who takes the broken pieces and puts them back together with a gold filling. I called in a favor."

Takes the broken pieces and puts them back together—
Like you do, Jack Gibson.

April's throat thickened, and her eyelids were not dry. She opened her mouth to say thank you, but no words came out, so she closed her lips. She'd assumed the vase smashed beyond repair, given the size of the gash in Travis's hand, but the pieces had fit back together, making it clear that it'd never been a total goner. Broken beyond normal repair, yes. But the artist had knitted it back together with a brilliant gold filling.

The purple vase was beautiful before. Really, it was. But now? Now it was stunning.

"So pretty." Harmony was enthralled, letting go of her anger for a moment. April did not hold out hope that even the prettiest of things would get Harmony past the few days she felt she'd been promised with Jack.

"Jack…" April lifted her gaze from the vase. "Thank you."

"It's you." Jack nodded to the gift, stuffing his hands in the pockets of his slacks. "When things break, they're not ruined. Fix them and they're stronger for it."

He held her gaze for the longest of moments. Yes, her

eyelids were not dry. Not at all.

Jack knelt so he and Rohan were at eye level. "I bet your mom won't mind if we FaceTime sometimes. I'll need to check in with the frogs."

"I don't mind," April said way too quickly. She paused, then said slower, "I really don't mind."

"Promise?" Rohan asked, holding up his pinky.

Jack linked his pinky with her son's in a binding pinky swear. "Promise."

"Banana," Rohan said solemnly.

"Banana," Jack replied, just as somber.

Harmony? Well, Harmony still looked ticked. April had seen that look on her daughter's face only a few times in her life. Usually, right before they went for flu shots or when her dad forgot to pick them up for his night.

She crossed her defiant little arms. "You don't *have* to go, Jack. You get to *choose*."

Oh dear. Bad. This was bad.

April closed her eyes and hoped the peace would wash over her. Nope, still numb. So she opened them.

"We don't *always* get to choose," April said gently. Was the gentle for her or for Harmony? She didn't really know.

The vase pulled her gaze back to the gold lines, mending it, strengthening it. Like her.

"I have a job and a life back in California," Jack said, his entire focus on Harmony. April understood the charge of his attention when it settled exclusively on a person. He spoke softly, like he was reading a story to Lola. "I just came to help your mom. But she's doing great." He stared at April for a moment that seemed to stretch on and on, even though it was probably only a few seconds, before giving the gift of his attention back to her daughter. "Your mom's ready to sing on her own. She needs to do that. So now, I get to go help somebody else."

Oh goodness. He got it. He understood exactly what she needed.

But of course he did—he was Jack. And if Jack thought she was ready to sing? She really was.

"Mom can't sing," Harmony said, her expression earnest. "Everybody knows that."

"Have you heard her?" Rohan asked, totally siding with his sister. "It's true."

"She'll surprise you," Jack said, the smooth tenor of his voice easing the ache he was already leaving behind. "Give her a chance. She always surprises me."

This man should be walking out the door, not wiggling into her heart.

Except. The numb chipped away the longer he stayed. The longer the vase held her attention. And the chipping away left a lot of feelings to sift through. Big emotions that April wasn't ready to face. *Oh dear God, what am I doing?*

He was already in her heart. A heavy pressure around that area proved it.

What had she gone and done?

"He's leaving because of you." Harmony clenched her jaw so tight as she turned to her mother, April worried she'd need to call the dentist. "You make everybody leave."

Yep, just like that—snap—the numb disappeared. Each of Harmony's words acted like a dagger in April's heart. She choked on nothing.

You make everybody leave.

April held her fist to her chest as though trying to keep her heart from breaking just like the vase.

"Hey." Jack braced his hands on Harmony's shoulders to draw her attention back to him. He shook his head and crossed his arms. All the butterscotch drained out of his voice when he said, "Your mom is the best person I know. Do you hear me?

You are so lucky you have a mom who loves you like she does."

Harmony's bottom lip trembled.

Sonofabitch, April's did, too. She turned away to study the drapes. Kitty waved to her from the StairMaster on her front porch.

Good to know that part of her life wouldn't change. April would start Life 2.0: a better version with stronger wings able to keep everything from falling.

"No one's making me do anything," Jack continued to Harmony. "Do you really think anyone could tell me what to do?"

"Mom," Lola whispered, tugging at April's hand.

April lifted her up.

"Your mom is doing everything to keep your family stable when I go," Jack continued. "It's hard for everyone, but it's our job to make people feel better. Not make them sad."

April held Lola tight against her.

"You should apologize to her," Jack said in a way that would've made anyone apologize for anything. "Because we all know she loves you."

April turned back, away from the window, the original wave of threatening tears ebbing.

"Sorry," Harmony mumbled. "I still don't see why Jack has to leave."

"He just told you, dummy," Rohan said, elbowing his sister in the ribs.

"Hey." April pointed to her son. "Not acceptable."

"Mommy," Lola whispered in her ear.

"One second, baby." April moved closer to the sofa, standing right next to Jack to address her eldest. "He has a job and a life in California. We have a life here. He's done what he came here to do, so we have to keep moving forward."

That was the only way.

She glanced at Jack. For what? Maybe help? She wasn't

sure—not really.

Jack apparently found the floor super interesting. He cleared his throat like he was about to say something, but the ensuing silence said everything.

Her throat thickened, and she gulped. There would be no promises that they could go visit him, and she couldn't promise he'd be back to visit them. He was like the Mary Poppins of influencers. He came. Then he left. That's how it had to be.

How could she possibly ask for more? She couldn't. She wouldn't.

She. Would. Do. This. By. Herself.

The kids always had FaceTime. That had to be enough, because she had to do the rest of this for her. The best thing was a clean break.

Clean breaks were easier to mend.

At least, that's what she used to believe. After the whole Kent clean-break thing, perhaps she shouldn't be so convinced. The vase *was* really pretty.

"We'll miss you," Rohan said without even so much as a ribbit. He'd firmed his chin, and that little show of fortitude made April want to give him a medal for being so mature about this.

Jack stood, his gaze traveling to Lola, Mayonnaise, and then resting on April.

He was leaving, so his eyes settling on her should not have felt like a warm, weighted blanket of comfort. Yet it did.

Fixing this. That's what he was doing for her. Filling her life with gold to hold it together.

"I'm lucky I got to meet you, and stay with you, and build a frog habitat, and hear Harmony's song." He held up his hand for a high five.

Rohan obliged.

Harmony crossed her arms exactly like Jack had after her

announcement that April made everybody leave.

He held his hand to her for a high five. She did not take the bait.

"This is bullshit," Harmony ground out instead.

April's mother instincts clicked into play, overshadowing her questions of all her current choices.

"Harmony." The word was steel plated. "We do not talk like that in this family."

Don't get her wrong, a lot of life was total bullshit. But Harmony could not go around just announcing that like she wasn't eight years old.

Harmony lifted her chin like a badass little miss, stood, and faced Jack with fists clenched. "Bye, Jack."

Then she strode to the naughty spot and planted her bum there. Glaring at April the entire time.

April swore she saw little dots dancing in her vision. She should talk to Yelena about what a stroke might actually feel like.

She shook the spots away, pretty sure a stroke didn't involve heartache because a woman's training wheels left for California.

She'd done this before—the goodbye thing. She'd done the hate thing, too. Harmony had blamed her for her dad's departure.

In Kent's case, he hadn't stuck around to say goodbye to the kids the night he decided to leave. He'd gone even more of the clean break route, not coming home again for a few weeks. Then he showed up with divorce papers. He'd decided to leave, so then he left.

Jack stayed because he couldn't leave without the goodbyes. He was probably right that this would make it easier on everyone. Leave it to Fix It Jack to know how to give April what she wanted.

And this was *exactly* what she wanted to happen. Jack was

leaving to go back to doing Jack things. She'd stay in Denver and do April things.

He would help someone else.

She would prove herself.

But with everyone winning, why did it feel as though she'd lost?

He gave Lola a quick kiss on the head. "Bye, princess."

Lola gave him a full princess smile.

"April." Jack didn't break the invisible thread binding them. He also didn't touch her. Not in front of the kids, even though her body was screaming for her to reach out for that last chance at contact. "You've got this," he said with such force that she absolutely believed him.

She nodded. She did. She knew she did. She had this.

So why did it feel so wrong?

With a quick clip to the invisible thread that she didn't see coming, he gave them all one last glance, and then he left. A quick, supposed-to-be-painless break that dissolved any residual numb.

"Mama," Lola said again, this time with more earnestness. She must've sensed her mother's need for solidarity. That was ridiculously sweet. Or perhaps Lola just needed reassurance when their world was going to go through another transition. Also very sweet.

"Give me a second." April closed her eyes, took a deep, deep breath.

She could breathe. Everything would be just fine.

"Mama," Lola said again, patting April's cheeks.

April leaned in to hear what she had to say, just as a warm liquid covered her hip.

"I needed to go potty," Lola said with a horrified look on her face.

And April? April cleaned it up.

CHAPTER THIRTY-FOUR

"You will never be the perfect parent. The moment you accept that and understand that doing your best in that moment is all you can do, the better you'll be."
—Amanda, Florida, United States

April

"I'm not nervous," April said for the third time. The words were mostly for her benefit, not Rachel's. Rachel, who leaned back to check April's level of forehead shine before the live started.

She squinted before she dabbed a bit more powder on April's forehead. Moved to a different angle. Then added a touch more.

At this rate, April should never, ever have forehead shine again. Ever.

The production guy had been in earlier to get everything ready, but it was a simple setup for this one. They ensured the lighting was good. There were a couple of umbrella things and some stand lights, but other than that it looked like a normal Zoom call set up in her living room.

No following her through the supermarket.

No celebrities teaching her to cook without common allergens.

Just April sharing her knowledge of meditative living and how to incorporate it into parenting.

She could so totally do this. A quick glance in the camera and she was ready to go. Her laundry-less couch, tidied living space, and Jack-vase on display was the backdrop for the show.

Rachel's phone buzzed. She glanced at the screen. "It's Jack."

April's heart did a high-dive jump to her toenails.

"He wants to know why you're not answering," Rachel said.

April had left her phone upstairs, so she didn't have to worry about Kent calling to cancel on the kids. In a rare show of fathering, he had asked if he could take them up to Estes Park for the weekend.

They used to do that as a family every autumn. Though she thought she'd be sad not to go along, really April found honest relief that she didn't have to spend the time with Kent making awkward conversation about things that didn't matter to her anymore. His new whatever-she-was could have him. Sure, April missed the promise of what they should've been. She did not miss who her ex had become.

Perhaps, though he'd turned out to be a crappy husband, maybe he could still be a good dad. She wouldn't hold her breath, but she'd hold on to hope.

"Tell Jack I left my phone upstairs." The excuse was valid, but it sounded weak even as she spoke.

Rachel relayed the message. Paused. "April's doing great."

She gave two thumbs up to April to illustrate her point.

"Uh-huh," Rachel said. "Sure." She frowned. "Yeah, I know. Okay." She held the phone away from her mouth asking, "Do you need to talk to Jack?"

April did. She so very much did. Her mouth parched at the thought of what Jack was doing in that moment. Which suit he wore. Whether he missed her.

"I'm okay," she said. Yes, the words sounded stilted even to her ears, but Rachel was intuitive enough to know that April struggled.

"She's finishing her makeup," Rachel said into the phone, ducking her head, listening to whatever her brother said. Finally, she added, "Of course. I'll tell her."

April's hands prickled with a desire to reach for the phone. To tell Jack he should come back when he wanted. She didn't do any of that before Rachel hung up.

"Tell me what?" April asked. This time, she actually was nervous about what Jack wanted to say.

Rachel squared her shoulders and tilted her head a little to the right. She had the same blue eyes as her brother. April should've noted that before, but she'd never really paid much attention to her friend's eye color. Not until right this moment. "He said to tell you he believes in you."

Oh. That was—

Was the air in the room thinner? It felt thinner.

"April." Rachel stuck the phone in the back pocket of her jeans. "I know I told you that Jack was a bad bet, that he doesn't stay. But you should know that the way Jack looked at you was special. I've never seen him like that before. I know you're doing what you need to do to move on, and that's what you want. But he's actually a great guy, and I think…"

"What do you think?" The air was absolutely thinner. *Sooo* much thinner. That's why those words had a subtle squeaky edge to them.

"I think he really cares about you and your kids. More than as just a guy who came to fix things." Rachel gnawed at the edge of her lips.

"There's something else you want to say." April could see it from a mile away.

Rachel went back to staring vacantly at her clipboard. But, since they'd already checked off all the boxes, there wasn't anything more for her to do with it.

"It's none of my business," she said.

"Rachel?" April asked. "Tell me."

Rachel set the clipboard down on the edge of the desk they used to set up the web cam. She pushed at it with her finger, aligning it to the corner. "He... You know, I think I should not be allowed to speak."

"Rachel."

"He fell in love with you while he was here, okay? He told me." Rachel went right on speaking even as April's heart stopped beating. "Before he left. And after he got back to L.A. And just now when he called."

April sucked in a breath and held it way too long because she had used all the oxygen in that air and didn't go back for more like she should've.

Her forehead tingled.

Jack loves me? How is that even possible?

She should breathe now. She pulled in just enough air to keep herself from passing out.

"I figured you should probably know that before you make any big decisions about not returning his calls," Rachel continued, apparently oblivious to April's current hyperventilation. "Please don't tell him I told you."

April dropped her head to her knees and begged her heart to stop racing. Begged the room to stop spinning.

"April?" Rachel asked. "Crap. I'm sorry. I didn't mean to—"

April couldn't hear what else Rachel said with the turmoil in her own head rallying all the chaos troops.

If Jack loved her, did that mean it was safe for her to love him, too?

If she loved him, too, why didn't she ask him to stay?

If she didn't ask him to stay, did she totally wreck the whole love thing?

Her experience with romantic love wasn't exactly a good example of normalcy, so how was she supposed to even figure this out?

The front door opened, and there was some rustling going on around her. She whispered the words, *peace* and *release*, over and over, trying to ground herself.

"What's going on with that one?" Kitty asked from some-where close by.

Oh, yay, Kitty's right on time, April thought with all the sarcasm possible. She pinched her eyes shut tighter. That meant it was almost time to log in for mindful meditation tips on *Practical Parenting.* This was a problem, given she wasn't feeling very mindful.

Emotional, absolutely. Mindful, nope.

Peace. Release.

In for four counts, hold for four counts—

"We should call Jack," Simone said from somewhere in the same direction as Kitty.

"Don't call Jack," April said, surprisingly clear for being mid whatever this thing was. She needed to figure out what the heck was going on inside her regarding the Jack feelings before anyone called him for anything.

Kitty settled next to her on the sofa. April didn't have to open her eyes to know it was Kitty there. Her arm wrapped around April's shoulders, her overly invasive citrus-based perfume saturating the air April desperately needed to get herself grounded.

"I think you're having a breakdown," Kitty whispered, pulling April closer to her, soothing, practically purring.

"Probably," April muttered, trying to shake it off.

"You're way overdue," Kitty said, still doing the comforting purr thing. "If you ask me, I think you've needed this for a while."

April opened her eyes to look at Kitty in disbelief.

"What started this whole thing?" Simone asked, gesturing to April, her rarely seen forehead lines showing.

"Jack called," Rachel said with a deep inhale. "I told her he fell in love with her."

Kitty and Simone both said, "Ohhh." In tandem.

"Didn't we agree to wait on that?" Simone asked. "Until after this big event that she's been preparing for since forever."

"You knew about this?" April asked, pulling herself together because, dammit, that's what she did. It's who she was. She reached for the powder and gave her skin an extra dusting in case she'd rubbed any off with the whole forehead to knees move thingamabob.

No one responded.

"Seriously," April said. "How long have you known?"

Rachel suddenly couldn't meet her gaze. Neither could Simone. She looked at Kitty.

Kitty absolutely met her gaze like a head-on collision about to happen. She looked her dead in the eye and said, "Since he told Beast he was thinking about staying in Denver and asked about office space."

"Yeah, I've known since right about then, too," Simone confessed.

"We thought we agreed to talk to you later." Kitty glared at Rachel. "Because, Gumdrop, you're in love with him, but you're trying very hard not to admit it."

April couldn't move. Her muscles seemed to have atrophied, which was a huge disappointment, because how could she teach other parents how to be calm on the biggest parenting web channel of them all when she couldn't even move her lips? Then again, how could she do it mid-meltdown? These were currently questions with no answers and—looking to the clock—she had approximately ten minutes to figure them out.

"I'm not in love with Jack." She didn't think so, anyway. She loved her kids. She loved her parents. She loved her friends.

Somebody like Jack?

Who makes you feel again.

"Oh shit," she said, dropping her forehead to her knees again. This wasn't about missing Jack's presence and his, well, extracurricular activities. Oh dear, no. With Jack, she'd seen herself as something other than a burned-out mess. How could she not fall in love with the man who had helped her see that?

A man who understood friendships and appreciated *her* friends. Including all the eccentricities they brought along as baggage. A man who kissed her good morning even when he was working. A man who built her son a frog habitat and drank Crayola water and wrote songs with her daughter.

The man who showed her how to see herself as something more. As someone who could catch the attention of a man like Jack and feel...worthy.

"I cannot believe I did this," she murmured, head still at her knees.

In for four counts, hold for four—

"I think we just had a teensy bit of what my mama would call a breakthrough." Kitty giggled and squeezed April, then stomped her feet like she was super giddy about this turn of events. "Now, what are we going to do about it? My vote is we call Rachel's Travis, convince him we need the company plane, and we all fly our tuchuses to Cali to bring that man home."

April turned her head to gape at Kitty. She couldn't just get on a plane and go to California. She wasn't Britney Spears.

"Beast has a lead on some office space," Kitty added.

"I can't go get him," April said, meaning every word. "I'm supposed to be here proving..." Proving she could live a life without training wheels.

Right now, that seemed kinda ridiculous.

Kitty took April's hands in hers. "Gumdrop, you *have* been doing this"—she waved around the room—"by yourself for going on a year now; what more do you have to prove?"

"That I can make it." Reluctantly, April sat up, giving the dizziness a moment to pass.

"Oh, sweet baby April, just because you *can* do it yourself doesn't mean you should." Kitty's expression was one of total sympathy. Like she'd just told April the worst news ever, and she was super-duper sorry about it.

April blinked. Holy Cheez-Its. Kitty was freaking right.

"Is she right?" April asked, directing the question to Simone and Rachel because she didn't trust herself at the moment.

Rachel was studying her clipboard again like it held the answer to how Travis made his margaritas taste so delish. Simone gnawed at her thumbnail like she did when she didn't want to say something that would sting.

They both nodded.

"Oh, dear goodness, she is right." And April had just completed what Kitty's mama would call a breakthrough. "I've been so wrong about everything."

She loved Jack. She could admit it, and the world didn't stop. Huh. Okay, then.

April wished she had a laundry pile to lean against. It was so very much wine o'clock even though it wasn't even five o'clock. She didn't, though. She had a livestream to get on with. Jack had never failed at fixing before. This he had shared with her. And damn if she'd be his first failure in the world of influencing.

No. She would not disappoint him.

"Maybe we should discuss this after my whole...." April gestured to the lights, the web camera, and the production guy gaping from the kitchen with half a sandwich hanging from his hand.

"You do your web cam whatever." Kitty pushed herself off

the couch. "I'll call Travis. This will be so fun. I've never been in a private plane before, and I have been waiting for just the right reason to convince him to take me on a ride. Do you even know how long I've waited to call that man and say, 'Fuel up the jet!'?"

"Maybe *I* should call Travis," Rachel said, sliding her phone from her pocket.

Kitty snagged the phone before Rachel could do anything but hold it.

"You take care of this." Kitty pointed to April. "While I deal with this." She held up the cell.

April needed somebody to put the brakes on this whole shebang until she could get her bearings. Did she love Jack? Yes. Was she going to talk to him? Also, yes. Did she know how she would make that happen? Not right now.

But given that Rachel and Simone were not making any moves to stop Kitty, it would have to be April. Of course it would.

"I'm not committing to anything." She stood, but the lightheaded, oh-damn-I-fell-in-love-and-didn't-realize-it feeling forced her to sit again. Which was fine. Sitting was better. She had to do it for the livestream, anyway.

The livestream that was starting in only minutes.

Calm. She was talking about calm and yoga as a family and definitely not backbends during sex or falling in love without realizing it.

"Yet," Kitty said all singsong, like this was the best day ever. "*You* haven't committed to anything yet." She sashayed to the front door. "But you will."

Just like that, the Kitty tornado moved to the yard and swirled across the street.

Simone shifted, looked to the door. Back to April. Then Rachel. "I should find a sitter, since Yelena and I will be leaving the state," she said.

Gah. Not Simone, too.

"Does Yelena know all this?" April asked.

"She knew before anybody else." Simone shrugged. "She's good at knowing things."

April's eyes misted. She put an immediate stop to that. No time to fix her eye makeup. Damn. Damn. Dammit. Damn.

"We're under control here," Rachel said, shooing Simone toward the door. "Go find a babysitter."

"No one is going to need a babysitter," April assured them, because they could not just pop on a jet and go find Jack. She didn't even know where his office building was located. Or his apartment. Or...if he still wanted to come back.

Her throat seemed coated with sandpaper.

"See if you can find a sitter for me, too," Rachel said. "Or scratch that, I'll call their dad. April's going to need one, though."

April was pretty sure her jaw touched the floor, it dropped so quickly. "I... Kent is supposed to take them for the weekend."

"I'll book one for her kids, too." Simone nodded along with her idea. "Because it's Kent and who knows."

"You would actually fly with us to L.A.?" April shifted gears because apparently babysitters were happening. But Rachel *hated* flying worse than she hated frogs, and she had a total aversion to amphibians since her kids stuck one in her shower without telling her first.

"With Travis as the pilot, yes," Rachel said, resigned. "I won't enjoy it, and I'll probably have to have Kitty fix me a grown-up juice box before we leave so I won't totally panic on takeoff."

"I'll have her start on that." Simone nodded before she left in the same tornado of what-the-hell-just-happened as Kitty.

"Weren't they my support team?" April stared at the now closed door.

Rachel gave a sly smile. "I think that's exactly what they are right now."

April's pulse evened out at that assertion. These ladies were so very much her rocks. And when the pieces had cracked, they'd filled them with gold long before Jack came to town.

She laughed because she wasn't a phoenix. No one burned her to ashes, even though Kent had truly tried. No, she wasn't a phoenix.

She was April.

And April may fall, but she always gets right back up again.

She steeled her spine. The little pieces of heart she'd grown back since Kent left her were strong enough to love again. Not that she really had a choice in the matter, since those pieces went rogue and fell in love with Jack all on their own.

"Are we...uh...ready?" Production Guy—Jim—asked.

April nodded.

Jim made a few minor adjustments to the lighting while Rachel flipped the deadbolt on the door—a good idea given, well...Kitty.

April inserted the earbuds and glanced at the microphone on her lapel.

They loaded up the talk show. She took a breath. Counted backward from ten, nine, eight, seven...until she was on.

CHAPTER THIRTY-FIVE

*"You, me, or nobody is gonna hit as hard as life. But it ain't
how hard you hit; it's about how hard you can get hit, and
keep moving forward. How much you can take,
and keep moving forward."*
—*Sylvester Stallone as Rocky Balboa*
(Clearly, not a mother figure, but he makes a good point.)

April

She was ambushed.

This was *not* good. Beyond not good and verging fast into horrible territory.

What April had expected as a nice *Practical Parenting*, Jack-approved introduction was so far south, they might as well settle down in Antarctica. April had, as requested, sent over details of her philosophy and a few samples of her motherhood meditations to use for her introduction.

This was not the introduction the show elected to use.

April was not an avid viewer, but like every other mother in the country with internet access, she'd seen glimpses of Paisley Sutton's *Practical Parenting* program. She'd enjoyed what she viewed. Always respected the hostess and the guests she brought on to illuminate the varieties of parenting philosophies.

Until now.

Now? She wasn't entirely sure she could keep her face from turning the same shade of plum as her shirt. April had gone with a purple blouse, because fuck it, Kent hated that color and she loved it. But no one cared about the color of her clothing during an ambush.

She forced her expression to remain passively neutral as the show veered from the agreed-upon topic of meditation and parenting straight into viral territory. Embarrassingly viral territory. Straight-up STD-level viral.

She didn't get why Paisley would do this—other than the ratings, obviously. Paisley with her red hair and green eyes highlighted by a pretty emerald cashmere sweater. She looked the part of any other mom friend. Paisley was a single mother in her own right. Two kids and one ex-husband who sometimes cohosted with her.

Single mothers should stick together, not backstab each other with butter knives.

As Harmony would say, this was bullshit.

"I thought we were discussing meditation and parenting today," April said evenly, though viral April still shopped on the screen. The webcam stayed on April in her living room as her video rolled in the background. They did that screen-on-screen drop-in of her watching the most embarrassing moment of her life because that made for more viewers.

Total bullshit.

"I'm not comfortable discussing this topic," she said, purposely avoiding focusing her gaze anywhere but directly into the webcam.

"Do you think parenting is about comfort?" Betsy Kelly asked with an overly long, high-pitched laugh. Oh yeah, the vigilante mommy blogger was a surprise guest on the program.

Do not throttle the hostess.

April doubled down on her soothing calm approach, ignoring viral April in the background shopping for cereal. "I think parenting is about doing our best."

"Obviously, we have different opinions on what the best is." Right. High and mighty, Betsy was at her *best* when she could be mean.

April had read her blog enough times to know this about her. If there were shock jocks on the radio, Betsy was the shock blogger.

"April, would you like to tell us what's happening here?" Paisley asked as Rohan dumped the coffee cans all over the floor.

April's entire body went hot, shame and fury melding into a heated mama mess. No, she didn't want to tell them what was happening there because she never expected Paisley would go for ratings above respect and bamboozle April into appearing under the falsest of pretenses.

She was wrong.

Keep breathing, April.

"I don't think I will discuss this," April said. Unfortunately, she didn't sound remotely serene as she spoke. She sounded sort of pissed. But given that she would much rather talk about all the things she'd prepared to talk about so she could get it done and find Jack, it made sense.

She couldn't, though. Not until the segment finished. Oh, sure, she could turn off the monitor and walk away, but that wasn't the answer. If she could survive the past year, she could more than handle Betsy and Paisley. No way would she turn off the camera and run. That's not who she was anymore. She could take the hits and she'd keep going.

Peace. Release.

Blah, not even her calming words were strong enough for this episode. Kitty needed to fix her a mommy juice box STAT!

"I think it's important to remember that children model what they are taught at home." Betsy pounced after viral Harmony cussed. "Our job as moms is to set the example."

Gah. Betsy was the worst kind of mommy blogger because

she was not open to alternative perspectives. She had one child who, by all accounts, was the perfect specimen of childhood. Her husband presented as perfect as the child. Though April called total bullshit on that. She'd lived with a man like him. Those who wanted the world to think they were perfection with a penis.

They never were.

Actually, April felt a little sorry for Betsy. She had a hunch that soon enough, Mr. Perfect would start going skydiving—if he wasn't already. She hoped she was wrong, because no one deserved what she'd gone through with Kent. Not even Betsy.

"Let's take a closer look at this choice with the cleanup," Paisley said as the screen in front of April filled with one of the most embarrassing moments of her life via the-video-that-should-never-be-mentioned.

April was sweating. And she didn't sweat.

Yes, she did actually sweat because she was a person with a body. But it was not a trait she normally had to worry about.

This moment was different. A trickle of moisture trailed along her spine, and she really wished she hadn't gone with purple silk. Every drop of sweat her body produced was going to show in Technicolor glory.

"This is the part that really gets my goat," Betsy said as viral April got to the portion where she lost her cool.

April's chest tightened, and she clenched her teeth, but she kept her passively neutral smile in place. She'd lived what happened on that video. She could live with having to watch and listen to it one more time.

Ethan Greene would probably have brilliant advice if he were there with her. He'd probably tell her again how everyone wanted to matter, and that's how she could turn this thing around.

He would be wrong, because how was she supposed to help moms matter when someone with Betsy's megaphone was there to knock them down a rung? Or twenty?

But I have a megaphone, too…

She straightened her shoulders. Betsy didn't have the backing of a firm like Jack's. April did. April had the platform that went beyond the blog.

Maybe she wasn't as loud as Betsy or as shocking, but she could help other mothers see they didn't have to feel the shame of Betsy's brand of opinionated.

"I'm sorry, can we just stop for a second?" April asked, leaning in toward the camera so her face filled her entire drop-in box. "We've all seen that video. If there are viewers who haven't, I'd invite you to save yourself the time: my kids aren't perfect. But they're perfect to me. I'm not perfect, but I love them and they know that."

"Children thrive best in an environment without the yelling," Betsy shot back. "Don't even get me started on the cussing."

"How did you feel about the cussing, April?" Paisley asked as though she was simply the one asking the questions, not the ringmaster of this circus.

"We are all on the same motherhood team here." April held her arms against her sides, even though she would very much like to talk with her hands. But…purple silk. Lotsa sweat. All that. "Of course I don't want my kids to cuss. But they're kids. They hear shit. I'm not the only mom who has survived a hellish divorce, and my kids are not the only children to process everything that entails. But we're moms. Our job isn't to make things perfect for them. It's loving them. Our job isn't to have no emotion other than happy around them. It's showing them that emotions happen. They're part of life."

Betsy opened her mouth, "I—"

"I'm not done speaking," April said, holding up her not-done index finger. "But I'll make sure you get your chance when I'm through."

She drew a breath that finally filled her lungs. "The thing about motherhood is that it's hard e-fucking-nough without other mothers telling us all the things we do wrong when we're doing our very best to make sure our kids know they are loved, and they are cared for, and they are important."

"I see where your kids get the cussing from." Betsy stood higher on her pedestal.

"I'm an adult," April assured her. "We get to have our voices, too, Betsy. Sometimes those voices include the word damn, or shit, or—other grown-up words."

"I've been known to enjoy a good grown-up word," Paisley said with a chuckle. "Whole strings of them, in fact."

"Betsy—with her opinions about the rest of us—doesn't get it. We are important, too," April said.

"I never implied others aren't important," Betsy said, but the fight had leached out of her voice.

"Your attempts to make me feel like a toad because I had a bad day caught on camera with the whole internet watching says a helluva lot more about you than it does about me. I know my worth. I don't deserve that."

God, she was wrecking this. She'd built her platform on patience, and she was showing none. But neither of the other women said anything and, since April was on a roll and her brand was toast, she kept rolling down this hill she died on.

Jack's first failure was not a title she embraced, yet it was the title she was earning. But the bitter taste of ruining Jack's winning streak didn't stop the fall.

"I came here today to talk about the importance of grounding ourselves," she said, "of making space in our minds so the chaos doesn't overwhelm us like it did to me that day. Sometimes, though, we need other women to help us so we can do that." April stopped, giving Paisley a chance to say something. She didn't, so April kept right on tumbling. "What we don't need is other moms tearing us down for simply existing."

She glanced up at Rachel. A clearly shocked Rachel, who did a soft slow-clap only for April. Production guy joined her.

Paisley started to speak, sputtered something about an apology, but stalled out.

April decided to keep taking the lead on this.

"Since you got to see my embarrassment, I think it's your turn to share yours. Paisley. Betsy." She added their names to be totally clear who she addressed. Betsy seemed the slippery type who would prefer to slip right out of anything unflattering. "Some other things *I* find embarrassing—my elderly basset hound eats my bras on the regular. Nice bras that actually fit are her favorite. My laundry is completely folded for the first time in *years*. I don't even want to admit how many times my kids have gone to school in wrinkled clothes because their Garanimals T-shirts sat in a hamper for weeks." She stopped. Paisley's eyebrows were nearly to her hairline, and Betsy seemed to play frog and catch flies. What the hell-o, April sallied forth. "And I mostly keep juice boxes on hand so I can mix cocktails with them." She heaved a breath. God, that felt good to get off her chest. "If you want to judge me, fine. But just know I refuse to judge *you*." April smiled a wary smile into the camera lens. "I'm done. You go, Betsy."

Betsy seemed to have atrophied. She didn't move. Her mouth finally closed, then opened and closed again. No sound emerged, however.

Like this episode had taken a direction she approved of, Paisley smiled a wry smile. "Last week, my son watched a video on MyTube and then announced at the grocery store that bananas are yellow tree dicks. The produce manager? Not amused." She lifted a shoulder. "It happens."

Betsy gasped. "I'm not comfortable with this conversation."

The weight of the world on April's chest straight-up disintegrated. Because, as Betsy had said before, *Motherhood isn't comfortable.*

Paisley chuckled. "Last week at the mall, my daughter opened the bathroom stall when I was…" She cleared her throat. "Still seated. The lady at the sink got a view neither of us planned. It happens."

"When my daughter was a brand-new baby, I took her for photos at a portrait studio. I went to change her diaper and she had a poop explosion. It was all up the wall. In my hair. We weren't welcome there again." April shrugged. "It happens."

"My son calls his penis a peanut, and it was cute until he told the teacher at his school he had a peanut. He had to come home that day because they don't mess around with food allergens. Even though he didn't actually have a peanut, they couldn't take the risk. I totally understood." Paisley pursed her lips. "It happens."

"I accidentally put my Elf on the Shelf too close to the floor and my basset hound thought he was a bra. It wasn't pretty," April said.

"I'm not even sure what to do with that," Betsy said.

"I had to make a quick run to Target for another Elf so the kids didn't know he got eaten." April pulled a yeesh face. "It happens."

Betsy's lips pursed into a flat, not-impressed line. Then her box went dark and disappeared.

"I guess she didn't want to play with us." April shrugged. Or her Wi-Fi picked the perfect moment to drop.

Either way, April wasn't sure quite what she'd just done to her career.

It didn't matter, though, because she regretted nothing she'd said.

"I'm important," she said. "Paisley is important. Betsy is important." She looked directly into the camera for all those watching the live feed now and the replay later. "And you're important. You matter, too."

CHAPTER THIRTY-SIX

"It's okay if you fall apart sometimes.
Tacos fall apart all the time and we still love them."
—Inspirational Sign

Jack

Well, screw him sideways and buy him a Snickers bar.

The pissed-off heat that flared, thanks to Betsy and Paisley, started to recede from Jack's extremities.

His cell was still pressed against his ear as he had attempted to triage this situation. But the situation no longer needed his assistance. Because...April had done it all herself.

Frustration turned to pride.

Slowly, he turned the phone off and set it aside. There'd be time to ream out the *Practical Parenting* producer later. Make no mistake, they'd be hearing from him about his thoughts on the editorial choices put into play after their last chat. Thoughts that would definitely include an abundance of Harmony-approved grown-up words.

That was for later.

Right now, April continued, wrapping up the end of the live feed with calm grace and genuine honesty. He would've clapped, but only Ben was there to hear him.

She'd gone totally off script. So far off script, she wasn't even in the same theater as the rest of the actors. And it was brilliant.

Jack clicked over to her social media stats, and they were rising steadily as he'd hoped, but for reasons he couldn't have guessed. This kind of spin would generally have Jack's fingerprints all over it, because this was perfection in public relations. The kind of thing they taught in business school.

But April wasn't spinning anything. And that's why it worked.

She'd been herself and, he just bet, the rest of Mommy Land was going to love her for it. How could they not? The woman was easy to fall in love with.

His stomach clenched at the thought.

"Are you thinking maybe you should've stayed in Denver?" Ben asked, seemingly unable to yank his eyes from the screen where the stats were still rising.

Jack didn't even have to think about that. "I figure it's a good thing I didn't stay, because I never would've allowed *that* to happen."

He would've shut it down before Paisley's trap even had a shot at snapping shut. Literally and figuratively pulled all the plugs. But April wiggled right out of that snare and into what his gut told him was a solid future as the next big mommy influencer.

She'd done it.

By herself.

On her terms.

What had just gone down on *Practical Parenting* was exactly the thing that would launch April's career. Like they'd planned. Yeah, he had a hunch this was the twist that would bring in viewers, followers, and sponsors to the real April.

Authentic April.

"What's going on with you?" Ben asked, concern clear.

"What's what?"

"That look on your face like somebody kicked you in the

nuts." Ben chuckled. "That's the look I had in the pictures from when I proposed to Sarah and waited for her to say yes." He stilled. Then he obviously got it. "Holy shit." Ben stared at his best friend, dropping more adult words under his breath. "April?"

Jack nodded.

"You didn't."

Unfortunately... "I did."

"Hot damn." Ben clapped his hands and let out a whoop. "Sarah's going to be so fuckin' happy, you don't even know." A smile stretched over his mouth. "This is the best news I've had since—"

"She's not..." Jack's shoulders slumped. "There's no future for us. She's still reeling from the divorce. "

She wasn't ready for a future. Probably would never be ready for one with Jack. His job was to read the room and go from there. In April's case, she needed lots of time to heal from the betrayal of her asshole ex. He'd arrived too soon, held her off too long. The state of his heart was his fault only.

"Since when does Jack Gibson not go out and get what he wants?" Ben asked, forehead scrunched. "Unless..." Then, because he was Ben, and he was a bright guy, he got it. "She said no."

"We didn't get that far." He hadn't given her a chance to say no. "What we had was temporary. She clarified that's all she wanted."

Then she'd practically shoved him out the door.

"You should talk to Sarah." Ben firmed his jaw. "Sarah always has ideas. I know she's going to have ideas about *this*." Ben was already grabbing his cell and typing a message.

Jack didn't stop him. He hoped he could join his buddy and his family for dinner. After weeks of a house full of noise, he didn't want to spend another night alone in his apartment with his brand new Crock-Pot. It cooked way too slowly.

He preferred April's terminator version.

"It's done, man." Jack stood. "I'm happy for her." He gestured to the buffering Web TV app. "She deserves the best."

"Good thing she's got you, huh?" Ben asked, eyebrows raised. His cell chimed.

"Given her history, I understand why she's got trust issues." He sighed and pulled on his suit jacket. "What's best for April does not include me."

"Wait to make that decision until we loop Sarah in on this." His phone chimed again. Then again. And again.

It sounded like Sarah was well and truly looped in.

That changed nothing. Or the fact he'd tripped over his own heart and fallen face first in love with April. Maybe that's what love was? A trip wire placed where a guy didn't expect it. Too bad for him, he tripped in the wrong place.

Jack's fingertips traced his cufflinks. Perhaps he should've told April before he left instead of Rachel. But he had to tell someone. Nah. He couldn't put that on April. The time had come for him to accept that she wasn't his. Wouldn't be his. Couldn't be his.

"Can I beg dinner at your house tonight?" Jack asked, swallowing any regret that threatened to breach the walls of his heart.

"You know it." Ben's expression crumpled. "Talk to me, Jack."

Jack toyed with the end of his pen, then set it back on his desk. "If you could tell Sarah I'm not interested in any more setups—"

"She knows," Ben said, full friend, not boss. "Judging by the number of messages she's sending—" His phone chimed again. "She's already got some thoughts."

"Probably none of those, either." Jack grabbed his briefcase.

Ben followed him to the door. "You're so into that woman, you might as well check your bachelor card with Carrie at reception."

Jack gave a subtle headshake. He may have found his someone, but it didn't matter.

Ben pointed to the now-blank screen. "What I just saw? She's looking for more. Give her some time to sort that out."

Jack would give her all the time in the world if it was his to give, but it wasn't. So he decided that he'd focus on his work and let that be enough. Work had always been enough.

Deep down, he understood there was no way it could fill an April-sized hold in his heart.

By the time he stopped at his apartment, showered, changed, and made it to Ben and Sarah's, she was already plating dinner from her slow cooker.

"Is that an All-Clad Gourmet?" He strode to the machine to check it out. He'd gone with a more traditional Crock-Pot, but he was already thinking of hitting up Williams-Sonoma for one of these babies.

"It is." Sarah looked at him like he'd lost his marbles and they were rolling all over the ground. "I bought it for myself for my birthday this year."

He ran his fingertip along the sleek edge of the nonstick aluminum insert. "Mine's been cooking way too slow, even on high. I'd like one with a little more oomph on the high setting."

"I like this one because it has the browning function." Sarah filled a plate and handed it over to him. "Braised lamb shanks."

"Oooh." He leaned in and inhaled the delicious scent of thyme and Cabernet Sauvignon.

"I thought about going full Ninja, since it's got the air fryer included, too." He glanced at Ben, who was cutting the crusts off a small stack of sandwiches. "What's with the peanut butter and jelly?"

"They're our backup after the kids try the lamb and decree it inedible." Sarah spooned a heaping of lamb onto another plate.

Jack set his plate aside to help Ben cut the crusts.

"Where'd you learn to do that?" Ben asked as Jack made a heart out of the crust he'd just hacked off.

Harmony had taught him. He should FaceTime the kids soon, since he promised he would. He'd figured he needed a bit of time to get used to being gone before he reached out.

Scratch that.

He'd been a chicken. Didn't want the kids to shoot him down because they'd rather hang out at the frog sanctuary.

"It's a long story," he mumbled.

"I've got time," Sarah said. He would bet she had all the time in the world.

Jack chuckled, forming another heart out of Ben's crust. "My friend taught me."

Sarah pulled at her bottom lip. "That's a good friend."

Yes, yes, she was. Since they already knew he'd fallen ass over slow cooker for April, he might as well tell them about her kids. So he did. He told them all about Harmony and Rohan and Lola. Frog sanctuaries and crayons and songs.

He stuck around to help clean up, dry the dishes with Ben and Sarah, while their kids got out all the pent-up energy in the backyard pool. Maybe he should borrow a pair of trunks and join them. Truth was, he still wasn't ready to go back to the quiet of his apartment.

The front door alarm chimed, alerting that someone had opened it.

Sarah glanced to Ben. "Are you expecting someone?"

Ben shook his head.

"Jack?" a woman's voice called from the foyer, and he swore it sounded like Kitty. Maybe he really had lost his marbles.

Sarah looked at him. "Are *you* expecting someone?"

"Jack!" the voice that sounded like Kitty said again. "Come out, come out, wherever you are!"

"Kitty, you cannot just barge into the house of someone you don't know. We don't even know if he's here." Was that Simone?

The actual doorbell rang this time.

"Oh, for goodness' sake, we're all going to end up in jail." That sounded like...Yelena. "Thanks, Kitty."

"Get back out here." Rachel? What was his sister doing here?

Jack rolled his tongue over his bottom lip and dropped the dish towel on the counter.

What, as April would say, the hell-o was going on out there?

"I think it's for me," he said.

CHAPTER THIRTY-SEVEN

"You can get glad in the same pants you got mad in."
—Kerrie, California, United States

April

It was official. April was going to kill Kitty. Not humanely, either.

They wouldn't find Jack if they were in jail.

April did not cross the threshold into the house because she wasn't entirely certain this was Jack's location, and there was the whole breaking-and-entering-equals-jail probability.

Simone didn't have that same concern, apparently, because she followed Kitty inside, yanking on her arm to get her to backtrack.

They needed Travis. They shouldn't have left him at the airport. He was the only one with a hope of physically removing Kitty.

Just when April was ready to explode, the world righted itself, because Jack strode into the living room. April's heart seemed to stop for a blip of a millisecond.

He moved straight into the tug of war between Simone and Kitty.

Two others followed. A man who looked sort of familiar—Black, bald, and about Jack's age. And a woman who seemed to be his wife? Probably?

This was likely their house. This wasn't Jack's house—they'd been to his apartment. Rachel had a key. That's where they'd found—after an abundance of snooping on Kitty's part—this address.

Oh dear God. This was Ben, the owner of the company she was signed with.

And his wife… Jack had mentioned her… Her name…

Sarah.

Ben and Sarah and holy, holy, holy shit.

"I told you he was here." Kitty tugged her arm free. She waved to the two who had come in behind Jack. "I'm Kitty."

"This is *the* Kitty?" the woman—Sarah—asked.

Well, apparently Kitty's reputation preceded her.

Sarah's smile was radiant. "I am so happy you're here. Why are you here?"

Simone turned three shades of red as she pointed to Kitty. "I am so sorry. She does whatever she wants and she's scrappy as all get out." Simone said the last part through clenched teeth.

April totally understood. Her teeth were clenched, too.

"How did you…?" Jack started to ask but then clearly didn't know what to say. *Get here? Find me? Find Ben and Sarah's house?*

"Jack," April said. She was pretty sure her face was as red as Simone's. And all the air seemed to be sucked from the room.

"April?" he asked, already moving toward her.

She'd changed clothes from earlier. This wasn't the purple sponsor-wear she wore on the show, and not her usual athletic wear, either. A black Henley with jeans and red shoes that matched her lipstick. The red was thanks to Kitty.

Jack seemed to focus on her shoes. That was weird. Totally weird. Why wasn't he making eye contact?

"This is April?" Sarah asked.

"Welcome to our home, April," Ben said, holding out his hand. "I'm Ben."

"You own the company." April struggled with a touch of hyperventilation. "Kitty just barged into your house."

"April." Jack moved to her, tilted her chin up. "It's just Ben and Sarah's place. It's okay. They're cool."

"We don't mind," Sarah added quickly. Which was nice. Jack had said she was nice.

April should breathe.

Really, she should.

"We've actually just been hearing about all of you," Sarah added, sweeping her arm wide. "Why don't you come into the backyard?"

April? April didn't want to go anywhere. Jack was here. She'd come to see Jack.

"Yes." Rachel looked like she'd recently finished a sprint. "Kitty, let's leave these two alone. Please. For the love of all that matters in this life."

Oh. Sarah had meant the others.

Not April.

April should stay put.

No. She shouldn't. She needed to make her point clear.

She stepped into Jack's chest, pressing her face against his pecs—they were great pecs—heaving with relief.

They had found him. *She* had found him. He was here.

"I totally messed everything up," she said, lifting her lips to his neck. Because, hey, she was too short to reach his ear.

Or he was too tall. Same thing.

He smoothed her hair as she soaked in the feeling of him.

She didn't need her training wheels anymore. But that didn't mean she didn't want him by her side.

"You messed nothing up. Your numbers look fantastic," he said with a press of his lips against her forehead, the whisper of his breath against her skin.

"Do they?" she asked. Because, well...after telling off Betsy and finishing the show, she'd had a one-track mind. That track being Jack.

"You haven't looked?" he asked, leaning back. Which was a bummer, because then his breath wasn't right there.

God, she wanted every part of him. His breath. His heartbeat. Everything. She'd never known a pull this strong before.

"I came straight to you." She heaved a huge lungful of air. "I haven't looked."

"I'm so proud of you," he said, like he meant it.

Like she hadn't screwed everything six ways to Tuesday.

"You did it," he whispered.

She nibbled at her bottom lip. "But I screwed up with you. The rest of it doesn't matter if I don't have you."

The air was definitely thicker at sea level. Stick-to-her-lungs thicker.

"April?" he asked.

She was starting to panic. More than a little.

"I don't know how this is going to work, and I have no idea how to do forever, but I want to try. I want you to come back. Rachel told me—"

Yes, definitely thicker.

He started to pull away. "My sister probably said some things she shouldn't have."

"Did she tell the truth?" April looked up at him with every hope molecule of her being.

He traced his fingertip along her cheek. "I guess that depends on what she told you."

April's throat worked as she swallowed. "That you fell in love with me."

Because, dear goodness, she'd also fallen head over heart for him.

"Then I guess she told you the truth, because I did," he said, earnest and honest.

Her eyes misted, and she rolled up on her toes to brush her lips against his. There were a lot of other words that needed to be said, but he was like a drug with his mouth so close to hers, and that trumped everything else. Oh, dear goodness, he was feeling her up. That was definitely a good sign. Right?

Well, two can play at that game, Mr. Gibson. She let the back of her hand brush across the fly of his pants.

"You don't have to love me back," he said when they came up for air. "Not yet. But let's give it a chance to happen?"

"I love you, too, Jack Gibson." Gently, she grazed her nose against his.

"Then that's plenty." He held her against him and...damn, that felt good. "Let's take it day by day? We don't have to think further ahead than that."

He would give that to her? Exactly what she needed when she didn't even know it?

April nodded, her cheek brushing against his chest with the movement. Then she pulled back so his gaze bound with hers.

"Banana," she said with firm resolve. She hoped beyond hope that that word from her lips—and the meaning it held— would say everything.

He threw his head back and laughed.

"Ribbit," he replied.

She pressed the back of her hand against her mouth. She loved him.

So. So. Much.

"Banana," he said, the word coming out rough.

Banana for forever and forever.

"What just happened here?" Sarah asked from somewhere near the kitchen.

"I'm thinking it's going to work out," Ben said, but the words were getting quieter, so she was pretty sure he was leading Sarah away.

April's forehead still pressed against his as she nodded. "He's right."

Life would probably be nutty with three kids and a try at happiness, but it would not always be bananas. Still, she knew without a doubt she loved this man. And it sounded like he might love her, too—her messy life. Her kids. Her...everything.

"I love you, April Davis," he murmured against the crown of her head like it wasn't a huge gift.

It *was* a huge gift. The biggest she'd ever received.

"And I love you." She glanced up at him, her eyes still misted. "Day by day, until we find forever."

She released him to hold up her pinky. He twined his with hers in a pinky promise she'd never break.

They'd found it.

They were forever. A forever they'd take day by day. That was the funny thing about forever—you could take all the time you needed to get there.

She'd just never noticed that before.

Turned out, for the right man? She was still a catch.

EPILOGUE

*"We used to cuddle naked all the time, then we had
kids and cockblocked ourselves."*
—Leanne, Yorkshire, England

Jack

TWO YEARS LATER...

When Jack had asked April to find a charity to support, he had
not meant Kitty's Cat House. Then again, at that time, Kitty's
Cat House did not exist. But then came Beast.

Beast sort of tamed Kitty. Not a lot—she was still Kitty. But
together the two of them founded the *mewest* Denver feline
rescue. A rescue that Jack had not visited because—

He sneezed.

Yeah, he was just going to take another few steps back. He
pulled the stroller with him.

April was cohosting the annual Ethan Greene and April
Davis Catoga Fundraiser. Catoga, seriously, was a thing April
started—yoga with cats. The whole concept really took off
among the mommy crowd.

That and their Cooking with Kids for Calm cookbook. April
was a household name. Just like he'd planned.

Today, Ethan and April set up at the baseball field for
yoga. This was so they could keep the cats confined and not
lose any of them. As he had pointed out when he made the
location suggestion, losing cats sort of defeated the whole

purpose of rescuing them.

April was very much into philanthropy after being pushed toward it. What could he say? He wasn't sorry he'd lit that fuse.

Also, not sorry Ethan hopped right on board with her.

Jack appreciated their collaboration because they did good work for the community. Also, it didn't hurt either of their brands one iota. Of course, that came second.

When April had decided to try a life with Jack, they'd committed to taking things day-by-day. Because that's what she needed.

The kids? They did not take things slow. In the beginning, there was an abundance of maneuvering on Harmony's part to get Jack to stay longer hours at their house. Lola and Rohan got involved. Jack loved it—the staying longer and hanging with the kids. April even came around. She'd wanted him there, too—it just took a bit for her to admit it to herself. He was patient about it, even when the kids weren't.

"Jack," Harmony called, searching for him with her gaze.

He glanced at her across the grass. Waved so she would see him.

"Over here," he hollered back.

This was their routine.

The thing with Harmony was that sometimes—times like now—he sensed a genuine fear in her. A fear that he'd disappear. He'd leave.

But he wouldn't be doing that, and if it took a lifetime for him to show her? Well, that's just what it'd take. He was in it for a lifetime.

Not just because of April and the baby, but because of all of them. They were his family.

But by the time the family welcomed baby Matt, they had all committed to forever as more than a team-building exercise.

Matt's older sisters and brother adored him. Of course they

did. He was easy to adore. Like his mama and his siblings.

Kent was still a wild card when it came to whether or not he would be active in their lives that day or not. But he was always invited. Whether he chose to attend? That was up to him.

The kids thrived within the family that April had created for them. The family she'd invited him into.

The family only a fool would leave.

Make no mistake, Jack was not a fool.

April hurried toward him. She got a funny, quizzical look on her face. "You're farther away than before."

"Cats do that to me."

She frowned. "The antihistamines didn't work?"

Not really, but he was still breathing, so he'd just keep his distance and everything would be fine.

"I'm good right here."

She drank him in like she did when she was worried. But she didn't need to be.

"You doing okay?" he asked, pulling her arm through his. During these events, she got going and sometimes forgot to stop to take care of herself.

"I have everything I ever wanted." She cooed at Matt. "Of course I'm okay."

Jack's whole world was here. April, Harmony, Rohan, Lola, and now Matt.

They did have it good. Even when things were bad—and with four kids it wasn't all sunshine and frog ponds. No, sometimes it was full-on muddy crayon water. But even then, things were pretty damn good. All things considered.

He still fixed things for influencers and loved his job, but he didn't work the same hours he once had. He also didn't travel much anymore. He supported April's business and he worked from home. He'd also figured out the laundry folding thing beyond the collared men's shirts. Folding didn't suck as bad as he used to think. The whole process of taking a basket of mess and turning it into piles of organized was somewhat cathartic.

What more could a guy ask for?

Especially a guy whose wife had found happiness and had no qualms sharing it with the world. She hit it big with the merging of meditation and reality, truthful and calm. Women flocked to her brand of *try to be calm but don't expect it to work all the time.* They loved her all the more because she didn't shy away from the swear words.

She'd become known for calling it as she saw it and including a "damn," "fuck," or "ass" when necessary. That's one of the reasons she'd become a regular guest on *Practical Parenting.*

Not the cussing. The calling it as she saw it.

Paisley had her come on and talk about it.

Rinse and repeat until April had a brand that made Jack wish he could do cartwheels to celebrate. He'd never been able to do a cartwheel. Though he had gotten fairly proficient at backbends.

He turned to gaze at his wife as she looked out at the field filled with people ready to do yoga with cats.

Then, because he could, he kissed the ever-loving bejeezus out of her.

She let him, since that was sort of their thing. One of them kissed the other, and they both rolled with it. She gripped his shoulders like a lifeline until Matt fussed and he had to pull away to move the stroller back and forth the way Matt liked. He was adorable, but he was awfully picky.

April patted at her lips. "Did I mess up my lipstick?"

"Maybe," Jack said. Just a little smudge to the left. "Could you kiss me again before you fix it?"

This time it was April who kissed the holy Hannah hell out of him. He let her. Of course he did. But he didn't let his hands roam, seeing as they were in public and all.

It seemed like only yesterday he was saving Captain Jack from the dryer and helping Travis fix his hand when they put furniture polish on the tile.

"April!" Kitty screeched.

That broke the moment. Jack grinned against his wife's mouth. "You're being summoned."

He pulled away as Kitty scurried toward them, parting the crowd. Her outfit was...tight. And he was pretty sure the neckline was cut specifically to show off her brand-new breasts. He hadn't checked them out on purpose or anything. The only breasts he was interested in belonged to his wife.

But April and Simone and, fuck it, even Kitty had told him *all* about them. He actually had to insist that Kitty keep her top on because he didn't need to see what she referred to as *the artistry*.

Also, Beast was huge and he didn't want to cross him.

"Did you see who had the balls to show?" Kitty demanded. Who she asked the question of, Jack wasn't sure. The murderous expression she threw was directed at both of them.

"Ah..." He had seen lots of people, so...

"Betsy Kelly is here." She pointed to the group of women with yoga mats.

"I know," April said, leaning into Jack. "I saw."

Well, didn't she seem remarkably okay with this?

"Here?" Kitty asked. She added, "At my fundraiser."

April nodded.

"And you're just over here kissing while she's over there—" She lowered her voice. "With. A. Yoga. Mat." Kitty's anger resonated. "Who had the cojones to invite her to the party? I would like to castrate them."

"I did," April said, totally throwing herself under the bus.

"Seriously?" Jack asked. What had his wife been thinking? Betsy scared him, and he didn't scare easily.

"She's having a hard time," April said. "I know what it's like to have a hard time."

Jack wasn't quite sure what to do with that. Betsy had always been the one who drove April up the wall.

"Damn." Kitty gnawed at her thumbnail. "I can't castrate you. You're the teacher."

Well...

"Just be nice to her?" April asked, because apparently his wife's heart truly was made of gold. "She really needs some friends right now."

Heart of gold. He loved this woman.

Kitty stomped off. It didn't seem like she was going to go make a friend, though.

Jack linked his hand with April's and raised it to his mouth, pressing a kiss to her knuckles, admiring the diamond he'd slipped on her finger when she'd said, "Banana."

That would be, yes, in banana language.

And looking at his wife, he tripped right into love with her all over again. Like he did every time his eyes found her.

In the morning, when the light streamed over her face and he was the first to get to see her that day.

When she showed up at his office in their house to drag him to an impromptu lunch.

In a crowd when he sought her out at Rohan's soccer field.

Late at night when he found her in bed and they showed each other just how much they needed the other.

Every single time, he fell in love all over again.

The way she looked at him? He was pretty sure that April Davis fell in love with him, too.

Scratch that.

He was certain of it.

ACKNOWLEDGMENTS

First up, I have to thank my eight-year-old daughter Sofia for allowing me to use her words for Harmony's song. When I was drafting this book, Sofia let me read her prose. Her words were so perfect, I asked if Harmony might borrow them. Sofia, thank you for saying yes and letting me pay you back in ice cream sandwiches.

Thank you also to all the wonderful readers who submitted mom wisdom for the chapter headings.

I learned long ago that creating a manuscript is often a lonely process, but I never felt alone when writing *this* story. My posse of family, friends, publishing team, and colleagues made this book a joy to write.

Emily Sylvan Kim, my extraordinary agent—seriously, she's the bomb diggity—went to bat for Jack and April as soon as I pitched the concept. Liz Pelletier, Stacy Abrams, Lydia Sharp, and the whole editorial team at Entangled deserve all the cookies for believing in me and helping polish this book until it shined.

Steve, my husband who didn't realize what he signed up for when we got together all those years ago—thank you for believing in me, being proud of me, and all the inspiration.

This is also where I give a shout out to my kids, without whom this story would never have been written and without whose arguments this book would've been finished earlier. (Drinking crayon water and hiding tooth fairy money in the sofa? Yep. Been there. Done that.)

My mom, Shirley, and my sister, Sereneti, always cheer me

on as I draft, edit, and cuss at my characters.

My best friend, Karie, who answers my calls even in the middle of the night even if the crisis is fictional. I'm so blessed you loved cupcakes as much as me and we bonded over that mutual love of carbohydrates.

Kiele, who is my person, always sees the best in me even when it's sweaty and gross.

Victoria, Angela, Jenn, SarahBeth, and Erika round out my girls. I adore you all.

Denise Allen, my fitness and nutrition coach, who helped me find balance between work, wine, and staying healthy while I worked on this book. It's because of her the wine and cupcakes didn't always win.

Massive thanks to Shasta Schafer, Deb Smolha, Becky Wesnidge, Dylann Crush, Renee Ann Miller, Jody Holford, C.R. Grissom, Patricia Dane, A.Y. Chao, Sara Celi, Diane Holiday, Kilby Blades, Serena Bell, Brenda St. John Brown, and so many others for commiserating, critiquing, and beta reading.

My publicist, Dani Sanchez, helps me keep my shit locked tight with all the phone calls, the marketing chats, and so much more.

The whole Entangled team made this experience so positive, especially Elizabeth, Nancy, Mira, Jessica, Curtis, Riki, the quality assurance readers, and sensitivity reader.

Finally, a huge thanks to *you*. Yes, you! The wonderful reader who picked up this book and joined me for the journey. I get to do my dream job because of you, and it's a pretty kick-ass gig I've got going on.

April May Fall is a hilarious, heartfelt romantic comedy full of relatable wisdom and steamy moments. However, the story includes elements that might not be suitable for some readers. Infidelity in a character's back story, talk of divorce, alcohol consumption, and open-door sex scenes are included in the novel. Readers who may be sensitive to these elements, please take note.

*Two powerhouse authors bring you a hilarious
tale of one woman's journey to find herself again.*

back
in the
burbs

by Tracy Wolff
New York Times Bestselling Author
and
by Avery Flynn
USA Today Bestselling Author

Ever have one of those days where life just plain sucks? Welcome to
my last three months—ever since I caught my can't-be-soon-enough
ex-husband cheating with his paralegal. I'm thirty-five years old, and
I've lost my NYC apartment, my job, my money, and frankly, my dignity.

But the final heartache in the suck sandwich of my life? My great-
aunt Maggie died. The only family member who's ever gotten me.

Even after death, though, she's helping me get back up. She's
willed me the keys to a house in the burbs, of all places, and dared me
to grab life by the family jewels. Well, I've got the vise grips already in
hand (my ex should take note) and I'm ready to fight for my life again.

Too bad that bravado only lasts as long as it takes to drive into
Huckleberry Hills. And see the house.

There are forty-seven separate HOA violations, and I feel them
all in my bones. Honestly, I'm surprised no one's "accidentally"
torched the house yet. I want to, and I've only been standing in front
of it for five minutes. But then my hot, grumpy neighbor tells me to
mow the lawn first and I'm just...done. Done with men too sexy for
their own good and done with anyone telling me what to do.

First rule of surviving the burbs? There is nothing that YouTube
and a glass of wine can't conquer.

AMARA

an imprint of Entangled Publishing LLC